T0209958

Deus lo Volt!

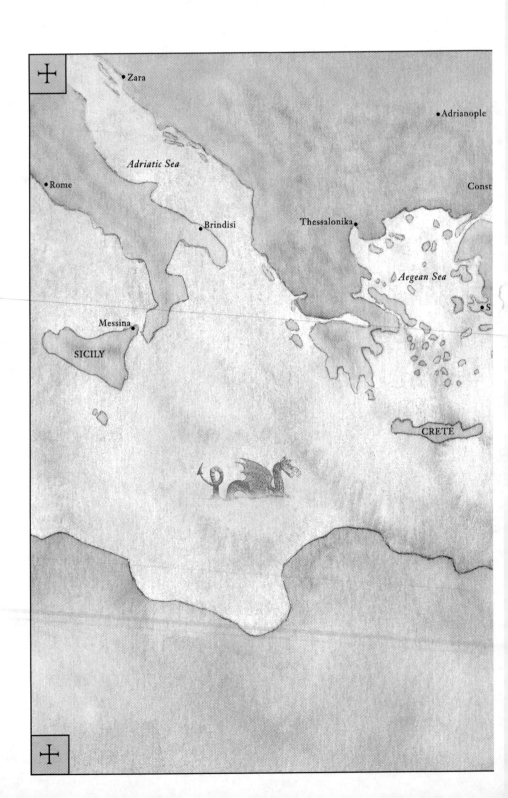

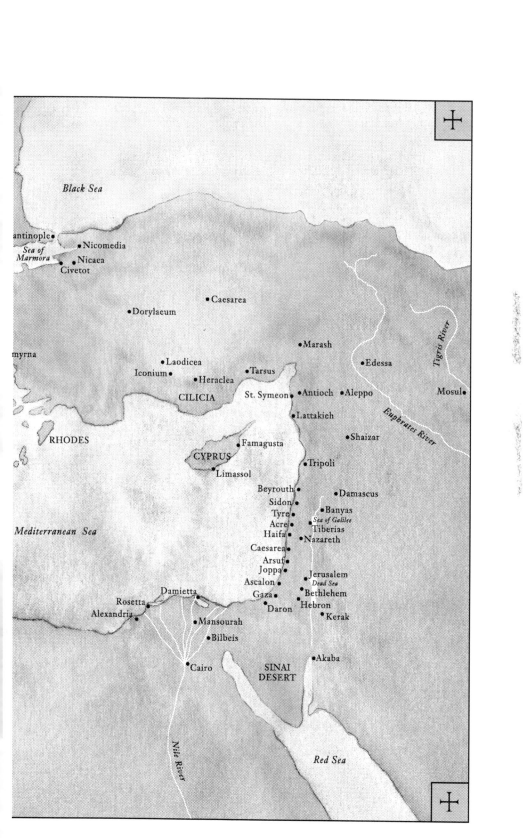

Also by Evan S. Connell

Deus lo Volt!

chronicle of the crusades

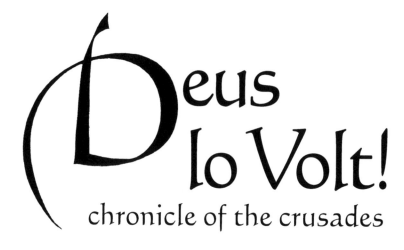

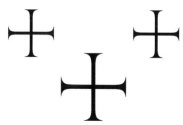

✝ ✝ ✝ ✝ ✝ Evan S. Connell ✝

COUNTERPOINT

BERKELEY

First Counterpoint paperback edition 2001

LIBRARY OF CONGRESS CATALOGING-IN-PUBLICATION DATA
Connell, Evan S., 1924–
Deus lo volt! : chronicle of the Crusades / Evan S. Connell.
        p.   cm.
ISBN 1-58243-140-X
1. Crusades—First, 1096–1099—Fiction.
2. Knights and knighthood—France—Fiction.   I. Title.
PS3553.05 D48 2000
813'.54—dc21
99-054831

Jacket and text design by Wilsted & Taylor Publishing Services

Counterpoint
2560 Ninth Street, Suite 318
Berkeley, CA 94710
www.counterpointpress.com

Printed in the United States of America

For Naoma and Webster Schott

The stream of Time, inexorable, constant, removes from our sight all things that are born and carries into the night deeds of little account, deeds worthy of notice . . .

PRINCESS ANNA COMNENA

IN THE YEAR OF OUR LORD 1189 my father's father, Geoffrey, died at the siege of Acre. That was before my birth. My uncles, Robert and Geoffrey, also took the cross. Robert accompanied Gautier de Brienne to Apulia, there ascending gloriously to God. King Richard of England honored my uncle Geoffrey, giving leave to quarter his arms with the Plantagenet lion. Geoffrey embraced our Savior during the battle of Kalaat al-Horn. This, too, happened before my time. My father, Simon, fought at Troyes and at Carcassonne to cleanse the earth of Albigensian heretics. Also, my father journeyed to Egypt where he fought valorously beneath the walls of Damietta. I, myself, when I returned from oversea, brought back the shield of my uncle Geoffrey to hang in the church of Saint Laurent at Joinville in order that men might pray for its owner, that his fame might not perish. There I placed a tablet upon which I had inscribed a tribute to the deeds of my illustrious family, both at home and while on pilgrimage.

Lord God, show mercy to the seigneurs of Joinville at rest in this place. Show mercy to one who, by Your grace, founded and built for You the abbey of Écurie, the abbey of Jouvillier, the house of Mathons, the priory of Le Val d'Onne, so that all descended from him may find themselves in Your presence, believing that he who builds the house of God on earth builds for himself a house in heaven.

How do such things come to pass? By the grace of providence two centuries ago Étienne Devaux, having grown wealthy on this land, espoused the Comtesse de Joigny. As her marriage portion she brought the fief so named, including various profitable manors. It was Étienne who built Joinville castle. I am myself descended from this man through my father's second wife, Béatrice de Bourgogne. I was betrothed to Alicia, daughter of Comte Henri de Grand Pré, during the lifetime of my parents, articles of marriage being agreed to in the month of June, 1231. Also, through the marriage of my great-grandfather to Félicité de Brienne was the house of Joinville allied with the twelfth king of Jerusalem. Therefore, I, Jean, speak as the present lord of a family distinguished throughout Champagne. May that suffice.

✝

Long ago near the village of Amiens lived a hermit called Peter, reputed to be from northern Gaul, diminutive, ill favored, with a gloomy countenance bonier than that of the donkey he rode, eyes so liquid and brilliant that some declared him lunatic. I have heard he was a soldier before assuming the cowl. Yet I have heard he was a distinguished scholar of noble lineage, mentor to Count Baldwin and Duke Godfrey. Syria, Hungary, Spain, Germany, and other countries now claim to be the land of his birth. Abbot Guibert de Nogent, who heard him preach, speaks of crowds glorifying Peter as a saint, urging gifts upon him. Whatever he was offered he refused or distributed among the poor. From village to village he wandered, homespun tunic flapping at his heels, bare feet embellished with dirt, regally crowned with a pointed hood. Neither bread nor meat did he accept, but lived on fish and wine. Those who gathered to hear him preach fought to pluck hairs from the tail of his donkey to worship as relics since the gullible covet novelties to assuage their need. Also, it is said that prostitutes who clustered around him would eschew their lewdness and, weeping, return to their husbands.

deus lo volt!

Ancient documents relate that he visited Jerusalem where he spoke with the patriarch Simon who told him of Christians held captive, holy sites dishonored. Peter wept, the blood boiled in his veins. He vowed to request audience with His Holiness Urban. Therefore the patriarch wrote a letter, sealed with his seal, which he gave to the hermit. And that evening Peter went to pray for courage at the church of the Holy Sepulcher but fell asleep on the floor. Christ appeared, telling him to rise up. Then down to the port he hastened, embarked, and sailed to Bari whence he proceeded to Rome. So much do chronicles assert. Some think he did not complete the journey since he was maltreated by infidel Turks and obliged to turn back. How much is true, God knows. Certain it is that Bishop Lietbert of Cambrai got no closer to Jerusalem than Laodicea because of abuse. There he with his entourage met Bishop Helinand who was returning and drew such a loathsome picture of what to expect that they quit the pilgrimage. And it is known that Abbot Géraud de Saint-Florent-les-Saumur fell among misbelievers who tortured him to death. Hence there can be no doubt that Christians oversea were harshly treated by enemies of the light. Babylonian. Turk. Arab. Still, what could dissuade them from reflecting upon that land where the Savior lived out His earthly life? What could prevent their feet from seeking that hallowed ground where once He preached the Gospel? For that is the essential of Christian life, to deny one's self in search of another and greater self.

That the Holy City lay in bondage could not be questioned. Clots of earth, dung, all manner of filth was hurled through windows of Christian homes. Daughters and sons of Christians were abducted, defiled, festivals prohibited. Yet these iniquitous pagans, dissatisfied with the boundaries of Arabia and Syria, traveled north to menace Europe. Thousands were slain in the Armenian capital of Ani and a cross surmounting the cathedral was melted to make a brick, set at the door of a mosque for infidels to step upon. Thus affronted, who could doubt the surpassing fury of God?

His Holiness Urban, moved by inexpressible pity, crossed the

Alps to Gaul in the year of our Lord 1095. At Clermont he met with the principal barons of France, entreating them to aid their brethren in the East. Present were three hundred abbots and bishops. For seven days they conferred while snow lay thickly on the ground. It is not I who beseeches you, he told them. It is Christ who commands. And during those days His Holiness excommunicated the bishop of Cambrai for simony. If this were not enough, he excommunicated King Philip for adultery with Comtesse Bertrade d'Anjou, a sentence of such inflexibility that all were astonished, making them at once fear and love a pastor so vindictive.

From many leagues came citizens high and low to see the pontiff, to hear his message. Those unable to find lodging put up tents. We are told that the fields near Clermont resembled a military encampment. Peter the hermit was seen, albeit chronicles from those days disagree as to whether he spoke.

All in good time His Holiness came forth, attended by cardinals and bishops, a tall man robed in white. When he lifted his hands the multitude fell silent. He spoke with sweet and persuasive eloquence.

O, Frankish men, in how many ways has our Lord blessed you. How fertile is your land. How steadfast your faith. How indisputable your courage. To you, accordingly, do we address our brief. We wish you to know what just and grievous cause has brought us hence. We hear ominous tidings. We hear of a malevolent race withdrawn from the communion of our belief. Turks, Persians, Arabs, accursed, estranged from God, that have laid waste by fire and sword to the walls of Constantinople, to the Arm of Saint George. Until now Constantinople was our bulwark, our rampart. Now it stands disfigured, imperiled. How many churches have these enemies of God polluted, torn asunder? We hear of altars desecrated by filth from Turkish bodies. We hear of true believers circumcised, the blood of circumcision poured into baptismal fonts. What can we say to you? Turks stable their horses in churches. Misbelievers force Christians to kneel and bow their heads, awaiting the stroke of the sword. Turks ravish Christian women. They ravish Christian children. What more can

4

we say? Think of pilgrims who crossed the sea, obligated to pay toll at the gate to every city, at the entrance to every church. How often are they falsely accused, humiliated? Those who trusted in poverty, how are they met? They are searched for hidden coins. Calluses on their heels are slit in search of coins. They are given scammony to drink until they vomit, until their bowels burst, while Turks examine what they disgorge. O, listen. Turks cut apart the bellies of Christians, slice apart their entrails so that what nature held secret must be disclosed. Turks perforate the navels of God's servants, pull forth and bind their intestines to stakes, lead them about while viscera discolor the earth. They pierce Christians with arrows, flog the suffering. What else can we say? What more shall be said? To whom, therefore, does the task of vengeance fall, if not to you? Are not these your brethren in Christ? O, Frankish men, are you not girdled knights? Step forward. Ye who have turned against one another, who cultivate fraternal strife, step forward. Ye who have been thieves, become soldiers. Be you now armed with the sign of the cross and step forth to battle enemies of our Lord. Let no obstacle dissuade you. Let controversy slumber. Let no possession detain you, nor family solicitude. Recall the words of thy blessed Savior. Whosoever shall abandon for my name's sake his house, or his brethren, or his sisters, or his father, or his mother, or his wife, or his children, or his property, shall receive a hundredfold and shall inherit everlasting life. If the Maccabees of ancient days earned glory because they fought for the Temple, likewise are you granted this opportunity to rescue the Cross, the Blood, the Tomb. In the past have you not waged unmeet war? Have you not ingloriously struggled toward mutual destruction? Avarice and pride directed you. For this you deserve damnation, perpetual death. Yet now we offer redemption, the reward of holy martyrdom. O, ye Franks. Palestine is a land flowing with milk and honey, precious in the sight of God, a place to be divided. Therefore we call upon you. Wrest from that accursed race the promised land, Jerusalem, fruitful above other lands, center of the earth, made illustrious by His sojourn, consecrated by His passion, redeemed by His death, glorified by His burial. The way is short, the struggle brief. Fear not. Fear not torture wherein lies the martyr's crown. A bed awaits you in Paradise. Fear not death wherein lies everlasting glory. Angels will present your souls to God. Now see before you, leading, guiding, He who is invisible, eternal. Therefore march assured in expiation of your sin. Go assured that after this world you shall know imperishable glory in the world to come. Let the host of the Lord rush against His foe. Let whoever would liberate Jerusalem bear the cross of our Lord on his breast or on his brow until he sets forth. And when he shall return from the journey, having fulfilled his vow, let him fix that holy emblem between his shoulders in memory of Christ who preceded him. Let him cover his shoulders with the mark of our redemption. Now may the army of God cry against His enemies.

Deus lo volt! Deus lo volt! Deus lo volt!

And the shout rang across the meadow. God wills it! We are told that while Pope Urban addressed the multitude an apparition of the Holy City glowed in the sky above his head. Does not a certain order embrace all things?

Bishop Adhémar of Le Puy knelt before the pontiff, asking leave to go. His Holiness decreed that Bishop Adhémar should go and rule the host. This was as it should be. Nine years earlier he had made the pilgrimage and now was first to accept the cross.

Next came envoys from Raymond, count of Toulouse, half-Spanish through his mother, Princess Almodis of Barcelona. He was fifty-three years old, scarred by ancient wounds, had lost one eye battling the Moors. Count Raymond would undertake the journey, his blue standard leading Provence mountaineers with saddles fashioned from soft Córdoba leather, reins weighted with gold ornament. He would bring his youthful wife Elvira, princess of Aragon, and their newly born son. Thus would they journey toward another life, realizing that duty imposed by Holy Scripture which bids us transcend the self.

News of this assembly at Clermont traveled across Europe faster than swift horsemen, more quickly than fire consuming a parched field. To the Netherlands, Scandinavia, Germany, Italy, hamlet to village to city. Thousands rushed to take the cross, noble and commonage. Ironsmith, groom, villein, carter, fletcher, knave, chandler, monk, fisherman, cleric, teacher, young, old, thieves absolved of crime through papal edict, debtors released from claims of creditors rising from the abyss of misery, touched by the light, impelled to take up arms against enemies of the Lord. Two brothers from Provence, Guy and Geoffrey de Signes, accepted the cross for the grace of pilgrimage, as they declared, but also to quench that immoderate madness wherein Christians are oppressed, made captive, slaughtered with barbaric fury. Since the creation of the world what has occurred so marvelous as this exodus toward Jerusalem? Abbot Guibert de Nogent disclosed how the Savior instituted holy war that all might find a new path to salvation.

Portents of divine favor blazed overhead. Mounted warriors, infidel and Christian, battled with fiery swords. Stars hurtled earthward, each a dying pagan. Clouds redder than blood darted to the zenith. In the east a comet was observed changing place by sudden leaps. A child was born with double limbs, another with three heads. A woman two years pregnant bore a child that knew how to speak. A foal emerged from its dam with uncommonly large teeth. Here and there people repeated what others said, that Charlemagne would rise from his grave to lead this army of the Lord.

Does not a wheel turn slowly at first? Now faster, faster. Knights mortgaged their estates, great or small, farmers sold their plows, artisans their tools, each after his fashion preparing to liberate the Holy Land. Some who felt reluctant or undecided got unwelcome gifts to express contempt, a knitting needle, a distaff. Meanwhile the clerics of France distributed swords, staves, pilgrim wallets. Yet dissident whispers and murmurs could be heard. How have Saracens troubled us? Why take arms against strangers that neither harry nor bait us? But these skeptics did not think rightly or they would perceive how everywhere Christianity lay wounded by Saracen misbelief.

As to women, thousands employed smoking hot iron in the form of a cross to sear themselves on the breast and stained their wound with red ointment. Whether burnt in flesh or cut from silk or woven gold to exhibit on mantles, tunics, cassocks, was it not appropriate that Christ's servants be thus identified? Since they made themselves known under this acknowledgment of faith did they not in truth acquire that Cross of which they bore the symbol? This emblem they adopted as a sign of pious intent and does not good intent warrant the accomplishment of good work?

How many pilgrims left home? Who counts the grains of wheat in a field? From mist-shrouded uplands came Scots clothed in shaggy skins, legs bare, each with his fleas and sack of victual. Now here came the Welshman out of his forest, the Dane who would forswear drinking to make a pilgrimage, the Northman turning his back on raw fish. From strange distant lands came unfamiliar men to disembark at Frankish ports, bawling a language so foreign that, unable to make themselves understood, they laid two fingers in the form of a cross to show in default of words how they wished to join this expedition. Many western Franks left home without regret because of civil war, famine, and plague spreading from the church of Saint Gertrude de Nivelle. Even today there is no help for this plague, which burns like fire until the victim must give up the afflicted part or his life. Neither leech nor physic nor corrective is any use, proof of sovereign displeasure.

Thousands marched toward Amiens lightly provisioned, crudely armed, taut with desire to swarm about Peter the little hermit, joyful and pious, eager to follow. They are said to have been ripe with laughter, full of badinage so confident were they, numerous as pebbles at a beach, fearless in their numbers, peregrini Christi. They busied themselves cutting scarlet crosses for their tunics while he preached. Yet what were these innocents who expected to vanquish a Saracen horde? Hapless peasants, mock monks, halegrins, ribalds, druggists, pick-thanks, beribboned harlots, sodomites, magicians, catamites, those with hairless shanks, cripples that begged a sou from the porch at Notre-Dame, those who chanted hymns for centimes and threw mad fits, night strollers.

How impatient to liberate Jerusalem were they? Frankish barons fixed the month of August for departure. But this shoal of blind fish, this bawling herd of misbegotten witlings refused to wait. Villeins fitted oxen with shoes as though shoeing knightly chargers, harnessed lumbering steeds to carts heaped with possessions until they might be taken for hayricks alive with children. In April they set forth to crush a pagan host, unwary lambs bleating on the track of their pastor.

Having marched to the land of Alemanni they were scorned as country folk loosed by folly, striving after uncertainties in lieu of certainty, having left for naught the places of their birth. And the children spying some village or castle would ask if it might be Jerusalem.

Easter Sunday they reached Cologne where again Peter stopped to preach. Some who felt impatient rode on, breeding disorder, looting, murdering. They assaulted a fortress but were hurled back. Some drowned while attempting to retreat. Others lost heart, withered by shame, and began walking toward Gaul, starved, penniless. Yet others sharply inveighed against a march on Jerusalem when all about lived those despicable enemies of Christ, Jews. Hence they searched out Jews, preceded by a she-goat and a goose. According to many, such creatures have been animated by God to identify unbelievers. Could this be the judgment of our Lord, or an egregious error of the mind? Israelites were led into captivity on account of numerous sins they committed, their term of deliverance fixed at one hundred years. Yet they had been held captive for centuries in divers places, which argues they have sinned past computation.

By the coat of our Lord may Israel be understood. As Jacob's coat was closer to him than any other garment, so at one time was the faith of Israel closer to God than any other. Yet the Jews tore apart His garment. Now, just as a furious man shreds his coat, throwing one shred this way, another that way, so did our Lord angrily cast aside the Jews, scattered them. While Christians labor to purify

9

churches and establish truth, Jews look to wicked ritual, circumcision, abstinence from pork.

Documents relate that Peter still preached at Cologne when Count Emich of Leisengen marched against Spier. A noble of low repute, a brigand, Emich burned a cross into his flesh. They say he felt inspired by the hermit. Also, he thought a display of religious fervor might put something in his pocket. However it was, at Spier he found the Jews sheltered by a Christian bishop. Nevertheless he rounded up ten or twelve, despatching them on the point of a sword since they would not gainsay their faith. Chronicles allege that a particular Jewess stabbed herself to avoid being taken by Germans. Later the bishop arrested several of Emich's men and chopped off their hands. Did our Lord's eye turn cloudy and dark?

Next to the city of Worms. It is said these Jews not long previous had drowned a Christian and kept his body in a cistern, poisoning the water, so quite rightly they feared the arrival of Count Emich. Soon enough he came knocking at the gate. His soldiers abetted by townsfolk stormed the Judengasse, which is to say Jews' Lane, butchered every Jew in sight, cutting them down like a reaper with his sickle, destroyed the synagogue, ripped apart rolls of the Torah to mock and litter the street. Meschulam bar Isaac snatched up his infant son, telling his wife he would offer the child to God. She implored him to kill her first. He would not. First he stabbed the child, then his wife. And a certain Isaac known as the son of Daniel was caught while leaving home, dragged to church, spitting, cursing, a rope around his neck. You may yet be saved, said Emich's men. Do you accept Jesus Christ? He refused to speak, or could not because of the rope, and motioning with one finger told them to lop off his head, which they did. In that city one thousand perished.

Count Emich moved north to Mainz. These Jews were terrified, knowing what happened at Spier and Worms. Two Israelites walking toward the synagogue heard ghosts praying, clear proof that all were doomed. They begged Archbishop Rothard to save them, slipped him two hundred silver marks and left Jewish treasure for him to protect. Therefore he shut the gates against Count Emich.

Mysteriously the gates opened. So all at once the courtyard of Archbishop Rothard sparkled with German lances. Emich's men hunted out those who crucified our Savior. Israelites draped fringed prayer shawls about their shoulders, huddled submissively, among them Rabbi Isaac ben Moses, renowned as a scholar, who was first to stretch out his neck, hastening to fulfill the intent of his Creator as if he did not wish to live another moment. Thus he met the blade. Willingly did these Jews accept the judgment of heaven and made no effort to escape, not while stones were flung at them, not while arrows struck. Those in the courtyard, one and all, took their final steps.

Others less devout rushed toward the palace for safety, entrusted their lives to Archbishop Rothard. But he did not like the look of things since he had been their spokesman and took to his heels, fled to his villa near Rüdesheim.

Emich's men went about the business with clubs and fire and swords while Jews howled insults, shrieked that our precious Lord was a flimsy god of nothingness, bastard son of a whore. They hurled coins from palace windows to distract or appease the Germans, but when this had no effect they lost hope. There is none like God! shouted these Jews. We can do no better than sacrifice ourselves! So they began to cut the throats of their wives and children. Blood flowed into blood, blood of women mingled with the blood of men. Sisters, fathers, daughters, mothers, brothers. Narratives speak of some Jewess who had four children and beseeched a friend to kill them lest they be baptized. The blood of her youngest she caught in folds of her cloak. Next, two daughters. Her fourth child, Aaron, crept under a chest but she seized his foot, dragged him out, offered him to the god of Israel. Emich's men found her weeping on the floor and put her to the sword. The husband, being told, stabbed himself. Mordechai the Elder slashed himself in the belly with a knife, his entrails gushed forth. Kalonymos, the principal rabbi, betook himself at full speed to Rüdesheim where he begged asylum at the archbishop's villa. This seemed a favorable moment to save Rabbi Kalonymos from hell so Archbishop Rothard proposed conversion, but Kalonymos snatched a knife and sought to murder him, which straightway cost his own life.

Documents relate that certain Jews were baptized through force but afterward, once Count Emich had gone, in defiance took up their wicked faith as dogs return to vomit. Isaac the Righteous, so called, led his son and daughter at midnight to the sacred Ark, slew them, sprinkled the pillars with their blood. This, said he, is reconciliation for the evil I have done. Next he set his mother's house afire. Next to the synagogue with his torch, chanting madly. Christians held out a long pole for him to grasp, hoping to save this Jew they had converted, but he would not accept it and perished in the blaze. Nine hundred or more died at Mainz. Carts heaped high with corpses went trundling through the night, which is piteous. Yet one should inquire, as did the bishop of Cluny, if Jews be not more guilty than Saracens toward Jesus Christ.

The bishop of Würzburg collected butchered Jews. Fingers. Thumbs. Feet. Hands. Severed heads. He anointed these bloody pieces with oil and buried them in his garden since it is the nature of a man to perform his office.

Count Emich's Jerusalemfarers marched along the Rhine to Cologne. Here, as elsewhere, Israelites scattered, disguised themselves. Some who were caught and refused to acknowledge the light of the world were slain, their synagogue wrecked, burnt.

Nor did English Jews escape. Many in London ran shrieking to the devil. York. Stamford. Norwich. Throughout the realm Jewish bloodsuckers were despatched, this according to Richard of Devizes. Winchester alone, says he, ignored its worms.

Count Emich marched toward Hungary. Why go to the end of the earth at huge expense, his soldiers asked, if those who deny our Lord live close at hand? Trier. Metz. Prague. Ratisbon. Nitra. How many Israelites tasted the blade? Coloman, sovereign of Hungary, would not grant permission for this army to continue and ordered soldiers to defend the bridge near Wiesselburg. For six weeks they skirmished, during which time Emich's men laid siege to Wiesselburg fortress. But they lost heart, fleeing in all directions when Coloman himself appeared. Count Emich with some few knights escaped on swift horses and rode back to Germany, very far from Jerusalem. It may be this was punishment meted out by God for slaughtering the children of Israel. And yet, since Jews are proven enemies of God what happened could not be homicide but malicide. With Jews, as with Saracens, albeit they manifest good works and great penance it is of no use since those who do not believe are damned. If enemies of the Church meet no resistance, how should Christianity survive? Therefore they must be bent with appropriate harshness, as the mad are shackled that the lucid may flourish. Christians who worship the Lord do not practice forbearance in false show.

Regarding the hermit, from Cologne to Oedenburg he straddled his donkey accompanied by the music of creaking wagons, errant knights, rabble beyond counting. On to Belgrade whose inhabitants wisely vanished. Seven days through the forest to Nish. One week later at Sophia here came envoys from Constantinople, from Emperor Alexius Comnenus, who greeted the hermit with respect. Peter wept for joy.

As rivers descend toward the sea, so did these pilgrims converge upon Constantinople, innocents looking to the Holy Land, crosses on their caps. It is said they were preceded by an army of locusts that ravaged vineyards but strangely ignored fields of grain. Soothsayers interpreted this to mean that Christians need not fear because they are symbolized by corn from which the bread of life is made. Saracens, however, would be annihilated because their nature is expressed by intermingling vines. Which is to say, Ishmaelites entangle themselves among the vices of Aphrodite, whom they call Chobar. They participate in orgiastic rites. Though they be circumcised their

13

passion overflows. They copulate without shame like camels or goats. Is it not vindicable for servants of God to march against unholy pleasure?

Toward the kalends of August here came Peter the hermit with his untidy host that would gather palm fronds on the banks of the Jordan, heralded by starving locusts. What awaited him at Constantinople? Italians. Ligurians. Lombards. These and more who did not feel strong enough by themselves to challenge the infidel.

Emperor Alexius Comnenus warned them. Do not cross the Arm of Saint George, he explained. Do not cross the strait until your Frankish barons arrive, for the land opposite swarms with Turks. But these palmers, indifferent to his counsel, unaffected by the hospitality he showed, went about his city doing as they pleased and behaved with utmost insolence, affronting citizens. They set fire to public buildings, stole lead plates from the roofs of churches. So after a while Alexius changed his mind and ordered them to cross the strait.

Nicomedia on the eastern shore marked the end of Greek authority. Pagans ruled the land beyond. For two months this rabble loitered about Nicomedia and the port of Civetot, daily expecting news of Frankish armies, stealing from houses, churches, orchards and fields. Alexius, to dissuade them from returning, despatched ships loaded with barley, oil, wine, corn, cheese, whatever they might need. Still they dreamt of Jerusalem. Capricious, dissatisfied, they explored valleys and slopes where they met shepherds whose language none could understand. They robbed the shepherds, drove flocks of animals to the coast for sale. Narratives relate that Peter admonished his pilgrims, but they were restless and tired of his leadership. Anna Comnena, the emperor's favorite daughter, told how they invaded a Greek village because they thought it was Turkish, mutilated and killed the people, roasted the bodies of infants on spits. Those who followed the hermit had become arrogant. They were bloated with pride.

Rainald de Broves led six thousand Alemanni through the countryside and took a fortress called Xerogord which they found stocked with provisions. But the instrument of God's wrath approached, a host of Turks ordered up by Sultan Kilij Arslan who was called the Red Lion. At the head of these Turks, Elchanes. Rainald hid some of his men outside the walls near a fountain. Elchanes discovered the trap and cut them down, after which he laid siege. Xerogord perched on a hill, so the Alemanni were deprived of water. According to the Gesta Francorum, those inside Xerogord had no water for eight days. They sucked the blood of mules and horses, drank their own waste, dipped rags into latrines and squeezed filth into their mouths, smeared shit on their bodies. Priests comforted them, urged them not to yield. Be strong. Be strong in the faith of Christ, said the priests. Be not afraid of those who would persecute you. Be not afraid of them that kill the body yet cannot kill the spirit.

After eight days Godfrey Burel, who was master of foot soldiers, vowed to fight alone against the Turks and rode forth to challenge them, spouting much brave talk. But instead of giving battle he bared his neck, miserably offering himself to these enemies of God. By certain accounts he agreed to surrender the fortress in exchange for his life. Whatever the truth, once the Turks occupied Xerogord they demanded to know which Christians would deny the Savior. Those who refused all at once sprouted arrows. Others marched into abject captivity like the animals they had stolen, marched away to Antioch, Chorosan, wherever their captors lived. These were the first pilgrims to suffer at infidel hands, the first to embrace martyrdom.

Elchanes turned against the Christian camp near Civetot. He directed spies to go and pretend that Germans had captured the city of Nicaea which was very rich. This excited the Franks at Civetot who thought themselves entitled to share the plunder. Trumpets began to sound. Soon enough five hundred knights accompanied by twenty thousand men afoot pressed noisily into the forest toward Nicaea. Only those who lacked weapons or felt too weak to march remained at camp. It is said they advanced in six battle lines, each with an up-lifted standard, boasting, shouting. Now here came the Red Lion himself, Kilij Arslan, leading his Turks through the forest. Hearing such tumult among the trees he paused to marvel. What is this? he wondered. Behold! he said. Are these not the Franks? Let us go back to the open field where we will meet them, where they have no refuge.

So when the foolish pilgrims got out of the woods they saw a field thick with enemies and were amazed. They began to shout, to encourage themselves in the name of Jesus. But the Turks, skillful archers, unleashed flight upon flight of arrows. Fulk, a soldier fa-mous in his own country, gave up the ghost. Walter the Penniless ascended to Paradise, ten or twenty darts piercing his chain mail. Walter de Breteuil fled through brambles and thickets. Godfrey Burel, according to some, did not bare his neck at Xerogord but turned from this battle and galloped back along the path to Civetot. God knows the truth. Now what remained of little Peter's army rushed desperately through the forest, Turks rejoicing at their heels. And when these heartless pagans got into the Frankish camp they rode among the tents killing the old, the sick, the feeble. Some they caught naked, others asleep, women nursing infants, all butchered. They found a priest celebrating mass, cut him down where he stood at his altar. Delicate girls or young boys and nuns agreeable to the eye they led off to captivity. How often we approve the beginning of things yet do not guess their end.

What of the hermit whose lugubrious face led thousands to this diabolic shore? He returned to France but never preached again, nor often spoke about what he knew. They say he brought back various holy relics and entered a monastery near Liège where he vanished in the depths of time.

Later that year a priest who accompanied the Frankish barons noted heaps of skeletons bleached by desert sun along the gulf of Nicomedia, pyramids of severed heads. Princess Anna Comnena, when she came to look around, observed twenty thousand skeletons or more, by her account a mountainous testament to folly. And it is related that years afterward when Franks built new walls for Nicomedia they used the bones of little Peter's soldiers in lieu of mortar, plugged chinks with Christian bones, made Nicomedia a tomb.

Exploits in which he took no part were attributed to the hermit until his reputation exceeded that of Godfrey de Bouillon, descended from Charlemagne, who held the richest fiefs in Lorraine. Why does Godfrey de Bouillon walk in the shadow of a monk with bare feet? This great duke sold estates on the Meuse to equip his army. He sold the city of Metz to its inhabitants for one hundred thousand gold crowns. He pledged Bouillon to the bishop of Liège. He bequeathed the castle of Ramioul to the Holy Church. All this born of his need to serve our Lord. Some say he vowed to avenge Christ's death with the blood of Jews during this pilgrimage. Concerning the truth of that, I have no knowledge.

In the spring of 1096 these barons set forth, some with falcons riding on their wrists, trailed by hunting dogs. And since the needs of such a multitude would cripple the land it was decided they should take different roads, converging and uniting at Constantinople. Those from the north, Lorraine and Brabant, as well as those who spoke Walloon, led by Duke Godfrey, would follow the route of Peter. Those from the south, led by Count Raymond, would cross Italy to the Dalmatian coast and proceed by way of Salonika to the court of Alexius. Yet another Frankish army would cross the Alps. And the Normans of Sicily, led by Bohemond with his nephew Tancred, would sail across the Adriatic to Macedonia.

Auspicious signs heralded the departure. A comet was observed, its tail streaming brightly toward the west. Some priest declared that while in the forest he heard a noise as though weapons clashed, and looking up saw a Christian sword amid a whirlwind. A monk named Sigger, of good repute, watched two horsemen in the sky ride eagerly to combat and one with an uplifted cross defeated his opponent.

When those who crossed the Alps entered Rome they went at once to pray in the basilica of Saint Peter, but were astonished by what they met. Advocates of Clement III, who was called Anti-Pope, clambering like monkeys or devils through the monastery rafters. Fulcher, an historian from Chartres who accompanied this army, relates how stones were flung at them while they lay prostrate in prayer. If this were not enough, Clement's disciples lurked beside the altar, swords in hand, to snatch up offerings. This Anti-Pope had conspired to usurp the office of His Holiness Urban, compelling His Holiness to seek refuge in Lucca. Therefore two pontiffs claimed the title and good Christians felt bewildered, not knowing which to obey. Thus, while stones dropped on them as they prayed in the basilica these Franks felt aggrieved but did not exact vengeance, which is a prerogative of God.

At Brindisi on the holy day of Easter this army was further tested. A vessel that had lain quietly at anchor rose up, cracked apart, and sank. Four hundred perished. Mules and horses swallowed by waves, chests of money lost. But when the corpses of the drowned had been recovered a very great miracle was observed. On the shoulder of each was imprinted a cross. Since they had fixed the cross to their garment in life it was God's will that this emblem of faith should accompany them throughout eternity. Shouts of joyous praise went up. But certain pilgrims felt afraid. They quit the journey, declaring they would not entrust their lives to deceptive water.

Count Raymond, who expressed a wish to die in the Holy Land, advanced by way of northern Italy, thence to the Slavic wilderness. Ahead and behind, plotting to attack, lay companies of Petchenegs, Cumans, and other cruel savages. Brutish people fled like deer when the Provençals arrived but followed at a distance to rob and murder any who loitered. Raymond captured six of these brigands. While returning with them to the army he found himself endangered. To horrify and delay those who pursued him, beseeching the help of God to deliver him from that accursed place, he ordered the hands of his captives mutilated, their noses chopped off, eyes gouged out. By this stratagem he contrived to escape.

For many weeks these Provençals wandered across Sclavonia, marching through clouds so thick they could be felt and pushed aside. Finally they got down to the seacoast where they expected to be safe. Here they met envoys from Constantinople bearing assurances of hospitality but the Petchenegs and others refused to disperse. Indeed, while acknowledging the sovereignty of Emperor Alexius they continued to harry the Franks. Prince Rainard was slain and his brother fatally wounded, both noble princes. Bishop Adhémar, having ridden his mule some distance from camp to pitch a tent, was attacked by savages who dragged him from the saddle, brutally beat him and robbed him. His life was spared through the power of Almighty God because so great a leader was necessary to the pilgrimage.

At Thessalonika he fell ill so there he rested with several knights for protection while the host advanced to a fortified town called Russa. Because these citizens proved stubborn and difficult Count Raymond ordered his men to break through the wall.

Toulouse! Toulouse! they shouted, doing as they were bid, and quickly the town surrendered.

Next, at Rodosto, shouting the war cry, they slew many soldiers and took some booty. Here they met emissaries Raymond had despatched to Constantinople. Alexius welcomed them, pressed gifts upon them, and gladly awaited his arrival, said these emissaries. Also, he was urged to hurry forward because Count Robert of Flanders and other princes had need of his counsel. Raymond therefore advanced with a few men, leaving the army behind, and came to the honey-colored walls of Constantinople. Alexius greeted him with honor and requested him to swear allegiance, thus making Raymond a vassal.

Count Raymond answered that he would respect the honor and life of the emperor, but said he had not journeyed such a distance to fight on behalf of any lord save Jesus Christ.

Godfrey de Bouillon, duke of Lorraine, arrived fitly clad, his gold and purple mantle edged with ermine and marten and similar fur white as snow. Alexius greeted him with the kiss of peace, whereupon the proud duke with his yellow beard went down on one knee.

I hear thou art the mightiest prince of thy land, said Alexius. I hear thou art a man to be trusted utterly. Thus I take thee for my adopted son. In thee I place my trust.

Next came Bohemond from Taranto, leader of those Normans who in times past wrested Sicily from Muslim hands. Never had the Byzantine court beheld such a prince. He stood almost a cubit taller than other men, which excited both admiration and fear. It appeared to Princess Anna that he stooped somewhat, not through weakness of the spine but a slight malformation present from birth. The skin of his body she thought strangely white, his features mottled red, tawny hair clipped at the ears so it did not lap against his shoulders like that of other Franks, his chin shaved smooth as marble and his eyes Celtic blue, crested with passion. His dignity she thought half spoilt by the terror he inspired, his glance wild and hard. In the way he stood she found something obdurate, savage, his arrogance manifest. His laughter sounded like a threat. She called his mind supple and rich in subterfuge, his speech calculated, his rejoinders ambiguous like one who meant to seize an empire if he could. In him, she wrote, love and courage stood armed, anxious for combat. She judged the natural gifts of Bohemond superior to those of other men, surpassed only by her father.

She mentions a certain Count Raoul who boorishly sat on the imperial throne. Alexius afterward retained this haughty knight, by means of an interpreter asking who he was. I am a Frank, said he, of most high and noble lineage. In my country is a shrine at the crossroads where all betake themselves who would display valor in personal combat. There I went and for a long time waited, but none chose to measure swords with me. To which the emperor replied that he would have his chance. Indeed, this malapert noble soon bled out his life on Turkish soil.

Anna did not set down what she knew about these Franks until years afterward when she was an old woman locked in a convent at her brother's command. I think with her husband Nicephorus Briennius she fomented some intrigue that was the cause of banishment. I have heard she tried clumsily to assassinate her brother. Whatever the fact, she was no more than fourteen when the Franks arrived. To her eyes they made up a violent host, impulsive, grasping, barbaric men followed by pale women, children, numberless animals, and quaint equipment. She named them Celts, albeit their homelands varied. Each leader she thought a count, whether duke or knight or baron or pilgrim of a different rank, confusing Longobards with Provençals or Flemings. She and other Greeks felt disdain mingled with hatred toward these intrepid servants of Christ who journeyed five hundred leagues.

As to the emperor, what sifts through ancient narratives? A man broad and squat, his curly beard glistening with oil, his gestures courtly, dark eyes alert with malice. Through some deficiency he could not quite enunciate the eighteenth letter, which is to say, R. He thought himself emperor of all Romans, paying homage to one who founded the city where he ruled, Constantine. Only when surrounded by torches did he expose himself to the people, gowned in the royal purple of dead Caesars. From the cross surmounting his crown dripped strands of jewels, from his shoulders loops of pearls to attest his radiance, attesting the radiance of Jesus Christ since he was Christo Autocrator. Yet he was bone and flesh and blood. During a game of polo an exceeding fat general, by name Taticius, fell against his leg. The injury did not seem important but later he got the gout. Owing to the abundance of my sins, he was heard to say, I deserve to suffer. And if he murmured with pain he quickly made the sign of the Cross. Wicked One, he would say, addressing the devil, a curse on you!

21

Turks made sport of his infirmity, believing it an excuse for cowardice. They thought it ripe for comic drama. Some would play at being servants or slaves while Kilij Arslan played physician. Shouting with laughter they would put the wretched emperor to bed and drunkenly attend his needs.

Nor did Franks show much grace. They petitioned him without respite, wanting this or that, nor limited their speeches by the water clock as did orators of times past. Shamelessly they invaded the palace trailed by subordinates, making a lengthy queue, each after something for his pocket. Alexius listened patiently to these requests. At dusk he would limp to his apartment. Still they followed, brisk with avarice.

Princess Anna wrote that he was expert at discerning the grain of a man, at penetrating secrets of the mind. Thus, when Bohemond arrived, Alexius inquired about the journey and had food brought to him. Bohemond gave the food to lackeys, neither tasting it nor touching it with a fingertip, and next day asked if any fell sick. Alexius tried him further. He ordered a room in the palace precincts set aside, stuffed with extravagant riches, brocade, silk, sumptuous clothes, hammered gold cups and urns. Jewels and coins so littered the floor that one could not walk through without trampling them. And the door opened suddenly. Ah! cried Bohemond. If I acquired such wealth I would be the lord of many lands! He was told that everything belonged to him, a gift from Alexius. Chronicles relate that he felt overjoyed but afterward changed his mind, claiming he was insulted. Then he regretted his pride, changing like a sea polyp. For this Princess Anna scorned him, writing that he as much surpassed in deceit all the Franks who visited Constantinople as he was inferior to them in wealth.

Fulcher de Chartres, who was present, declares that the emperor excelled at caution. We could not visit, says he, but in little companies of five or six, at hourly intervals. As one group of pilgrims emerged, another entered to pray in the churches. All because Alexius feared mischief.

deus lo volt!

What of those emperors who preceded him? Ghosts sunk in pravity. Here was Monomakh, surpassing fat, held upright in the saddle by slaves to either side, who bestowed his diadem and purple mantle on the jester, who endured the gout as did Alexius but called it an excellent thing since otherwise he would squander himself among women. He showed his mistress to the populace, gold serpents entwining her naked arms. Here also his aged consort Zoë wallowing on carpets in senile lust, clutching jeweled icons to her flabby breast. Here, too, Emperor Michael entranced by races at the hippodrome while a beacon winked ominous news from the Asian shore. When high office falls to decadent rulers who shall measure corruption? The city is called by some a mindless old hag eternally renewing herself, magically becoming a maiden lustrous with gems.

Why should not rude Franks be dazzled by Constantinople? Here lay the severed head of John the Baptist in a golden casket. Here was the rod of Moses. The crown of thorns. The cerement of our Lord. Five drops of His precious blood. These and other relics of high significance might be seen within the walls. Here were lamps of light for those who believe.

Toward the end of April in that year of providential grace 1097 orders were given to embark, to cross the Arm of Saint George. Taticius, whose clumsiness at polo caused the emperor's gout, went with the Franks. He had lost his nose during some battle and thereafter, much ashamed, wore a golden nose. Or it may be as William of Tyre relates that his nostrils had been slit, sign of an evil nature, mangled in virtue, treacherous, chosen to serve as guide because he knew the land. The emperor would depend on his cunning. Taticius therefore accompanied the living host like a snake among eels, a goose among swans, reporting privately to Alexius.

In the legions altogether were six hundred thousand of both sexes afoot or mounted, one hundred thousand cuirassed knights.

They crossed the strait and proceeded to Nicomedia without opposition. From here they looked south to Nicaea, home of Kilij Arslan. By chance the Red Lion was two hundred leagues distant fighting insubordinate princes. When he learned of the Christian army he sent word to Nicaea, telling his people not to be afraid. These invaders have traveled so far, said he with contempt, that even their horses stumble.

Duke Godfrey put three thousand men to work with swords and hatchets because the road was narrow. These faithful servants of our Lord erected crosses of iron and wood to encourage those who would follow. Here and there on the plain, in the forest, they discovered little cemeteries where pilgrims of the hermit's army lay buried, a fruitless end.

Duke Godfrey was first to view the walls of Nicaea. One by one here came the barons. Guy de Possessa. Bohemond. Tancred. Roger de Barneville. Robert the Fleming. Bishop Adhémar. They encamped, wondering how to attack Nicaea, which could not be surrounded because it stood at the edge of a lake. Nor could the inhabitants be stopped from going out to collect wood, fodder, grain, whatever they needed. But the city must be taken since it was situated between Constantinople and Jerusalem. Logs were hauled from the forest to make battering rams. Perriers, mangonels, ballistas, and similar engines were constructed.

When all seemed ready they undertook the siege. Stones flew at the wall and over the wall. Defenders answered with fire, stones, poisoned arrows. Men on both sides died groaning, pierced, crushed, bleeding, invoking their God. Count Raymond set a company of men to work burrowing at the foundation while archers defended them from Turks overhead. These miners pried out stones and dragged them away, replacing them with wood beams that were set afire. If Satan's disciples managed to injure a pilgrim beside the wall they let down iron hooks to catch him and hoist him up where they would strip off his armor, mutilate him, and throw down pieces of his body at his friends.

Anon the wall crumbled but those inside hastily bolstered it. And here came enemies rushing from the gate with ropes to tie up captives. By the grace of God all were slain, their heads tossed back into

24

the city. Now the wife of Kilij Arslan was at Nicaea and grew exceedingly terrified in the manner of women and thought to escape. Taking her children and her maids she embarked. However the Franks wisely had posted guards in little boats, so they caught her and brought her to the barons.

On the sixteenth of May during a sharp engagement many Turks were killed. Archbishop William of Tyre asserts that one thousand infidel heads were delivered to Emperor Alexius, a gift that heartily pleased him and moved him to reward the barons with silk garments and not a little money.

Day after day some Turk of gigantic stature stood insolently on the battlements. Using a bow of prodigious length he wrought havoc among the living host. Christian arrows launched toward him would drop at his feet, thus word spread that here was the Arch Fiend against whom no mortal could prevail. Duke Godfrey then took a crossbow and loosed a bolt at his heart. Without a cry the pagan fell dead. Anguished groans could be heard inside the walls. Shouts of vindication arose outside.

Deus adjuva! Deus adjuva!

Yet they were unable to subjugate Nicaea. They met in council, after which they sent to Emperor Alexius requesting ships. Presently here came a little fleet, which cast anchor at Civetot, two leagues distant. The Franks lashed wagons together according to the size of each vessel and with the help of ropes, using men and horses, drew them up on wagons and during the night hauled them to the lake. By this stratagem Nicaea was encircled and would have been forced to surrender. But just when the Franks prepared to attack they saw the blue and gold standard of Alexius floating above the city. Unknown to them, the emperor had made a pact with these Turks. Nicaea would submit to him if he spared the citizens. Alexius arranged this not for the inhabitants whose lives meant less to him than the lives of ten thousand cats, but to regain control of provinces along the coast. Further, when the wife of Kilij Arslan was delivered to him at Constantinople he released her. By doing so he ingratiated himself with

25

the Red Lion. Which is to say, when the hour seemed ripe he might more easily call upon these Turks to battle the Franks. Was ever a more devious sovereign?

Those who had fought to capture the city felt betrayed. They wished to loot Nicaea and make bloody sport of the citizens. Alexius tried to placate them, saying he would give the barons equivalent treasure if they would return to Constantinople and receive it. Further, he said, those who had not sworn fealty might do so at that time. Count Raymond would not. He who vowed to fight for no lord save Jesus Christ chose to stay at Nicaea until the army might continue along the road to Jerusalem.

As for Tancred, he went reluctantly, seduced by the promise of wealth. Princess Anna saw him there and later wrote that he was a spirited, haughty youth. When asked to swear loyalty he pretended indifference. But then, glancing toward a pavilion behind the emperor, he said he would take the oath if he were given such a tent filled with money. Whereupon a member of the court, George Palaeologus, roughly shoved him. Tancred drew his sword. Alexius himself intervened, rising from the throne. Lord Bohemond also intervened, rebuking his nephew, saying it was improper to threaten a relative of the emperor. They say Tancred felt ashamed because he had acted like a man who was drunk. Then he took the oath.

Comte Stephen de Blois spurned the emperor's request. This noble lord had married Adela, daughter of William the Conqueror, and observed in a letter to her that every prince excepting himself and Raymond hurried off to congratulate the emperor on a splendid victory. Alexius receives them with much affection, he wrote, and bestows upon them opulent mantles, jewelry, horses, gold and silver coins. When he learned that I remained at Nicaea to defend the city he was most grateful, esteeming my service more to be treasured than a mountain of gold. From Nicaea we march to Jerusalem in five times seven days unless the city of Antioch withstands us.

As things turned out, Stephen wrote better than he knew.

efore all had been settled, governance of Nicaea and other matters, the Turks let go some captives, including a nun from the convent of Saint Mary at Trier who claimed she was with the hermit's army. In bitter terms she lamented her fate, how she was abducted, forced into wicked union not only by a particular Turk but others all at once with scarcely a pause. Tearfully she appealed to the barons for help in purification. Bishop Adhémar counseled her and she gained absolution because the defilement was against her will. But who shall bridle a shiftless mind? Here came word from the Turk inflamed by this nun's inestimable comeliness and he was full of coaxing, expert at cunning lewdness, imploring her to come back, offering gifts, vowing to become Christian himself if she would return. So what did she do but rush off to her filthy bridegroom and their abominable marriage. As to her reason, God knows, save that nothing but this Turk might slake her lust.

Toward the end of June, hearts set upon Antioch, the living host marched away from Nicaea. And since they had embarked on a holy expedition it seemed the Turks could not oppose them, for this would oppose the will of our Lord.

Anon they came to a marsh thick with reeds close by the city of Dorylaeum and there were Turks in ambush. Kilij Arslan had gathered three hundred thousand fighting men captained by such redoubtable emirs as Lachin, Caradig, Amirai, Boldagis, and Mirath. At sunrise here came these Turks down the hill chattering, whistling, launching clouds of javelins and poisoned arrows. As soon as the first rank of Turks emptied their quivers they made way for a second rank. Then another. Another. Various high lords had not arrived. Duke Godfrey, Count Raymond, and Hugh Vermandois were misdirected at a fork in the road.

Now those trapped beside the reeds huddled like sheep in a pen fearing death at each moment while Turks rode jubilantly among the tents, slashing, butchering, disdaining pleas for mercy. Christians fell to earth groaning, weeping, confessing their sins.

But all at once Hugh Vermandois charged into view. Next, Bishop Adhémar. So the beleaguered Franks thrust aside their doubts in order to challenge the enemy of God. Women followed, bringing water. All fought courageously, except one. Stephen de Blois could not be found.

Kilij Arslan had thought the Christian army surrounded and he rejoiced. Then came Hugh Vermandois, Godfrey, Raymond, with Bishop Adhémar leading an army of southern Franks. So the Red Lion fled away to the east without stopping to gather his tents. Muslim chronicles say he asked himself what let slip such fury. Their lances sparkle like stars, said he to himself. Their shields gleam. The clash of their swords echoes more terribly than thunder. They lift their lances when they advance, silent as though they knew not how to speak. But when they draw close they loosen the reins and charge fiercely, thirsting for blood. They grind their teeth and shout. The wind itself would retreat from their cries.

Until dusk God's army pursued the green banners of these Turks, capturing many camels loaded with baggage, weapons, brocaded garments, silver and gold. They took innumerable oxen and sheep. Such was the victory at Dorylaeum at the end of June. Even so, four thousand Christians arose to glory in our Savior. Not least among them, Tancred's noble brother William.

Two days later they resumed the march. Thirst and hunger beset them. Inhabitants of the country vanished or would not sell food. They found little to eat but thorns whose branches they chewed for liquid. Salt marshes in the desert provided no water to drink. Cisterns had been destroyed by the Turk. Men staggered, dropped, gasped for air with open mouths. Women cast forth babies too soon. William of Tyre asserts that during the first days of July five hundred pilgrims gave up the ghost. Sumpter beasts which carried baggage, parched to the vitals, refused their usual obedience. Chargers with gleaming teeth that once gloried in their estate, that once took pride in tossing their heads, stumbled clumsily to their knees and would not get up. Falcons accustomed to soaring when their lord deigned to hunt now drooped and faded. Armored knights lurched on foot across the desert. Dogs, pigs, sheep, goats were saddled to carry baggage. Yet it is said that hardship brought the pilgrims together, this varied camp of Gauls, Normans, Aquitanians, Bretons, Armenians, Greeks, and others. They had come from divers lands speaking many tongues, but marched like brothers toward Jerusalem.

They arrived at some desolate village whose people wondered why they traveled without waterskins. Here the pilgrims learned how to make them and gave thanks.

Deeper in Saracen land they discovered a plant not unlike a reed that produced a sort of honey for which reason it was named canna mellis. They swallowed as much as they could, albeit this did not assuage their hunger. They killed donkeys to eat. They ate camels and dogs. Presently the autumn rain began to fall. Even as gold is thrice tried with fire and seven times purified, so were these servants of the Lord subjected to manifold torment. In their path stood a precipitous mountain, the route narrow and foreboding. None was anxious to go first. Pack animals were jostled or slipped and plunged screaming into the abyss. Those roped together dragged each other down. Valiant knights benumbed with cold lost hope and cast aside their shields.

At length our Savior rescued them from adversity and brought them to Marash, a settlement of Armenians in a fruitful valley where they obtained food.

It was here that Baldwin de Boulogne resolved to conquer Cilicia. They say he did not feel much need to visit the Holy Sepulcher but often spoke of governing a Turkish province. Therefore he commended his wife and children to the army of God, took five hundred mounted knights and two thousand sergeants afoot, and departed. Fifty leagues west he came to the city of Tarsus. But there he saw to his amazement the Norman banner of Tancred flying from every tower. Bohemond's nephew with a small company of one hundred knights had captured the city. So, being furious, having more knights at his command, Baldwin charged Tancred to withdraw. Seeing the disadvantage and no help for it, Tancred led his knights away to besiege Adana. The monk Albert of Aix relates that during the night here came three hundred Normans expecting a welcome at Tarsus and Lord Baldwin did not unbolt the gate. He listened to every plea without hearing. Perforce these Normans camped outside the wall where Turks descended, cutting them to pieces. Many pilgrims held this against Baldwin.

When he returned to Marash he learned that his children were dead of plague and his beloved wife Godehilde, an English lady of noble birth, lay dying. Truly does a certain order embrace all things and whatever deviates unjustifiably must fall back into order, conscious of the retribution it has earned.

He found also that his brother Godfrey was gravely hurt while fighting a bear. Duke Godfrey had ridden into the woods for exercise and recreation when he heard someone cry for help and there was a pilgrim laden with firewood chased by the monster. Duke Godfrey rode to save him. Then the beast flung itself with teeth and claws against this enemy's horse and clawed until it fell to the ground. Then with his left hand the duke clutched the bear and with the other hand plunged his sword hilt deep into the struggling animal, which roared and died. Yet it was a costly triumph, Godfrey stretched on the earth and blood leaking from horrible gashes. The pilgrim called for help so people came running. They put Godfrey on a litter and took him to camp where remedies were administered. Thus his life was saved, showing how the mercy of our Lord prevails.

Baldwin stayed at Marash just two days following the death of his wife. He had in mind to visit Edessa, a fortified city governed by a prince of Armenia named Thoros. This prince was extremely old and afraid of Turks. Some say he invited Baldwin to visit because he heard that Kerbogha, the atabeg of Mosul, had levied a vast army. Chronicles relate that Thoros, who was childless and much in dread of Kerbogha, proposed to make the Frank his son and heir. Baldwin for his part thought Edessa well worth owning. The voluptuous ritual of adoption looked alien to Frankish eyes. Baldwin, having removed his blouse, was instructed to creep inside the flowing blouse worn by Thoros. Thus concealed they rubbed their bodies as if they were lovers and the prince kissed him. Baldwin next performed this duty with the old princess.

Some conspiracy was hatched. Citizens objected that Prince Thoros failed to protect the harvest from brigands. Also, they said, they were taxed too much. By certain accounts Baldwin approved this revolt, seeing himself the legetary. However it was, Thoros came to him in great mistrust, saying he would escape with his old wife to Melitene. By the archangels and on the holiest relics Baldwin swore that his venerable head was not at risk, no matter if a crowd outside was howling for his death. Thoros abjectly offered his people the cross of Varak and the cross of Mak'enis, but they and the senators of Edessa shouted with one voice that he should not escape. He attempted to lower himself from the palace by a rope because he understood that nothing he might do would appease them. But the furious citizens shot him down with five hundred arrows and lopped off his head which they fixed on a spear to carry about the streets. That may be how it was. By other accounts the terrified old prince and his consort were each pulled apart, limb from limb, near the palace gate. Who can look through centuries of dust?

Baldwin, finding himself now count of Edessa, married a rich and highborn lady called Arda because the union might prove advantageous. It is said her father Thatoul promised a dowry of sixty thousand bezants, then all at once rode away to the mountains, so much was he alarmed by this violent Frank. Beyond doubt Lord Baldwin was one of those who would have a fortune, no matter how. And where he finds it, that place would he call home. Many hold this up as rank ambition, believing it turns the iniquitous heart to evil. For myself, Jean, I do not pretend to know.

Now, Antioch is the principal city of Turks and to it has been ascribed the third or perhaps the second seat of dignity, since there is much argument, after Rome itself. Antiochus, who succeeded Alexander of Macedon, gave it his name. Here may be found three hundred and sixty monasteries with a patriarch holding sway over one hundred and fifty-three bishops. Of such authority is Antioch that during its existence seventy-five kings have sat enthroned. At one time it was called Reblata. Here the king of Judah, Zedekiah, together with his sons came into the presence of Nebuchadnezzar who ordered the youths slain under their father's eyes. Then the king, Zedekiah, was blinded.

Here occurred the first gathering of true believers. Here also they adopted the name Christian. Prior to this they were called Nazarene. Eagerly and voluntarily did the city embrace this faith and disseminate the Name, a name diffusing fragrance like precious ointment. Therefore a new name was appointed. Theopolis. Hence, a city that had borne the name of a wicked man saw fit to honor Almighty God. By what means it reverted to Antioch, mistress of error, I have not heard.

So thick are the walls of Antioch that wagons may be driven along the top and pass without touching. Four hundred turrets surmount these walls, which are the color of biscuit. Within their compass rise four mountain peaks. Antioch is magnificent to behold. It has been called a sister to Constantinople. It has been likened to a fabulous orchard blooming with myrtle and pine, enhanced by a multitude of flowers. Among its many wonders is a church dedicated to the apostle Peter who sat enthroned after receiving the keys to the kingdom of heaven from our Lord. Also, there are numerous public baths watered by ancient Roman cisterns and a theater paved with marble by King Herod. Villas and palaces of wealthy merchants embellish the hillsides.

Antioch scornfully rejected the insidious dogma of Mahomet

while Eastern lands shuddered, while millions breathed miasmic falsehood. Among errant or subjugated cities Antioch by itself sustained the true faith. But at last, enfeebled, distressed, unable to combat the wickedness of God's remorseless enemies, Antioch surrendered. Nevertheless her citizens continued to worship the Lord, for which they were mistrusted. No Christian might have weapons. No Christian might participate in military exercise. None might hold high office. Nor could they leave their homes except at certain hours.

Very often it happens that men know the bays for succulent fish or where to look for mollusc, or which strand is rich with pearl, yet in their blindness they do not know where to look for the good they seek. Thus, when the living host approached Antioch what did the governor do? He imprisoned the Christian patriarch, stabled horses in the cathedral of Saint Paul. If this were not enough, he drove impoverished citizens out of the city lest they become a burden. As for Christians he suffered to remain, they envied the lot of exiles. They carried beams of wood, cement, stones for catapults, labored to strengthen the walls. They got little rest, meager food. And in secret council the Turks resolved that on a particular night every Christian should feel the sword.

Nevertheless, divine vengeance advances, step by step. Albert of Aix tells how the Frankish army marched toward Antioch with purple and gold banners unfurled, sunlight on their helmets, splendrous the painted shields. When they came out on the plain there was the gleaming river Orontes, which originates near Heliopolis and flows grandly past Shaizar. Beyond the Orontes they saw five principal gates to the city. Gate of Saint Paul by which one travels to Aleppo. Bridge Gate by which one crosses the river. Gate of Dogs. Gate of Saint George. Gate of the Duke among a nest of marshes.

Antioch could not be taken from the opposite side because of precipitous slopes and ravines thick with laurel. Therefore the knighthood of Christ encamped on the plain. Here was a babble of voices. Flemings, Frisians, Bavarians, Allobroges, Iberians, Scots, Dacians, Greeks, Alemanni, with others of wonderful strangeness.

Should a Breton or Teuton address me, writes Fulcher, I could no more respond than understand.

Now the lords began to debate. Count Raymond urged immediate attack, arguing that by the mercy of God they captured Nicaea and should fear nothing. Others protested because they had no siege engines and to scale such a mighty wall would cost hundreds of lives. Others argued they must press forward because already they had spent one winter on the road to Jerusalem. Thus divided, querulous, they halted. Cattle and horses grazed nearby. Pigeons fluttered about the rooftops of cottages. Here was a lake roiling with fish, waterfowl swarmed in the reeds. Sheep were visible on the hills, orchards slung heavily with fruit. Thinking there could be no end to such abundance they stuffed their bellies on figs, quince, lotus fruit, white bread, wine, birds, and ate little of the animals they slaughtered, choosing only what fastidious appetites suggested. But all things obey their ancient law. So after a while, because these pilgrims succumbed to gluttony, famine succeeded exuberance and prodigality. They had nothing to put on their bread nor bread to put it on. These servants of the Lord munched thistles that pricked their lips, herbs unseasoned with salt, bean stalks, rats, dogs, camel hide, seeds picked from shit. Companies of soldiers explored the countryside, having vowed to share what they found, but on account of the gluttonous host not much remained. Anon the plump general Taticius departed, explaining that he would hasten to Constantinople and inform the emperor. Princess Anna recalled matters differently. Lord Bohemond, said she, coveting the city of Antioch for himself, would not honor his oath of allegiance, would not concede Antioch to the imperial representative, Taticius. Rather, he contrived a scheme. I am much alarmed for your safety, said Bohemond, I have heard of a plot to murder you. Do now as you think best. And upon these words Taticius hurried to the port and embarked for Cyprus. However it came about, the Greek slipped away.

Bishop Adhémar wisely gave orders to plough and sow the fields, understanding how those inside Antioch expected the Christians to retreat. But if they saw grain being planted they must admit to them-selves that nothing could dissuade these servants of Christ. Crops would be sown and harvested until Antioch was taken. It happened that during this time God's enemies dangled a cage outside the wall. In this cage sat the patriarch for everyone to see and pity. Yet our God remains forever a wall of strength to those who trust in Him.

Syrians are wont to speak of Antioch as a pissoir because rain so often falls. Now indeed the sky darkened and lowered. Marshes flooded. Armor rusted. Mud seeped through rugs and blankets, rot-ted tents. Bowstrings slackened. Next came pestilence creeping out of the marshes, bearing away the sick or discouraged. As many as one thousand died on a single day. Bodies putrefied, the air stank. At night here came archers through the Bridge Gate launching clouds of arrows. Muslim narratives tell how the citizens could hear Franks in their tents pray to God for mercy.

Muslim spies reported to the governor, Yaghi Siyan. They said a Frankish baron lay ill with plague and twenty thousand soldiers had marched away in search of food. Yaghi Siyan ordered cavalry across the bridge, which surprised some Provençals who rushed back and forth not knowing how to escape. Only when Bishop Adhémar came to help did these Provençals regain their wits. During this skirmish the bishop's standard with an image of Blessed Mary was captured. And the Turks, having stolen as much as they could, mutilated bodies and rode triumphantly back to Antioch. That night candles burning at the altars gave feeble reassurance. Pilgrims looked for signs, omens, and beheld visions that cheered or depressed them ac-cordingly. A comet in the shape of a cross blazed overhead, which presaged victory. Yet a gust of wind blew apart the tents of puis-sant lords. The ground underfoot grew restless. Surely men are not granted the power to comprehend in thought, nor to expound in speech, the majestic course of our Lord's divine work.

Bishop Adhémar now wrote to his bishopric at Le Puy that the army of God had fought three battles, had marched from Nicaea to Antioch, and had stormed many fortified outposts. Although this army numbered one hundred thousand knights and sergeants it was threatened by infidels more numerous than locusts. Pray for us, Bishop Adhémar concluded. Pray for us.

During Lent the barons considered a gate situated between them and the sea. Turks very often rushed out this gate to assault pilgrims going to the port of Saint Symeon five leagues distant, or when they returned with supplies. It was decided to build a fort. Lords Raymond and Bohemond should go to Saint Symeon with knights and sergeants to fetch carpenters, mattocks, whatever materials might be required. So they departed. But the watchful Turks, who could not guess why these knights were going to Saint Symeon, guessed that in a little while they would come back and laid plans to intercept them. Narratives from those days tell how whistling chattering infidels surrounded the Christians. Some escaped, riding frantically out of sight, but those afoot or otherwise limited could not do much. According to the Gesta Francorum, one thousand knights and sergeants ascended to heaven gowned in white, clothed in the white robe of martyrdom. From the Gesta we learn how Bohemond rallied his followers, how they called upon Christ, how they armed themselves with the sign of the cross fixed on their foreheads and in their hearts, how they scattered the pagans, drove them across the narrow bridge. So frightened were God's opponents that many leapt head downward to hell, yielded deformed souls to ministers of Satan. They succumbed howling to Christian steel, plummeted screeching into the river Orontes. If any wounded or drowning Turk sought to climb up columns of the bridge or struggled to gain the bank he was assaulted by servants of God who stood around waiting. Twenty Turks at least were struck with planks from the bridge until they sank and the water flowed red. Shrieks of anguish could be heard from the ramparts. But at windows in the wall appeared the faces of Christian women who lived in Antioch, who fed ravenously upon the spectacle, stealthily applauding with their hands this massacre of our Lord's enemies.

According to Raymond d'Agiles, the governor Yaghi Siyan ordered a host of Turks to defeat the Franks or perish, and shut the gate behind them. Now when they came against each other Ysoard de Ganges, sinking to his knees, called upon God for aid. Soldiers of Christ! he shouted. Soldiers of Christ! With no more than one hundred and fifty sergeants he attacked these Turks, who felt astounded by such audacity, horrified, and no longer wished to fight.

With victory achieved the Franks collected as much spoil as they could. Impoverished knights came back proudly wearing silk garments. Some boasted three and four painted shields. Some went prancing around the tents on Arab chargers. They did not stop to gather enemy heads because this happened at dusk. Very soon one and all were overwhelmed by darkness.

No more was it light than Turks crept out of the city to gather corpses on the river bank. Many were half obscured by sand. These they buried in a mosque outside the wall, which they name the Mahometry, buried them with arrows, jewelry, cloaks, bezants, whatever belonged to the dead. No sooner did they retreat than here came Franks who rushed into the diabolic sanctuary, dragged cadavers out of tombs, chopped off heads, searched for gold. Peter Tudebode relates how these heads were carried to the Frankish tents so they might be counted. Four horse loads of enemy heads went as gifts to the emir of Babylon since he had promised to become Christian.

Turks watching from the ramparts grieved openly when they observed their dead mishandled. They put aside all shame. They screamed aloud. Pagans lament an unburied corpse much as Christians lament a soul en route to hell. Christians perish for the sake of futurity, Turks for the wickedness of misbelief, since Almighty God who creates and sustains, who makes and destroys, has ordained that at the cost of suffering to Christianity the false light of Islam should be extinguished. Therefore did the bishop, wishing to excite their grief, promise twelve deniers for the head of each Turk. And having got a supply he mounted them on poles to display beneath the walls and freeze the hearts of those inside. So the Turks, gazing down upon these bloody prizes, squirmed with anguish.

Three days later the fort was begun, using stone from the Mahometry. Carpenters, masons, puddlers, lackeys, and others who had fled when attacked, being now delivered from a thicket of infidels, seeing the enemy dead, lifted up their voices to praise our Lord. This was appropriate and just, since by His disposition a pagan throng at whose hands numerous Christians had fallen became themselves victual for birds of prey and savage beasts.

These Turks chose to parade on the walls a most valiant knight they captured during the month of March and kept in a donjon, Rainald Porchet. They ordered him to ask of his comrades how much they would pay so he did not lose his head. From where he stood on the wall he shouted that they must not pay ransom. If I die, he shouted, it is no matter. You have slain twelve emirs and the bravest men of Antioch. Be assured in your love of Christ that God is with you now and evermore.

When the misbelievers asked what he had said the interpreter replied that it was nothing good. Yaghi Siyan had him brought down from the wall and inquired if he would live honorably among Turks. Rainald Porchet asked how he might do this without sin.

Accept the teaching of Mahomet, said Yaghi Siyan. Deny that Lord whom you worship and believe. If you do that we will give you horses and mules and gold and whatever else you desire. We will give you wives. We will give you land.

As our Lord was tempted by Satan, Rainald Porchet felt tempted. He prayed with clasped hands, iunctus manibus, imploring God for assistance. He knelt in prayer to the east, humbly asking that his soul might be transported with dignity to the bosom of Abraham.

Yaghi Siyan demanded to know what was said. The interpreter replied that Rainald Porchet denied the faith of Mahomet and would not accept the goods he was offered. Yaghi Siyan ordered his head struck off, which was done. Next, because he failed to make this knight turn apostate, he brought forth the Christian prisoners from Antioch and bound them in a circle. Firewood, hay, and chaff was stacked around them, the torch applied. While their flesh burned they screamed and shrieked. Their voices resounded in heaven and they came into the presence of our Lord wearing white stoles. This according to Peter Tudebode.

Once the fort was built Christians could travel among the hills or to Saint Symeon for merchandise. Also, the activity of Turks was restricted, not only those within Antioch but those outside who attempted to provision the city. A Syrian caravan approached through the mountains expecting quick passage but had not reckoned on Tancred who captured it and took everything, oil, wine, barley, and other valuables. Tancred often rode unexpectedly here or there with his knights, so the enemy learned to dread his name.

During this time Christian law took root. Those found guilty of sexual crime were punished harshly, which was fit and just since these servants of God exposed to pagan swords ought not to wallow in lustful thought. What value has bodily congress where death seems imminent? Therefore to mention prostitutes was intolerable. Guibert de Nogent speaks of a monk who fled his monastery to join this expedition, more out of caprice than piety, who being caught with a woman was tried by fire and convicted. The monk and his whore were stripped, drawn naked through the ranks while being savagely whipped to the terror of all who watched. Neither feast day nor Sunday passed that Bishop Adhémar did not preach the authority of Holy Writ to every corner of the camp, enjoining abbots, priests, and clerics to hold themselves above reproof. He exhorted men to be patient in their deprivation.

Comte Stephen de Blois again wrote to his wife Adela. Having assured her that he was safe with the army of Christ, drawing ever nearer to the House of Jesus, he observed that for twenty-three weeks they had besieged Antioch and he had managed to double the amount of gold and silver she bestowed upon him when he withdrew from her embrace. He recounted the battle against Turks at Nicaea, after which by God's help they conquered the whole of Cappadocia, seized castles belonging to a prince called Assam and made him flee. By the river Euphrates they had defeated other Turks, driven them backward toward Arabia, forced them to abandon sumpter beasts and baggage. Yet a great many contrived through hurried marches night and day to reach and enter Antioch. Inside were thought to be five thousand Turkish soldiers, not counting Arabs, Syrians, Turcopolitans, Saracens, Armenians, and divers others who caused much evil. Under the walls numerous Christians were slain, their souls lofted to Paradise because their blood was that of martyrs. And so Comte Stephen bade his wife farewell, counseling her to watch over his lands, to act with lenity toward her children and the vassals.

This letter was composed on Easter Day by his chaplain, Alexander. While it was being written a skirmish took place during which sixty Turks dropped screeching into hell, their bloody heads exhibited that the knighthood of Christ should derive joy therefrom.

Now by the Aleppo road came seven thousand enemies. Lord Bohemond met and defeated them, mounted fresh bleeding heads on stakes facing Antioch to challenge and terrify Yaghi Siyan. In response, the Turk flaunted Bishop Adhémar's standard of Blessed Mary upside down.

Spies crept through the Frankish camp, Syrian, Turk, Armenian, each adopting the language, demeanor, and custom of the role he played. Because of such mischief Bohemond brought out several prisoners. In view of Antioch they got their throats cut, after which the bodies were smeared with butter, spitted and roasted. Bohemond's captains were told to reply, if asked what this portended, that henceforth infidel spies would serve as nourishment. If the story is true, I could not say, but it swept the Levant, gripping with terror all who heard it, and every spy in camp got out as soon as he was able.

Thanks to the indulgence of our Lord, who does not fail to hear and judge the pleas of His children, Antioch was delivered from

40

bondage through trickery. How did this happen? According to Raymond d'Agiles, fourteen years earlier when Turks got control of the city they compelled Greek and Armenian youths to labor as servants and gave them wives to make them tractable. Still, these youths would escape when they could and they brought word of a captain named Firouz, charged with defending the Tower of Two Sisters, who would betray Antioch. Yaghi Siyan had punished this captain for hoarding and selling grain, which enraged him and impelled him to seek revenge. His name, Firouz, is said to mean Victorious One. He came of a distinguished family, Beni-Zerra, which means sons of those who fashion breastplates, which is to say armorers. Albeit he was raised Christian he had converted to the evil faith of Mahomet, thereby comitting the sin of apostasy. But one night the Lord appeared, rebuked him and commanded him to deliver Antioch into Christian hands. They say Firouz wondered at this apparition. Once more the Lord commanded him to betray Antioch. Now Firouz went to Yaghi Siyan and revealed what he had been ordered to do. Are you not a fool? the governor asked. Would you obey a ghost?

For a third time Firouz beheld the Messiah. Then he was terrified and ashamed and sent word to Bohemond, who played upon his guilt. Bohemond promised to restore him to the faith of Jesus Christ if he would surrender his post, meanwhile through flagrant cajolery hinting at wealth and honor. For seven months they negotiated.

Being closer to me than life itself, Firouz declared, very well do you know how I have loved you since we undertook this common friendship by authority of God. So do you creep ever more deeply into my heart. With earnest care I have pondered the subject of our discourse. Here is what I believe. I will rejoice eternally in heaven if I deliver my native land from the dogs that govern it and introduce a people who love God. I will enjoy the society of blessed saints forever if I lift the yoke of oppression from Antioch. It is clear that should I fail at this task my house and the honor of my distinguished family will cease to exist. Even the name Firouz. Therefore I urge you, be attentive. Here is what I will do. I will give up the fortified tower that I

41

am charged to defend in order that you with your people may breach the city. So much will I do.

Yaghi Siyan during this period had appealed to the Muslim ruler of Jerusalem, to Rodoan who was prince of Aleppo, to Docap who was prince of Damascus. He had sent further to Arabia and to Chorosan seeking aid from Bolianuth and Hamelnuth. Hence these emirs came marching toward Antioch with twelve thousand choice knights led by the atabeg of Mosul, Kerbogha. Here were Agulani, Publicans, Azymites, Kurds, and others from distant lands. This news alarmed the Franks. In particular they dreaded the Agulani whose horses were sheathed in iron. Bohemond now urged Firouz to consummate their understanding without delay, saying they had agreed upon a meritorious act and the moment was at hand.

In the course of supreme enterprise it will happen that events occur which are impossible to foresee. Just so, Firouz one day took his son to the tower he was charged with guarding but all at once told his son to hurry home. There the boy saw his mother embrace a Turk. Horrified and disgusted he rushed back to his father, who spoke with deep bitterness. If I live, said he in allusion to the Turks, I will repay those filthy dogs. Now more than ever did he mean to carry out the plot. Truly does God order each event from inception to end.

Saracen histories tell how the citizens of Antioch began to suspect treachery, more from divination than any proof. Certain principals therefore obtained audience with Yagi Siyan. They reminded him that numerous Christians lived or worked inside the walls and at this council the name of Firouz was mentioned. They knew this Armenian for a convert. Thus he was invited to the meeting because all hoped to discover by his words if he was justly or unjustly suspect. Firouz, being quick to understand, praised the foresight of the governor and these citizens. Your mistrust is laudable, said he, and overcaution does no harm. The duplicity you fear may be thwarted by those who keep watch from the turrets and those who patrol the ramparts. Let them be changed often so they do not remain anywhere long enough to negotiate with the enemy. This would eliminate all chance of treason.

His words satisfied everyone. They agreed that his advice was sound and that what he proposed should be effected. Firouz, then, having escaped the trial, knew he could hesitate no longer. He notified Bohemond that they must act. Tomorrow, he said by way of messengers, you will sound the trumpets and ride out of sight, pretending that you go to pillage the land. But at night you must return quickly, silently. I will be at the tower I command and will direct you.

Bohemond now told a servant, Malacorna, to advise the cavalry and have them prepare.

Anon, a herald proclaimed that all should obey orders. So the Franks rode noisily out of sight. Before day they quietly returned. And by the Tower of Two Sisters was a ladder fixed to projections from the wall. Bohemond directed his boldest knights to ascend. If it please God, said he, we shall hold Antioch in our grasp. Thus in a short time sixty knights stood atop the wall.

Firouz, however, began to tremble because they were so few. Micro Francos echome, he said in his native tongue and asked where was the most fierce knight Bohemond. Why did Bohemond stand on the ground?

At this a Longobard descended the ladder and ran to ask why Bohemond did not join the others. Bohemond is said to have felt ashamed because he ought to have gone first. Very nimbly he climbed up and more knights followed. They ran around killing everyone they met. The ladder broke under the weight of so many armored knights but there was a postern gate nearby and certain Franks exploring in the darkness came upon it and broke through and entered the city. Thus at dawn the people awoke to see Bohemond's red banner on a hill. By the account of one who participated that is how Antioch was taken.

Yet another relates how seven hundred knights were chosen to climb the wall. The plan was kept secret, a herald rode through camp announcing that they were going to face Kerbogha. Then at the appointed time Bohemond sent his interpreter who returned saying Firouz urged them to hurry because watchmen with lighted torches had just gone by, and Firouz lowered a rope that the Franks attached to a ladder made from strips of hide. When this ladder had been secured Bohemond climbed a few steps, after him Godfrey de Bouillon. Next, Robert the Fleming. They were saved from discovery by the howl of wind rushing through mountain gorges, by the tumult of the swollen river, by the noise of rain dashing madly against the wall. Whatever the fact, these Franks triumphed who set their hope in God Almighty who knows not how to be conquered.

According to William of Tyre, Firouz had a brother who despised the army of Christ, so Firouz did not confide in him. About the ninth hour when the Franks rode out of camp these two stood side by side on the ramparts watching. Firouz, anxious to know his brother's thoughts, said he could not but pity such misguided people who would meet a bitter end. Behold how confidently they ride forth, said he. Little do they know what snares have been laid. Little do they know what tomorrow will bring.

Would that already they had fallen beneath Turkish swords, his brother replied. From the day they marched into view we have had no rest.

At these words the spirit of Firouz shrank. And lest the will of God be thwarted he began to plot his brother's death.

According to William the rope was made of hemp, secured atop the wall, fixed below with iron hooks. Midnight was past when the interpreter crept forward. Firouz spoke through an opening in the wall. Go quickly to your lord. Tell him to come without delay. Firouz then hurried into the turret where his brother lay asleep and stabbed him. Bohemond, upon seeing the corpse, embraced Firouz who had slain his own brother, who demonstrated that he loved Christianity above all else.

When those who had gained the wall saw the light of an approaching torch they hid behind a buttress and as the Turk came in

44

reach they murdered him before he was able to cry out. Next they hurried down the staircase and opened a portal to admit their comrades. Raymond, waiting for a signal, brought up his legions so almost at once Frankish knights crowded the streets. Thus, Antioch awoke to shouts and screams of terror. Many Franks outside the wall thought Kerbogha's army had arrived, but others said those were not the shrieks of exultant Turks. As the sky lightened it was possible to make out Frankish banners on the southern hill. Antioch, capital and glory of Syria, had fallen.

Eagerly the pilgrims searched for gold and jewels and broke through alabaster screens to get at Turkish women. They ran through apartments looking for silk, velvet, coins, treasure of any sort. In mosques where enemies of God congregate, where the false writing of Islam is worshipped, where prophets of the Antichrist hold forth, they gathered and burned deceitful works. They slit the bellies of iniquitous Saracen priests, drew out the entrails and led them by their own entrails around heaps of burning parchment. In this way the exuberance of wickedness was checked. And how could acolytes of the Lord feel other than they did? They saw with dismay what Saracens had done. Eyes gouged from images of the saints, noses plastered with shit.

Armenians, Syrians, and other true believers in the city wept for joy. They picked up weapons and guided the Frankish host through unfamiliar streets, pointing out the homes of wealthy Turks, and helped to slay the guards. They who had so long borne the yoke of servitude now saw fit to exact revenge, bathing the stones of Antioch with the blood of tyrants. Raymond d'Agiles relates how infidels hoping to escape dashed back and forth but were cut to pieces. Some on horseback got through the gates but were followed into the hills and driven over a precipice. The jubilation of these Franks who pursued the Turks was boundless, yet they felt grieved to look down upon thirty dead or dying horses with broken necks.

Antioch being gloriously rich, pilgrims stuffed their pockets.

However they did not find much to eat. They learned that the citizens had been as hungry as themselves. And they learned that in darkness they had slain many of their own.

Streets, courtyards, and houses soon began to stink since ten thousand infidels rightly met the sword. Pilgrims scarcely could walk a dozen steps without sloshing through pools of blood or trampling on bodies alive with insects. But what of Yaghi Siyan? He wakened to the blast of oliphants and fled on horseback. At some mountain village he was recognized by Armenian woodcutters who lopped off his head, which they delivered to Bohemond for a reward. These woodcutters sold the governor's ornamental belt and the sheath of his scimitar for sixty gold bezants. Is it not a tribute to the omnipotence of our Savior that he who caused many Armenians to lose their heads should be deprived of his own by one of them?

Yet according to the monk Albert, three Syrians traveling through the mountains recognized Yaghi Siyan a long way off. Behold! said they. Is Antioch captured? Our lord and governor looks intent on flight. Considering how we have sustained tyranny and sharp practices he will not escape our hands. So these travelers approached thick with deceit, showing false reverence. And coming near they snatched Yaghi Siyan's sword out of the sheath, flung him down from his mule and sliced off his head, which they put in their bag. They took his head to Antioch for Christians to see. Yaghi Siyan's head was enormous, ears broad and hairy, while from his chin a white beard flowed down as far as his navel.

The second day after Antioch was subjugated, while Christ's army searched for provisions and labored at strengthening the walls, being much afraid of Kerbogha, several Turkish knights appeared on the plain. They came near the city, riding splendid chargers. They trotted insolently to and fro, which angered the Christians. And since it would be disgraceful not to refute this challenge Roger de Barneville rode fiercely out the gate accompanied by fifteen knights. And the Saracens, pretending fright, whirled and galloped off with Christians at their heels. Then unexpectedly three hundred more

deus lo volt!

Saracens rose up. Roger fell with an arrow through his heart. He was a most valiant knight from the retinue of Count Robert the Norman and faithfully had carried out the aims of pilgrimage. The Turks made off with his head. As soon as they were out of sight Roger's comrades brought back his corpse, which they entombed in the basilica of Saint Peter, a holy place containing the chair once occupied by the Prince of Apostles.

Next day at sunrise here came the black banners of Kerbogha. His multitude of cavalry in white robes astonished all. The wide plain scarcely was large enough to accommodate his army. When they encamped their tents reached up toward the hills. Some few separated themselves and rode close to Antioch where they dismounted as though in contempt before launching arrows. Tancred charged from the east gate and killed six. Because Roger de Barneville ascended to glory near this place Tancred cut off the heads of these six and bore them into the city for consolation.

Now as it suited him, Kerbogha advanced. Presently those who had besieged Antioch and took it through force of arms were themselves encircled and menaced. Nor had they food enough. Before long a single egg cost two sous. Intestine of a goat, five sous. One denier for a nut. Rotting carcasses of dogs fetched huge prices. Head of a horse without the tongue, three silver deniers. Fig leaf, thistle, vine, camel hide, all were boiled and eaten. Low people as well as knights who had once been rich could be seen hobbling about, leaning on sticks. Some asked feebly for bread. Others withdrew from sight, starving in private rooms to hide their shame. Next to arrive was that brother of famine, plague. Out of three hundred thousand Franks who undertook this pilgrimage, no more than sixty thousand could be counted.

What of Stephen, Comte de Blois? While the battle raged at Dorylaeum he could not be found. Here, one day before Lord Bohemond scaled the wall, Stephen pretended to be sick and retreated to the fortified town of Alexandretta, taking with him four thousand soldiers. There he meant to await the outcome. Should the army of

God triumph, he would return to Antioch claiming his health had much improved. Or if heathen force prevailed, then would he quickly embark to France. But as he waited with folded arms beside the port he learned of Kerbogha. They say he climbed a mountain to observe the enemy camp and seeing the number of tents thought it best to retreat toward Constantinople. Why he did so has been much discussed. According to Fulcher de Chartres, all in the pilgrim army felt aggrieved because Stephen was a man of eminent virtue. Nor could he afterward explain to his wife Adela why he avoided the battle of Antioch. She is said to have berated him without mercy as they lay on the conjugal bed. Fulcher, making note, chose to call Stephen sagacious and high born, yet declined to call him brave.

This defection gnawed at the vitals of those he left behind. They asked one another why they should be trapped like vermin inside Antioch while Stephen de Blois brushed his hair beside the sea. They contemplated their misery and wondered what to do. They saw themselves languishing from plague and hunger, encircled by Turks. Outside the wall, a sword. Desolation within. Lord Bohemond attempted to revive their spirit, but losing patience set fire to a district where many were billeted, burning hundreds to death while their comrades watched indifferently. Some thought to escape over the walls at night, lowering themselves on ropes, for which they were villified as rope-dancers. Most plopped into the arms of Turks who welcomed them to slavery. Not all who plotted to escape were low born. William de Grandmesnil, a noble married to Bohemond's sister, wished to save himself. But while preparing to descend the rope he saw the face of his brother Albericus, recently dead, who asked where he would go. Stay, Albericus reproved him. Stay and fear not. God will be with you. And your companions who preceded you in death will fight with you against the Turk. William felt amazed at these words from one already departed. He let go of the rope and told what he had heard.

And the Lord, not unmindful, spoke to a cleric who was greatly terrified, Stephan Valanti. Where goest thou? inquired the Lord. I would flee, the cleric answered, lest unluckily I perish. Return, said the Lord. I will be merciful to the Franks in battle. They suffer because they have neglected my precepts. Let them repent their sins and they shall have victory. Let their trust in me endure. For I am the Lord.

Stephan Valanti returned full of shame and spoke to others.

Lambert le Pauvre and Guy de Troussel, illustrious men of rank, slipped down ropes, burning flesh from their hands. Also, William Carpenter, viscount of Melun, fled in disgrace. He was called the Carpenter because in battle he chopped down men like trees. Yet his reputation stood on boasting, he excelled more at words than deeds. Once before he took flight but Tancred pursued him and brought him back. All night he waited outside the court of Bohemond and next day faced the prince.

What sort of Carpenter have we? Bohemond asked. Has he worn out a thousand swords by the strength of his arm? In this fashion did Prince Bohemond mock the timorous viscount.

Altogether how many fled is not known. Some got to the seacoast where they clambered aboard vessels and slashed the anchor ropes, demanding that the crew hoist sail at once. Kerbogha, said they in fright. Kerbogha has come out from Mosul like the wind. Antioch has fallen, our barons murdered. By the help of Almighty God we escaped. Now while there is yet time let us quit this accursed place.

Others without pride sought to join the heathen, beseeching mercy, denying our gracious Lord and Savior, which is abomination.

What of Hugh, Comte de Vermandois? Some allege that he, like Stephen, fled before the battle opened. Others argue that he went to reproach Emperor Alexius at Constantinople and charge him with neglect, with failure to send help. It is known that Hugh loitered at the Byzantine capital showing little concern for the Holy City until he embarked to France, albeit he once declared he would not come home with breath in his body. Some say this great lord, goaded by the contempt of lesser men, retraced his steps toward Jerusalem. Perhaps. I neither deny nor avouch the truth of it.

Saracen chronicles relate how Kerbogha made sport of the Franks when he was shown an ancient sword flaked with rust, a wretched bow, a darkened lance taken from poor pilgrims. Kerbogha began to laugh. Would Christians armed with such shining instruments drive me past the boundaries of Chorosan? he asked. Such weapons could not strike a sparrow to the earth. And when he finished laughing he ordered a scribe to address the caliph.

To the Caliph, our Pope, our King, Lord Sultan, most valiant knight, greeting and honor immeasurable! Behold these arms we took from a squad of Franks. See how perfect they are. How fine. With such weaponry will the Orient be scourged?

In this wise did Kerbogha continue, asserting that he had shut up the Franks in Antioch like a bird caught in his hand, boasting he would lead them to harsh captivity or sentence them to death because they had threatened to expel him and cast him beyond upper India. By Mahomet, he swore, by the gods of every name, he would not return until he acquired the regal city of Antioch and all of Syria and Romania and Bulgaria even to Apulia. Yet these proud words by which he thought to earn praise would augment his disgrace. For as he soon would take wing from those he despised, to that extent was the humiliation greater. Who does not find ignominy easier to bear if defeated by a noble adversary? Just so, when the ignoble triumph, is not discredit doubled?

Anon here came Kerbogha's mother who lived in the city of Aleppo, hurrying to ask, weeping, if what she heard was true. He answered that she knew the truth. Then she pleaded with him not to engage the Franks. In the book of Islam and in the book of the Gentiles, said she, it is found that a Christian host will come against us and conquer us and everywhere make our people subject. Miserable woman that I am, I have followed you from Aleppo where, gazing and contriving rhymes, I scrutinized the planets and stars and the twelve signs. In all I have seen the Christian host victorious, so I fear greatly that you will be taken from me.

Ah! said Kerbogha. Is not Bohemond mortal? Is not Tancred

mortal? Do not these with their host of Franks at one meal eat two thousand heifers and four thousand pigs?

Bohemond and Tancred are mortal, she answered. But their God loves them and gives them valor. He has made heaven and earth and established the sea and prepared a dwelling throughout eternity. His might is to be feared.

Nevertheless I will fight them, Kerbogha said.

When his mother heard this she returned sadly to Aleppo with as many gifts as she could carry.

Three days afterward Kerbogha rode toward Antioch, his Turks shouting blasphemy, hooting, whistling. A Christian knight whose name has been forgotten shook his lance and cried aloud.

Whoever would sup in Paradise, let him eat with me!

And spurring toward the enemy he overturned and killed the first Turk he met. Of an instant he himself was slain. Yet he died rejoicing, emboldened, strengthened by his love of Jesus, finding glory in Heaven while he lay bleeding on earth. So others rode out to give battle but could not overwhelm these Turks and were forced backward through the narrow gate. More than one hundred suffocated. As noble Boethius has written, at the price of glorious death shall men earn fame that future generations venerate.

Now occurred a miracle. A servant from Provence, by name Bartholomew, lay alone in his tent when the earth began to shake, whereupon he cried out to God. Then he beheld Saint Andrew, who said he should go to the church of Saint Peter where he would be shown the lance that pierced the side of our Lord as He hung upon the cross. And suddenly, as if they had flown hand in hand, they entered the north door of the church. Saint Andrew vanished. Presently he came back with the lance that opened the side of our Lord, whence flowed the salvation of the world. This inestimable relic he offered to the servant who wept for joy.

When the horror of battle threatens, Saint Andrew said, this shalt thou turn against the enemy. And he took back the lance.

At that moment Bartholomew awoke in his tent, hearing the cock twice acclaim morning.

Bartholomew sought and obtained audience with Count Raymond and Bishop Adhémar to recount the vision. He said he had been told by Saint Andrew to search the floor of the church in the company of twelve pious men. By every account Bishop Adhémar was unimpressed, knowing Bartholomew as one who frequented taverns. Count Raymond, being cut from different cloth, resolved to explore the dream. Five days later they proceeded to the church at sunrise, twelve pious men, Bishop Adhémar, Count Raymond, and such lords as Pontius of Balazun and Faraldus of Thuart. When they asked Bartholomew where to dig, he hesitated. Then adopting a look of authority he pointed. So they commenced, broke through the floor and dug until the hour of vespers to no avail, as though the earth could not yield what it never received. Bartholomew disrobed, excepting his shirt, and leapt into the pit with a spade.

Here is the place, said he, leaning toward a corner. Here lies hidden what we seek.

Then they heard the clash of metal against metal and Bartholomew cried out, for the point of the lance was seen, leaf-shaped hammered iron. Raymond d'Agiles, chaplain to the count of Toulouse, declares in his chronicle that he himself kissed the point where it stood half revealed, the point that Longius thrust into the side of our Lord.

Some would not believe. Arnulf Malecorne, chaplain to the duke of Normandy, thought it the rusty point of a Muslim spear. Mockingly he inquired when Pontius Pilate or the centurions visited Antioch. Bishop Adhémar also withheld approval. Lord Bohemond detected a trick, wondering aloud at suspicious things, by shrewd conjecture throwing doubt, casting shadows. By what vagaries of thought are we molded? Bohemond asked. How is it that Saint Andrew would visit a man who, so I hear, prowls the streets and devotes himself to public houses? Why has the apostle disclosed to such a man the secret of heaven? How came the lance to this church? If some Christian hid it, why not at the nearest altar? Or if some Jew or Gentile concealed the lance, why bury it within a church? Does not darkness abet deceit? For at the moment of cozenage this Provençal sprang into the hole, turned his back and found what others vainly sought. Why should any man be vouchsafed in darkness what was denied to others in the light? Thus did Lord Bohemond belittle the relic. Just so did Arnulf Malecorne, the counts of Normandy and Flanders, Tancred, and more who peeked beneath the shell. Here began that sullen dispute between Provençals and Normans. Those quick to believe, those who doubted. It is said that Count Raymond felt bitterly aggrieved and considered vengeance, digesting a thousand plots in the sanguine depth of his heart. With what ambiguous success does fate unfold the course of affairs.

Now the lance swaddled in gold cloth was borne triumphantly through the streets of Antioch while ecstatic pilgrims followed, chanting, singing, paying homage. According to some, the Holy Shroud lay in this self-same trench and was secured by Adhémar, that it rests enshrined at the abbey of Cadouin.

How often may God's favor be revealed? Saint Andrew reappeared to Bartholomew on the second night after the lance was found, accompanied by a radiant companion, radiant beyond the children of men.

Draw near that you may kiss His foot, Saint Andrew commanded.

And Bartholomew perceived that the foot was freshly wounded, bloody.

Behold our Lord, Saint Andrew said. Behold our Lord who suffered on the Cross, whence this wound. The day you were given the lance, that day would He have you celebrate. And since it was given you at vespers, and that day cannot be celebrated, therefore will you celebrate on the eighth day in the following week, and each year on the day of discovery. Let clerics sing before the lance. Let them conclude the hymn on bended knees. Let all deport themselves as is taught in the epistle. Humble yourselves beneath the mighty hand of God.

Moreover, the Lord appeared to a priest while he knelt in the church of Our Lady grieving at the expected death of himself and his brothers. He had put on the garb of confession, obtained absolution, and was reciting psalms when he observed a light greater than the sun and a visitor of indescribable beauty. It seemed to the priest that he was asked who now occupied Antioch. Christians, he replied. Those who believe Jesus Christ was born of a Virgin, suffered and died on the Cross and was buried, but arose on the third day.

Knowest thou me? the splendid visitor asked.

I do not, the priest replied. But at his words a cross shone on the face of the visitor.

Knowest thou me? the visitor asked again.

I do not, said the priest. Except I see on thy head a cross like that of our Savior.

I am He, said the Lord.

Then the priest dropped humbly at His feet, beseeching help for the oppression upon them.

I have given you the city of Nicaea. So far have I attended you, said the Lord. I deplore your adversity and have brought you into the city of Antioch. Yet you take evil pleasure with corrupted women, whereof arises a stench unto heaven. Now go and tell the people. Return to me and I will return to them. Let them chant the response to Congregati sunt, including the verse, each day.

Men wept for joy throughout the ranks when they heard of our Lord's intervention. Now overhead blazed a star, dividing into three parts that fell on the Turkish camp. Thus encouraged and reassured, the pilgrims consulted. They resolved to send Kerbogha a message demanding to know why he encamped haughtily before Antioch, why he assailed the servants of Christ. There was a Frank called Herlvin who could speak both languages, so the barons addressed him. Go to this Turk, they said. Tell him we wonder at his insolent conduct. Has he arrived for the purpose of molesting us? Or does he wish to be converted?

Away went Herlvin to the assemblage of Turks and spoke as directed, demanding to know why they invaded Christian land. Our leaders would have you depart at once, said he. They grant you leave to collect your possessions, your mules, horses, camels, cattle and sheep. Take them with you as you wish.

And when Herlvin returned he told how Kerbogha answered fiercely.

Your God and your religion we neither seek nor desire. Both do we spurn absolutely. We have come hither because we reject your claim to this land, which we took from weak and effeminate people. Therefore if you wish to become Turks and deny the God you worship with heads bowed, and renounce your laws, we shall generously give you this land and more, castles and cities. If you do so you will become knights and we will esteem your friendship. But if you do not, know this. You will be led captive in chains to Chorosan where you will serve us and our children and their children forever.

Then the Franks prayed and fasted for three days, after which they swung open the gates and in unison marched forth, singing as one, led by clerics and bishops in surplice and cap who invoked the saints and held up crosses. They called on God to strengthen His children, granting them victory to affirm the sanctity of His blood. Documents from those days relate that few Frankish knights were mounted on chargers, most bestrode donkeys or camels, so impoverished were they. Behind this army walked servants and peasants armed with cudgels, bills, pikes. And among pilgrims of low estate marched women carrying rocks in their sleeves, accompanied by children who meant to die with their parents.

Kerbogha remained in his tent playing at chess after a black flag hoisted from the highest tower of Antioch gave notice that the

55

Franks would sally forth, such was the contempt he felt. But when he saw them outside the walls he sent for Mirdalin, a noble celebrated for courage. Did you not tell me, Kerbogha asked, that the Franks were few in number and afraid to fight?

I did not say so, Mirdalin replied. But I will consider them and tell you if we may defeat them.

When Mirdalin saw how they advanced in serried lines, foot soldiers preceding the knights, commanded by the counts of Normandy and Flanders and other brave lords, when he had observed them he returned to Kerbogha. These Franks may be killed, he said, but I do not think they can be put to flight.

Kerbogha asked if they could be driven back.

They will not yield, Mirdalin replied.

Kerbogha notified an emir that if light burned at the head of the Turkish army he should sound trumpets and retreat.

Amid a shower of arrows and clashing swords this battle was joined. Mules brayed, camels grumbled. Down from the hills rode dead Christians bearing white standards who uttered no battle cry, astride white destriers, preceded by Mercurius and Demetrius and Saint George. Then the Franks knew they would triumph. And the Turks, understanding that they could not prevail, set fire to the grass, which was a signal to flee. Thus the siege of Antioch was broken, the devil's army scattered.

Mahometans, too, behold resurrected knights at perilous times, albeit they wear the pagan color of martyrdom, green. Similarly, as Christians wear amulets around their necks beseeching the help of our Lord, so do unbelievers wear amulets addressed to Allah. Moreover, both copy sacred verse on parchment. Yet afterward the heathen washes ink from his parchment and drinks blackened water, expecting thereby to consecrate himself, which is false and abominable.

What of Kerbogha? Amply provided with warriors, why should he give up the field? Because he endeavored to contend against God. And the Lord discerning his arrogance, observing his pomp, crushed Kerbogha.

deus lo volt!

Franks who inspected his vast pavilion were overcome by amazement since it was constructed like a castle with ramparts and turrets, with sumptuous silk furnishing. In the midst they found his private quarters while partitions extended like rays of the sun, forming miniature streets with sleeping places that resembled hostels sufficient to accommodate two thousand men. Colorful rugs, splendid saddles, and other costly items were discovered along with grain, wine, sheep, butter, camels, and good horses. Also, many women had been left behind. According to Fulcher de Chartres, pilgrims did not abuse these women save to pierce their bellies with lances.

Bishop Adhémar, riven with plague, died at the kalends of August. Charitable, tolerant, modest, shrewd, wise in strategy, courageous, he ascended peacefully to the Lord. Such sorrow engaged the Christian host that few were able to comprehend their grief. Lord Bohemond vowed to carry the husk of this saintly bishop as far as Jerusalem, but after some argument he was laid to rest in the trench where the lance was found. Now by the helm of goodness does God Almighty rule, thus on the second night Bishop Adhémar was observed in the private chapel of Count Raymond standing next to Saint Andrew and Jesus Christ. The bishop was heard to speak.

Most gravely did I sin, for when the lance was discovered I withheld approval. For this I was led down into hell and punished. See how my beard and the side of my face are burnt. My soul writhed among flames from the hour it departed my weak body until my body was given to dust. There was I clothed in the garment you see, for when I received the order of the episcopate I bestowed it upon a poor man. And though the heat of Gehenna raged and ministers of Tartarus did their worst, no harm could they do beneath it. And nothing has been so precious to me as this candle that my companions offered, which restored me while I suffered in hell. Bohemond who is prince of Otranto would carry my body to Jerusalem, but let him not disturb me, for the blood of the Lord who accompanies me is there. And should Prince Bohemond doubt what I say, let him uncover my tomb that he may see my head and my face scorched. And

57

let not my brothers on earth grieve that I am done with life since I shall dwell among you and prompt you better than hitherto. Bear in mind the castigations of hell. Serve God who redeems you from these and other evils. So much does the Savior grant all who embrace His precepts. Keep what remains of this candle in the morning and give a cloak of mine to the church of Saint Andrew.

Having spoken, Bishop Adhémar vanished. And when those in the chapel looked to where Lord Jesus stood they perceived an unwonted splendor.

Some argue this was diabolic work, saying Bartholomew cast a spell, for he is known to have taken offense at those who mocked him. Yet are we not privy to divine intervention? Bohemond demonstrated the sharpness of his knife by slicing a taper in half, only to see the unlit half miraculously light itself. How could such marvels obtain if not from the hand of God?

Withal, have we not met charlatans? Mountebanks who daub their foreheads blue or green with fruit juice and call themselves subject to heavenly supervision. Consider the abbot who burnt a cross on his body and claimed an angel put it there, flaunting his stigma before Antioch, who got himself named archbishop of Caesarea. Or those who shout with praise if clouds pile up to the likeness of sheep and bearded prophets. Or an old hag trailed by a white goose that waddled toward the altar at Cambrai, hence talk leapt quick as lightning that our Lord directed a goose to liberate the Holy City. Thus would pretenders lower our dignity as Christians.

How often are limbs, toes, portions, ungodly bones foisted on the credulous? How many fraudulent bargains sealed? Bishop Odo of Bayeux longed for the corpse of Saint Experius, paying one hundred pounds to the sacristan of the church that owned it. What did the sacristan do but dig up the carcass of a peasant called Experius. Now the bishop demanded an oath to prove he was buying the saint, to which the sacristan replied that he would swear these were the bones of Experius. As to his sanctity, the sacristan went on, I could not swear, Your Grace, since many who receive the title of saint are less than holy. By this cunning argument he assuaged the bishop's doubt. Thus did peasant bones make their way to the altar of God. Or the bishop of Amiens who would house the bones of Saint Firmin in a new reliquary but found no letter nor anything to certify the wizened corpse. Still he would write on a lead plate that here lay Firmin the martyr. Enough. Enough. Let charlatans be punished for harmful inventions of the heart.

Eight months and a day did these Franks besiege Antioch, after which they themselves were shut up inside by Kerbogha for three unhappy weeks. After his defeat they rested five months and as the kalends of November approached they had not moved toward Jerusalem. Some in the army grew restless. Why, they asked their companions, do we not proceed toward the Holy Sepulcher? If the barons prove reluctant to lead us, then must we choose a valiant knight we trust. Is it the will of God that so many armed men should loiter? Let those who cherish the revenue of Antioch pocket it. Let us take the journey upon which we embarked. Let those who treasure Antioch flourish inside its walls, as those who recently held it plunged head downward to hell.

Now the high barons agreed it was time to march. They agreed to convene at the church of Saint Peter on the kalends of November whence all should depart for Jerusalem, the Holy City for which they hungered, toward which they had traveled so far. The duke of Lorraine while en route to Antioch with twelve knights was assaulted by a host of pagans. Yet these twelve acquitted themselves without fear, knowing they would prove victorious because their number equaled the number of apostles. Our Lord awarded them thirty dead, as many captive, while others fled howling to the swamp and drowned. Hence the duke of Lorraine proudly entered Antioch with captive Turks bearing the severed heads of comrades, a welcome sight.

When all were assembled at the church of Saint Peter they consulted. Some who had gained castles in this region, or collected revenue, wished to know what should be done with Antioch. If we depart and the Turks reclaim it, they said, things will be worse than before.

59

Some proposed that Antioch be given to Bohemond who was brave and wise, whose name inspired terror among the Saracens. Others, including Count Raymond, objected. So now these barons raised such discord contradicting one another they almost came to blows. The question of Antioch remained in dispute, but at length they settled upon a day to continue the pilgrimage. Jerusalem lay ten days south, although some said if they did not repent their ways this march would take ten years.

Is it not true that visions breed quicker than mice? The ghost of Saint George addressed a priest, Peter Desiderius, bidding him enter the church of Saint Leontius, saying he would find within it the relics of four saints that he should carry to Jerusalem. John Chrysostom. Cyprian. Omechios. Leontius.

Peter Desiderius did not fully believe the specter, entreating God if it were false or true. But at this Saint George threatened him and said he must do as he was told or things would go ill for him and his lord, the count of Die. Much affrighted, the priest went scurrying to chaplain Raymond d'Agiles, who consulted the bishop of Orange, Count Raymond, and others. So they proceeded to the church where they lighted candles to God, praying mightily. And next morning they discovered a chest stuffed with bones. Yet no one could guess who these bones were. The priest of Saint Leontius wanted to keep them, whereupon Raymond d'Agiles said if the saint wished to go with the army to Jerusalem he ought to disclose his name. If not, he should be content with his niche in Antioch. For, said Raymond, why burden ourselves with strange bones?

No voice being heard, the relics were bound up in cloth.

That night a youth of surpassing radiance came to visit Peter Desiderius and inquired angrily why his relics were not set aside with others.

Who art thou? Peter asked.

Dost not thou know? the youth demanded. Dost not know who bears the standard of this army?

Saint George, Peter replied.

deus lo volt!

I am he. Now set aside my bones with the rest. And close by thou wilt find in a small ampule twelve drops of the blood of Saint Tecla the martyr, which likewise must go to Jerusalem.

Peter did as he was instructed and afterward chanted mass.

Is not our Savior an irrefutable fountain whose munificence enriches all? Gerbault de Lille obtained from a monastery in Greece one arm of a saint. Robert the Fleming in Apulia acquired numerous holy bones. Ilger Bogod in Jerusalem was privileged to see a tangle of hair the Virgin clawed from her head while mourning. And in ancient times a king of Britons by name Quilius got for himself a length of rope that bound our Lord to the whipping post, a bit of the scourge that furrowed His body, thorns from the Crown, a splinter from the Cross, a shred of the garment His mother wore while giving birth. Thus do they benefit who truly believe.

Anon, the living host marched from Antioch. But what followed? Tafurs. That is to say in our language Trudennes, those who skulk and wander about killing time. Jackals. Vagabonds. Dregs of Gaul. Sluts. Ribalds. Clapperclaws. Brigands. Who could describe such offal? Breeches undone, leaking ulcers, reeking of Paris gutters, born with a need for poverty. Weeds and grass they munched. For a crust of bread they would hold a bridle, carry a log. Leather they chewed, gobbled roots, sucked raindrops out of rock. Mice they relished, clubbed bony dogs to death, trotted with flaming eyes toward putrid mounds of camel flesh. Pagan burials they searched for corpses that they strung up in the wind to dry, pounded rotten bodies with flails, thrust moldy arms and legs into bubbling cauldrons, claimed the meat of a Turk superior to pork. So sang the minstrel Robert le Pèlerin. Barefoot did these Tafurs march, pouches slung at their necks by plaited cords,

61

menacing with pointed sticks, jaw bones, mattocks, never a lance or sword but common daggers. Unpaid, looking to no reward save the benediction of our Savior, a chance to sleep in heaven. Like mangy lions they attacked the infidel, overturned ballistas, hurled stones, boasted Le Roi Tafur as king, some Norman petty noble who traded sword and breastplate for scythe and sackcloth. Indigence to this chuff seemed godly. And did their grimy sovereign meet a vassal parading in filched robes, straightway was he drummed out of the wretched kingdom.

Twenty leagues from Antioch stood Maarat al-Numan whose citizens were haughty because in times past they had killed or enslaved numerous Christians. God's army bivouacked among the olive groves and set to work constructing huts roofed with grapevine and branches. They built hurdles, rams, siege engines. Each day at sundown they looked up at Turks climbing a hill toward a mosque on the summit. Here the pagans would assemble for evening worship, persisting at wicked misbelief, led astray by ignorance, by obdurate depravity.

These Turks cursed the living army of God, vilified the barons. They dangled crosses outside the wall to infuriate Jerusalemfarers. When scaling ladders were placed against the wall they let down iron hooks to catch any who set foot on a ladder and drag him up where he would be stabbed with curved knives, yateghans, or slashed to death with scimitars. The knights climbed timidly because the ladders were fragile, so they were repulsed. Many in the host despaired, thinking they would starve before escaping this accursed land. Some turned homeward. Others trudged through the fields, pausing to search out beans, roots, grains of wheat.

Our Lord observing His troubled children resolved to comfort them. In Count Raymond's chapel the servant Bartholomew lay fast asleep when he awoke to find a man with a ripped tunic standing beside the chest of relics. Bartholomew, mistaking him for a thief, demanded to know what he wanted. But this was Saint Andrew, envoy of God, who replied that he manifested himself thus garbed to show how it profits a man to serve the Lord devoutly.

In this season and poor garb, said the apostle, have I come to Him.

At these words Bartholomew noticed a light more beautiful than anything. He dropped to the ground, terrified.

Thou didst fall easily, Saint Andrew said, and lifted him up.

It is so, Bartholomew replied.

In like manner do they fall who do not believe or who transgress the commandments of God, said the apostle. But if they cry out and are penitent they will be raised, even as I have raised thee. And as the fluid of thy body sinks into earth, so will He wipe away the sins of those crying out for grace. Tell me, how fares the army of God?

Bartholomew answered that the pilgrims were overcome by sadness, miserable, with bellies empty.

Do they not recall the perils from which He has delivered them? asked the saint. For when you were beaten and troubled before the gates of Antioch you cried out to the Lord. Your plea was heard in heaven and He gave you victory over your enemies. But now you offend God. Will caverns or mountains preserve you? Among you is murder, theft, rapine, injustice, adultery. Yet will the Lord out of compassion grant you the city you besiege.

In the morning when Bartholomew made this known to the bishop of Orange and to others they chanted prayers. They gave alms. Then they built more ladders and Count Raymond sent a wooden castle on wheels up against the wall. Inside this castle were several brave knights with Everard the Huntsman to sound his trumpet. Saracens tried to burn the castle with Greek fire but failed. They flung stones from catapults, threw javelins, slack lime, hives filled with bees. William de Montpellier and other knights inside the castle threw down stones at those on the ramparts, breaking their shields. Some toppled backward into the city. Priests and clerics meanwhile beseeched God to assist.

63

On the eleventh day of December, which was Saturday, in that year of our Lord 1098, Goufier de Lastours gained the top of the wall. The ladder cracked beneath him and the weight of those climbing after him, so these few by themselves confronted the enemy host. Saracens attacked with lances. At this several pilgrims lost their wits from terror and leapt off the wall to death. Those on the ground now undertook to sap the wall and when the pagans understood what was happening beneath their feet they turned and fled. This happened about the hour of vespers. Soon thereafter Maarat was taken.

Next day at dawn the Franks went looking for valuables but did not find as much as they expected. Neither did they see many infidels because thousands were hiding in caves underground. Accordingly the soldiers of Christ descended to explore these caves, thinking that must be where the treasure was hidden. Again they were disappointed. Hence they tortured every citizen they caught, demanding to know where the silver and gold was concealed. It is related that some of these people would lead the Franks to cisterns as if intending to disclose what they had hidden, but instead would leap into the depths. They did this to escape worse torture. Bohemond, thinking to gain their allegiance, told the Saracen leaders they should take their families and valuable possessions to a palace near the gate where he would defend them. But after a while he changed his mind. He took everything they had. Some of these important people he killed, others he despatched to Antioch where they could be sold into slavery. This was God's will, a penalty exacted for the anguish His children had endured.

It is said that Bohemond's knights took little part in the siege yet they obtained many captives and lodged themselves in the best houses, hence quarreling broke out between his soldiers and those of Count Raymond. Also, Bohemond had laughed aloud when the servant Bartholomew spoke of being visited by Saint Andrew. Therefore the army was riven with dissent. Soldiers complained and grew restive. Look you, said they to one another, the barons quarreled about Antioch, now they quarrel about Maarat. When will it please our leaders to continue the journey? Come, let us destroy the walls and put an end to this argument. The Gesta tells how these disgruntled Jerusalemfarers armed themselves with staves and clubs to dislodge the stones, how even those who were sick got up from their beds to help. The bishop of Albara ordered them to stop but they resumed work when he was gone. Those who lacked courage to work during the day would apply themselves at night. Meanwhile they had less and less to eat.

It is evident that the sun, moon, and other planets with all their heavenly motion incite men to behave as they do. Yet these do not control or direct the will and desire of any man. Each is expected to chart and govern his course. But in extremity what shall he do? Radulph de Caen tells how starving pilgrims sliced meat from the buttocks of dead Turks as though they were oxen. Also, corpses dredged from the swamp, members chopped off to put in stewpots. Heathen children impaled on spits to roast. Albeit every man is expected to chart and govern his course, in extremity what shall he do? During the pontificate of His Holiness Innocent some pilgrim called Robert was caught by Turks. Anon, captives with children were told to butcher them for food. It is said this pilgrim, urged by hunger, did kill his child and eat the body. Anon, Turks bade him slay his good wife to eat. But with her flesh served up, Robert could not put it in his mouth. Afterward, having made his way to Europe, he sought absolution. Then did His Holiness Innocent assign penance, that among other deserts Robert the pilgrim should not remarry so long as he lived, nor again eat meat.

Now concerning Tafurs, abominable to man and God alike, these villains devoured human flesh not to assuage grumbling bellies but proclaimed it new manna that would sustain them till they entered the promised land of milk and honey. Therefore they sliced up pagan corpses to share with brethren a hideous sacrifice, thinking thus

to reach the heavenly abode of God. And while the living host encamped at Maarat the bishop of Orange gained his just reward. So
ended that providential year.

Before setting out to Jerusalem, for which they had pledged their
lives, Count Raymond gave orders to burn Maarat. Raymond himself departed from Maarat barefoot, having vowed to approach the
city of Jesus humbly.

Some few leagues south the host encamped by Hosn al-Akrad.
And here came envoys from the learned emir of Tripoli, celebrated
for prudence if not courage. He invited Count Raymond to discuss
the conditions requisite for truce and friendship. He proposed that
Count Raymond send ambassadors to make arrangements, bringing
with them a banner of Toulouse, which might float above the city.
This seemed good to Raymond, who sent three knights. But the
magnificence of Tripoli addled the wits of these ambassadors. When
they got back they counseled Raymond to besiege nearby Archas. By
doing so, they explained, the emir of Tripoli will grow alarmed and
will pay as much tribute as you wish.

Unwisely the host laid siege to Archas, which had been constructed by Aracaeus, son of Canaan, grandson of Noah. Because the
pilgrims had grown proud they were unable to subjugate this stronghold. Sergeants proved indolent and useless. Many nobles relinquished the ghost, including Pontius of Balazun.

Lord Engelram, son of the Comte de Saint Paul, ascended to
glory at Maarat, yet during the siege of Archas he manifested himself
to Anselme de Ribemont.

How is it, Anselme wondered, that you whom I saw dying on the
field of battle now stand before me filled with life?

You must know that those who fight in the name of our Lord do
not die, said Engelram.

Whence comes this radiance surrounding you? said Anselme.

For answer the youth pointed upward. And when Anselme lifted
his eyes he beheld a palace sparkling with crystal and diamond.
There do I dwell, said Engelram. From that mansion derives the

splendor that astonishes you. But a far greater dwelling has been provided for you. Tomorrow we shall meet. Farewell.

At these words Lord Engelram faded from sight. Anselme assured his comrades it was not a dream since he had been awake. They were amazed and speechless because they saw him unhurt, glorious in manhood. Next morning he sent for priests to confess his negligences and take the sacrament. Hours later the Turks sallied forth. Anselme de Ribemont went out from his tent to battle, sword in hand. A stone from a Turkish sling crushed his forehead. Thus perished a valiant knight holding up his gauntlet to God. His bones rest near Archas.

Now those suspicions concerning Bartholomew that took root in Antioch had surged beyond control, entangling adherents of Count Raymond with adherents of Bohemond. One believed in the holiness of the lance, another did not. Some argued openly what many privately thought, that Bartholomew had through sleight of hand buried and extracted a rusty bit of iron. All agreed that he who instigated the difficulty should put an end to it. Thus, Arnulf Malecorne, chaplain to the duke of Normandy, called upon the servant to undergo trial by fire.

I beg and wish that a large fire be made, Bartholomew replied angrily. I will pass through the flames while carrying the lance. I will pass through uninjured if this truly is the lance that wounded our Lord. If not, I will suffer.

It was thought this trial should occur on the day our Lord was pierced in the side. Accordingly two windrows of olive branches were heaped up stretching six times the length of a man's body and a narrow passage between. On the appointed day countless pilgrims gathered, including numerous priests with bare feet. And when the fire blazed vehemently Raymond d'Agiles, who was chaplain to Count Raymond of Toulouse, held forth.

If Almighty God hath addressed this man, and if blessed Andrew hath revealed to him the lance, let him pass through unharmed. But if it be otherwise, let him suffer with the lance he carries.

67

Ancient documents say this olive wood burned so hot it scorched the air for thirty cubits. A bird flying overhead plunged headlong to death as testified by Ebrard the priest, by a son of William the Good, and by an esteemed knight from Béziers, William Maluspuer. Many others witnessed the falling bird. But then, as now, three credible witnesses suffice for any cause.

Bartholomew knelt before the bishop of Albara, calling upon God to verify that he had seen Jesus Christ face to face. When he was given the lance, wrapped in embroidered cloth, he stepped boldly toward the fire and entered without hesitation, pausing just once amid the flames, and emerged shouting with joy. Then a host of pilgrims rushed forward, each hoping to snatch a thread from his tunic. They overwhelmed him and trampled his backbone and he would have breathed out his soul but for a knight who pushed through the crowd to save him. This knight carried him to the house of chaplain Raymond. There he was asked why he paused in the fire, to which he replied that the Lord had met him, took him by the hand, and spoke.

Since thou wert afraid and doubted the finding of the lance when Saint Andrew first offered it, thou shalt not pass through unhurt. Neither shalt thou see hell.

Look therefore, Bartholomew admonished those attending him, and find how I am burnt.

They looked and observed one of his legs scorched. Others came to inspect his face and head and members, and when they found that he was whole they glorified our Lord. They marveled, saying to one another that an arrow could not pass through such a fire. They marveled to see the embroidered cloth undamaged. They said among themselves that the Lord who delivered Bartholomew would assuredly protect them from Saracens. The knight William Maluspuer avowed that he saw a man wearing priestly garb, save for a robe folded back across his head, advance into the flames as though leading Bartholomew. The pilgrims wondered at this. They snatched up glowing coals, fiery brands, ashes, and it is said that various good deeds worked through these relics afterward.

Concerning Bartholomew, although he had been vigorous and

robust, twelve days later he succumbed and was buried at the place where he underwent trial, giving up his body to worms near the citadel of Archas. Some thought he died from the pernicious effect of fire while attempting to validate a falsehood, others that he died from injuries caused by so many pressing against him in a transport of devotion. As for the lance, Count Raymond ever afterward carried it about in a jeweled casket guarded by priests.

Now the emir of Tripoli, informed through spies of Frankish discord, thought to himself he would not pay tribute. Who are these Christians? he asked himself. How great is their strength? Behold, they camp but four leagues distant and do not assault me. Let them come hither. Let them demonstrate their skill. Why should I become tributary to those whose faces I have not seen, whose bravery I doubt?

This being reported to the host, they talked furiously. See what we have accomplished by quarreling! The emir of Tripoli blasphemes God while we are despised! Therefore all agreed that Tripoli should be attacked.

However, the people of this city are content to remain inside if threatened because they are nearly surrounded and protected by the sea while a capacious aqueduct delivers water from land. According to the Gesta, numerous Turks and Arabs discovered outside the walls were sent flying or quickly tasted the Christian blade. So much pagan blood flowed that water in the aqueduct turned red, frothed and bubbled with headless corpses of those who did not believe. Indeed, the cisterns of Tripoli changed color. We are told how the scornful emir, thinking his numbers adequate, sent forth his knights to confront the living host. Out from Tripoli they rode, thrusting from the gate like a stag thrusting his antlers, but our Lord cast fear against them. How many wicked lives ended sharply may not be known. They were choked by sinfulness.

This day, said the Frankish princes, have they met us and learned what we are. Tomorrow, because we have acquired knowledge of roads and fortification, the emir will learn to pay tribute.

Next day no Turk ventured outside, albeit the emir sent word. If

69

the siege were lifted he would supply food, garments, horses, fifteen thousand gold coins, and he would provide a market and would release every Christian captive. This seemed good to the princes. Besides, all were anxious to pursue the journey.

According to chaplain Raymond, they inquired how best to reach Jerusalem and learned of three roads. Inland through Damascus was level, with food enough, but they would not find water for two days. They might go south through the mountains of Lebanon with safety, yet this was very hard on camels and sumpter beasts. Or they might proceed south along the coast but would find such narrow passes that fifty or a hundred Saracens might hold the road against all mankind. They learned also of Christians who lived among the mountains close by the city of Tyre, or as many call it Sur, whence they were called Surians. These people had managed the land for centuries until dispossessed by Turks. Now they were prohibited from observing Christian law. If by the grace of God one persisted he must give up his sons for circumcision or be killed and the mother of his child corrupted. These Turks riddled holy images with arrows, gouged out eyes, overthrew altars. If some true believer kept an image of our Lord in his home it was flung down into the dust, broken, mutilated. Christian boys were sold to brothels, their sisters exchanged for wine.

How shall we reach the Holy City? Count Raymond wondered.

In the gospel of Saint Peter, the Surians replied, it is written that if you are meant to take Jerusalem you will pass along the coast, however impossible that seems to us.

On the sixteenth of May, therefore, the living host marched

south from Tripoli and came at length into Palestine, to Caesarea, in which city Saint Peter once preached at the house of the centurion Cornelius. Also in this city Herod Agrippa wretchedly gave up the ghost. And while they were encamped they saw a hawk attack a pigeon that dropped wounded to the earth. A silver tube had been fastened to one of its legs. Inside was a scroll with writing.

To the Lord of Caesarea the Emir of Akka sends greetings. A pack of quarrelsome dogs hath in disorderly fashion passed by here. As thou lovest Allah, send word to other citadels and fortresses that every injury be done to them.

Thus, God in heaven by means of the very birds had chosen to warn and protect these travelers during the arduous journey.

Until the thirtieth of May the host remained at Caesarea in order that Whitsun might be celebrated, after which they continued south to Ramlah, eight leagues from the Holy City. Ramlah they found deserted except for Samaritans. Advocates of the devil had fled after burning the White Mosque so it could not be torn apart and the timber used to make siege engines. Under the marble floor of this mosque lay the spotless body of Saint George who happily embraced martyrdom. The Franks purified this place of unholy worship, consecrated it anew, made it a bishopric dedicated to our Lord. Some now argued they should not proceed to Jerusalem but go instead to Egypt and capture Alexandria and Babylon and kingdoms all around. For if we besiege Jerusalem but do not have sufficient water, they argued, we will accomplish nothing. But others claimed it would be folly to venture toward unknown and distant regions since they had scarce fifteen hundred knights. Let us hold our way, they said. Let us trust the Messiah to provide for His servants. Accordingly they loaded up camels and oxen to continue marching. Yet of that multitude which besieged Nicaea two years earlier, less than thirty thousand remained.

Presently they reached the castle of Emmaus where a bold plan was conceived. Tancred and Baldwin du Bourg rode ahead. Before daybreak they passed Jerusalem and rode on to Bethlehem. Greeks

71

and Syrians who lived there at first mistook them for Turkish cavalry, perhaps Egyptians who had come to defend the Holy City, but when it became clear from crosses on their mantles that here were Frankish knights the citizens of Bethlehem wept for joy. They held up rosaries and banners and crosses. They kissed the hands of Tancred's followers and sang hymns, praying that the hour of deliverance had arrived when Christianity would prevail against those who threatened it.

These intrepid Franks made haste to visit the basilica of Our Lady where they offered supplications. They visited the place where Christ was born. Tancred by himself rode two leagues nearer Jerusalem and dismounted on a height from which he could see the Holy City. To his eyes and within his mind surely it appeared as it once appeared to Saint John the Divine, descending out of heaven from God, having the glory of God, more luminous than crystal, within a mighty wall having twelve gates where angels waited. Chalcedony, amethyst, emerald, jasper, topaz, of such were the foundations garnished, all manner of precious stone, and twelve gates made of pearl. And the streets were gold. And the city had no need of the sun nor of the moon, for it was lightened by the glory of God. Tancred is thought by many to have stood on the Mount of Olives.

Before returning to join the Christian host Tancred set his banner above the church of the Nativity as though it were a lodging house, which moved some to anger.

Albert of Aix reports in his chronicle how the nearness of Jerusalem excited these pilgrims. Few could sleep. Indeed, rather than await the dawn they resumed the march shortly after midnight. And they saw the power of the Lord manifest because the moon sank into eclipse, foretelling the eclipse of the pagan crescent.

At sunrise they could see minarets, domes, towers, and white houses of the city that hitherto they had seen only in their hearts. Many knelt to pray. Others wept, screamed, hurled themselves face down with arms outstretched to kiss the earth. Jerusalem, they could see, did not compare with Constantinople or Antioch, but not for quotidian profit did they undertake this journey.

deus lo volt!

Eight days before the ides of June they encamped. And because they had need of wood to construct siege engines the barons despatched foraging parties. Tancred accompanied them, though ill with flux and often obliged to seek privacy. Once while voiding himself he looked into a cave and saw four hundred timbers, which seemed miraculous. He shouted to his companions. Now they were able to erect ballistas, mangonels, trebuchets, wheeled castles, wooden sows that they protected with hide, mantlets, and other devices. With tent rope, olive branches, and palm stems they assembled scaling ladders.

At last, hearing in its soul a thunderous command, the boundless army of God advanced. Count Robert of Flanders laid siege near the church where Saint Stephen was stoned to death in the name of Christ. Duke Godfrey laid siege from the west, a gold image of our Lord affixed to his catapult. Count Raymond attacked from the south near the church of Saint Mary. All this through the lawful covenant of things.

Arrows descended like hail from the ramparts of Jerusalem, yet no less terrible were those enemies long familiar to the host, starvation, thirst. By direction of Iftikhar, who governed the city, fresh water springs had been concealed or muddied, nearby cisterns poisoned. Shepherds were instructed to drive their flocks away. Christians whose families had lived for centuries in Jerusalem were expelled, told to scavenge what food they could and drink what water they found. It is related that some few inhabitants of Thecus or Bethlehem came to visit the host and led pilgrims to water, but there was not enough. The Pool of Siloam where a blind man regained his sight had not been poisoned, although Turkish arrows reached that far and the spring replenishing this pool flowed weakly. Once, they were told, the water flowed each Saturday yet otherwise lay stagnant, which could not be explained except that our Lord so commanded. People of the region used this water for washing clothes and tanning hides. The Franks in desperation crowded together, the strong thrusting aside the feeble as they fought toward a juncture in the rock whence trickled a salty liquid. Sick or dying pilgrims fell, unable to speak, mouths open, stretching out their hands. Beasts in the field stood like creatures made from stone, fell down and rotted. The smell of death corrupted day and night and a burning wind tormented all. The Gesta relates how pilgrims sewed ox hides together by means of which they carried fresh water several leagues. But the water putrefied, turned rank, fetid, loosened the bowels. And the watchful Turk, noticing how groups went unarmed to watering places among the hills, rose up to slaughter them and dismember the bodies. During this chastisement few felt mindful of the Lord nor took heed to beseech His grace, so in their agony they could not recognize God amid them.

Now all at once came news of two Genoese galleys anchored at Joppa, captained by the brothers Embriaco, and four English ships. Since the port lay half in ruins and the city desolate, these ships were endangered. Count Galdemar started at once with thirty knights and fifty sergeants, but while en route the Turk surprised him. Various Christian knights ascended to glory including two brave youths, Achade de Montmerle and Gilbert de Trèves. Albeit many pagans plunged shrieking into the depths Count Galdemar decided to withdraw. At this moment a rising cloud of dust was seen, stirred up by Raymond Piletus leading fifty mounted knights who called loudly upon the Holy Sepulcher and Jesus Christ. Then the Turks made haste to scatter, thinking an army approached, dreading in their hearts the fiery pit of Gehenna. Count Galdemar's men pursued them a while, killing more, then paused to collect and divide the spoil before proceeding to Joppa, which is the oldest city on earth. According to Solinus it was founded prior to the Flood, and at Joppa one may see a rock bearing traces of the chains that bound Andromeda when she was exposed to a monster. Marcus Scaurus, when he was aedile, exhibited the bones of this terrible creature at Rome. They say each rib was eight times the length of a man.

Be that as it may, Count Galdemar was boisterously welcomed at Joppa since these mariners felt themselves much exposed. They

74

rejoiced when he arrived. They got up a banquet of fish, wine, and bread. But that night, feeling secure, they neglected to post lookouts and in darkness here came an Egyptian fleet. So the Genoese, electing to sacrifice their vessels, hurriedly dismantled everything, collecting sails, ropes, and other equipment and quickly got ashore. Count Galdemar escorted these mariners to camp outside Jerusalem, making the best of it, having defeated quite a few enemies on land but losing his grip on the port.

Archbishop William declares in his narrative that these Genoese and English sailors with mallets, spikes, axes, and hatchets brought great joy to the legions surrounding Jerusalem because they were skilled at the art of building, expert at felling trees, smoothing and fitting beams. Which is to say, much that had seemed difficult or impossible was soon accomplished.

On the ides of June this army of God once more attacked. They breached the first wall and they set a ladder against the principal wall, enabling a few knights to gain the top and strike furiously at unbelievers, but they had not ladders enough to take the city by escalade. Throughout that month they continued to assault Jerusalem, enduring much hardship for the love of Christ. Barley bread made with poisonous water caused ague. Infidels surprised and killed many going in search of fresh water. Yet some went down to the river Jordan for baptism a second time, gathering palm branches to celebrate the journey.

Curious events were noted. Guibert de Nogent relates how besiegers and besieged, exhausted by slaughter, promiscuously intermingled. Battalions of children under the direction of child captains would engage in mock struggles, armed with sticks in lieu of swords, using reeds for spears, carrying shields woven of twigs, battling on the plain while their parents watched, Franks emerging from tents, Saracens looking down from the ramparts. It is said the children charged like men, uttering shrill cries. Their captains impersonated adults, one calling himself Bohemond, another Hugh Vermandois. If these little captains saw their soldiers hungry they would go to beg food from the princes after whom they were named. Now and again these childish struggles incited the hearts of adults who could no longer rest quietly but must rush out to continue fighting.

Presently came news of a huge Babylonian army to break the siege. Those in the Frankish host looked at one another and did not know what to think or say because they numbered twelve hundred knights with some nine thousand soldiers afoot. Then through divine intercession Bishop Adhémar manifested himself to the visionary Peter Desiderius.

Speak to the lords and to the people, Bishop Adhémar commanded. Say they must purge themselves of wickedness. Remind them how they have come from distant lands to liberate the Holy City. Then with feet bare let the host march around Jerusalem invoking their Savior. After they have done this, let them attack on the ninth day. Let the pilgrims attack with fury and Jerusalem will be captured. But if they do not, then will the Lord God multiply their trials.

When the priest had spoken of this with Count Ysoard and William Hugo and certain clerics, they summoned the people and the barons.

We have been negligent, said they. We have not reconciled the Lord to us. In various ways we have affronted Him. By wicked deeds have we driven the Lord from our side. Now let each of us be reconciled to his brother. Let those who are offended forgive those who offend them. Let us humble ourselves before God. Let us beseech Him who assumed the flesh, who rode into Jerusalem mounted on an ass to suffer death for our sins. Let us beseech His aid. If with contrite hearts we go in procession around the city of Jerusalem, then will He open the gates to us. Then will He deliver judgment against His enemies who contaminate and corrupt the place of His burial, who withhold the blessing we seek, who deny entrance to the site of our redemption.

Thus it happened on the eighth of July, announced by trumpets. Preceded by clerics and bishops holding aloft sacred relics and crosses, all together the living host marched with feet bare around Jerusalem, which caused Saracens to parade likewise about the walls carrying an emblem of Mahomet on a standard. The infidels shouted insults, blared horns. They made a wood cross like that upon which our merciful Savior poured forth His blood to redeem the world. They beat upon it with sticks, spat upon it, smeared it with filth. Frango agip salip? they screamed, by which they mockingly inquired if the Franks thought it a good cross.

When the host got to the Mount of Olives it seemed they could do no more to purify themselves. They said anew that each should forgive his brother that the Lord might forgive them. Unbelievers clustered on the ramparts of Jerusalem to watch without concern, imagining themselves secure.

If people assert they are not permitted for any reason to take up arms against enemies of the Church, to fight bodily in defense of their belief, it becomes clear that they have been inspired and directed by Satan. If they misuse the authority of Scripture to produce false interpretation, that must be Satan's voice. So egregious arguments are brought forth to debauch and seduce the credulous or inattentive. Certainly the Church would be devastated by heretics if these were not annihilated since they are without number, past counting, because they renew themselves. What could be more evident? For this reason do we excise decadent flesh, sever putrid limbs. Otherwise what is substantial would deteriorate. Hence the wicked must be destroyed that the good may flourish. Is not the strength of a man's right arm bequeathed by God? Surely. Therefore the good do not seek peace in order to make war, but rather to arrest the wicked so that all may enjoy the fruits of peace. Consequently the good do not shrink from shedding blood nor inhibit the power of the sword.

Again, some that oppose holy war declare it not in accord with Christian principle since our Lord told Peter to sheathe his sword. Yet has not the Church two functions? Surely. One of production, one of conservation. When the vineyard is planted and bears fruit, must it not be defended? Surely. Or again, has not Christianity differing stages of growth? Does not a man develop out of infancy to old age? Is not this evident? At first our Church was poor and defenseless, now she is rich and able to defend herself. When Christ bade Peter to put up his sword He spoke for that occasion only since the time for use had not arrived. Thus, to make war against Saracens, who are enemies of the Messiah, must not be incompatible with Christianity.

Roger Bacon avows that to attack the infidel will but hinder and delay his conversion, yet such argument is lamentably weak. Just as every man learns through adverse experience, so will the Saracen learn to distrust Mahomet when he is wholly defeated. Nor does any Christian wish him ill but desires to see him get what he deserves, as a judge decrees merited punishment to a thief. Hence, for Saracens to be slain is good and necessary that their turpitude not increase.

Now the living army of God advanced, the hearts of all fired by a single purpose. They would restore Jerusalem to the righteous or give up their lives. Nor could one be found in that zealous host, sick, aged, feeble, young, who did not anticipate what was to come. So did women, disdaining their natural weakliness, pick up arms to fight beyond their strength. And the host marched, holding wicker screens and shields to guard against arrows, stones, and iron darts. They brought forth siege engines but Muslims on the ramparts hung bags of straw and chaff from the walls, tapestries, nets, mattresses stuffed with silk to thwart Christian missiles. The pagans fought bitterly, flung spears, hurled wood bolts wrapped in fiery rags with protruding nails that clung to every surface. Through the air flew clumps of hay drenched in oil and wax, burning pitch, sulfur, clots of flame.

deus lo volt!

Saracen and Christian missiles crashed against each other making a noise that afternoon like the death of Satan. But at nightfall the city held.

Next day two sorceresses leapt and capered among the turrets because of a catapult inflicting much damage. They gesticulated, pranced, shrieked, by evil incantation seeking to bewitch it. And while they summoned the acolytes of darkness a millstone came down, crushed them together with three apprentices. So a hideous spectacle vanished from sight. Exultation filled every Christian heart. Applause was heard throughout the ranks. Groans and sighs emanated from Jerusalem.

Anon a spy was caught because a Greek pointed him out. Ma te Christo caco Sarrazin! said he. By Christ, there goes a filthy Saracen!

They demanded of the spy to know his business. He replied that he had been sent to learn what machines the Franks were building. So they trussed him and laid him in a petrary to throw him back where he came from. What happened but ropes broke when the machine hurled him out. Halfway to Jerusalem the spy came apart, feet, legs, arms flying all directions. What led him astray? Ignorance of our Lord.

Atop the Mount of Olives stood a knight holding a luminous shield. Duke Godfrey and his brother Eustace called attention to this. Then the host, its spirit renewed, surged impetuously toward the wall, wishing to be tried again, to sway the course of battle, believing they should draw a better lot and earn the palm. Those who turned away because of wounds or suffering from exhaustion returned to fight with increased ardor. Sacks of cotton and straw were set afire. Black smoke poured into Jerusalem. The defenders felt sickened. Dazed, coughing, they lost hope. They closed their eyes, blind to the glory of God.

At the ninth hour Lethold de Touraine scaled the wall. Was it not ordained that those who fought for Him should consummate their yearning at the very hour when He suffered to reclaim this world? And the pagans, seeing Lethold among them, broke and fled.

Down came the drawbright of Godfrey's castle. He sprang to the
wall followed by knights of his train. Tancred, Baldwin du Bourg,
Gaston de Béarn, Gérard de Roussillon, Thomas de la Fère, Ludovic
de Moncons, and others whose names are lost.

Godfrey directed certain of his men to Saint Stephen's Gate,
which they unbarred so those waiting outside could enter. The army
of Christ rushed into Jerusalem shouting with jubilation, swords unsheathed. Nor did they hesitate to strike all they met, recalling how
their faith was insulted. Striking, slaying at every turn, God's name
upon their lips, they washed through streets and courtyards faster
than the tide. Unbelievers drowned in the blood of unbelievers, since
our Lord commanded this to be. Blood splashed the fetlocks of
Frankish chargers, splashed against bridle reins. Each drop contributed to the glory. Bodies sprouted arrows. Heads dropped like fruit.
Pilgrims chopped off hands, feet, private parts, weeping and mad
with lust and joy after the gall they had swallowed. Not since the
world began was more blood spilled. Thus did God compensate
those infidels who inflicted such anguish upon the living host. Could
it be other than His just and splendid judgment? What was this, if
not retribution equivalent to the crime? Were not these people in-
volved with error, choked by sin?

Jews beyond number ran screaming and lamenting to their synagogue. Soldiers of Christ put it to the torch. These Israelites burned,
every one, even as the prophecy of Daniel told how their anointing
must fail. They had not obeyed the voice of our Lord to walk in His
laws. So were they reimbursed for helping to defend Jerusalem. In
them were united the treachery of Judas, the impiety of Herod, the
cruelty of Nero, their hearts exuding ashes of avarice.

Ten thousand heathen sought refuge in the mosque al-Aqsa. Gaston de Béarn and Tancred beheaded them like sheep at market, harvested them like corn. With superstitious ritual had they polluted
His sanctuary, the Temple of Solomon. Now, delivering up their
lives, they cleansed the sacred precinct. Some fled to the roof hoping

to escape but finding no outlet hastily surrendered, pledging silver and gold in exchange for life. Tancred left them secure beneath his standard and proceeded to the Dome of the Rock. There he laid claim to eight precious silver lamps plus other valuables, a good and deserved fortune.

God's army searched Jerusalem for gold, jewelry, donkeys, horses. They looked for Saracens to kill, looked under beds, opened closets, dragged infidels out of obscurity into public where all might watch them expiate the sin. What is this but a parable of our time? And the host marveled because Jerusalem flaunted such splendid streets, squares, and courts. Once the city was called Aelia Capitolina in homage to Aelius Hadrian who lavishly embellished it.

At sunrise next day, this being one day after Lethold from Touraine accomplished what others dreamt about, certain pilgrims without allegiance to Tancred, some say these were Provençal, climbed to the roof of the mosque. Infidels huddling beneath Tancred's banner cried out for mercy to no avail. Heads dropped like melons until all were slain, albeit many leapt to death. Narratives say Tancred grew indignant when told of this, having pledged himself to their custody. Also, the gold and silver ransom was lost.

What of Iftikhar? He fled to the Tower of David whence he sent word to Count Raymond promising a heavy purse if he might go free. This seemed good to Raymond. So the governor of Jerusalem and those next to him earned safe passage to Ascalon.

Thus was the Holy City released from bondage on the ides of July in that year of our grace 1099, which is called Dies Veneris for on this day Jesus Christ redeemed the world.

Our Lord did not undertake to liberate Jerusalem but to scatter seeds that grow against the wickedness of Antichrist. This day hath He made, wrote the chaplain Raymond d'Agiles. Let us rejoice and be glad. This day will endure to future ages since it marks the justification of Christianity. And in truth these Franks rejoiced. How they exulted, offering songs of praise to the King of Kings. Bishop

Adhémar who ascended to heaven from Antioch was seen by many as they explored Jerusalem. Some allege he was first to scale the ramparts, beckoning his knights to follow.

Now the barons clad themselves in fresh garments. Hands washed of blood, feet bare, contrite, humble, singing a new canticle to the Lord, they visited places the Messiah had deigned to glorify. Tearful, sighing, they pressed kisses upon the stones His feet once trod, kissed memorials of His sojourn among us. Reverently they approached the Church of the Holy Sepulcher for which they had endured such deprivation. Here they felt they had entered Paradise. To them it seemed they could almost see the body of Christ while they accepted the blessing of Greek and Syriac priests among the burning candles and the sweet odor of incense. They worshipped and supplicated the Lord. They sobbed with profound emotion.

They visited Bethlehem to kneel beside the cradle where the Infant had lain. They saw the stone that felled Goliath. They saw the anvil upon which the nails of the Passion were forged. They visited the shop where thirty pieces of silver were coined. Much else did they see, including the star that guided the Magi and fell into a cistern on the day of Epiphany. At these places everything our Savior did or taught while he lived among men was recalled, refreshed the memory of true believers.

With prayers complete, when they had rendered homage, the high barons decided to cleanse Jerusalem of decaying bodies. Some few pagans that had been found in prison were assigned the task. However they were not enough so a daily wage was offered to pilgrims who would help. Torsos, arms, heads, legs, all were carted outside the wall and flung together. According to the narrative of Fulcher de Chartres, Provençals who arrived late for the sack of Jerusalem went about splitting the bellies of corpses to pull out entrails and inspect the folds. They did this because many infidels had tried to keep their wealth from Christians by swallowing gold bezants. Or it might happen that six or eight bezants popped from the mouth of a corpse if struck on the neck with a fist. Also, which was shameful, Saracen women hid gold inside their bodies.

Archbishop William with his account of those days relates how pyramids of severed human parts terrified all who gazed at them, yet more hideous was the spectacle of pilgrims resolute in their faith, swords dripping blood. How many citizens of Jerusalem bent their necks? God knows. Neither before nor since has such a multitude felt the blade. To this day, it is said, Muslims draw strength from ancient memories of the Holy City splashed with gore.

Abbot Guibert argues that all should look narrowly upon Christians who participated, who took pride in this exploit, who delighted at crime, perfidy, and turpitude, because having feasted their eyes on Jerusalem they thought themselves exempt from natural law. But what of Muslims? Were not they themselves responsible? Did not these black souls seethe with hatred toward Christians lighting the lamp of truth? Where is the seed and root of wickedness?

When the Holy City had been purified, bodies set afire, Frankish lords retired to houses they had selected. Jerusalem they quickly learned was filled to abundance with goods of every sort. Embroidered robes, gems, silver and gold coins, oil, grain, wine, more than enough. On the second day they held a public market, again on the third day. So they passed this time in amiable celebration. Pilgrims refreshed themselves, eating what they liked, idling, giving thanks.

It is said that people in Baghdad wept incessantly. These unbelievers follow a calendar of their own devising and in the ninth month, which they call Ramadan, they do not eat or drink from sunrise to sunset. But upon learning how Jerusalem was seized by Christians they violated the feast of Ramadan by swallowing their tears. So it is alleged. The truth of this, I, Jean, do not pretend to know.

Very long ago Charlemagne conquered Jerusalem. When I was a child I learned that twelve peers and eighty thousand Franks accompanied him but did not have to battle enemies along the way. When they got to the Holy City they entered a church and saw a throne prepared for Charlemagne, with twelve thrones for his knights. No more did they seat themselves than a Jew arrived. Mistaking these Franks for Christ and His apostles, the Jew submitted to conversion. Which is to say, Charlemagne may be likened to God's representative on earth. Anon came word of a very great monarch, Hugh the Strong, king of Constantinople who tilled his fields with a golden plough. The Franks marched off to see for themselves. Hugh greeted them honorably but challenged them to demonstrate their prowess. Because of this insult they raped his daughter and went about destroying his palace. Hugh begged them to leave his country, which they did, having proved themselves superior to Greeks. While in Constantinople they saw astonishing things, gilded birds that sang, statues of men that could move and speak. Yet these were foolish marvels wrought by a decadent race.

Charlemagne might well gaze with pride upon a host of illustrious descendants, not least Duke Godfrey de Bouillon. This great lord was born in the province of Reims at Boulogne-sur-Mer next to the English sea. We are told by a monk of Wast that his mother Ida had been endowed with angelic grace, that she was assiduous in attending church, that she worshipped with extreme and devout humility. Hence we do not wonder if Duke Godfrey remained so long on his knees that mealtime often came and went, obliging those of his entourage to swallow cold food. Yet none spoke ill of him by reason of his perfect nature. Count Eustace, his father, wrought many notable deeds and to this day the mention of Count Eustace evokes favorable memories. He fought with great valor in that year of our Lord 1066 when Normans invaded England. They say he rescued the Conqueror at a moment of desperate peril, when his third horse was slain, therefore we see Count Eustace on the majestic tapestry at Bayeux alongside William.

Thus, by virtue of lofty character and noble lineage, Godfrey de Bouillon was elected to defend and rule the Holy City of Jerusalem. This responsibility he accepted, but declined to wear a crown of gold in the city where Jesus Christ had worn a crown of thorns. The title he chose for himself was Advocate of the Holy Sepulcher.

Very many tales are we told of Godfrey. How at one stroke he cut a Turk neatly in half, so the Muslim steed galloped off with only the legs and hips of its rider clinging to the saddle. Also, narratives speak of a Mahometan lord who arranged a truce in order to visit because he had heard of Godfrey's matchless strength. He brought into Godfrey's presence an enormous camel, beseeching him to smite off the creature's head. They say Godfrey unsheathed his sword and lopped it off as easily as though the camel were a goose. Then the pagan stepped back, amazed, knowing the stories were true. And returning to his own land he proclaimed the mightiness of Godfrey, for he had witnessed it himself.

Now here came anxious Turks riding down out of the mountains of Samaria with bread, figs, wine, raisins and other gifts, seeking Godfrey's approval. These suppliants found him at rest on a bale of straw in his tent, the earth bare, without carpets. Nor were there guards to protect him from assassins, so they were dumb with astonishment. Why, they asked through interpreters, did a prince who seized a kingdom and caused the Orient to tremble sit thus ingloriously? Why did he not loll among tapestries and silk? Why was he not flattered by attendants? And when Godfrey understood what they were saying he replied that the earth would suffice as a seat for any man since after death it would be his abode forever. Then these misbelievers thought about his words and concluded that he was a man devoid of pride who knew the poverty of his nature. They were filled with admiration. When they departed they said he deserved to be lord of the Franks.

Anon came word of an Egyptian host ten leagues distant. Al-Afdal, vizier of Babylon, overflowing with rage, vowed to kill every Christian male above the age of twenty, to seize every woman and child, giving the women to youths of his race. Nor was that all. He would proceed to Antioch and do likewise. Further, he meant to place upon his head the diadem of other cities, including Damascus. Nor was that enough. He blasphemed against God, claiming he would annihilate the place of our Lord's nativity and Golgotha and the site of His burial and other sacred places, avowing he would tear these up by their roots from the earth, break them and cast their dust at the sea. And when he had done this the Franks would find no memorial to guide them.

Such news having reached Jerusalem, the people huddled uneasily, citizens, clerics, princes. Around the Holy Sepulcher they marched, chanting psalms, beseeching God to deliver His children since the enemy host camped near Ascalon. Next the lords consulted among themselves, how best to defend the city, how to confront al-Afdal. Duke Godfrey with Count Robert of Flanders set out on the ninth day of August to observe these Babylonians and sent back word by the bishop of Martirano that so far as they could see the plains were spangled with tents.

On the tenth of August, beseeching God's mercy, Count Raymond set forth accompanied by the duke of Normandy, Robert Curthose. They came to a river where they saw a great many Arabs tending herds of cattle, sheep, and camels, which made them think the army of al-Afdal must be near. Two hundred knights rode ahead prepared for combat. When the Arabs saw these knights they deserted their animals and fled. Had God regarded them as He regarded us, said the chaplain Raymond d'Agiles, they should have fought, since they were three thousand armed men. Some few herdsmen these knights slew, others caught and forced to divulge information. So the Franks learned that al-Afdal was encamped not five leagues distant. Therefore, confessing their sins and negligence, persuading themselves that the enemy must be timid as hinds, docile as sheep, certain that God would deal with unbelievers on His own account, they passed the night wakefully.

Horns and trumpets announced the dawn. God multiplied this army, said chaplain Raymond, so its numbers did not seem inferior. Animals came to join these pilgrims, miraculously forming herds albeit no one drove them, halting if the army halted, advancing when it advanced.

Al-Afdal's soldiers loitered in camp, having been informed that the Christians were few, wretchedly armed, riding feeble horses. Also, stargazers and soothsayers admonished them not to move until the seventh day of the week. Such was the hubris of these infidels that when the battle commenced each hung a water bottle around his neck so he might slake his thirst while pursuing Christians.

But what they envisioned proved false. Tancred, whose name terrified misbelievers throughout the Holy Land, burst into their camp and sent many flying. Count Robert, seeing al-Afdal's standard adorned with a gold apple on the tip of a silver lance, rode furiously against the bearer and struck him down. Blinded by terror, stupefied, Satan's troops looked with vacant eyes at these knights of Jesus Christ. Horrified, fearing to advance, some in the excess of fright climbed trees. Others groveled on the earth to be speared like fish. Others crouched, pretending to hide. Many rushed to a sycamore grove, which the Franks set afire, so they were all burned. Others scattered and fled toward the sea, dashed into the waves. On every side they were butchered, drowned, burned. Voices of corruption silenced.

Al-Afdal, distraught with grief, watched what happened. He asked himself if ever such a thing had occurred since the world began. How is this? he asked. We are destroyed by a regiment of Christians that I might crush in the hollow of my hand. I have brought every manner of instrument and weapon and machine. Here I have assembled two hundred thousand Islamic knights, yet with loose bridles they flee down the road. Alas, I am ruined by a poor and beggarly race. Alas, it will be told throughout the land. Whereupon al-Afdal escaped the wreckage, leaving a field strewn with bucklers, daggers, shields, quivers, lances, arrows, to say nothing of innumerable proud and wicked soldiers whose tainted blood discolored the earth, whose black souls plunged screeching into eternal night.

His fanciful painted tent, his jeweled sword, his concubines, all were seized by the living host. For twenty silver marks Duke Robert Curthose bought the vainglorious standard. Truly this battle attested the power of divine intervention since the Cross of our Lord, mighty against enemies, accompanied these Franks. Therefore the pomp of Egypt could not prevail.

Archbishop Daimbert, Duke Godfrey, and Count Raymond, laboring as one, composed a message to His Holiness. They described how a vast Christian army marched upon Antioch, how this army was so immense that it might have covered all of Romania and drunk up all the rivers and eaten every growing thing. And although the Saracens resisted, they were easily defeated. Yet some in the army being puffed with conceit neglected to thank God, for which reason He detained the army for nine months beneath the walls of Antioch and so humbled it that nearly all the good horses died. And when Antioch succumbed there were many who did not worthily magnify Him but attributed victory to their own strength. Therefore came such a multitude of Turks that none dared venture outside the walls. And hunger weakened them. But God, having chastised them, mercifully consoled and fortified them and revealed the Lance that had lain buried since the time of the apostles, so they were able to overcome the enemy and proceed into Syria where they captured many strongholds. Yet they suffered again from lack of food and were obliged to eat the bodies of heathen. And they suffered grievously for lack of water during the siege of Jerusalem, but God delivered up the city on the day when the Dispersion of Apostles is celebrated. And should His Holiness wish to know what was done to these unbelievers, know that in Solomon's Porch the knights rode through Saracen blood as high as the knees of horses. But while they considered who ought to hold the city they learned that the King of Babylon with a host of soldiers encamped before Ascalon, whose purpose was to lead the Franks into captivity. Therefore the army of God went out to meet him. And God was present. Christian soldiers rushed against the infidels with such alacrity that one might have taken them for a herd of deer rushing to quench their thirst in water. So all the treasure belonging to the King of Babylon was seized while one hundred thousand Moors perished by the sword. Those drowned in the sea surpassed counting. Likewise, many were slain among thickets of thorns. Nor should it be omitted that on the day preceding this battle the army captured untold thousands of camels, oxen, and sheep, which were divided among the pilgrims. And when the army proceeded, glorious to relate, these animals organized themselves into squadrons to accompany the soldiers, and halted or charged as did the host. Meanwhile the clouds overhead protected and sheltered these soldiers from the heat of the sun. And when the victory had been celebrated the army returned in triumph to Jerusalem. Therefore all those of the catholic Church of Christ and of the Latin church should exult in the bravery and devotion of their brethren. May they sit down at the right hand of God who lives and reigns eternally.

This letter they despatched to His Holiness Paschal, who became pontiff at the demise of His Holiness Urban II, following the memorable victory of Ascalon.

How is it that we know the beginning of things but not their end? Less than one year after Jerusalem was liberated Duke Godfrey fell ill at Caesarea, having attended a banquet given by the emir. Some think he ate poisoned fruit. Whatever the truth, he continued to Joppa but there his spirit failed. He asked to be carried to the Holy City. In the pleasant shadows of Jerusalem he improved, if not much. Remedies were sought far and wide, to no advantage. On the eighteenth day of July in the year of our Savior 1100 he went the way of all flesh to accept perpetual life. He was buried at the entrance to the chapel of Adam near the foot of Golgotha. So passed from view the first Latin ruler of Jerusalem.

For three months the throne stood vacant. At length, perhaps by agreement among certain lords, or in deference to Godfrey's last wish, his brother Baldwin was elected. The bishop of Ramlah with an escort of knights rode hastily to Edessa but did not find Baldwin. They were told he had set out to rescue Lord Bohemond who was captured by Turks.

It so happened that Armenians in the city of Melitene greatly dreaded an attack by the emir Malik Ghazi and appealed to Bohemond for help. Since he had numerous Armenian friends such as the bishops of Marash and Antioch, he responded gladly. With three hundred knights he went marching up the river Euphrates toward Melitene. By all accounts he marched inattentively through the hills. Malik Ghazi caught him unaware, massacred the reckless knights. Bohemond himself, seeing no escape, cut off a lock of his hair, entrusting it to a sergeant who slipped away and got to Edessa. In that way Baldwin learned what happened. And there was Bohemond's yellow hair to prove his sergeant spoke the truth.

Malik Ghazi large with success rode to the very walls of Melitene where he shouted insults and displayed bloody Frankish heads. But when he found out that Baldwin was en route he withdrew toward the mountains. Baldwin followed Malik Ghazi for three days. Then, not liking the look of things, and because he doubted Bohemond could be saved, he turned around. By this time, say Arab chronicles, Bohemond dressed in chains was on his way to the distant castle of Niksar.

So it was not until Lord Baldwin got back to Edessa that he learned his brother Godfrey was dead and he, himself, would be king of Jerusalem.

September passed arranging for this new estate, deputizing a cousin to act as regent of Edessa. In October, grieving somewhat upon his brother's death, all the same rejoicing at such good luck, he set out for Jerusalem. From Antioch he sent his wife with her ladies by sea to Joppa.

deus lo volt!

Fulcher de Chartres relates that two leagues above Beyrouth they came to a narrow place in the public road, no more than a ledge on the cliff. One hundred thousand soldiers could not get through, he writes, if sixty armed men resolutely blocked the way. From ancient times this has been a famous passage. Every general who forced it has left some inscription on the cliff. Here may be seen the writing of Pharaoh Ramses, Nebuchadnezzar, Septimius Severus, and others. Lord Baldwin proceeded cautiously. What lay in wait but a great many Arabs and Turks commanded by Ginanhadoles and Ducath. We pretended one thing and thought another, says Fulcher. We feigned boldness but feared death. I very much wished to be in Chartres or Orléans, as did everyone else.

Baldwin retreated a little. Next morning a little further. Enemies of Christ followed. But when the passage narrowed he turned swiftly to attack and by nightfall had sent them flying. Many in despair hurled themselves from rocky crags into the sea. Others met the point of the sword. Others dispersed quicker than rabbits bounding away to the mountains or scurrying to safety behind the walls of Beyrouth. After this Baldwin was not molested.

When he approached the Holy City all came forth to honor him. Greeks, Syrians, many bearing crosses and lighted candles. They escorted him to the Church of the Holy Sepulcher and with ringing voices praised God.

Lord Baldwin rested six days in Jerusalem after which he set out to explore his kingdom, albeit he was not yet crowned. The domain was small and menaced by pagan hordes from Syria to Egypt, but he thought a display of spirit might intimidate them. After posting three hundred knights to guard the city he rode forth and pressed on to a wide country through villages whose terrified inhabitants hid themselves in caves. But the Franks would light a fire in front of each cave, which brought up the Saracens gasping and coughing and choking. Among them were Syrian Christians who pointed out brigands responsible for murdering pilgrims along the Jerusalem road.

According to Fulcher, nearly one hundred of these malefactors were beheaded as soon as they emerged. Afterward, thinking the Syrians could be murdered in reprisal, Lord Baldwin had them escorted to Ascalon.

Next he resolved to visit Syria. Therefore the Franks crossed the hills of Judea at Hebron, visiting a mosque built over the cave of Machpelah. Here lie entombed the earthly remnants of Abraham, Isaac, Jacob, Joseph, Sarah, and Rebecca. Thence to the valley where Sodom and Gomorrah were consumed by flame. Here is a vast lake called the Dead Sea because it does not move, although some call it Asphaltite because now and again asphalt floats to the surface. Sodom and Gomorrah are thought to be submerged in its depths. The length of this accursed lake is five hundred and eighty stades. No animals come to drink, nor any bird. Fulcher asserts that he made a trial of the water, getting down from his mule to cup a little in his hand, finding it bitter as hellebore. The Jordan empties into this lake. Next to it rises a mountain white as snow from which rocks made of salt break off and tumble to the base. Rainfall streaming through ravines carries this salt into the lake. Or perhaps there exists some channel underground by which the salt sea enters. The truth is not known.

Close by is the village of Segor, happily situated, abounding in palm fruit that is sweet to taste. Baldwin's army spent a day eating this fruit because they could find little else, the Saracens having all vanished except some people dark as soot who harvested seaweed from the lake. Here the Franks encountered another fruit with a thick rind or husk, but when the shell was broken they saw nothing inside, nothing save black dust. Some construed this as a warning.

Next they rode through the valley where Moses twice struck a rock and brought forth good water, enough to supply Israel. On a summit where the oracles of God were given to our fathers stands a church. Baldwin entered to pray and his army drank from the fountain of refutation. Beyond, as far as Babylon, this land is said to be uncultivated and desolate. Baldwin decided he had seen enough.

deus lo volt!

Passing by that lifeless sea and the tombs of patriarchs, by the tomb where Rachel lies, he returned to Jerusalem on the exact day of the winter solstice.

Latin documents assert that when Baldwin was a youth he nourished his spirit on liberal arts. He became a cleric, holding prebends in churches of Cambrai, Liège, and Reims. Later, troubled at heart, he became a soldier. Anon he married the English lady Godehilde and with her at his side he chose to follow his brothers Godfrey and Eustace. He is alleged to have been tall and dignified, larger of frame than Godfrey, serious in aspect, oddly pale, with a reddish beard. He lived splendorously and had a gold shield with the image of an eagle borne ahead of him as though he were some infidel potentate. If he entered a village there were knights to blow trumpets in front of his chariot. He wore a mantle or toga, making him resemble a bishop more than a soldier, and took his meals seated on a rug while accepting homage from admirers. Yet he inherited the curse of Adam, struggling mightily against cravings of the flesh. Withal, none but a few servants understood the frequency of his habit for he was most circumspect. Should one seek to excuse King Baldwin's lechery, as certain narratives do, justification mayhap is possible, if not at the bench of our strictest Judge.

Now, finding himself absolute, he prohibited Greek and Syriac rites in the Church of the Holy Sepulcher. Thereby he committed the sin of hubris for which Almighty God chastised him. Easter Sunday the lamps in the Sepulcher refused to burn. It is well known how pilgrims wait outside this most holy site during the vigil before Easter when lights are extinguished and the patriarch emerges bringing a new flame from the darkness of our Savior's tomb. Hence this is both miracle and reality, visible sign of our central mystery, the Resurrection. None in the Latin world could say when this began save that it was long ago, some think during the fourth century when pagan feet trampled Jerusalem. Unbelievers invaded Christian homes to stamp out fire, leaving ashes on the hearth, knowing this miracle must be a consequence of trickery. It is said they marched through the basilica with drawn swords to extinguish the light of Christianity. Still the passionate request of those who arrived to pray could not be denied, quickly the lamp was lighted. Old men avow that Turks once removed the wick, nevertheless light blazed anew in empty metal since nothing prevails against the truth. However that may be, when King Baldwin with his excess of pride forbade all but Frankish rites the lamps refused to burn. Nor could anyone make them burn again till those who had been dispossessed beseeched the Lord to forgive him. And so, when he understood, Baldwin restored these privileges.

During the second year of his reign a cavalcade of wealthy Arabs passed through outer Jordan. Baldwin at once crossed the river, falling upon them while they slept. Few escaped. Most died in their tents. Slaves, camels, booty, women and children were seized. Presently he learned that the wife of a sheik was about to give birth. She was riding in a woven basket on a camel so he ordered her brought down and had a bed fixed for her in the shade of some palms. He arranged that she be supplied with food, two skins of water, two female camels filled with milk, and gave orders that a maid should attend her. Baldwin himself supervised these preparations and wrapped his mantle around her. Then he continued toward Jerusalem because she would be found soon enough. In a little while here came this woman's husband, the sheik, who rode courageously through the soldiers to thank Baldwin, promising that one day this merciful act would be rewarded.

That summer he moved against Caesarea. For two weeks the citizens resisted, but without experience at war and through protracted leisure they had grown effete. When true believers placed ladders against the wall and mounted eagerly toward the ramparts these eunuchs succumbed to fright. As happened elsewhere, some gulped down jewels and gold coins, which roused the cupidity of Baldwin's soldiers who split them apart to inspect their vitals. It is said that Baldwin wished to show he could be pitiless toward any who opposed him, therefore he authorized his men to do as they liked. Still, he and his captains were astonished by what occurred. Infants and lovely women escaped the sword, all others had cause to regret their misbelief. Hundreds fled to the mosque, which in ancient days had been the synagogue of Herod Agrippa, mistakenly hoping since it was a chapel of prayer they might be safe. In rushed the knighthood of Christ, Saracens pleading for mercy to no avail. Carpets in the mosque changed color. Much spoil was obtained, not least a quantity of pepper, so much that sergeants were allotted two pounds each. Archbishop William tells of a certain Genoese who found an emerald bowl that is regarded by some as the Holy Grail.

No more did Baldwin subjugate Caesarea than news arrived of a Babylonian army menacing Ramlah. At once he hastened to challenge them but they declined and withdrew, awaiting help. Not until September did they feel confident, what with eleven thousand horsemen, twenty thousand afoot.

King Baldwin assaulted them at sunrise near Ibelin close by Ramlah although he commanded fewer than three hundred knights and nine hundred sergeants. Bervold, a valiant knight, ascended to Paradise with all his men. Geldemar Carpenel, lord of Haifa, was embraced by the loving arms of Jesus while trying to rescue him. Hugh, prince of Galilee, turned and fled like a dog. It seemed the battle had been lost, the day forfeit. King Baldwin confessed his sins in view of his army before the True Cross. Then, mounting his splendid Arab charger Gazelle, he rode toward the heart of the enemy.

God help us! shouted his knights while dashing among these pagans like fowlers into a mass of birds. Christ conquers! Christ reigns! Christ rules!

95

King Baldwin shook his lance from which fluttered a white banner, pierced an enemy, knocked him to earth, and the flag lodged in his gut. Fulcher de Chartres, being very near the king, observed this.

Misbelievers looked all around and suddenly cared for nothing except themselves.

King Baldwin chased them to Ascalon. Such was the punishment meted out by God on account of their absurd belief and wicked nature, which blinded them to the sovereign light.

Fulcher writes that he feared such deeds might be forgotten. Thus I set them down, says he, wishing to publish these marvelous works of our Lord, albeit my learning is rude, my ability slight. I have collected what I saw with my own eyes or have learnt through assiduous questioning. I relate what happened for the benefit of those who come after me. Let any man rectify what I have done, but let him not superimpose fictive symmetry or dignity, lest he adulterate the truth.

Now, Egypt is huge and rich and to the south live men with black skin who are fierce in battle. Hence the vizier al-Afdal summoned these warriors to expel the Franks. In May of the following year these accursed Egyptians moved once more against Ramlah and King Baldwin rode forth in high spirits because he did not know how numerous they were. This display of hubris alarmed Stephen de Blois, who urged caution. But all remembered how Stephen retreated from Antioch. Not until they rode out on the plain did they see the devilish host, by which time they could not retreat. Some few knights cut through the enemy and escaped to Joppa. Most gave up the ghost. King Baldwin with those nearest him fought his way to the citadel of Ramlah and then it was dark.

At midnight here came that Arab sheik whose wife King Baldwin succored when she was ready to give birth. He presented himself at the citadel asking to see the king, so he was let inside. He recalled that great charity to the king and declared himself obligated to repay such kindness for he loathed the sin of ingratitude. He warned King Baldwin to leave at once, saying the fortress would be overwhelmed at daybreak and all inside put to death. He said he would lead the king to safety, claiming he knew this region well. Therefore, taking a groom and three comrades, Baldwin put his faith in the Arab.

At daybreak here came Egyptians swift as roaches swarming

across the wall to heap faggots around the citadel and set everything ablaze. The Franks charged out, led by Constable Conrad, since they thought it more honorable to die sword in hand. Few survived. Conrad and more than one hundred Franks were led away. What became of these, no chronicle relates. Geoffrey from Vendôme, Stephen from Burgundy, Hugh from Lusignan, all joined the fellowship of martyrs. Here, too, Stephen de Blois perished. At Dorylaeum he could not be found. News of Kerbogha caused him to retreat from Antioch and climb a mountain, caused him to excuse himself as far as Constantinople. Nor could he explain to his wife Adela, daughter of William the Conqueror. We are told in Historia ecclesiastica by Oderic Vitalis how she abused him. My Lord, said she, no longer can I submit to the insult you receive from every quarter. Gather up that courage for which you were renowned as a youth. Take arms in a noble cause for the salvation of thousands. Let Christians exult throughout the world to the terror of infidels and to the perpetual disgrace of their false religion.

Thus, in that year of our gracious Lord 1102, Stephen de Blois fell at Ramlah. It may be his wife thereafter slept content. The Lord passed judgment on Stephen according to His great lenience, allowing this wealthy prince to compensate for doubtful conduct.

Arab histories say King Baldwin eluded capture by hiding flat on his belly in a thicket of reeds. They set fire to the reeds but he escaped and for two days wandered about north of Ramlah, his body scorched. At length he got across the plain to Arsuf where he found an Englishman called Goderic with a boat.

The queen of Jerusalem and her ladies were at Joppa when they heard of King Baldwin's defeat. Thinking him dead, they planned to board ship while they could before Egyptians came to seize them. But an Egyptian fleet broke the horizon so all in the city commended their souls to God. That same day al-Afdal's cavalry rode to the very walls of Joppa and they saw what looked to be King Baldwin's severed head on a lance. Next, down from the north sailed Goderic with King Baldwin's standard at the mast and the king

97

himself aboard, for the head was that of Gerbod de Winthinc who narrowly resembled him. All at once a fortuitous breeze favored the passage of Goderic's boat, carrying it swiftly inside the harbor. What is this if not benevolent Providence?

Ibn al-Athir tells how the vizier sent forth a new expedition which failed. Yet another. Each failed because those who are one with Him, who hold Him close, cannot be overcome. The wickedness of their belief robbed and punished these Babylonians, sowed disarray among their forces. Nor could they slip the hand of fate. It was prophesied of a Saracen general that he would meet death by falling off a horse. Therefore he ordered paving stones removed from the streets of Beyrouth where his horse might stumble. Yet during combat the animal reared for no cause and threw him. He fell dead among his troops. Who shall cheat so vast a thing?

Baldwin moved to secure the land. He entrusted the fief of Galilee to Lord Hugh of Saint-Omer who had been his neighbor in France. This lord built castles from which to raid Muslim caravans. Toghtekin, atabeg of Damascus, came down like a storm while Hugh was returning from a raid, fatally wounded him and scattered his people. Baldwin next entrusted the fief to Gervase de Basoches, a knight celebrated for audacity. It is said that when Gervase with two other knights encountered a large troop of infidels he ripped apart his undertunic and fastened it like a banner on his spear. Then beseeching God for aid, ordering his companions to do the same, they cried out loudly and spurred forward. The pagans turned to flee, leaving themselves mortally vulnerable to three bold pilgrims in the service of Christ. However, Toghtekin managed to capture Gervase and sent word that he would be released in exchange for three cities. Acre. Tiberias. Haifa. Baldwin thought such terms extravagant. Therefore, during some Turk festival Gervase was urged to repudiate and abjure the true faith. He said he would not. So he was bound to a tree in the midst of a field, his body torn by a hail of arrows from every side. They cut away the crown of his head to make a drinking cup for Toghtekin. This according to Abbot Guibert. Or it may be that the atabeg himself slew this valiant knight, scalped him because of his flowing white hair and carried the scalp on a pole. However it was, Gervase de Basoches entered that pantheon of martyrs whose name will be honored throughout eternity.

In the year of our Lord 1106 while King Baldwin was engaged on the frontier of Galilee these enemies of God surprised and murdered certain Christians near Joppa. Roger de Rozoy, who was governor, rode out against them but unluckily fell into ambush. He got back to Joppa with his head on his shoulders where it belonged, yet forty of his sergeants entered Paradise. Misbelievers next surprised Chastel Arnaud, an unfinished castle near Jerusalem, and slaughtered the workmen. Later they felt bold enough to assault Jerusalem itself and touched the walls, after which they retired with little show. There could be no doubt these black gentiles meant to recoup what they had lost.

One day when as usual King Baldwin fought his enemies it happened that some Ethiop lurked behind a rock and struck the king very hard in the back, wounding him almost to death. Yet the leeches attended him well, and being the steward of God's ministry he recovered. How equitable the judgment of our Lord.

King Baldwin suffered many wounds. According to Abbot Guibert, he generously rode forth to rescue a foot soldier whose bravery delighted him and was dealt a blow piercing him to the vitals. Then the leech who was summoned did not want to apply a soothing cataplasm for fear the skin might grow smooth on top while putrid matter rankled within. This he foresaw partly through conjecture, partly through experience. He besought the king to have some captive likewise injured and afterward slain, by which he might inspect the corpse and perpend how things might be with the king's deep wound. King Baldwin shrank from this, repeating the words of Emperor Constantine who declared he would not be the cause of any man's death, however evil, for some faint benefit to his own good health.

Then the leech addressed King Baldwin. Sire, if you resolve to

99

take no man's life for the sake of thine own I beseech you to provide a captive bear, which is a beast of no use except to be baited. Let this animal stand erect on hinder paws so that steel may be thrust into him. Then after he is dead I may by inspecting his vitals measure the degree of his injury at bottom, and to some degree thine own.

To this the king responded. If need be, do as thou wilt.

It was done. Thus the leech discovered how perilous it would be if King Baldwin's injury drew together before the rudiment healed. Again we perceive how our Lord most graciously extended His hand.

During the seventh year of Baldwin's reign it became customary to exchange tokens of spiritual friendship with churches in Europe. Anseau, who was precentor of the Church of the Sepulcher, despatched to the canons of Notre-Dame a splinter from the True Cross. This inestimable relic had belonged to the king of Georgia who adored and guarded it. Upon his death the sorrowing queen shaved her head, took the veil, and retired to Jerusalem accompanied by this holy sliver of wood. Also, she carried a huge amount of gold that she distributed among various monasteries. And to the poor she gave innumerable alms. Because of her saintliness the patriarch of Jerusalem asked her to govern a community of nuns, a request she dutifully honored. These nuns at length fell into want. They lacked food and other necessities. So in order to sustain them the widowed queen of Georgia sold the most precious item known to mankind. By the helm of goodness does our Lord govern His universe.

During the summer of 1110 there came to the port of Joppa a Norse fleet numbering fifty or sixty vessels. Their captain a handsome youth named Sigurd, son of King Magnus Barefoot. This youth with his brother Eystein ruled Norway after the death of their father, slain while pillaging Ireland. These adventurers wintered first in England as guests of King Henry. Next winter they spent in Galicia and battled the Moors in Portugal. Next they sailed to Apulia, thence to Palestine. Baldwin greeted them joyously, conversed, and escorted them to Jerusalem. He ordered a fine banquet and gave Sigurd many relics. Later he accompanied Sigurd to the river Jordan.

deus lo volt!

He entreated these Norse to remain, if only long enough to help capture Sidon. For if they did, he said, they would go back to their own land offering praise to our Lord. So the Norse agreed. Documents relate how they fought valiantly at Sidon. Now, the governor of Sidon plotted to murder King Baldwin but did not succeed, thanks to native Christians who launched an arrow with a message into the Frankish camp. All the same, having no use for a dagger in the back or tainted meat, Baldwin looked about shrewdly while the siege continued. Anon, Sidon was captured. In this way, helped by Norse warriors, King Baldwin established himself on the Syrian coast.

Presently it seemed to the Norse that they should go home. They embarked for Constantinople, which in their language they call Micklegarth. It is said that Alexius entertained them at great expense. They in return gave him their ships. Certain of these Norse chose to become vassals of the emperor and live out their lives in Constantinople. Others traveled north through savage countries to Denmark, whence they sailed to their icy homeland. And since they had been inspired by God to visit Jerusalem, Sigurd was called Jorsalfarer. The head of this devout sovereign, Sigurd Jorsalfarer, rests forever in Oslo, lodged in a wall of Akershus Castle.

King Baldwin during the year of our grace IIII thought to seize the ancient city of Tyre. So he constructed among other engines a tower on wheels equipped with a battering ram. Misbelievers in the city commended their black souls to Allah because walls trembled when struck by the ram. But according to the narrative of Ibn al-Qalanisi there was some mariner who devised grapnels to catch the ram and Turks pulling on ropes affixed to these hooks contrived to wrench the tower aside. Now the Franks brought up a ram sixty cubits long with an iron head. Turks emptied jars of excrement on those who operated it, which sickened and choked them. If that were not enough, the mariner called for baskets of asphalt, resin, oil, and reed bark, had them set afire and dropped on Christian soldiers. Sergeants threw water and vinegar at the flame, Turks threw boiling oil. A Frankish knight wearing chain mail was seen rolling across the stones like a blazing torch. No chronicle preserves this martyr's name. We wonder at such inequity, yet it is not within us to measure the compass of God's work.

After several months at Tyre but little accomplished, with news of Toghtekin approaching from Damascus, King Baldwin thought better of his idea and retreated.

Some years having gone by since he married the Armenian princess, he wearied of her. She had not brought the dowry he expected, nor had she borne children. He dismissed her as adulterous, charging that she had given her body to infidels on a voyage from Lattakieh to Joppa. Who can be sure? Abbot Guibert speaks of how contrary winds swept her vessel to an island peopled with Barbars who murdered a bishop in her retinue, murdered others, and for a long time held the queen captive. As for the truth, God knows. However it was, King Baldwin pushed her from his bed, compelled her to go and live with nuns at the convent of Saint Anne in Jerusalem. It is known that she escaped this constraint and made her way to Constantinople where she wallowed in unspeakable vice. Such are the narrow streets of destruction.

In the providential year 1112 came word that Countess Adelaide of Sicily, a dowager whose wealth surpassed calculation, might be persuaded to remarry. Nor would she mind becoming queen of Jerusalem. Therefore the king, who anguished over money, being at times unable to pay his knights their monthly stipend, sent to ask for the lady's hand.

Countess Adelaide sailed to Acre most grandly, her entrance unmatched since Cleopatra came to visit Mark Antony. Latin narratives describe the beak of her galley as plated with silver, a carpet of spun gold beneath her throne. In her wake numerous vessels bearing precious fabric, engraved suits of armor, coins, gems, whatever wealth Sicily could provide. Arabs in handsome white robes looked out for pirates.

King Baldwin met her at the port, he and his entourage dressed in costly silk. The streets had been carpeted, purple banners hung from balconies, mules and horses draped with purple and gold. And people rejoiced throughout the Holy Land. Yet some whispered that Countess Adelaide was tricked, not knowing about King Baldwin's other wife. They declared he should first have divorced the Armenian. Still, the patriarch of Jerusalem united them. Three years afterward King Baldwin wearied of the countess, having spent the treasure, and ordered her back to Sicily. Almost alone she embarked, impoverished, humiliated.

Tancred refused to acknowledge Baldwin as king, mistrusting so much authority vested in such a man, nor would he consult him except on the banks of a stream called Nahr al-Aiya while water flowed between them. Yet few could be more dissembling and ruthless than this Norman from Sicily who boasted that one day he would pierce the walls of Baghdad with a lance, who fancied himself Islamic and wore a turban, styled himself Emir Tankridos, issued coins with his own likeness, dreamt of a principality in the Orient. Sooner than most he passed from view, aged thirty-six. His remnant they bore to the cathedral of Saint Peter. Greatest of the faithful, according to Matthew of Edessa. Otherwise, not many wept.

ive years after Tancred gave up the ghost a plague of locusts swept across Jerusalem. Vines, leaves, crops in the field, all devoured. As if they had agreed upon it in council these insects approached, hopping, creeping, others flying. When they had feasted on everything green and chewed the bark from trees they moved along by companies. And each day like pilgrims they came to rest. So does the Creator admonish and instruct us, reproach us through merciful lessons. Now, on the fifth night of December all observed the sky suffused in reddish light from the center of which streamed white ribbons. What this signified, no one could say. All wondered, expectantly awaiting the dispensation of our Lord. His Holiness Paschal soon ascended to glory, as did the patriarch of Jerusalem, the Armenian wife of King Baldwin, and Emperor Alexius Comnenus. Each assumed his place in the covenant of things.

Princess Anna with deep sorrow wrote about the illness afflicting her father, of the pain he experienced while breathing. Also, he was seized by fits of yawning. What troubles me? he would ask the empress. The ablest physicians were summoned. Nicolas Kallicles, Michael Pantechnes, and Michael the eunuch. They felt his pulse, conceding that they found irregularity at each motion but could not assign the cause. He ate frugally, moderately, hence there could be no aggregation of humors from rich food. They thought his heart inflamed by incessant worry, by concerns of government, therefore excess matter accumulated from the rest of his body. He could not lie on either side, but had to sit upright. The illness choked like a halter, giving him no respite. They cut his elbow, which did not help. They gave him pepper to swallow, which dispersed the humors but afterward forced them into cavities of the arteries so his belly puffed up, as did his feet. The disease invaded his mouth, obstructing his throat. Anon, the movement of blood stopped. Then suddenly the empress uttered a frightful shriek, took off her purple shoes and laid aside her imperial veil. She cut off her hair with a razor, asked for black sandals and a dark veil. The soul of Alexius had gone to God. Thus does inimitable order embrace the universe.

Tancred's nephew, Roger, succeeded as governor of Antioch. Chronicles assert that he was lecherous and quick to fight. Before long he subdued the enemy strongholds of Marqb, Azaz, and Biz'a. Looking to further conquest he marched against Aleppo with seven hundred knights and four thousand sergeants. These proud Franks, imagining themselves braver than lions, pitched their tents at al-Abat, which afterward was called the field of blood, Ager Sanguinis. Pagan spies pretending to be merchants eased into camp, so the Turk, Ilghazi, kept himself informed. Eight days he loitered, waiting

until hunger and thirst weakened Roger's men. Then at night he surrounded them with forty thousand Turcomans. At daybreak the
Franks understood they would not see Aleppo except in chains, if
ever. The archbishop of Albara preached to them, confessed Roger
privately in his tent, granting absolution for manifold sins of the
flesh. Soon enough Turkish arrows began to fly. Kamal al-Din declares that Muslim arrows darkened the sky, stiffened the morning.
Walter the Chancellor tells how these doomed Franks brandished
lances, drew their shields in close, set spurs to their mounts and
charged. Many Turks crushed by the timber of death hurtled into
lower regions, but the forces of Ilghazi assembled like wasps and like
wasps could not be contained. Roger's pilgrims were mutilated in
different ways, beaten with stones, pierced by javelins and arrows,
which delighted the Turk. And when it ended Ilghazi ordered those
clinging to life brought out for destruction. Five hundred or more he
had bound like dogs with iron chains, naked, hands cruelly twisted
behind their backs. Some felt the skin flayed from their faces. Ilghazi
commanded others to be led half a league through bramble and thistle to the vineyard of Sarmedan where they fell down eagerly, biting
at grapes in the dust. So, according to the judgment of God, they
met death abominably.

Tancred's nephew Roger was found among innumerable dead at
the foot of a great jeweled cross, his skull split to the nose. Ilghazi
made off with his head, his armor, and the cross, carrying these tro-
phies to Aleppo. News of the battle preceded him. The citizens of
Aleppo butchered sheep and danced in the street when he arrived.
They saw naked Franks dragged over stones, Christian heads displayed on lances. This much to the delight of those who recalled
how Jerusalem was sacked.

When news of this defeat reached Antioch the people thought
Ilghazi would come to murder them and raze the city, but he did
not. Muslims say he drank so much wine that he was seized with a violent ague and could not get out of bed for twenty days. Meanwhile
he sent word of his victory to the caliph who honored him with a

splendid robe and a title, Star of Religion. Three years later Il-ghazi dropped shrieking into the fiery pit when the true and un-biased voice of God was heard.

Ibn al-Athir wrote in his account of the Arab world how Turco-mans such as fought the pilgrims were brutal nomads oblivious to the teaching of Islam. They enrolled beneath the banner of cupid-ity, each with a pouch of flour and dried sheep flesh, and consented to follow Ilghazi only so long as they were paid. They put jugs of water in front of captive Franks, killing those who tried to drink. Numerous soldiers of Christ taken alive on that sanguine field gave up the ghost in such a way, yet we know they came face to face with Him.

Pilgrims who determined to visit the Holy Land would travel un-easily by ship past Saracen castles. Should our Lord deign to guide and protect them, at length they came to port at Joppa where they were met with joy by Christians eager for news of the distant West, for news of loved ones in Gaul or England or the Netherlands or Germany. These newcomers told what they knew of kingdoms and families, which was a source of grief or bewilderment or rejoicing. Many perished en route. Albert of Aix declares that in a single year three hundred ships fell victim to pirates. How many servants of Christ were hurled into the sea, sold into bondage? But if they got safely to Jerusalem and Bethlehem and other holy places they were able to fulfill their vows, grateful they did not see the vile crescent of Islam defiling the domes of churches. Most returned to their homes with glorious accounts of what they had seen, such as splinters from the True Cross found beneath the shrine of the Sepulcher. They had seen water that gushed from the rod of Moses, shreds of Blessed Mary's robe, two thorns from the crown that Jesus wore, and in a glass vial they beheld some darkness from one of Egypt's seven plagues.

Certain pilgrims chose not to return but settled in the East. And with the passing years these Franks, Lombards, Germans, Scots, and Danes who lived in Outremer grew increasingly Asiatic. They forgot the cities of their birth, Marseilles, Düsseldorf, Genoa, Canterbury. They became men of Antioch or Galilee. They wore slippers and loose clothing. Their women wore veils. They slept in the long noon heat. They established fresh codes of law and new tribunals, inherited servitors, possessed homes. Some chose to marry Christian women of Syria or a Saracen that had received the grace of baptism. Therefore Turks might live at a Christian house, related through marriage. Indeed, while speaking various languages they learned to understand all. Hence they asked themselves why they should go back to the West that had been their home, since the East proved generous. Those with few coins in Europe now fondled more bezants than they could count. This seemed a great miracle, enough to amaze the world. Surely the Lord wishes to enrich all of us and draw us to Him. And because that is what He desires, that is what we also desire. What is pleasing to Him, that would His children do with loving and submissive hearts, for we would live in Him throughout eternity.

It happened when King Baldwin neared his sixtieth year that he resolved to punish Egypt for egregious wickedness. Therefore with two hundred knights and four hundred men afoot he marched south to Pharamia, an ancient city close by the mouth of the Nile. Here, too, is an old city called Tanis where long ago the Lord worked signs before Pharaoh through his servant Moses. The inhabitants of Pharamia fled in terror when King Baldwin arrived so he took it without a blow. Next morning he went to contemplate the fabulous river, which is called Gihon by Israelites, which he had not seen. He gazed upon it with delight, marveling at the water because this river originates in Paradise. Yet how could that be? We are told that Paradise is found to the east, but to the east lies the Red Sea. Has the Gihon a second source? Or if it does emanate from Paradise to the east, how shall it resume a course west of the Red Sea? As good Boethius notes, when we observe a thing contrary to expectation there must be error and confusion in our thought.

The Red Sea is red because of discolored rock, yet if its water is poured in a vessel it remains pure and limpid. What better witness to the inimitable strength of God? The Red Sea derives from an ocean to the south but extends like a tongue almost to Mount Sinai, one

107

day's journey by horse. From this sea to the Great Sea, or Mediterranean, is thought to require five days on horseback through a parched and desolate region encompassing much of Egypt, Numidia, and Ethiopia. As to where the Mediterranean originates, some point to the Straits of Gades with no source but the surging ocean. Others trace it to the Straits of Pontus because tides flow out but do not return. Accordingly we praise the Creator who excels mankind with unimaginable knowledge, who in His wisdom fixes limits and bounds and entrances. We may ask what prevents the Red Sea from joining the Mediterranean across the plain of Egypt since it is lower. Does heavenly law inhibit? The explanation we leave to Him who gives water to the cloud, who appoints the mountain to sustain and nourish countless lakes, who commands the stream to search for one that is larger until, miraculous to relate, all discover and blend with the obedient sea.

We are told by parchment from those days how King Baldwin meditated by the river Gihon while his knights who were deft with lances contrived to spear a number of fish. These they carried back to Pharamia for breakfast. But as King Baldwin arose from the meal he complained of distress in his belly. Also, an old wound began to stir. His spirit flagged. Then a herald was instructed to proclaim that all should at once make ready to depart for Jerusalem. The king was unable to ride so they placed him on a litter made from tent poles and traveled as far as the town of al-Arish where he lost hope. He asked that his body be carried to Jerusalem because he did not want infidels to dig him up and do him some dishonor, saying that he wished to be laid next to his brother Godfrey. Those attending him fell silent and he understood why they would not speak, because in such heat the corpse would putrefy. He told them he should be embalmed. I entreat you to open my stomach with a knife, said he. Take out my entrails. Rub my body with spices and balsam generously in the mouth, nostrils, and ears. Wrap what is left of me in a hide and carry it to Jerusalem for Christian burial. The nobles were hard put to restrain their grief. They answered that he placed on them a heavy burden. As you love me, said the king, or as you loved me when I was in fair health, you will not refuse this task. Then without delay he summoned his cook, Addo, and bound him with an oath to handle the business.

For two days King Baldwin lay motionless in his tent, but at last quit breathing. Then the cook Addo slit his body and took out the organs, which were salted and buried, the poor shell smeared with pungent oil and spices, sewn into a hide adorned with hangings, tied firmly to a horse. Mournfully yet cautiously, since news of Baldwin's death might incite the pagans, they carried him to the Holy City.

By chance, which is the will of God, on that same day when it is customary to bring palm branches from the Mount of Olives the body of King Baldwin met a procession descending toward Jehoshaphat. And the dead king was brought up in the midst of their singing. So, rather than songs of joy and triumph, groans of sorrow could be heard throughout the valley. Even those Saracens who observed the cortege were seen to weep.

All agreed that since the body had been kept a long while and was stinking it should be given a funeral at once. Now King Baldwin lies in Golgotha alongside his brother Godfrey. The tomb is said to be wondrously crafted of polished white marble.

A cousin to these men, Baldwin du Bourg, ascended the throne. He was not first choice among the barons. By repute he owed much to Count Joscelin of Edessa. Valorous enough, displaying a full beard yet little presence, of such piety that his knees grew callused from kneeling in prayer. Withal he had a tight fist, his virtue tarnished by cravings for silver. Such was Baldwin du Bourg.

His advocate Joscelin was caught by Turks in our year of grace 1122. Joscelin and his cousin Galeran went riding with a small force when they dropped into the arms of Balak. This occurred on the thirteenth of September amid showers of cold rain. Frankish horses floundered in mud, hence the Turks rounded them up without difficulty. Joscelin, Galeran, and sixty knights were captured. Ibn al-Athir tells how Balak wrapped a camel skin around Lord Joscelin and sewed it tight and carried him off to the fortress of Kharpurt. Nor would Balak exchange him for ransom, demanding instead the city of Edessa.

King Baldwin du Bourg rode north in April of the following year to see how Count Joscelin might be liberated. Knights from Edessa guided him to a muddy field near the Euphrates, that same field where Joscelin was trapped. With little thought the king encamped. Next morning he resolved to enjoy some falconry, which art he had learned from Eastern nobles. But all unexpected, once again, here came Balak. Turks say the king of Jerusalem flung down his sword. Perhaps. However it came about, Baldwin du Bourg soon enough joined Count Joscelin in the wretched dungeon of Kharpurt. There they loitered miserably, bound with shackles, hidden from every light save that provided by our Lord.

Anon the count of Edessa contrived a plan to escape. Through promised rewards he got in touch with Armenian peasants and some time later here came fifty Christian Armenians disguised as pedlars with goods to sell, or disguised as monks or beggars, all carrying knives hidden in their clothes. One by one they drifted through outer gates of the citadel, day by day making themselves familiar to guards until they did not seem suspicious. One day while the officer in charge was playing chess they approached to complain about some pretended insult. And as they got close they stabbed him and took spears that had been left unattended and began killing other guards. More Turks rushed up but were likewise slaughtered. Now the captives were freed. Some, hobbled by chains, nevertheless climbed ladders and hoisted a Christian standard to the summit of the citadel.

Fulcher de Chartres relates that Balak in a vision beheld Lord Joscelin tear out his eyes, so he asked his priests to interpret. Truly, they answered, this will happen, or something equally bad, should you fall into his hands. Balak at once despatched men to kill Joscelin, but they arrived too late. What is this if not proof that our Lord contemplates and protects His subjects?

deus lo volt!

Soon enough every door to the citadel was shut, bolts shot into place, carts rolled against the gates.

During the night, after commending his soul to God, Joscelin crept out followed by three servants and with the aid of divine intercession succeeded in passing through the Turks. Once beyond the walls he entrusted his ring to a servant. Go to the king, said he, with this proof that I have escaped.

Joscelin traveled by night to avoid being seen and got to the Euphrates but did not understand how to swim. Discouraged, weary, he consulted his servants. They had two goatskins of wine so these were emptied, blown full of air, and affixed to him with rope. Thus, helped by lackeys experienced at swimming, he crossed the Euphrates. Now, feeling exhausted, he lay down beneath a nut tree and pulled brambles over himself and told a servant to look for something they might eat. By God's grace this servant met a peasant carrying dried figs and clusters of grapes. The servant approached cautiously, fearing betrayal. We are told by Odericus Vitalis that the peasant was a Saracen who in his youth had been Count Joscelin's vassal. Whatever the truth, when they got to the river bank where Joscelin was resting the peasant hailed him by name and dropped at his feet. Joscelin said he had escaped from the castle of Balak in Mesopotamia and was a fugitive, a wanderer about to perish. If you help me so I do not fall into the hands of Balak, he said, you may spend the rest of your days with me at Turbessel. Let me know the value of your house and I will give you a better house.

The peasant replied that he asked nothing but would guide Count Joscelin to safety. Then he went away. After some time he came back with a donkey, two oxen, a pig, his wife, infant daughter, and two brothers. Joscelin who customarily rode a splendid mule got on the donkey and the child was given him to hold. Thus they continued the journey. It is said that Joscelin grew distraught when the infant screamed or cried and thought of abandoning this company, thinking it might be safer to proceed alone, but he did not want to offend the peasant. At length they got to his castle and he gave the peasant two yokes of oxen.

Next he assembled his knights and rode to Antioch, thence to Jerusalem where he praised God and made an offering of the shackles he had worn in Balak's dungeon, hanging them reverently upon Mount Calvary in recognition of his captivity and glorious liberation. One shackle was made of iron, the other silver.

After three days in the Holy City he set out to rescue his king. But when he reached Kharpurt he learned that Balak had stormed the citadel. King Baldwin du Bourg and Lord Galeran were once again captive and had been sent under close guard to the distant city of Harran. As to the Armenians who helped Joscelin escape, Balak cruelly tortured them, ordering them burnt, hanged, flayed, thrown from ramparts, buried alive, bound to stakes as targets. Balak's harem was quartered at the citadel and by various accounts these brave Armenians, succumbing to allurements of the flesh, delighted in Balak's women. God knows the truth. However it was, Lord Joscelin went mad with rage and devastated the countryside.

Sixteen months or more Baldwin du Bourg languished in chains while the Franks negotiated his release. Turks demanded a kingly ransom, eighty thousand gold dinars with certain lands belonging to Antioch. After twenty thousand dinars had been paid, King Baldwin was freed, leaving hostage his youngest daughter Joveta, aged five. Midsummer of that year 1124 he rode away from prison on the handsome charger he was riding when he decided to camp in a muddy field near the Euphrates. Turks had kept this animal well. Also, they lavished gifts upon him. Gold helmet, a rich robe, embroidered buskins. Accordingly he rode to Antioch like some Oriental sultan.

Bernard, who was patriarch in those days, pointed out that while Baldwin might be overlord and regent of Antioch he had promised to surrender land that was not his to give. The king heard this with great satisfaction and hastily notified the Turk that he would, as agreed, remit the full amount of gold. However, he could not lawfully cede the land. Documents assert that in reprisal the child princess Joveta was handled lasciviously. If so, we can but ask with others from ages past. Why thus, Lord God?

Joveta was at length ransomed, in due time after she had grown to womanhood becoming abbess of the convent of Saint Lazarus in Bethany. Therefore we note how the Creator determines each event from beginning to end.

Anon the heathen governor of Manbij, puffed with pride, thinking himself superior to Balak, decided to revolt. Soon enough here came Balak with five thousand horsemen, invited the governor to a conference outside the walls. Then what did Balak do but perfidiously take the governor's life. So the people, believing their own lives forfeit, sought help from Christians. Lord Joscelin hastened out of Antioch. Fulcher tells how a desperate battle took place. Horses whinnied, asses brayed, camels grumbled. Fields and roads glistered in fresh blood. Three times did Lord Joscelin repulse the Turks. Three times they returned to fight. Thirty Frankish knights and sixty footmen who were driving sumpter beasts went to sleep with the Lord while three thousand advocates of the devil plunged bellowing into the fiery pit. So much according to Fulcher. Yet, as we in our day could attest, chroniclers are wont to praise their countrymen, by shameless mistruth exaggerating the number of enemies slain while misprizing their own. Be that as it may, here came a Turkish arrow from the ramparts of Manbij to strike Balak. Kamal al-Din relates that he wrenched out the shaft and spat with contempt, saying this would be the death of Islam.

Count Joscelin, fearing he had escaped, ordered Turkish corpses to be examined. By insignia on his armor they found him so his head was lopped off. The soldier who brought it to Joscelin got forty nomismata, which is to say forty pieces of gold. Joscelin despatched Balak's head to Jerusalem as proof that he would trouble the Holy Land no further. And the squire who brought such joyful news found himself elevated to the rank of knight. And all who contemplated the bloody face in the sack gave thanks because a raging dragon that feasted on pilgrims had lost his appetite.

Archbishop William relates that Count Joscelin himself met the Turk, hurled him to earth and took his head. Through the mist of centuries what may be resolved? Only that Balak's vision came true since he had dreamt of Joscelin scooping out his eyes and whoever cuts off a man's head destroys his sight.

In the following year King Baldwin erected a castle near Beyrouth at a place called the hill of the sword, Mons Glavianus, because those condemned to death are brought here for execution. He did this to convince Saracen peasants they ought to pay taxes, which they had been reluctant to do. And when these unbelievers looked up from their fields at a castle bristling with Christian soldiers they amended their habit. Is not the coercion of a sword to be admired? Has not Almighty God so enjoined us? Thou shalt rule with a rod of iron.

Now in the year 1127 since the birth of our Savior, in the fifth indiction, a host of rats marched across the Holy Land. They were observed to seize an ox by its hindquarters and smother and eat him. They devoured seven powerful rams and numberless small creatures, then scurried up the mountain of Tyre to quench their thirst. Savage wind and rain drove them into the confinement of valleys where multitudes perished. For a long while those valleys stank with corruption. What is this, if not some allegory of our time?

Are not the articles of Christian faith described with pictures and with letters? Yet no man is able to describe the Trinity, nor the Holy Ghost, nor anything so vast because of many sins and evils we commit, which weigh down mortal life, which blind us to the sovereign light. Hence, disaster befell the Franks. Bohemond's son marched along the river Jihan and proceeded carelessly. They say this prince was of great stature, tall, in aspect like his father, with an air of high

breeding from his mother Constance. He expected to recoup Ana-
zarbus, which was lost. But all at once Danishmend Turks surprised
him and destroyed his army. He was slain because these Turks failed
to recognize him, otherwise they would have made him captive for
the huge ransom he would fetch. As it was, they embalmed the handsome blond head, fashioned a silver box, and presented this trophy to
the caliph. Some argue that Prince Bohemond now wears a finer
crown than any he might have worn on earth. Others say that if we
but acknowledged the power of Jesus Christ, recognizing how we live
beneath His feet, we should never do wrong.

One year later King Baldwin du Bourg lay dying. At his request he
was borne to the house of the patriarch close by the Holy Sepulcher
so that his spirit might bask in its radiance. He summoned the nobles, together with his eldest daughter Melisende and her husband
Fulk d'Anjou, bidding all to honor them as sovereigns upon his dis-
solution. He requested the habit of a monk, which was put on him,
and he was admitted a canon of the assembly. No more was this complete than the second crowned king of Jerusalem ascended to glory.
Ibn al-Qalanisi, a misbeliever, took note, calling him an old man polished by time and bad luck, remarking that Frankish authority now
descended to the inexperienced hands of Fulk d'Anjou who had but
recently arrived.

That same year Count Joscelin gave up the ghost. While exploring the province he came upon a turret of sundried brick with enemies of the true faith inside. Therefore he instructed his men to dig
at the foundation and most unwisely examined the shaft they dug.
Now the body is a vulnerable, worthless master and when bricks
dropped into the tunnel he was at once buried, bones cracked. They
pulled him out half-dead and returned to the castle at Turbessel.
Here for a long time Joscelin's body lingered, detaining his spirit,
which struggled to depart. Then all unexpected came a messenger.
Turks on the northeast frontier were moving toward the fortress of
Kaisun. Lord Joscelin told his son to call up the army but his son
offered excuses, saying they had not enough men, saying this Turk,

115

the sultan of Iconium, had brought a mighty host. With sorrow and bitterness the old count understood what sort of a man his son would be. Therefore he himself called up the army and directed that a litter be prepared, since he was unable to ride or march. It is said he traveled some distance on his litter when here came Geoffrey the Monk with news. These Turks, hearing that Count Joscelin advanced, conferred among themselves, lifted the siege of Kaisun and fled. So when he learned they were gone he had himself lowered to the earth. He raised both arms to heaven and with tears and sighs he spoke. Lord God, I praise and give thanks as best I can that You have thus honored me, that You have been so merciful and generous that enemies flee at my approach, though I am nearly dead.

Having spoken, he commended his spirit to God and expired. Thus do men, like events, rise and fall, waves of an inland sea. Mortal crises reach their apex merely to decline. Others follow, each within the boundary of inimitable Providence. Therefore we rejoice at logic and natural succession.

The less than valiant son of Count Joscelin is said to have been of slight stature, dark face pocked like the Devil's own, bulging eyes and a monstrous nose. Licentious, drunken, dissolute, this youth fell heir to the properties but governed foolishly, by reason of which he lost control. Although he bore that name, Archbishop William notes, he was not his father's equal.

Similarly, disorder came to threaten Jerusalem. Fulk d'Anjou governed by virtue of marriage to the heiress Melisende. The marriage net could not hold. Queen Melisende grew enamoured of a cousin, Hugh Puiset. She lay with him. King Fulk understood, but meekly swallowed the bitter draft. Others would not. Lord Walter Garnier stood up in assembly to denounce Hugh Puiset, charged him with plotting to murder the king, which charge Hugh denied. It was thought best to adjudicate this matter through combat, according to Frankish custom. On the appointed day Hugh Puiset could not be found, having skipped away to Ascalon where he took refuge among Mahometans. While there he made some perfidious compact with

God's enemies, which was high treason. Still, Queen Melisende and the patriarch of Jerusalem counseled mercy. King Fulk obliged. Hugh Puiset would be pardoned after three years in exile, small payment indeed.

Hugh Puiset returned to Jerusalem while waiting for a ship that would carry him into exile. And one day as he played dice in the street of the furriers a Breton knight stabbed him. At once the crowd began muttering against King Fulk. How could this happen, said they, without knowledge of the king? Did not the king order it?

When Fulk heard this sentiment he moved to exonerate himself. He put the knight on trial. And there being no doubt of guilt the knight was sentenced to mutilation. First, his arms and legs were chopped off. However, King Fulk directed that his tongue be left in his mouth, which was shrewd. If the knight were unable to speak he could not make full confession, whereas with his tongue he might incriminate the king. But he did not. While life stirred in the bloody stump he declared that he stabbed Hugh Puiset in hope of gaining the king's approval. In this way King Fulk acquitted himself. As for Hugh, upon recovering his health he sailed away despondent to live three years in Apulia.

This king of Jerusalem was by repute shorter than most men, affable, ruddy-faced like David whom the Lord found after His own heart, with a memory so exceeding poor he did not recognize his own domestics. Or if someone he had honored the previous day should arrive unannounced then he must ask the visitor's name. It is said, too, that he was compassionate and generous, which traits are unusual with men of choleric hue. There was at court in those days some Genoese who had brought from Europe a large falcon and a bitch that was taught to hunt cranes. They worked together, the dog racing after the falcon, which would strike down a crane. Then the bitch would seize it. Emir Mu'in al-Din, when he visited King Fulk, greatly admired this falcon so the king took it away from the Genoese and presented it to the emir. Along the Damascus road, according to the chronicle of Usama ibn Munqidh, this fierce bird attacked gazelles. Although when they got back to Damascus it did not survive long enough to go hunting.

Be that as it may, King Fulk's reign ended quickly during the year of our Lord 1143. This occurred in late autumn. Queen Melisende wished to go for a ride in the country, to the Springs of Oxen where once upon a time our father Adam found those beasts that enabled him to till the soil. Now as they rode along they startled a hare asleep in a furrow. The hare leapt up and bounded away, followed by shouts. King Fulk seized his lance to join the chase, urging his mount forward. However, God determined that his mount should stumble. King Fulk lunged headfirst to the ground, the saddle crushing his head so his brains gushed out from both ears and his nostrils. The king's entourage, all overcome with horror, came rushing to his side but he was unable to speak or understand anything. And his queen felt pierced to the heart, shrieking, pulling her hair, tearing at her garments. She flung herself down beside him and embraced him. Crowds of people appeared, eager to behold this tragedy. Then the king was brought to Acre where he lived three days, unseeing, never moving. On the tenth day of November, during the eleventh year of his reign, King Fulk ascended. His remnant they carried from Acre to Jerusalem where he lies among his predecessors in the Church of the Sepulcher of our Lord at the foot of Mount Calvary, by the gate as one enters on the right.

He left two sons. Baldwin, aged thirteen. Amalric, seven. Thus it came about that a child was anointed and crowned Baldwin III, albeit during the minority of this child his mother ruled.

They say of Baldwin III that he was a graceful and slender youth, seemingly fortunate from birth, with a silky beard and a fresh vermeil complexion. He delighted in reading. History gave him pleasure so he would inquire of learned men about the deeds and character of kings from days past. Unlike his father, he remembered names, down to the lowliest servant. He did not trouble the endowment of churches, neither did he lie in wait for wealth of any sort, except games of dice at which he played more than was thought appropriate.

deus lo volt!

Roiled by hunger of the skin, all too often he violated the marriage ties of others. Strangely, though, excessive food and drink disgusted him, calling such indulgence touchwood for the worst of crimes. Archbishop William of Tyre, who knew him in and about Jerusalem, since they were much the same age, said the youthful king's hair was long and yellow and he behaved with infallible courtesy.

During the second year of his reign Edessa fell to unbelievers. This noble city had been among the first captured by Franks and so it remained for half a century owing to thick walls capable of withstanding bombardment. Mercenaries had been engaged to defend it because the citizens were Armenian and Chaldean traders, which is to say merchants not given to combat. As for Count Joscelin II, he did not live in the city but amused himself at Turbessel castle.

Zengi, atabeg of Mosul, appeared in November leading a host of vermin. His engineers dug under the walls of Edessa, buttressed tunnels with vertical beams and joists, smeared animal fat, sulfur, and naphtha in crevices to nourish the flame. Because the Franks had been guilty of intolerable sin a breach opened near the Gate of Hours on Christmas eve. A north wind pushed thick smoke into the eyes of defenders. Citizens fled to the citadel for protection but found the gate barred. This happened because Archbishop Hugh went out to organize a defense and instructed guards to admit no one until he returned. Thousands pressed against the locked gate struggling to breathe while the garrison followed orders. How many died is not known. They say the mound of corpses rode higher than the gate. Archbishop Hugh was slain. If he fell beneath a Turkish sword or smothered in the crowd has been argued to this day. Elsewhere in the city aged priests felt the Turkish blade while chanting prayers and holding up relics of martyrs. Zengi commanded his men to stop. He noticed an old bishop of the Jacobite church dragged around naked at the end of a rope, inquired who he was and learned this was Basil, a Syrian. Zengi reproached him for defending the city.

It is all for the best, said this aged bishop.

Why so? Zengi demanded.

You have gained what you wanted, the bishop answered, you have conquered Edessa. As for us, we have gained your respect.

Zengi gave Basil a robe and invited him to discuss how the city should be administered since the bishop was courageous and could speak Arabic. Further, he commanded his men to return what they had stolen, including a pubescent girl seized by one of his emirs. Through such clemency he expected to reassure Christian cities and persuade them to surrender. He razed every Frankish church in Edessa, but did not molest those belonging to Greeks and Armenians. He appointed a governor, garrisoned the citadel with Turks, and moved on to attack Saruj.

The siege of Edessa lasted four weeks, during which time the youthful Count Joscelin did not step outside his castle at Turbessel. Archbishop William denounced him for sloth and cowardice, yet others say he had not men enough to challenge the Turk. He sent word to Antioch and Jerusalem, but help arrived too late. So the pride of northern Syria was lost.

Muslims say of Zengi that when he paused at some hospitable city he would reject offers to sleep comfortably inside the walls but would choose a tent among his men. They say the honor of women concerned him and he was heard to remark that wives of soldiers ought to be sequestered during long absences to preserve them from corruption. Theological schools flourished while he was atabeg, schools that counseled against frivolous books, lewd jokes, cavorting on swings, and the wearing of satin robes. When this fierce Turk laid siege to Baalbek the garrison surrendered after he swore on the Koran to spare them. What did he do but crucify every man, selling wives and daughters into slavery. The governor he flayed and burnt. As the words of a madman are understood with difficulty, or not at all, how should Christians understand this Turk? Some think he was part Austrian. They believe his mother was Ida, that famously beautiful margravine captured alongside the river Eregli and secluded in the harem of Zengi's father. What none dispute is that Yaruqtash, a eunuch of Frankish descent, murdered him. They say Zengi drank too much wine and fell asleep. Some noise wakened him and he saw Yaruqtash furtively sipping from the imperial goblet. Zengi cursed him, vowed to punish him on the morrow, rolled aside in drunken sleep. Then the eunuch thrust a dagger into his bowels and rode away to Jabar. Almost at once the second son of Zengi, Nur al-Din Mahmud, entered the tent, withdrew the ring of authority from his father's hand and placed it on his own. What afterward became of the eunuch Yaruqtash, chronicles do not relate.

News of Zengi's death brought joy to Christian Syria. Now the timorous young Count Joscelin called up an army, thinking that with Armenian help he might overwhelm the Turkish garrison at Edessa and win back his capital. Jubilant Christians opened the gates at his approach. He slaughtered every Turk excepting a few in the citadel and quickly appealed to Jerusalem for help because Nur al-Din would hear about this soon enough. Not one Frankish soldier arrived from Jerusalem, nor Antioch, nor any Christian enclave.

What of Nur al-Din Mahmud? Swarthy, tall, with luminous eyes, a goatee or neatly sculpted little beard to accentuate his features. He carried two bows and two quivers stuffed with arrows when riding into battle, so impatient was he to kill Christians. He dressed roughly and seldom thought of comfort. His wife objected, complained about such austerity, so he gave her three shops in the city of Hims from which she might collect twenty dinars a year. She complained this was not much. No more do I have, said he, for I am but the custodian of Muslim wealth. Nor would I deceive my people, nor cast myself into hell on your account. Yet it seems he could be liberal enough, granting huge amounts for public works at Shaizar, Aleppo, Hamat, Baalbek, and other cities, endowing hospitals and dervish monasteries and caravanserai along the roads. It is said that he would stand up when scholars or priests came into his presence and bade them sit beside him, nor contested their opinions however much he disagreed. Ibn al-Athir, who proudly claimed to have read

121

the history of many sovereigns, declares that except for caliphs long past he could think of no man so virtuous and just as Nur al-Din. Unlike his father, he drank no wine and forbade his soldiers to drink. He would not listen to the tambourine or flute, calling such music offensive to Allah. Very often he got up at night to pray. Angrily he rounded on those who reproached him for distributing so much to Sufis, doctors of law, students of the Koran, dervishes and the like. With them, said he, rests all my hope. And having learned that Mahomet carried his sword in a scabbard, unlike his own warriors who carried swords in their belts, what did he do but insist they emulate the Prophet as best they might. Few men ever saw him smile. He loved the game of polo, otherwise but one desire suffused his heart, to kill Franks, to reconquer what was lost. He scorned the radiance of Christian belief, spurned the beauty that was offered.

On the second day of November he appeared beneath the walls of Edessa. That night Joscelin's little army slipped away hoping to cross the Euphrates. Nur al-Din followed. Next day he caught them and the Franks scattered. Count Joscelin, wounded in the neck, escaped to a castle beyond the river. Nur al-Din returned to Edessa. Thousands met the sword, thousands more enslaved. That emir who seized an attractive girl when Zengi took Edessa now went looking among the captives and there she was. Zengi, considering her youth, made him let the child go, but Nur al-Din did not. Where she was taken, what became of her, ancient chronicles do not relate. Lord God, since Thy aid goes out to one and all, how should such things be?

Patriarch Michael the Syrian speaks of Edessa as a charnel house inhabited by jackals, vultures, rats, lizards. At night came vampires to suck and chew the flesh of murdered citizens. No living men approached, none except those in search of treasure. A city mutilated, abandoned, silenced. Who but Jeremiah would lament further on this?

We know our Lord is a mighty fortress, the music of His voice like thunder. And so the onslaught of doubt receded. And people spoke of the Holy Land, thinking that with God's help they should banish evil from the bounds of His commonwealth. Pope Eugenius III in his bull, Quantum praedecessores, called for a new expedition.

In the year of our tuition 1146 it came about that Bernard de Clairvaux stood preaching on a hillside at Vézelay. As happened before when His Holiness Urban spoke at Clermont, multitudes listened. Few could restrain their tears when Bernard spoke of Turkish infamy, ravagement, oppression, misusage. Edessa was taken. Edessa, bulwark of strength, was lost. If, therefore, Saracen tides engulfed the Holy Land where might Christians turn for hope and revelation?

God's unsleeping enemies mock the broken glory of Christ's endeavor, he declared. So I consider you a blessed generation since you have been caught up in a year pleasant to the Lord, a year of jubilee. That cross cut from cloth does not fetch much if sold, but worn on the shoulder it is worth the kingdom of God. As lords on earth invest their vassals with some slight token, does not the cloth and thread of the Cross represent God's ineffably greater gift? Has He not placed Himself in a position of necessity? Yet is not this for the benefit of His children? He wishes to be thought the debtor so that He may offer wages to all who serve, perpetual riches. Is it not true that many hustle to market when there is cheap pork to buy, yet dawdle toward Christ's kingdom in Heaven?

Sanctified by the purity of his nature, armed with apostolic authority, speaking with the voice of a trumpet, he exhorted those listeners to undertake the journey, granting absolution, remission from sin. Nor should those on pilgrimage encumber themselves with vain superfluities, nor high lords travel with dogs, with falcons on their wrists, in expectation of temporal delight. Many who listened felt persuaded. They cried aloud vociferously for the insignia of faith, cried out to mark themselves with the vertical and horizontal sign, so many that the parcel of crosses he had brought proved inadequate. They say Bernard gave up his red sacerdotal vestments to be cut in the shape of crosses.

King Louis VII, Queen Eleanor of Aquitaine by his side, resolved to accept the sweet yoke of Christ, as did numerous Frankish barons. Abbot Suger, the king's minister, strove to dissuade him, arguing that he should address the needs of France, but King Louis like men everywhere sought invisible things. Some dispute with Count Thibault once led him to invade Champagne. At Vitry-sur-Marne he set fire to Thibault's castle. Flames leapt to the village. Citizens rushed into the church for sanctuary but King Louis put it to the torch. The roof tumbled down on those inside, which crushed a thousand or more. Shrieks of the dying rang in his head until he thought he must beg absolution at the Holy Sepulcher. Otherwise he saw little hope of eternal bliss. Therefore he took the cross at Vézelay.

Odo the monk describes how King Louis en route to Saint Denys entered a leper house to purge his mottled soul, humbling himself in search of grace, appealing the severity of God. And because our Lord responds to all, surely He did not fail to succor a troubled king of France.

At Saint Denys, in the presence of Abbot Suger and His Holiness Eugenius, King Louis prostrated himself to adore the saint, after which the pontiff unfastened a gold door and with Abbot Suger lifted out a silver reliquary that King Louis kissed, which his soul loved. Then from above the altar Louis took the imperial oriflamme in lieu of a common pilgrim staff and received from His Holiness the purse, symbol of pilgrimage. Next he withdrew to the monks' dormitory to prepare himself. He dined in the refectory with these monks, obtaining from them the kiss of peace. Then he departed amid tears and prayers.

Abbot Bernard, frail of body yet robust in spirit, flew hither and yon to make himself heard and God's army multiplied. Women roused by the silken eloquence of his tongue vowed to accompany husbands or lovers. Many forsook the hearth to undertake this blessed journey. Stories were told of Frankish women who girded their soft bodies with chain mail and wore plumed helmets, whose captain had golden spurs. Some said Queen Eleanor would lead a company of Amazons. In Belgium and Germany, engulfed by thousands, he preached with surpassing loftiness, albeit few understood the Frankish tongue. Devils fled howling when he began to speak. Malignant ulcers shrank. Numerous miracles occurred. Philip, archdeacon at Liège, kept count of wonders, which exceeded three hundred.

But as he could not visit every Christian country he addressed the faithful by letter. To the people of England he wrote.

May the warrant of Christ excuse my presumption. I am myself a person of small account, yet my desire for our Lord is very great, which is my reason and motive for writing. The earth shudders. The earth is affrighted because that land in which our Lord manifested Himself, where He lived among men for more than thirty years, which He made glorious through miracles, which He blessed with His blood, is menaced and threatened and compromised. The enemy of God like a serpent lifts his head to strike, to devastate that blessed land. Alas! Should there be none to withstand this evil, then will he overturn the arsenal of our redemption. Then will he desecrate holy places. He casts greedy eyes upon the sanctuary. He longs to violate that couch upon which Our Gracious Lord fell asleep in death. Therefore, you mighty men of England, rise up! O mighty soldiers of England, O men of war, rise up! Now comes the day of abundant salvation, now is the acceptable hour. In this cause may you fight without peril to your souls. Beneath the banner of His name is it glorious to conquer, when death is not loss but gain. And the Evil One beholding the glitter of your swords will gnash his teeth and shrivel.

To Bavarians and eastern Franks he wrote. O, what are you doing? Servants of the Cross, why do you hesitate? Do you not know how many sinners have obtained forgiveness in Jerusalem because the swords of your fathers have cleansed the temple? O my brothers,

what darkens and clouds your minds? Do you think the hand of Our
Lord has shortened? Do you think He is powerless to save? Could
He not send twelve legions of angels? For you know He has the
power. But I say that He wishes you to gain merit by setting aside
earthly consideration. He looks down on you. He waits. He wishes
to know if any among you understand His plight and seek Him and
grieve. O sinners, gaze into the depths of His love! For what is this
but a chance to obtain the salvation that God alone can provide? He
wishes to be the debtor who bountifully reimburses those who labor
in His cause. He will reimburse you with everlasting glory. He will
remit your terrible sins. For this opportunity are you called a blessed
generation. You live in a year agreeable to the Lord, rich in remission.
If you are a prudent merchant fond of goods, behold! I show you a
wondrous market. If the cross of cloth is sold, does it fetch much?
But its value exceeds a kingdom if worn on the shoulder of one who
serves God. Those who have taken the heavenly emblem have felt the
power of His touch. O my brothers! Seize what is provided for your
salvation!

He wrote to citizens of Bohemia. I speak to you about the business of Our Lord, wherein lies redemption. I am, like you, an ordinary man, yet I am not ordinary in my desire for Jesus Christ. To you,
therefore, do I deliver my heart in spite of the distance between us. I
would speak to you of divine mercy, of a new abundance. Blessed are
they that walk the earth in this year of remission, of veritable jubilee,
for the Lord has not bestowed such munificence upon previous generations. He has not lavished upon our fathers such copious grace.
Listen! O listen, my brothers! Wickedness occupies the land of promise. Evil men feast their eyes upon the sanctuary of our belief. They
would stain the very bed of Jesus. They would corrupt a dwelling
purpled with the blood of the immaculate lamb. Why, therefore, do
you hesitate? Be quick to accept the gift that is promised. Seize the
opportunity of apostolic indulgence. Listen! Listen! Next Easter will
the army of God set forth and I say to you that it will pass through
Hungary. You have with you the lord bishop of Moravia, a learned

and holy man who will impart to you the wisdom provided by God, who will encourage and direct you in these matters. No pilgrim shall wear silken garments, nor miniver, nor multicolored clothing. None shall fasten gold or silver ornaments to the trappings of his horse, only to his shield and to the wood of his saddle. But when the army marches into battle any man is free to wear silver or gold so the sun may shine upon him and reflect his courage and melt the courage of pagans. I would expand on this, were it not for the lord bishop of Moravia. Obey him. Be attentive, be diligent. Glory awaits you.

Multitudes enrolled. Bernard could write to His Holiness that castles and villages stood deserted while seven women looked hard to find one man for company.

Thus, high-born Nivelo announced by charter that to expiate wrongdoing he would go on pilgrimage.

Whoever earns pardon through the grace of heavenly atonement, who would free himself from the onerous burden of misdeeds, whose weight bears upon his soul and prevents its flying up to heaven, must look to the end of malfeasance. Therefore, I, Nivelo, born to a nobility that often engenders ignobility of mind, do renounce oppression of the poor, a custom bequeathed me from my father. In a manner that was usual I did tread and trample upon Emprainville by seizing the goods of inhabitants. I, taking with me a troop of knights, would descend upon foresaid village to make over their goods. Therefore, in hope of divine acquittal, I go to Jerusalem. Toward expenses the monks have given me ten pounds in denarii and gave three pounds to my sister Comitissa in return for her consent. Forty solidi did they give my brother Hamelin, this being acceptable to my son Urso and other relatives. If, in the course of events, any shall be tempted to break the strength of this concession, may he be transfixed by the thunderbolt of anathema. May he drop into hell with Dathan and Abiram to suffer egregious torment forever. In confirmation of this I make the sign of the cross with my own hand. I pass the document to my son called Urso, and other relatives and witnesses, for all to endorse by making their signs.

Monarchs enrolled. Conrad, emperor of Germany, took the cross, which was splendid and wonderful because the Turks did not live close by. More dangerous were Jews all around. Würzburg annals relate how the body of a man chopped in bits was discovered, two pieces of him fished from the river Main, another close to Thunegersheim, yet another found among the mills toward Bleicha, other pieces in a ditch opposite Katzinwichus tower. Hence the citizens of Würzburg as well as pilgrims who gathered in the city were seized with frenzy and rushed through the streets impetuously killing Israelites, children, women, old and young. Also, signs had been observed at the grave where the victim's parts were buried. The mute could speak, the lame could walk, the blind could see, and other miraculous things. Accordingly the pilgrims began to venerate the slaughtered man and carried leavings of him and thought he should be canonized. Bishop Siegried, however, resisted this importunity, which aroused such indignation that he hid himself in a turret to avoid being stoned. And the canons lived in such dread that on the most holy night of Maundy Thursday they would not ascend to the choir to sing matins. Also, in Norwich it was rumored that Israelites had murdered a Christian child. Also, in France many complaints sounded that Israelites contributed nothing toward the relief of the Holy Land. Our Lord was delivered to death on behalf of these people, to frightful death, that of the Cross, where in those days thieves were hung as now we hang them on gallows. How should pilgrims march great distances to behold their sanctuary and wreak vengeance on Muslims if all around live Jews whose forefathers slew our Lord and crucified Him for no cause? We would attack God's enemies in the East, said they, yet here are God's worst enemies, Jews, before our eyes. So we are doing the work backward.

Be that as it may, with kindly spring rain warming the earth Emperor Conrad boarded ship at Regensburg to lead his troops along the Danube. So mighty an army accompanied him that the river seemed not broad enough nor fields wide enough for those on foot. This according to Otto of Freisingen. Through Hungary and Bulgaria they went without offense. But when they came to Greece, home of double-faced knaves, petty disputes and turbulence hobbled their progress.

At Constantinople these Germans broke into the wondrous pleasure garden of Emperor Manuel Comnenus where captive animals wandered peaceably through woods and drank from streams as if enjoying their natural surrounding. The Germans butchered these creatures or turned them loose while Manuel Comnenus watched from a palace window. Whether Germans proceed to sin through love of evil is a matter of dispute and futile exercise.

Emperor Manuel wished to expel these barbaric travelers. Because they had not kept faith and violated their oath he thought to play the role of scorpion whose face looks benign but whose tail stings viciously. He offered guides to lead them past the Golden Horn to the wild desolate land of Cappadocia where they would find little water and less to eat, where they would be destroyed by Seljuk Turks. Some say he instructed these false guides to sicken the Germans by mixing chalk into their bread. Whatever the truth, at Dorylaeum here came Turks on light fast horses and the weary Germans encumbered with armor floundering through swamps and hollows. Of all who served under Count Bernhard, not one escaped. Before the sun went down at least eighty thousand Germans lay dead and Conrad himself, wounded twice, riding as fast as he could toward Nicaea. Michael the Syrian declares that overnight the price of silver in Cappadocia sank to the price of lead, so much booty did these Turks harvest.

King Louis advanced on Constantinople ignorant of what happened to Conrad, ignorant of Byzantine malice. A deputy from the scorpion Manuel greeted him at Ratisbon to deliver letters overflowing with such flattery that while listening to them read aloud he blushed. Manuel expressed the hope that King Louis would march through Greek land in a seemly and peaceable manner.

These Franks entered a world they could not understand. Odo from Deuil relates that in the village of Branitchevo where they bought provisions they saw coins made from pewter, which they considered unnatural. For each of these strange coins they must pay five centimes. They had done business at villages and castles along the way, but now they found every gate closed so they had to camp outside the walls. Whatever they wished to buy was let down in baskets. And since they could not get enough to eat they began to forage and steal, all because of German misconduct.

At Philippopolis a company of Germans from Conrad's army went to loiter in taverns and drank and made noise. A juggler who did not know their language sat down with them and paid his share and began to drink. Presently he drew out of his jacket a snake and set down a glass, laid the viper on top and began to perform conjuring tricks. But the Germans flew into a rage because his tricks did not satisfy them. They pounced on him and tore him apart. Or it may be the Germans accused him of sorcery, saying he had been hired to kill them with poison. This brought the governor of Philippopolis to investigate. Now the Germans, excited from wine and fury and thinking they would be punished for murdering the juggler, hurled themselves at the governor's men. This brought other men with bows who killed several Germans and drove off the rest. But they came back freshly armed and set everything on fire.

At the money exchange near Constantinople some Fleming lost his wits before unimaginable wealth, seized what he could and rushed about shouting wildly for his comrades to do the same. Gold and silver trampled in the mud, screams of rage, tables upside down what with vendors and pilgrims running back and forth. The count of Flanders remanded this unruly soldier to King Louis, to be flogged with rods or burnt, as the sovereign chose. King Louis had him hanged in public. Further, everything stolen must be returned, delivered to the bishop of Langres. What could not be recovered the king himself would make up.

Some days afterward this army crossed the Arm of Saint George, invading Turkish land. Duke Frederick of Swabia, who was the emperor's nephew and heir, came riding into camp and told what happened. Not much of Conrad's turbulent host survived. They were swollen with hubris.

Beyond Laodicea on mountainous slopes fouled by German corpses the army of King Louis was assaulted. Turks high above them on a narrow pass shot arrows and sent tree trunks and stones rolling down to crush them. Sumpter beasts went mad with fright, pressed against one another, reared and plunged, fell screaming into the abyss. At every death the vile Turks rejoiced. Many pilgrims who left home and family for the sake of Jesus Christ found martyrdom at this snowy pass. Documents do not explain how it was that King Louis got separated from the imperial guard. However it came about, he attempted to climb a slope by clutching roots that God exposed to ensure his safety. Turks pursued him. Archers from a distance shot arrows at him. But he was protected from arrows by his cuirass and with his sword he cut off the hands of those who tried to capture him. Yet the valor of King Louis was not enough. His efforts bore dry fruit. After this defeat he relinquished command to Everard, third Master of the Temple, and made his way seaward to Attalia, whence he journeyed to Antioch. I have heard he got to Jerusalem where he stayed a while, long enough to celebrate Easter. At last, yielding to the importunity of Abbot Suger, he returned to France. So ended a wretched pilgrimage where once they had thought to subjugate Damascus. The vices of this army drew our Lord's wrath, according to the bishop of Freysinghen. Yet another cleric, Geoffroi of Clairvaux, declared the result no less than favorable since this endeavor populated heaven with a throng of illustrious martyrs.

Some disparaged King Louis, saying he acted against the counsel of Prince Raymond of Antioch. They said he wished to humiliate Prince Raymond whose conduct toward the king's wife provoked whispers. Thus we see how things that are one become several through the aims of human perversity.

As for Abbot Bernard who prophesied success, he addressed a letter to His Holiness Eugenius.

Most Holy Father, we have fallen upon grave times. The Lord, provoked by our sins, forgetful of His mercy, has laid low in the desert many of His children, cut down by the sword or depleted by famine. Therefore some call us immoderate. Yet I did not proceed like a man who questioned his goal, since I have acted with the authority of God as decreed by you. And the judgment of God is true indeed. Who does not know that? How, then, should anyone reprove what exceeds all comprehension? When Moses wished to lead his people out of Egypt, he promised them a better land. If he had not, would they have followed? He led them, but he did not lead them to the land he promised. Yet he acted at the Lord's command. Who does not know that? How, then, should it fall incumbent upon me to justify what befell the host? Would anyone say that the fate of those lost in the desert was contrary to our Lord's promise? These few matters I invoke, most Holy Father, since the perfect and ultimate apology for any man must be the testimony of his conscience.

God's kingdom Outremer now manifestly decayed. The fruit of barons and high lords withered. With delight Saracens mocked the crumbling pediment of Christian enterprise, with impunity looked toward those whose names once had riven them with fright. Their boldness rose proportionately.

Nur al-Din raised a fearful army to pick apart the castles. He resolved to invest the fortress of Inab. This news brought Prince Raymond furiously out of Antioch with not enough men, but narratives from those days call Raymond a prince of impetuous courage who disdained advice. He encamped near the fountain of Murad and during the night was encircled. Next morning, when he saw how they must escape or be massacred in the hollow, Raymond ordered his knights to charge. But suddenly the wind blew dust in their eyes. Not many escaped. Raymond's head was sliced off, preserved in a silver casket as was usual, and despatched to Baghdad. It is said the caliph exhibited Raymond's head throughout the Muslim world to prove this formidable adversary would trouble them no more. His death occurred on the feast day of apostles Peter and Paul in the thirteenth year of his seigneury. What the Saracens left of him was carried sorrowfully to Antioch, entombed among his predecessors. Then the people of Antioch lost themselves to wretchedness and grief.

Before long Nur al-Din rode by the very walls of Antioch, pillaging, burning, insolent, looking to the death of Christians. He attacked the monastery of Saint Symeon high up in the mountains, after which he rode down to observe and contemplate the sea, which was a new experience. He immersed himself in salt water and exulted, studied by the men of his army. Next he confronted and took the fortress of Harim. Christians everywhere now yielded to helpless fright because the flower of Latin knighthood was delivered to the palm of a Turk. Who in the country roundabout would govern them, protect them?

Next came the sultan of Iconium leading a powerful column across Syria to threaten Christian strongholds. So the land was dazed, sick with apprehension. He laid siege to the castle of Turbessel. Count Joscelin persuaded the sultan to depart by freeing every Turkish captive and giving him twelve suits of armor. Many believe the pigeonhearted son of Lord Joscelin met a worthy end. One day en route to Antioch he turned aside to empty himself and while going about the business was captured by Turcomans who led him to Aleppo dressed with chains. They blinded him and there he languished nine years before giving up the ghost. Or it may be as the pagan Sibt relates, he went to meet some Turkish girl. Syriac narratives claim a Jew pointed him out. Others think the limb of a tree knocked him senseless. Whatever the fact, this Joscelin did not stand as high as his father's belt.

Now, with Antioch and Edessa deprived of leadership in that summer of grace 1150, Christian Syria weakened.

Divine providence roused the Holy Land from fatal apathy. Three leagues south from Ascalon stood one of ancient Philistia's five cities, Gaza, with splendid churches and marble homes. For centuries it stood proudly, but at length fell apart. On that hill the servants of Christ erected a fortress and garrisoned it with Templars. By

133

doing so they threatened Egyptians to the south who were in the habit of victualing Ascalon. Hence, some faint equilibrium prevailed.

But the lash of the Lord is restless. In the year of our grace 1153 here came Baldwin III with all the siege engines he could muster, accompanied by knights of the Temple and Hospital, by great lords of the realm, by the archbishops of Tyre and Caesarea and Nazareth and the bishops of Acre and Bethlehem. This mighty host encamped along the circuit of walls and Lord Gérard de Sidon made ready to blockade the port with fifteen beaked ships. Citizens of Ascalon looked to defend themselves. Every night they marched around the ramparts, which had been lighted bright as day since they put lamps with glass covers here and there.

One morning at sunrise after five months of bombardment a section of the wall came tumbling down with noise enough to rouse the army. Pilgrims seized their weapons and rushed joyously toward that place where fortune decreed they should enter. Bernard de Tremelay, Master of the Temple, got there first and occupied the breach so his people might have first chance at looting. Forty Templars pushed through, consumed by greed, but were hacked to pieces. And the Saracens patched the wall with great wood beams, dangled Templar bodies from ropes in full view, jeered, whistled, and boasted. This infuriated God's servants who forgot all fear of death and hurled themselves against Ascalon until those inside could not mistake the terrible wrath of our Lord. Lamenting, groaning, they chose to surrender, at which a shout arose from the Christian host. Many wept, gave thanks, lifted up their hands and eyes to praise the Creator. Thenceforth, while His standard floated from the towers of Ascalon, that province of the Holy Land seemed secure. Had Turks in the north united with Babylonians in the south, how could Jerusalem survive?

The conquest of Ascalon brought grief and fear to Egypt. Caliph al-Adil despatched troops to the mouth of the Nile and with this army went his grandson, Nasr. Because these Mahometans record events as do Franks or Scots or Alemanni or Lombards, albeit using letters few servants of God understand, the cruelty, intrigue, malice, and corruption of their lives has been preserved. The youth Nasr wearied of garrison life and returned to Cairo, whereupon al-Adil ordered him to rejoin the army. What did this rebellious youth do but get into the harem and stab his grandfather. Afterward, he showed his grandfather's head on the point of a lance.

At first a wheel turns slowly, yet the angle grows steeper. Twenty trays of gold, thirty saddled mules, forty camels loaded with grain and other gifts did the next caliph bestow upon Nasr. It is said they would disguise themselves and slip out of the palace at night to mingle with common people.

You must visit me, said the youth to his royal patron. You must visit my home in the bazaar of sword-makers.

The caliph accepted. But all at once here came assassins out of hiding. It is related that Nasr himself threw his patron's body into a vault beneath the house. And a black slave, Sa'd al-Daula, who witnessed the crime was put to death. Where is the light of this dark and heathen world?

Citizens howled for the death of Nasr but he escaped and fled along the Damascus road where Frankish troops caught him. Now, as wicked people do when caught, he repented his villainous life and wished to be reborn. Therefore, clanking with chains, he was instructed in the true faith of Jesus Christ and learned to write Roman letters. Nevertheless, when Cairo offered sixty thousand gold pieces for him the Franks accepted. Away went Nasr, stripped of dignity, locked in a cage on the hump of a camel. And no more did he get to Cairo than citizens tore him apart and chewed his flesh. What little remained they hung outside the Zawila Gate. Has the Prince of Demons conceived a more odious tribe?

Or as happened once in Aleppo when a mad prince ascended the throne. Alp Arslan, son of Ridwan, sixteen years of age and stuttering so much they called him the Mute. No more did he come to rule than he chopped off the heads of his brothers, various officers, counselors, servants, any he disliked. He led certain nobles to the citadel, to a trench in the cellar. How would you like it, he asked, how would you like it if right here I cut off your heads? Narrowly they escaped the sword, feigning amusement, assuring the mad king that he might do as he wished since they were loyal subjects. Thereafter all avoided him save the royal eunuch Loulou, which is to say Pearls. These infidels bestow sweet names upon eunuchs. Murjan, which means Coral. Fayruz, which is Turquoise. Kafur, meaning Camphor. Mithqal, which is Sequin. However that may be, Loulou considered the past and the future and one night strangled Alp Arslan. But what was his reward for killing the tyrant? As he wandered through the fields beyond Aleppo on a pleasant afternoon the men of his escort drew their bows. After the hare! they cried. After the hare! But this hare was Loulou and he struck the ground with his last breath, showing more bristles than some hedgehog. How could it profit such malignant spirits to gain the world, which straightway they must lose?

Now with Ascalon secure, Christian banners flying from turrets, King Baldwin in our year of enlightenment 1157 found himself persecuted by creditors. Turcoman shepherds pastured their flocks near Paneas and the king looked greedily upon these animals and gave orders to slay the shepherds. He gathered sheep and donkeys as well as many splendid horses. However, this brought Nur al-Din raging down out of the north to fall upon the king's army near the Sea of Galilee and destroy it. King Baldwin himself escaped to Safed, but infidels delight in telling how Nur al-Din rode through Damascus displaying severed heads and Frankish captives. Christian knights on red camels rode through the streets, standards unfurled as though victorious but in truth were captive, the banners stained by Christian blood. Prisoners of high estate rode in seeming triumph through the city, behind them naked sergeants roped together, four, five, six, eight. Arab chronicles relate that Muslims danced, hooted, shouted insults, gesticulated, convinced that Allah punished these Franks. Archbishop William, disturbed by the king's imperious act, wrote that our Lord visited upon him what he had visited upon peaceful shepherds.

Certain it is that the King of Kings waxed furious with Frank and Saracen alike, furious at the conduct of His children. Throughout Syria the ground trembled. Watchtowers above the walls of Aleppo shook and fell apart. Beyrouth. Tripoli. Homs. Tyre. Buildings crumpled, thousands died. Citizens of Harran peered into a crevice and saw the ruins of some ancient city. A teacher in Hama left the school to relieve himself and got back to find every student dead. Munqidhites at Shaizar assembled for a royal circumcision when the earth cracked and the citadel fell inward. Of this dynasty no more than two survived, one a princess of Shaizar. The other was Ushama ibn Munquidh, author and diplomat, who chanced to be traveling. With great bitterness he wrote that death did not advance step by step, nor catch his people one by one, but in a wink their homes became their tombs. Blessed Saint Augustine teaches how God does not idly strike mountains, which are innocent, nor without purpose cause the ground to shake. God does so to signify His terrible wrath at sinners. Thus it behooves us, who are from birth choked by sin, to purge our souls of impurities and rivalries.

Now in those days Emperor Manuel was the wealthiest, most generous sovereign on earth. Whoever asked of him got one hundred silver marks. If counselors reproached him for such benefaction he would answer frankly. There are but two with the right to give, our Lord and I.

King Baldwin, seeing how it was, resolved to ally himself with the mighty house of Comnenus. He thought to ask for the hand of a Byzantine princess. Therefore he despatched two envoys who came back rejoicing. Manuel Comnenus had selected one of his nieces, Theodora, aged thirteen. The child was alleged to be tall and elegant, her skin compared to burnished gold. Presently she was delivered to Jerusalem roped with pearls, accompanied by an escort befitting the majestic house of Comnenus, bringing innumerable gems, fabulous carpets, spices, unguents. And no more did King Baldwin set eyes upon the child than he forsook other women, of whom there had been more than enough. So they were married.

In this way, Emperor Manuel became uncle to the king of Jerusalem through marriage.

Down from Constantinople to the land of Syria he rode in our year of grace 1159. Baldwin with his greatest lords hurried north to Antioch, whence he sent ambassadors to convey salutations in a most courteous fashion and to inquire if he should present himself. Being informed that he should do so, he set forth at once. He was met by two nobles of the highest rank, nephews of the emperor, who conducted him to the tent where Manuel Comnenus held court. It is said the emperor welcomed him graciously, gave him the kiss of peace, and seated Baldwin at his side, albeit on a throne less elevated than his own.

For ten days the monarchs discoursed pleasantly, after which Baldwin returned to Antioch carrying twenty thousand gold nomisma as well as brocade, jewelry, fine silk, vases, and other gifts.

Anon, here was Manuel Comnenus with his vast army approaching the gates. King Baldwin emerged, attended by notables, followed by citizens. To the music of trumpets and drums Emperor Manuel passed through the gates and was escorted to the cathedral of Saint Peter through streets adorned with carpets, strewn with flowers. Then to the palace. He wore chain mail beneath his robes.

Emperor Manuel luxuriated at the baths and otherwise sampled the pleasures of Antioch for several days. Now he wished to go hunting. So on the day of our Lord's Ascension these two monarchs with their attendants went riding toward the forest. But as they galloped across uneven ground King Baldwin's horse stumbled and pitched him from the saddle. When he struck the earth he broke one arm. The emperor at once dismounted, knelt beside him and took up the duty of physician, ministering to the king as if he himself were a common leech. Seeing this, Greek courtiers stood amazed, dumb with shame, for it was unseemly that the most powerful sovereign in the world should disregard the majesty of his office. And when they had returned to Antioch the emperor visited the king each day to change poultices and ointments, displaying as much solicitude as if Baldwin were his son. Narratives agree that he took much pride in his skill at physic.

Shortly thereafter Manuel Comnenus returned to Constantinople. King Baldwin, troubled by discord and Saracen threats, returned to Jerusalem.

Queen Melisende, his mother, wasted from long suffering that no remedy could palliate, the wall of her flesh broken, ascended to celestial glory in the providential year 1161. She was entombed in the valley of Jehoshaphat, to the right as one descends toward the sepulcher of Blessed Mary. She rests in a stone crypt with iron gates. Close by is an altar where mass diurnally is celebrated for her soul, for the souls of all who trust in the Lord. King Baldwin lost himself in grief. For a long time he would not be comforted.

One year later while sojourning at Antioch he swallowed certain tablets, that being his custom when winter approached. He obtained these from a Saracen medicaster called Barac. On the advice of wives and daughters many Christian lords Outremer disdained the practice of Latin physics, submitting instead to the care of Syrians, Jews, Samaritans, or what pagan horse leech may be known only to Allah. Ushama ibn Munquidh speaks of one called Thabat who came to treat the abscessed leg of a Frankish knight. This Turk made a plaster and the leg began to heal. But here came a Latin who said Thabat did not know how to cure the cancer. Would you live with one leg or die with two? he inquired of the wounded knight. Certainly I prefer to live, the knight replied. So the Latin ordered his leg hacked off with a battleaxe, marrow spurted, and the knight went to sleep in God. Also there was a consumptive woman for whom Thabat prescribed refreshing food. But the Latin said a devil wanted her so he chopped off the woman's hair. Then she went back to eating Frankish food with mustard and got sick. A devil has slipped into her brain, said the Latin. With a razor he drew a cross on her skull to expose the bone, which he rubbed with salt, whereupon she followed the knight to glory. This according to Ushama. It is possible that certain unbelievers have better knowledge of such matters than the shrewdest physicians in Europe, albeit I do not claim to know, nor avouch the truth of infidel writing.

Be that as it may, King Baldwin had no more swallowed these tablets than fever and flux attacked. Nothing could be found to alleviate his distress. When he perceived that he was failing he went to Tripoli where he rested several months. At length, knowing he must die, he had himself carried to Beyrouth and directed that lords of the realm and prelates of the Church be assembled. In their presence he acknowledged his faith, humbly confessed his sins. Having done so, he was mercifully released from this ephemeral flesh. Some think the medicine he got from Barac was poison. Certain it is that several tablets were put in bread and fed to a dog, which very soon died. Whatever the truth, his spirit ascended on the tenth of February, less than two years after his mother Melisende, during the twentieth year of his reign. Because he expired without issue he was succeeded by his brother Amalric.

The funeral cortege of King Baldwin traveled for a week between Beyrouth and Jerusalem, attended by frantic displays of grief. Not only Christians but Muslims felt saddened. In the Holy City he was entombed among his royal predecessors. When it was suggested to Nur al-Din that during this mournful time he might lay waste to Christian land he declined, saying the Franks had lost such a prince as could not be found elsewhere in the world.

Concerning Amalric, this much has been preserved. His greed was notorious, he intervened at courts of justice for his own profit and pocketed ecclesiastic benefices. Archbishop William of Tyre, who knew him, declares that he was egregiously fat so his breasts dripped down to his belly like those of an old woman. His blond hair receded. Storms of discordant laughter would course through him, which caused his fat body to shake and lessened his dignity. He wallowed in female flesh, seducing married women without guilt. Yet he displayed commendable taste, abjuring theatrical performances and gaming while delighting at the sweep of herons and falcons. Neither curses nor reproaches troubled him, even when uttered by contemptible men. He would listen eagerly while Archbishop William read to him about foreign customs or strange beliefs. Above all, he imagined himself king of Egypt.

One day in the citadel at Tyre, being feverish, he summoned the archbishop and for a time they conversed on various subjects. Then he asked whether, beyond the teaching of our Lord, there could be proof of resurrection.

At this Archbishop William felt perturbed, wondering that an orthodox prince should debate fixed doctrine or question it in the depth of his heart. He replied with much agitation that the teaching of our Lord should be sufficient. Plainly, he said, the Gospel teaches future resurrection. Beyond doubt He promised to come and judge the quick and the dead. To the elect will He give a kingdom prepared from the rudiment of the world. To the wicked will He consign everlasting fire. Without doubt the testimony of holy apostles and of ancient patriarchs suffices.

This I firmly believe, said King Amalric. Yet I search for a reason whereby these things might be demonstrated to skeptics.

Imagine yourself a man so afflicted, said William. Then let us peer into the matter.

Having thought about this, King Amalric consented.

Do you acknowledge that our Lord is just? William asked.

Nothing could be more true, said the king.

Do you acknowledge that good shall be met with good, evil with evil?

That is true, said the king.

In this life it does not often happen, said the archbishop. Many good people suffer inordinate distress while the wicked enjoy unlimited happiness.

Again the king said this was so.

Then, said the archbishop, retribution must occur in another life since it is impossible for God to act unscrupulously. If those who merit good shall be rewarded, while those who merit punishment shall be punished, there must be resurrection of the flesh.

This seems good to me beyond expectation, said King Amalric. You have withdrawn all uncertainty from my heart.

Now their discourse turned upon other subjects and King Amalric felt much refreshed, even as Emperor Charlemagne refreshed himself through conversation with the learned Alcuin.

During King Amalric's sovereignty occurred an iniquitous act that would bring signal harm to the empire and to the Holy Church. In the diocese of Tortosa lived a community of sixty thousand pagans who chose their leader not as Franks do, by hereditary right, but according to his qualities. This leader was called simply the Old Man. And no matter what he commanded them to do, that would they do with utmost fidelity. If some prince, Muslim or Christian, incurred the wrath of this Old Man he would present a dagger to one of his subjects, perhaps to more than one. And they who had been so designated would hasten to murder the offending prince, whence they were called Assassins. These people for at least five centuries adhered to Saracen law with such rigidity that by comparison others seemed heretic. But during Amalric's time they chose a leader of acute intellect who obtained and valued the books of our holy apostles. While reading these books he attempted as best he could to understand the wondrous precepts of our Lord. And as he pondered the noble doctrine espoused by Christians he could not but reject the false dogma of that despicable seducer Mahomet which he had swallowed along with his mother's milk. So he came to abominate filthy works. He taught his people what he had learned of the true faith. He dissuaded them from loathsome habits, restored the eating of pork and drinking of wine, destroyed places where they were accustomed to kiss the toes of a noxious prophet, and in other ways sought to rescue his people from the bottomless pit where they had been cast by Mahomet. Next, desirous of advancing toward the infinite mysteries of Christian law, he despatched an emissary by name Boaldelle to King Amalric.

The king greeted Boaldelle courteously and found him to be not only wise but eloquent and sincere, anxious to form some bond. If this might be accomplished, said Boaldelle in the name of his master, Assassins would embrace Jesus Christ as their savior, would receive baptism and from that moment onward behave with brotherly kindness.

To this speech King Amalric listened with delight. And when Boaldelle made ready to go back to his people King Amalric provided an escort. They had gone beyond Tripoli, traveling incautiously since Boaldelle relied on the good faith of Christians, when certain knights of the Temple rushed at him with drawn swords and murdered him. The king was roused to anger since this brought infamy upon himself, imperiling the dignity of his throne, and by an atrocious act would that increase so pleasing to God be lost. Mad with rage he summoned his barons. Such wickedness merited retribution, all agreed. Then two high lords, Seiher de Mamedunc and Godescalous de Turout, went to confront the master of the Temple, Eudes de Saint-Amand. A one-eyed Templar, Walter du Maisnilio, was held responsible. Now the master, Eudes, sent word to King Amalric that he had enjoined penance upon this guilty brother and would remand him to the pope. However this did not satisfy King Amalric who traveled to Sidon and found the culprit, had him dragged forcibly out of the house, dressed with chains and banished to prison at Tyre. Thus, Amalric contrived to exonerate himself in the eyes of the Old Man whose emissary was slain without cause. Yet the death of Boaldelle was but a harbinger of evil to come, as though in the eyes of God this matter stood unresolved.

Between watchful enemies His kingdom on earth lay at risk. To

143

the north, Turks, Saracens, whose masters governed from Aleppo to Damascus. In the south, Egyptians. King Amalric decided to look for some alliance with Egypt that would guarantee safe passage for vessels to and from Europe. Also, Egyptians might then have little stomach for a pact with cousins to the north. He charged Hugh from Caesarea to go and carefully observe this degenerate land. With Lord Hugh went a Templar, Geoffrey Fulcher, to interpret.

From very ancient days it has been known how Egypt lies between two inhospitable deserts condemned to sterility, for which reason the land could produce no harvest were it not fertilized by the abundant Nile. This river seeks to expand itself and seasonally washes through adjacent regions. Hence it contracts or enlarges, bringing with this deluge the blessing of agriculture. Upper Egypt the people call Seith because long ago there was a city named Sais of which Plato makes mention. Lower Egypt they call in their language Phium, albeit no one could say why. At one time this region was called Thebiad because of opium cultivated there, a remedy physicians call Theban. And from top to bottom, where some assert the world ends in darkness, all agree that Egypt overflows with marvels. Here live horrific serpents and lizards, most fearful being the dragon, which makes a commotion in the air while slinking from its cave. Whatever the dragon grasps must die. Indeed, the elephant is not safe despite his monstrous bulk. They say the dragon inhabits Ethiopia or mayhap India where it lurks near footpaths used by elephants and ties them in knots to suffocate them. Yet we should remember that God creates all and what He is pleased to create should please us and we should render praise to Him. His manifold works exceed reckoning.

Scythia is the home of griffons, which are savage birds, mad beyond insanity. In Hyrcania live panthers marked by delicate spots. Also the beast leucocrotta, which surpasses others in speed, with the haunch of a stag, head of a badger, and cloven hooves. There is the mantichora, which exhibits the visage of a man with sparkling eyes, the body of a lion, and a spiked tail enabling it to sting like the scor-

pion. The voice of a mantichora is reputed to be musical and sibi-
lant, causing listeners to think of a flute. There are skinks and lacer-
tae, which do not experience passion unless hurrying in search of
their mates. The amphisbaena, which vaunts two heads. The yale,
whose two horns sway back and forth during battle. But who could
account for the infinitude of animals, birds, and fishes? All being the
handiwork of God must be marvelous. Yet infinitely more wonderful
is He who imagined and composed them.

Latin parchment tells how Lord Hugh and Geoffrey the Templar
were guided through Cairo by imperial attendants who displayed
swords and made a huge noise, how they were escorted through the
palace, each gallery more astonishing than the one previous, each
guarded by Nubians with gleaming black skin. The Franks were
amazed and did not know what to think. They saw water spouting
from gold pipes, marble pillars, fish basins inlaid with carving. They
walked across patterned floors, heard the warble of songbirds captured from all four corners of Africa. They saw the peacock spreading jeweled wings and creatures like those dreamt by men asleep.
Quadrupeds glaring, howling, gibbering. Afreet. Gyascutus. Bar-
ghest. Wivern. Harpy. The fearsome basilisk whose body is striped
white, who crawls on his lower half while his upper half stands erect,
whose glance brings death and subordinate vipers tremble. Such
wonders did Lord Hugh and Geoffrey the Templar behold, such
prodigies cavorting through gardens, such curiosities chained or
caged as would tempt a painter to represent or a poet to rhyme. Solinus who traveled through Egypt in very ancient days remarked similar things.

The sultan of Cairo led these Franks into a room boasting a silk
curtain thickly encrusted with pearls, rubies, and emeralds. The sultan approached humbly, removed a jeweled sword dangling from a
gold chain around his neck and placed it on the carpet. Twice he
prostrated himself, exhibiting reverence akin to terror. Whereupon
with astonishing rapidity the silk curtain flew aside. On a throne
fashioned from gold, surrounded by eunuchs and counselors, sat the

caliph. The sultan, after kissing one of his slippers, told the purpose of these Franks.

In those days Caliph al-Adid was no more than sixteen or seventeen years old, in the flower of youth, his skin very dark, his features girlish. Thrice yearly he showed himself in public for the adoration of citizens. They called him lord and thought the Nile must rise at his command. The number of his wives exceeded calculation. Each day he took a different woman, idling away his life in dissolute games, leaving the administration of Egypt to his vizier. What man is master of himself when shackled by chains of lust?

It is said that he listened cheerfully while the sultan explained provisions of the treaty and the urgent need addressed therein. To all of which the youth responded that he would accept and fulfill the stipulations, with a most liberal interpretation, out of regard for King Amalric.

The Franks sought reassurance. They asked Caliph al-Adid to confirm the pact with his own hand as was usual in the West, which horrified the counselors grouped about him. To them such a request was beyond understanding. Finally, urged by the sultan, after much deliberation, the caliph extended one hand draped with a veil.

Lord Hugh then addressed the caliph. Sire, in matters of trust there can be no deviation, since when princes bind themselves to one another they conceal nothing. Therefore, unless your hand is freely offered, we must think there is some lack of honesty on your part.

At last, much averse, yet displaying a faint smile that humiliated members of the court, Caliph al-Adid gave his bare hand to the Frankish knight. Then he repeated, syllable by syllable, each word spoken by Hugh, thereby promising that he would honor the stipulations without fraud or evil intent. Later he sent generous gifts to the ambassadors, which greatly recommended him, causing Lord Hugh and Geoffrey the Templar to depart for Jerusalem more than a little satisfied.

At that time no city was richer than Cairo. And being a nest of pagan intrigue, why should it not be annexed to consolidate Christ's protectorate on earth? King Amalric marched out of Ascalon in October of the year 1168, a splinter from the True Cross hanging about his neck. Templars opposed this invasion, mindful that Lord Hugh and the caliph had reached accord. Also, they served as bankers to Italian merchants who dealt profitably with Egypt. However, knights of the Hospital joined Amalric and pledged everything they owned to equip the troops. Some think he offered the province of Bilbeis as their fief. Whatever the fact, a Muslim emissary found King Amalric marching across the desert and reproached him for perfidious conduct. But the king said he was justified and would not turn back, not unless Egypt paid heavy tribute.

The city of Bilbeis resisted with desperate fury. When at last it had been taken every inhabitant met the sword. This was to horrify and intimidate the people of Cairo and other cities. Yet according to the narrative of Ibn al-Athir, had King Amalric behaved magnanimously he would have taken Cairo with ease because the nobles had decided to surrender. The massacre at Bilbeis changed their minds. In the old part of the city they set twenty thousand jugs of naphtha afire, destroying markets, houses, stalls, mosques, whatever might be useful to invaders. And here came that same emissary, Shams al-Khilafa, to say they would burn up Cairo with all its wealth before they would deliver it to Frankish hands. And the caliph wrote hastily to Nur al-Din, enclosing a lock of female hair, explaining that he took this hair from one of his wives, all of whom beseeched Nur al-Din to rescue them from the Franks. Nur al-Din agreed to help. So the king, observing how these people in Cairo would do anything rather than submit, thinking he might be attacked from another direction by Turks, considered it prudent to withdraw. He demanded one million dinars in order to seem victorious, but did not wait for payment because of infidels gathering on the horizon. And most bitterly he reproached the Hospitalers for bad counsel.

The sea afforded clear passage to vessels from Europe while Egypt brought to the realm strange commodities. Further, moneys spent by unbelievers enriched the treasury and benefited private commerce. Now all was changed. Into what turbulence had immoderate lust for wealth plunged the Holy Land. William of Tyre laments that wherever one looked there was anxiety, fear, misfortune wrought by the cupidity of one man, Amalric, whose avarice clouded the serenity vouchsafed to Christian Jerusalem.

Perhaps the greed of Amalric did not exceed that of Nur al-Din. He, too, coveted the fabulous treasure that was Egypt. When the Franks threatened Cairo he despatched his most trusted general, Shirkuh the Lion, to defend the city, but also to obtain some purchase there. Shirkuh, they say, was blind in one eye, short and sturdy, given to howling rages, lowly born as was manifest in his features.

With the army went Shirkuh's nephew, Saladin, whose name means Protector of the Faith. He was born in Mesopotamia of Kurdish descent and called Yusef, meaning Joseph, for these people bestow a Hebrew name when a boy is circumcised. As a youth he lived in a monastery where he studied and could recite the genealogies of Arab tribes. He knew the lineage of celebrated horses. Later in life he pondered curiosities and marvels so that whoever talked with him would learn things impossible to learn elsewhere. What he liked most to discuss was holy war.

He first became conspicuous by exacting tribute from Damascus whores, selling them licenses. Some palmist or haruspex, a Syrian whose name is lost, prophesied that he would one day be lord of both Damascus and Cairo. He was no more than twenty when he accompanied Shirkuh the Lion to Egypt. He went reluctantly, objecting, complaining that his heart had been pierced by a dagger. Were I granted the whole kingdom of Egypt, said he, I would not go. All the same, when Nur al-Din ordered him to take the road with his uncle, he obeyed.

No sooner did this Turkish host bivouac outside Cairo than here came the vizier of Caliph al-Adid, whose name was Shawar. Almost daily Shawar arrived bearing gifts. Who knows what happened next? Many stories are told. It may be that Shirkuh disappeared, leaving instructions to kill the vizier.

deus lo volt!

He has gone for a walk beside the Nile, said the instruments of death when Shawar arrived with more gifts. Then all rushed to stab him and sliced off his head.

Or it may be that he was invited to accompany some emirs who wished to visit the tomb of a saint. Saladin rode beside him feigning cordiality, then all at once seized his collar to arrest him. Caliph al-Adid demanded it. Why should the caliph want his vizier murdered? Because weak sovereigns hate and dread inferiors.

Now as the vizier plunged shrieking into that horrible abyss reserved for unbelievers, what did Shirkuh the Lion do but present himself to the caliph and got himself named vizier. So he dressed in the silk brocade of office and went to occupy the home of Shawar but found it empty as the day it was built. He could not find a pillow to sit on. Everything was stolen the moment people learned that Shawar was dead.

Three months later Shirkuh the Lion, having gorged on rich food, discovered he could scarcely breathe. Almost at once he followed Shawar to the dolorous house of hell.

Now here came Saladin into the presence of Caliph al-Adid and was named vizier because the caliph did not imagine he could be dangerous, and gave him a title, Victorious King, with sumptuous badges of office. A flowing robe lined with scarlet silk. A white turban embroidered in gold. A jewel-crusted sword. A fine chestnut mare, the saddle and bridle adorned with pearls. Some believe that Saladin carried a stick while going to pay homage and shattered the caliph's skull with one blow. Next, he put al-Adid's children to the sword, making himself undisputed master of Egypt. Others say he got control by murdering the imperial guard, fifty thousand black men from Nubia. He set fire to the barracks at Fostat where they lived with their wives and children. So the black men thought about their families burning to death and were horrified and rushed to Fostat where the Turkish army waited. Perhaps. We can be sure only that men act out what seems natural to them. However it was, Saladin prevailed.

God has chosen me to govern Egypt, said he, although I did not expect it.

Fortune elevated a Kurdish youth, making him wealthy who was poor, making much from little, a sovereign of a peasant. He who gained entrance to court as patron of Damascus whores, who ruled over stews, who ate garlic and played at dice in low taverns now was lifted up to sit among princes, to exceed princes, to govern over Egypt. He would occupy the lands of Gesry, of Roasia, carry his strength to India Citerior. He would assault and subdue each neighbor, one through deceit, one by force, arrogating to himself the prerogative of kings, molding divers scepters into one. With all his nature would he seek to reduce and usurp that provenance bequeathed by God to Christians.

Those who knew him best called this infidel compassionate. They tell of the grief expressed when Taqi al-Din, his nephew, died. They say he wept, asking God's forgiveness, but asked courtiers not to mention how he wept and sent for rose water to bathe his eyes. They speak of a Frankish woman who came to him sobbing and clawing her breast because thieves had stolen her little daughter. Saladin despatched a retainer to the market and presently a horseman appeared with the infant riding on his shoulders. The woman flung herself to the ground at Saladin's feet and smeared her face with sand, muttering Frankish words. Then she with her child were escorted to the Frankish camp. They say he was a melancholy little sovereign with a neat beard, always pressing food upon visitors, invariably courteous, anxious that none should leave his presence disappointed. Assassins more than once tried to murder him.

Turks and Egyptians opposed each other like tarantulas in a jug while strife and discord roiled the Holy Land from Kerak to Nicomedia. Sedition spread. Armenians abhorred the proximity of Syrians, Syrians detested the bellies of Greeks, not one able to countenance the next. Prince Kakig of Armenia would take Caesarea and thrust the Greek bishop into a sack with a mad dog. Greeks would lure Prince Kakig into ambush and murder him. So this tapestry unrolled, adumbrating the evil of our time.

During the providential year 1170 two patriarchs would compete for spiritual supremacy. Athanasius, patriarch of Constantinople, arrived to minister Antioch. But this enraged the Frankish patriarch, Aimery, who suspended service and retreated to his castle at Qosair. Presently the earth began to tremble as if lashed by the King of Kings. Churches shuddered. Stones came loose in the cathedral of Saint Peter while Athanasius was celebrating mass, tumbled down to bury him. Now the prince of Antioch dressed in sackcloth, shaved his head and hurried to Qosair begging forgiveness of Aimery. But the Frankish patriarch sulked and would not emerge from his castle, not while Athanasius lived in Antioch. So they put the injured Greek on a litter and took him outside the walls to die.

Such was the lowering state of affairs. God's enemies found new inspiration while Christianity appeared deficient in prudent leadership. It seemed a new generation had grown up steeped in wickedness, caring neither for purpose nor result but squandered in disgraceful ways the legacy of their fathers. All could watch the kingdom deteriorating. King Amalric summoned his nobles to discuss how this might be remedied. They answered that Christianity had sunk to a wretched estate because of sin.

Appeal to the West, said they. Appeal to Europe for help in contesting the powers of darkness.

Amalric and his counselors then resolved that a delegation of high lords be sent to petition the kings of France, England, Sicily, and the Spains, to beseech the pontiff at Rome, to solicit influential dukes and counts. Also they resolved that Emperor Manuel Comnenus be approached since he was nearby and eighty times wealthier than the rest. This envoy, they thought, should be a paramount lord. And because none seemed so well suited as the king himself it came about in the year 1171 that he traveled without much enthusiasm to Constantinople. He was greeted better than he expected. Civil festivities, displays of dancing at the hippodrome, religious rites, an excursion on the Bosporus. The kingdom of Jerusalem puzzled Manuel

Comnenus, yet he felt sympathetic since all were brothers in Christ. He had caused the Church of the Nativity at Bethlehem to be redecorated with mosaic by the artist Ephraim and generously repaired the Holy Sepulcher. No chronicle preserves what accord was reached, what contract signed, but it is known that King Amalric departed full of admiration for his host.

Now it seemed to Amalric that he might once more invade and this time emasculate Egypt. To the south lived people who called themselves Coptic and embraced the teaching of our Lord centuries ago, albeit in strange fashion. Amalric therefore thought he might restore Christianity to its rightful heritage along the Nile. But while he debated this he succumbed to bloody flux and filled up with noxious water. In a little while he flew to the arms of Jesus all blackened and discolored.

Saladin ordered his brother to learn about these Christians in the south. It is related that he marched as far as Wadi Halfa where he killed the bishop, as many Copts as he found, and seven hundred pigs. When he returned to Cairo he told Saladin it was an odious place.

In the very year of Amalric's death the life of Nur al-Din had run its course. While riding with companions through the orchards of Damascus he remarked on the fragility of existence and nine days later plunged screaming toward the flames of hell. What afflicted him? Perhaps congestion of the heart. He lay helpless in a room of the citadel where he often prayed, unable to speak. Physicians decided to bleed him, whereupon he recovered his voice and said they should not because he was sixty years old. They took other measures, all in vain. First they entombed him at the citadel. Afterward, on account of his piety, they deposited the shell of him at some theological school near the osier market. No Christian wept.

Amalric left as heir to Jerusalem's throne a leprous boy of thirteen, Baldwin IV. Archbishop William, who became his tutor, wrote that the child possessed a quick and open mind, forgetting neither insults nor kindness. He resembled his father in gait and in the timbre of his voice. He played vigorously, as children do, but when pinched or scratched he felt nothing. William found the boy's right arm and hand to be insensitive, and upon consulting medical books he saw in the work of Hippocrates how this predicted grave illness. Fomentations, anointings, and poisonous drugs were administered to no avail. As the malady progressed, growing ever more obvious, the people of Jerusalem felt sick with grief. The child himself, understanding that he had not long to live, resolved to be a mighty advocate and rake the Saracen. That he should suspect malefactors all about is little to be wondered, knowing as he did how they awaited his death and plotted among themselves to seize the crown. It is said he trusted his constable, Humphrey of Toron. But the constable would fall, seething with arrows, near the forest of Paneas.

So this was Saladin's opponent, a crippled, stricken boy who already had used up more than half his life.

Beneath his standard Frankish Syria gained new heights. At Montgisard with eighty Templars and five hundred knights supported by foot soldiers the leper king defeated thirty thousand mameluks under Saladin. These Franks rose up baying like dogs, agile as wolves, to attack and pursue the astonished pagans. At such moments does not our Creator express His will?

During our year of edification 1180 the patriarch of Jerusalem went to sleep in God. Archbishop William, who spoke Arabic, Hebrew, Greek, and other tongues, was proposed to succeed him. Few Syrian Franks rivaled this archbishop for learning. He possessed intimate knowledge of Syrian manners and was agreeably rich, owning two thousand olive trees. Yet the leper king favored a cleric of no repute from Gévauden, by name Heraclius, who was scarce able to read, handsome and chattering with the brain of a sheep, making him sought by ladies of every rank. He is said to have been more dissolute than a grunting hog. Beyond doubt he touched the king's mother. Through her patronage he had become archdeacon of Jerusalem, archbishop of Caesarea, and now patriarch of Jerusalem. Thus do long past events anticipate our own.

Heraclius kept at his palace a woman named Pasque de Riveri, wife of an Italian draper from Nablus ten leagues distant. He would send for her to come and stay with him. She would stay a week, two, three, four, wandering the streets dressed in such finery and jewels winking on her bosom that a stranger might take her for a duchess. Up and down the realm she was called Madame la Patriarchesse. The draper did not mind because through Heraclius he was getting rich.

One day with the king and his barons assembled at the patriarchal palace in marched a lackey shouting that he brought good news if the patriarch would give him a reward. Very well, wretch, said Heraclius, thinking it would concern Jerusalem, tell us your news if it is good. Aye! brayed the servant. Lady Pasque has given birth to a daughter! No reward did the lackey get but Heraclius cursing him outright.

As for Archbishop William, Heraclius excommunicated him. This happened Maundy Thursday when Heraclius went to make the chrism on Mount Zion. Nor would he permit the archbishop to appeal. It is thought Archbishop William sought justice from the Vatican. Some think he traveled to Rome where he obtained audience with His Holiness Alexander. Others say he prepared to go but was poisoned, murdered by a leech in the employ of Heraclius. Whatever the truth, our Lord keeps count.

Some years previous King Baldwin had thoughtfully allied himself through marriage with the powerful house of Comnenus. So now in the year 1180 did Emperor Manuel think to arrange a high marriage for his son, who was ten years old. To King Philip Augustus went emissaries charged to learn if the king's little sister, Agnes, might be available. It is said that Philip Augustus, marveling over the dignity and sumptuous garments of Emperor Manuel's envoys, did not take long to decide. Thus the Frankish child, aged nine, journeyed to Constantinople where she was greeted with honor. Emperor Manuel wished his niece Theodora to attend the wedding so he charged a kinsman, Andronicus Comnenus, to go and fetch her from Jerusalem. Andronicus accepted willingly. By most accounts he was charming, eloquent, and less upright than a serpent. Queen Theodora was now more beautiful than when she had been King Baldwin's child bride. As related in the narrative of Robert de Clari, when they got well out to sea Andronicus lay with her by force. In fact he did little else but love the queen, who was his cousin. Therefore, since he dared not return to Constantinople he bore her away to Konia where they lived among pagans.

In that same year, albeit soothsayers prophesied that he would enjoy fourteen more years of earthly existence, Emperor Manuel Comnenus ascended to heaven.

Andronicus now considered restoring himself to grace. From exile he sent word to the child emperor, Alexius II, that everything whispered about him was a lie. I beseech you in God's name, said he, to put aside your wrath. So he insinuated himself, deceived the boy and got back to Constantinople. There he flattered young Alexius and gained his confidence, subtly, as serpents move at their own discretion. When the hour seemed ripe he had the boy stuffed into a sack and carried out to sea and hurled overboard. Next he summoned all those related to the house of Comnenus and they arrived at the palace not knowing what had occurred. He imprisoned them, scooped out their eyes, sliced off their lips, and crowned himself emperor. Next he raped as many beautiful women as he could find, nuns in abbeys, wives and daughters of lords, taking by force a huge number of women, so everyone longed for his death. Next he claimed the child empress for his wife. She was now twelve years old, Andronicus five times her age. He asked if any citizen of Constantinople bore him ill and so learned of three young men descended from Constantine Angelus, which is to say the noble lineage of Angeli. He therefore despatched his steward Langosse to catch them but Langosse caught only one, whom he blinded. Another escaped to Syria. Isaac, the last, fled to the land of Vlachia.

Isaac crept back into Constantinople because he was very poor and took refuge in the house of his widowed mother. It was about

155

this time that soothsayers told Andronicus he had but five days to live, which terrified him. He asked who would become emperor after his death and they said the name of the man was Isaac. Then his steward Langosse found out that Isaac was hiding in Constantinople. If you kill him, said Langosse, you have nothing to fear.

Go at once, said Andronicus.

Langosse with a company of sergeants went to kill this last descendant of the Angeli. When he rapped on the door of the house where Isaac was concealed the widow pretended to be alone.

God's mercy! cried she. No one hides within!

Langosse told her to make Isaac come out or she herself would be seized.

At this she became alarmed and went to speak with her son. Ah, fair lord, the emperor's steward waits. You are a dead man.

Isaac went outside. Langosse struck him across the face with a whip and vowed he would hang. So then Isaac drew a sword from beneath his cloak and cleaved the steward's head down the middle so his teeth and brains flew out and the sergeants ran away in all directions. Isaac mounted the steward's horse and rode toward the church of Sancta Sophia shouting that he had slain a devil. When he got to the church he rushed inside to embrace the cross. Now here came citizens to throng the streets, exclaiming that Isaac was very brave and should be made emperor. They crowded into the church to admire him and sent for the patriarch to crown him. But the patriarch replied that he would not do as they wished. You act badly, said he. Besides, I dare not since Andronicus would have me torn apart. The people answered that if he did not do as they wished they would cut off his head. So the patriarch went to Sancta Sophia where he found Isaac gripping a bloody sword and his cheap garments splashed with blood. Then the patriarch vested himself as required for the ceremony and, though he did not want to, made Isaac the emperor.

Andronicus being told about this could not believe it. He ran through a passage to the church and climbed up to the vault where he could look down. At the altar stood Isaac. Andronicus asked his

followers to give him a bow. He fitted an arrow and drew the bow,
but the string snapped, snapped by the hand of our watchful Lord.

Andronicus fled to the palace, escaped through a postern with
some of his followers and boarded a galley, thinking he would find
safety at Trebizond. But who can escape from Almighty God? A
storm arose, driving the galley backward. He sent men to explore the
coast and they returned full of dismay. My lord, they said, we are
near Constantinople. They led him to a hostel where they told him
to hide among the wine casks. But the keeper looked suspiciously at
these people seeking refuge from the storm and bade his wife go
among the wine casks. There she found Andronicus wearing imperial robes. Then the keeper sent to a noble whose wife Andronicus
had raped. The noble gathered his men, came to the hostel and
seized the emperor. Next morning they took him to the palace where
Isaac sat enthroned.

Andronicus, said he, why didst thou betray thy lord, the emperor
Manuel? Why didst thou murder his son? Why didst thou ravish the
queen of Jerusalem? Why dost thou delight in evil?

Against such charges Andronicus replied that he would not deign
to speak.

Isaac gave him to the people, saying they should do as they
wished since he could not administer justice that would satisfy them.
The citizens were glad of this. Some wanted to burn him. Some
wanted to boil him in a cauldron. Others wanted to drag him
through the streets until he fell apart. Then a man said he had a
camel that was the most loathsome beast on earth and they should
strip Andronicus naked, bind him to this camel with his face in the
creature's ass, and lead him from one end of the city to the other.
All the citizens thought this was good. So they tore away his clothes
and shaved his head, leaving a cross of hair on top. They crowned
him with a chaplet of garlic stalks. They plucked out one of his eyes
but not the other because he should see what was done to him.
They strapped him to the camel and went parading about the city.
Women emptied buckets of urine and shit on his head. Some whose

157

daughters he had ravished would scream and pull his beard. Some rushed up to stab him or cut off strips of his flesh to eat, meanwhile telling him what they had suffered, eating his flesh to save their souls by avenging the wickedness he had done. And by the time this camel walked across Constantinople not much remained of Andronicus except gristle and bone. What little was left they thrust into a dung-heap near the forum of Theodosius. And here amongst stinking offal they found a porphyry chalice with an inscription declaring that at this place an ignoble emperor would be entombed.

None could forget how Isaac miraculously escaped death when the bowstring snapped, so this was pictured above the portals of numerous churches. Our Lord stands beside Isaac while Blessed Mary places a crown on his head, meanwhile an angel cuts the bowstring. On such occasions we note how providence invests good men with authority.

Chronicles relate that Isaac began to think about his brother Alexius who had fled to Syria and wondered if he might be alive. He learned that Alexius was held captive by Muslims who would not let him go except for a huge price. Out of love for his brother Isaac sent all the gold they demanded, and when Alexius returned to Constantinople the brothers joyously embraced. However, some at court persuaded Alexius that he was more fit to rule, flattered his ambition and pride until he agreed with all they said. Moreover, his wife told him she ought to be empress and would not share his bed unless he obtained the crown. Isaac scoffed at reports of conspiracy, so much did he love and trust his brother. According to Nicetas Choniates, Isaac consulted a diviner named Basilakios who poked out the eyes of a portrait and tried to knock off the painted cap. Still, Isaac would not believe.

From exemplary tales we learn how adversity like a dog licks the hand of a trusting master. Thus, when Isaac decided to go hunting he invited his brother. Alexius excused himself, pretending to be ill. And in the forest Isaac was attacked. Understanding at last, he got across the river Maritza and fled along the road but conspirators overtook him. They carried him off to a monastery, grabbed his hair

and gouged out his eyes. The wicked brother now thrust Isaac Angelus into prison and told people that henceforth he, himself, would
rule. Such are the Greeks. Do they not kick at the sweet yoke of
Christ? Have more knavish Christians walked the earth since time
began? What is the root of such evil? Yet we acknowledge the limita-
tion of perplexity and complaint. Thou who art Creator of all creation, we would not question Thee nor doubt Thy intent.

We know that just as a man engulfed by raging
water will be drawn to the bottom, so may he be
sucked into the abyss of perversion. Thus, during
the reign of Emperor Manuel a certain Reynauld de
Chatillon arrived in the Holy Land. He was by all accounts a penniless rogue born to some Angevin family of slight estate. With no
prospect in France he resolved to settle oversea, mayhap to enter the
service of a puissant lord, by this or that to fill up his pocket. Simple
by nature, brave enough, a feral dog, here came Reynauld de Chatillon. Turks called him in their barbaric language Brins Arnat.

What did this wretch do but quickly make himself a lord through
marriage to the widowed princess of Antioch, Constance. They say
she had been espoused at nine to a prince four times older and was
little more than twenty when he departed to join the celestial host.
Now, to the bewilderment of all, she took delight in rejecting suit-
ors. Ralph de Merle. Walter de Saint-Omer. Yves de Nesle who was
count of Soissons. A Byzantine noble whose veins leaked gold. None
pleased Lady Constance. Why did she favor Reynauld de Chatillon?
Chronicles do not explain save to call him handsome, the lady dazzled. This match pleased few in Antioch. All thought she demeaned
herself. Emperor Manuel heard the news with little grace. In those
days he was busy chasing Seljuk Turks.

The island of Cyprus thirty leagues offshore seemed to Reynauld

159

worth pillaging. Therefore he approached the patriarch of Antioch for money to equip a fleet, but the patriarch looked at him with disgust. Reynauld cast him in prison. Still the patriarch would not unlock his treasury. Reynauld ordered him flogged and chained naked on the roof of the citadel, his bald head smeared with honey and no relief from a blistering sun but flies to suck his wounds. One day proved enough. The terrified patriarch agreed to pay for ships and troops. Thus furnished, Reynauld invaded Cyprus, not caring that it was subject to Byzantium. Fields burnt, villages looted, nuns ravished. Old men and women, being useless, forthwith got their throats cut. Greek monks and priests lost their private members and got their noses slit, after which Reynauld sent these mutilated clerics to Emperor Manuel. Truly does Abbot Guibert observe that one may in good conscience speak ill of a man whose wickedness transcends malediction.

Now being well supplied with captives, gold, jeweled icons stolen from churches, precious fabrics, animals, whatever he fancied, Reynauld de Chatillon embarked for the Holy Land. Among his captives was the governor, John Comnenus, nephew of Emperor Manuel.

Soon enough Manuel Comnenus marched toward Antioch. Reynauld hastily took himself to the emperor's camp near Mamistra to ask forgiveness. They say the bishop of Lattakieh prevailed upon Manuel, allowing Reynauld to come before him as a suppliant in a wool tunic, feet bare, a rope around his neck, sword in hand. Holding the sword by its point, he offered the hilt. When it was accepted he flung himself down in the dust, awaiting his fate. He wept so abjectly that all who were present felt embarrassed. Emperor Manuel for a long time did not bid him get to this feet, but instead prolonged the degradation. At length he did raise up this knave, kissed his lips and forgave him. Many expressed disbelief at such gentle punishment.

Not long afterward the Saracens caught him stealing horses. Thus he entered Aleppo in grand style, bound to the hump of a camel. There he marked time in chains for sixteen years. Neither the king of Jerusalem nor Manuel Comnenus nor the citizens of Antioch

seemed anxious to buy his freedom. During those years the lady
Constance died.

No more was Reynauld out of prison than he contrived to wed
Lady Étienne de Kerak, by which he acquired the vast and remote seigneury of Moab. He had long dreamt of capturing Muslim traffic on
the Red Sea. Further, he wished to assault Mecca. So now with trees
cut from the forests of Moab he transported five galleys, plank by
plank, on the backs of camels, to the gulf of Akaba. Once they were
assembled he went about doing what he liked best. Down the coast
of Africa he went to sack Aidib, seized merchantmen from India,
destroyed a pilgrim vessel bound for Jedda. Saladin's brother, Malik, sent the admiral Husam al-Din Lulu in pursuit. Reynauld's fleet
was caught near al-Hawra. Certain of these Franks were beheaded in
Cairo, others ceremoniously executed in Mecca. Reynauld himself escaped capture and traveled by land to the fortress of Kerak. It is reported that Saladin vowed to kill Brins Arnat with his own hands.

During the month of November a host of Turks surrounded
Kerak. By chance they arrived when lords and ladies had gathered to
celebrate a royal wedding. Humphrey, son of Lady Étienne, would
marry Isabella, sister of the leper king. So there was dancing and
feasting high in the keep when Saladin's army appeared beneath the
walls. Lady Étienne sent a message to let him know her son was mar-
rying. And she reminded Saladin that when she herself was a child he
had carried her in his arms. After such a long time who could avouch
the truth of this? According to a Syrian Frank attached to the house
of Ibelin, the Turk was for a while held captive at Kerak. However
it may be, Saladin wished to know where the young couple would
spend their wedding night and he forbade attacks against this turret.
So the Lady Étienne sent out to him delicacies from the wedding
feast, such as mutton, bread, wine, and roast beef. Meanwhile fighting continued along the ramparts, merriment within the castle.

By repute Humphrey was gentle and attractive, some said girlish,
who got from his ancestors a talent for scholarship but little courage.
He learnt Arabic with ease, interpreting if Turks and Franks needed

161

to converse. Lord Conrad de Montferrat years after this marriage resolved to have Isabella for himself and Humphrey did not know what to do. They say that a champion of Lord Conrad, one Guy de Senlis, threw down a glove at Humphrey's feet and the miserable husband did not dare pick it up. Much is made of Helen surreptitiously abducted in ancient days, yet some thought it more infamous that Lord Conrad took Isabella with her cowardly husband present.

Now as bombardment continued those who were defending Kerak lost hope. However, Saladin withdrew when the count of Tripoli approached. With this Frankish host was the dying leper king, mute, nearly blind, with neither hands nor feet, carried on a palanquin to celebrate the wedding of his sister. The curtains of his litter were drawn when they brought him through the gate, his flesh poisoning the air. Those nearby held their breath.

From throughout the realm high barons arrived to await King Baldwin's death. In our year of grace 1185 he went to sleep with God. They buried him between the Holy Sepulcher and Mount Calvary where kings of Jerusalem have been laid to rest since the days of Godfrey de Bouillon. Many wondered at the source of his leprosy. Some ascribed it to the incestuous marriage of his parents because his mother Agnes, a lascivious woman panting for men and gold, was third cousin to his father Amalric. Who shall decide? Are we not girdled by falsities of superstition?

Ibn Jubayr, a Spanish Muslim who traveled in those days from Andalusia to Damascus, observed with grave surprise how Arab caravans would pass unmolested through Frankish land, even as Christian merchants did business in Syria. Perhaps wiser than sovereigns, they went about buying and selling while armies surged to and fro. Unluckily, here was Reynauld de Chatillon. When he learned of a caravan passing not far away he rode out from Kerak and took it, an hour Christendom would lament because it carried the sister of Saladin. Woe to the Holy Land. Some assert that Reynauld de Chatillon by himself roused greater fury in the Saracen heart than one hundred years of war.

Now with the leper king in Paradise the crown of Jerusalem went to a foolish knight, Guy de Lusignan. Histories from those days account him skillful in the use of weapons, well versed at flattery, excelling at courtly gestures. Because of such attributes he caught the eye of Baldwin's elder sister, Sibylla. She loved Guy de Lusignan and slept with him. How the leper king heard of this is not recorded, only that he knew. He had Guy de Lusignan tortured and would have stoned him to death but for certain Templars who counseled moderation. Then he granted life to Sibylla and to this knight she loved. And because no son or daughter would succeed him on the throne, he permitted them to marry. This ill suited noble and citizen alike. They despised Guy de Lusignan as much for the vacancy of his soul as the impoverishment of his mind. Therefore in the city of Nablus barons of high lineage gathered to consult, worried that a simpleton might be their governor. Next came word from Sibylla, commanding them to be present at her coronation. They refused. And since Nablus was but ten leagues distant, the gates of Jerusalem were shut. Patriarch Heraclius and the grand master of Templars did not like the sound of things. Then the obstinate lords instructed a sergeant who was born in Jerusalem to disguise himself as a monk and go there to spy on the ceremony.

Imperial regalia were kept safe in a coffer with three locks. The keys were held one each by the patriarch, by the master of Templars, and by the master of the Hospital, Roger. And when Roger was asked to produce his key, he would not. The patriarch and the Templar went to see him. But when he heard of their approach he concealed himself. Not until noon could he be found, clutching the key because he was afraid somebody might give it to the patriarch. They stood outside the Hospital wheedling and threatening until Roger flung his key out a window, but said he would not attend the coronation nor would any Hospitaler. So the master of the Temple and Heraclius proceeded to the treasury where they unlocked the coffer and got two crowns.

And when it came time for the ceremony Heraclius placed one crown on the altar. With the second he crowned Sibylla, Queen of Jerusalem. Lady, said he, because you are a woman it is not fit that you reign alone. Take this crown that you see beside you. Give it to such a man as you would have govern the kingdom.

Sibylla beckoned forth her lover, Guy de Lusignan. Sire, the queen addressed him, I would have you wear this. I do not know where better to bestow it.

Guy de Lusignan knelt and she placed the crown on his head. Then the patriarch anointed him. This occurred on a Friday in the merciful year 1186. Never had a king of Jerusalem been crowned on Friday, nor with gates to the Holy City shut.

Thus it happened that a piddling courtier with the mind of a goat was expected to contain Saladin.

King Guy ordered Reynauld de Chatillon to release the Muslim lord's sister. Reynauld answered that by virtue of marriage to Lady Étienne he was master of Kerak and had made no pact with Saracens. By this insubordinate response, by refusing to acknowledge the sovereignty of Guy de Lusignan, it may be that he hastened the fall of the Holy City.

No one knew what Saladin might do next. King Guy despatched messengers to Count Raymond at Tiberias, since Raymond was highly experienced at warfare. While these messengers were en route it chanced that Saladin's son, al-Afdal, requested leave for seven thousand mameluks to ride through the fief of Tiberias. Why they wished to enter Christian territory is much debated. Some think they were bent on pillage, others think they wished to vaunt their strength. Raymond gave permission, stipulating that they must not appear before dawn and must depart before sunset. And when these mameluks rode by Tiberias they found the gates closed, indicating that Count Raymond would respect the truce. However, news reached the castle of La Fève and ninety Templars with various other knights resolved to attack these enemies of Christ. But the Templars hesitated when they saw this multitude of Saracens watering their horses in a valley behind Nazareth. Jakeline de Maille, who was Marshal, advised retreat.

Gérard de Ridfort, who was Grand Master, challenged him. Do you so love your blond head that you wish to keep it?

Marshal Jakeline replied with disgust. I shall die a knight, but you will flee.

What the Templar prophesied came true. Gérard de Ridfort escaped.

Marshal Jakeline, seeing all around him dead or dying, faced the enemy by himself. The mameluks, admiring such valor, were filled with compassion. They shouted earnestly at him to give up his sword so they might spare his life. He would not. According to the narrative of Geoffrey de Vinsauf he was with difficulty slain, falling beneath a load of javelins, stones, and lances. Then his soul fled in triumph bearing the palm of martyrdom.

These Templars gained eternal bliss on a field that had been planted with corn and reaped, hence it was thick with stubble, and so many Saracens rushed to fight that the field was trampled to dust. Once the battle ended here they were sprinkling dust on the corpse of Marshal Jakeline, afterward sprinkling dust on their own heads to honor his courage. It is said that one chopped off the private member to keep, as though a poor scrap of flesh might generate a son of equal fortitude. And because Marshal Jakeline rode a white horse and dressed in white armor, Turks with knowledge of Saint Gregory boasted they had vanquished the greatest knight in Christendom.

Late that afternoon al-Afdal again rode past Tiberias, his knights exhibiting on lances the heads of Templars they had killed. They crossed the river Jordan before sunset, as agreed. But who would counsel peace after God's enemies rode through Christian land flaunting the severed heads of Christian soldiers? Still, has not a sword two edges? Did not these Templars vex the Turk? How does our Creator adjudicate?

Now it became apparent that a decisive battle must take place, as the Bible foretells conflict on the plains of Armageddon. And the infidel lord, as if he were Antichrist spreading impenetrable darkness, called upon the armies of Damascus, Aleppo, Egypt, and Syria. Various in name or sect or birthplace, they assembled swiftly to annihilate the living army of God. Bedouin. Arab. Parthian. Cordian. Babylonian. Mede. According to the chronicle of Abu Shama, camel skin tents surrounded Lake Tiberias like the ocean. Muslim banners fluttered in the sunlight. Here or there stood pavilions of bright fabric embellished with verses from the Koran.

Soldiers of Christ assembled near Saphori close by Nazareth. Lords of the great fiefs arrived, leaving only a few knights and sergeants to defend each castle. Mercenaries hastily enrolled. Pilgrims. Mariners. Hospitalers and Templars gathered. Patriarch Heraclius, when invited to join the host, replied that he did not feel well enough to go but would send the True Cross. Some muttered aloud what others thought, that Heraclius preferred battle in the fragrant arms of Madame la Patriarchesse.

Geoffrey de Vinsauf relates how the king's chamberlain had a vision. He dreamt of an eagle flying past the army, in its talons seven missiles and a ballista, and the prophetic bird cried with a loud voice.

Woe unto thee, Jerusalem!

What is this if not fulfillment of Scripture? It is written how the Lord hath bent His bow and in it prepared the vessels of death. What are these missiles but seven sins by which the Franks should perish?

Saladin besieged Tiberias and stormed the lower town, which could not hold. Then the wife of Count Raymond, Eschiva, fled to the citadel. It is what Saladin expected and what he wished, believing in his heart that Count Raymond would try impetuously to save his wife. Indeed, when news reached the army that Countess Eschiva with her attendants had locked themselves in the citadel a huge cry went up. Templars, Hospitalers, sergeants, pilgrims, all demanded that they march upon Tiberias. Accordingly they proceeded to Saphori and bivouacked for the night. Although they found good water it is said the pack animals refused to drink and behaved like grieving men. Now a dispute arose between Count Raymond and King Guy.

Sire, I would give counsel, said Raymond, but you will not heed me.

Speak on, the king replied.

Let the citadel be taken. Tiberias is mine. The lady of Tiberias is my countess. Yet I would rather see Tiberias razed to the ground, my wife enslaved, my soldiers killed, than to know the Holy Land was lost forever. If we march against Tiberias we must be defeated. Here is why. Between us and Tiberias there is but one spring of water, at Cresson, which is by no means enough. So what will become of men and horses? They will go mad with thirst. And next day the Saracens will take us. For in the past I have seen many a Saracen army, but none so numerous or powerful as that which Saladin commands this day.

You would frighten us, said Reynauld de Chatillon. You would frighten us because you prefer their company to ours. For myself, I say the fire is not dismayed by the amount of wood to burn.

I am one of you, Count Raymond answered. I will fight at your side, but Saladin will take us.

Gérard de Ridfort, Grand Master of the Temple, spoke angrily. I smell a wolf, said he. For a long time Gérard de Ridfort had nourished himself on hatred of Count Raymond. When he arrived in the Holy Land he at first took service with Raymond, who promised him some heiress for a wife as God so determined. Presently the lord of Botron expired, leaving all to his daughter Lucia, and Gérard put forth his claim. But here came a merchant from Pisa, by name Plivano, who admired the shape of Lucia and offered Count Raymond her weight in gold and made her step on a balance, heaping gold on the opposite scale until her value was calculated at ten thousand bezants. As this seemed good to Count Raymond, he granted her to

167

Plivano. So then Gérard de Ridfort left his service to become a Templar but did not forgive the insult. Now at this extremity, encircled by a Muslim host, Gérard crept into the royal tent near midnight to admonish King Guy.

Count Raymond has made a pact with our enemies, said he.

The king, rotted by misgiving, did not know what to do since he would believe whoever spoke to him last. And when a call to arms sounded in the depth of night the Frankish barons asked one another the purpose. Wondering, dumbfounded, looking at each other in surprise, they hurried to the royal tent. King Guy would not explain why he sounded the call, saying only that they must obey.

At dawn the Frankish host marched away from Saphori, hearts fixed upon Tiberias. The bishop of Acre, escorted by priests and monks, held upright the Holy Cross sheathed in gold encrusted with jewels so that all might draw comfort and strength from the presence of our Lord. Since the day King Baldwin first carried the cross to victory at Ramlah it had accompanied the knighthood of Christ.

Anon, they overtook some hag riding a donkey and when they asked where she was going she would not answer. When they threatened her she admitted to being the slave of a Syrian in Nazareth and was going to ask Saladin for a reward, considering the service she had rendered. They tortured her to learn what service this was. Then she admitted to being a sorceress who had cast a spell on the host, having for two nights encircled the army and cast her spells by the devil. Had they not marched away she would have bound them so close that Saladin would take every one. A fire was kindled of thorns and couch grass, the hag thrown in. She hopped out. They tossed her into the flame again. Nimbly she hopped out. Then a sergeant with a Danish axe struck her such a blow on the skull as to cleave her almost in half. A third time she was tossed in the fire. It is related that when Saladin heard of this he felt dismayed because he would have ransomed her.

And learning how the army moved upon Tiberias he rejoiced, for the day would be hot. He was heard to say that Allah delivered these

Christians into his hands and scarcely controlled his glee, knowing they would not find water. Therefore he waited in comfort along the pleasant shore of Lake Tiberias.

By midafternoon the Franks had climbed to a rock-strewn plateau between two summits that are called the Horns of Hattin. They could see the ground fall steeply away toward the village and the lake and a luxuriant plain with fruit orchards. Word arrived from Templars behind the army that they were troubled by Muslim cavalry and could ride no further. Certain lords urged King Guy to press ahead to reach the lake, but he would not. He gave orders to halt. When Count Raymond learned of this he rode back from the vanguard crying aloud that the battle was over.

Ah, Lord God! he cried. We are betrayed unto death! The kingdom of Jerusalem is finished!

King Guy then asked Count Raymond what they should do. To which Count Raymond answered that had his advice been taken they would not be where they found themselves. As it is now too late, he said, I have no better advice than for the king to pitch his tent on the summit of this hill. With God's help the enemy may think we cannot be dislodged.

Yet there could be no worse place to camp or fight, exposed like fowl, the earth studded with volcanic rock that made it difficult for men and horses to move. So all night these Franks peered toward the lake by starlight and saw death in every shadow.

During the night they were surrounded. Saladin ordered his mameluks to collect brushwood and stubble and make a palisade. At dawn he set this afire to blind and choke the Christians and punish them with heat. Soon enough the Franks heard Saracen bows creak, arrows pierced the smoke. Camel caravans brought jars of water from Lake Tiberias and God's servants watched this water emptied on the ground. What did Saladin do but give them the wine of remorse to drink. These errant knights were plagued by havoc of their own making.

Until high tierce the Jerusalem army waited, encircled by a pagan

169

horde so dense that not a cat could escape. Five or six knights followed by sergeants rode down to consult Saladin. These were Laodicius from Tiberias, Ralph Buceus, Baldwin of Fortuna, and I do not know the others. Why, they asked, did Saladin choose not to fight? The Franks are all but dead, said they. And by certain accounts these knights renounced our Lord to save themselves. As for the sergeants whose mouths hung open, tongues protruding, miserably they bared their necks. King Guy observing this ordered Count Raymond to attack.

Therefore, calling upon Jesus and Our Lady, Count Raymond did as the king commanded. And the experienced Saracens feigned retreat, opening a path, only to close swiftly around him. Many of his knights, burdened with axes and maces, bodies swollen inside coats of mail, gave up hope and surrendered. Ten or twelve fought through the Saracen ranks, among them Reynald of Sidon, Balian d'Ibelin, and Count Raymond himself. It is said they charged so impetuously that nothing could withstand them. Or it may be they deserted the field, trampled their comrades, fled in panic to Tripoli. The truth is not known.

King Guy retreated to the summit where his men began digging trenches, which caused Saladin's son to exclaim that the Franks were destroyed. Chronicles relate that Saladin plucked his beard and frowned. Be quiet, he said, they are not defeated until the king's banner falls. But even as he spoke these words the Jerusalem banner fell. He dismounted, prostrated himself and wept for joy, praising Allah while his soldiers tore apart King Guy's red silk tent. Later in gratitude for this victory he constructed a mosque on the summit.

From that great army of Jerusalem less than two hundred got out. Count Raymond died some months after the battle, wracked by fearful dreams. Frank and Muslim alike regarded him as the true master of Christian Syria, scorning King Guy, and thought him destined for the crown of Jerusalem. He ascended to Paradise thinking infidels and Christians might equably share the land. He had learnt Arabic, studied the pagan faith. His skin was dark and his nose like that of a vulture. Excepting his great size he could pass for a Syrian emir. They say his body showed evidence of circumcision, undeniable proof that he rejected our Lord. If so, what impels honorable men to recant? How does apostasy creep into creation?

As to misbelievers, they fought with the strength of pilgrims. Mangouras, who some thought related to Saladin, charged by himself against the army of God. Franks promptly cut him down and displayed his head. Turks argue that Mangouras through intemperate courage succeeded to the abode of the merciful, which is fallacious and wrong. They are evil who hold evil opinions and will become godly only as they perceive the truth. We who have been led toward the light do not fear to give up earthly things since we are instructed by Jesus Christ and the examples of numerous saints.

This battle took place in the providential year 1187 on the fourth day of July, which was the feast of Saint Martin Calidus. How bitter that on this very summit our Lord preached his most famous sermon of peace.

Imad al-Din served as secretary to Saladin as well as to Nur al-Din and compiled a narrative of those days which delights at butchery. He went among the Christian dead noting Trinitarians cut in two, bowels drained, the stench more intoxicating than perfume, bellies slashed, skin flayed, limbs scattered, genitals sundered, ribs splintered, faces pressed to earth, spirits flown, no longer animate with desire, stones among stones. And how should this Turk respond to Christian death but quote from the villainous book they worship. It is said, too, that pagan alchemists crept around the field plucking out the eyeballs of knights or sergeants since they believe the eyes of young men hold nutritious elixir. And such people believe our Lord suffered crucifixion in appearance only, claiming that God so loved the son of Mary that He would not countenance torture, and any who assert that He emerged from a woman's private parts must be mad, having neither faith nor intellect. Yet we firmly accept these points and articles that are witnessed and taught us by saints of both Testaments, from the mouth of our Lord. Let us not forget the debt we owe to a spring so bounteous.

On the slope of Mount Hattin they captured that vivified wood of our salvation upon which the Redeemer hung, bled, and gave up the ghost, down which His lifeblood flowed, the emblem that devils fear and angels adore. With the Cross fell those two valiant bishops of Acre and Saint George, one slain, the other seized. Impious hands now would soil the sacred Cross. How terrible, therefore, must have been God's wrath, how numerous the iniquities of His children, that He should account them less worthy than Saracens to embrace it. I, Jean, do not know where the pagans bore this hallowed emblem. Some say they buried it in Damascus at the entrance to their mosque. Thus, all who crossed the threshold should trample it.

Among those seized with the Frankish king were his brothers Geoffrey and Amalric, Gérard de Ridfort, Reynauld de Chatillon, and the aged marquis William de Montferrat. Muslims boast there were so many captives that one could scarce believe any were slain, yet so many lay on the slope that one could scarce believe any were captured. Imad al-Din relates that when Franks saw the True Cross was taken they quit fighting, for to venerate the Cross was their obligation, to which their mouths sang hymns of worship, before which they touched their heads to the earth and talked of nothing else if it was displayed. But when it was lost they sank into despair. Turks claimed they could not find ropes enough. They claim that fifty naked Franks submitted to a single rope like domestic animals to be led away unprotesting. How many once proud men were seized?

They allege that Saladin now encamped on the plain of Tiberias like the moon in splendor or a lion on the desert. Throughout the army it was cried that captive nobles should be brought to his pavilion. Yet he would receive only two. King Guy de Lusignan. Reynauld de Chatillon. Arab chronicles say this pusillanimous king of Jerusalem seemed about to faint, head dangling, unable to speak, intoxicated with terror. I have heard he claimed descent from the water fairy Mélusine, for such does the house of Lusignan believe. Whatever the truth, Saladin addressed him gently, trying to assuage his fright, and offered him a goblet of rose water cooled with snow from Mount Hebron. So the king, having eased his thirst, handed the goblet to Reynauld whom Saladin hated beyond any man on earth, who took his sister. Reynauld drank. Then to the interpreter Saladin addressed these words.

Tell the king that he, not I, has given the man a drink.

He spoke in this manner because infidels have a custom that prohibits taking the life of a captive who has eaten or drunk at the table of his captor and Saladin had vowed to Allah that with his own hands he would kill Brins Arnat. Now he fell upon Reynauld with a scimitar and slashed off an arm which plopped in the dust. Then as King Guy watched in horror the stump of Reynauld was dragged away. Others have it that Saladin lopped off Reynauld's head and the corpse tumbled at King Guy's feet while Saladin tried to comfort him, saying that kings do not kill one another. Or it could be that Reynauld disdained the goblet, saying arrogantly that as it pleased God he never would eat or drink anything of a misbeliever. At this Saladin called him a pig, drove a sword through his body and dipped his fingers in the blood to prove he had consummated the vow to Allah. However it came about, Reynauld's head embellished the point of a lance and was dragged behind a camel through Damascus.

As to knights of the Temple and Hospital, numbering almost three hundred, Saladin ordered them held apart. Some now belonged to Muslim warriors but he purchased them all, giving fifty gold pieces for each. When they were his property he assembled them outside the walls of Tiberias and spoke.

You see that I have taken the Holy Cross and have taken your king. I have killed or captured most of the high lords. I have retaken lands that in earlier days Christians took from us. I have pitied you because you are brave knights who may live to profit greatly. Here is

173

what I will do if you accede to my wish. I will provide you with wives, with fiefs, with gold. I will give you lands that I have conquered. So much will I do for you.

They asked what they must do in return. He said they must supplant their faith in Jesus Christ with the faith of Mahomet. To this the knights responded that they would not ever forsake Jesus, saying that as He suffered for them on the Cross, so would they suffer death for Him, knowing the faith of Mahomet to be false.

When these words had been interpreted for Saladin he gave orders to behead the knights.

Imad al-Din records how there were present numerous ascetics, Sufis, austere men versed at law, savants, all requesting permission to slay a Frank. Those granted the honor rolled back their sleeves and approached with sword in hand, anxious to demonstrate their skill. Some cut or slashed proficiently and were congratulated. Others who sought clumsily to behead a knight heard themselves jeered. Some were excused by reason of blunt swords. Saladin watched indulgently, smiling, for to his mind the butchery pleased Allah. By causing Christian heads to fall he thought he earned great merit. He thought to glorify pagan misbelief by assaulting the Trinity. So was it prophesied. A time shall come when those that kill you may think they render God a service.

How eagerly these knights flocked to the executioner, joyously offering their necks to the blade. What ardor and faith they exhibited. Among them a Templar called Nicholas who so inspired others to martyrdom that, by virtue of their wish to be first, he could hardly obtain the stroke he wanted. And for three nights afterward celestial glory shone on these unburied corpses. All know how the serpent to protect its head presents its body to the assailant, which throws much light upon our Lord's command that we should be wise as serpents. For the sake of the head, which is Christ, we should freely offer the body to those who persecute us, lest by vaunting this mortal scrap of flesh we deny our God.

Caracois was a very ancient Turk who had seen Godfrey de Bouillon during the conquest. Now observing these Templars beheaded, he addressed Saladin. Do you think, Sire, what you have done will put an end to bloodshed? You should know that Templars are born with their beards and their deaths will be avenged by Christians who demand recompense.

Saladin indulged just one, Gérard de Ridfort, Grand Master of the Temple, whom he sent shackled to Damascus. It has been said that Gérard bought his life by spitting on the Cross, which is not so. As Grand Master he was useful because of various castles held by Templars. He would in time purchase his liberty by ordering the fortress at Gaza to surrender.

Muhammed al-Kadersi relates how carts piled high with Christian heads rolled through Damascus, so numerous they might have been watermelons. A glorious and beneficent year, writes Imad al-Din, a blessed age anticipated by previous ages. How many knights and common sergeants marched off to servitude is beyond computation. At auction some fetched a paltry three dinars. One Frank was sold for a pair of shoes. And to delight the citizens an image of our Lord was carried about the streets upside down that they might think the glory of Saladin suffused the earth by drowning Christ's army in waves of blood. Yet there is a chain of necessity over which Almighty God presides, which banishes evil from His commonwealth.

Ibn al-Athir speaks of a Frankish woman captive in Aleppo who one day accompanied her master to visit a friend. When the door opened there stood another captive Frankish woman. They embraced and began to weep and flung themselves on the ground to talk because they were sisters. Al-Athir himself owned a young Frankish girl with an infant son who had been seized at Joppa. One day the child fell out of her arms and the mother wept. Al-Athir sought to comfort her by showing that her baby was not hurt. It is not for him, she said. My six brothers are dead and I do not know the fate of my sisters and my husband. Thus, grief and fear blazed across Syria for a multitude of Frankish sins.

Saladin returned to attack Tiberias. Before long he took the citadel. Toward Countess Eschiva it must be said he displayed chivalry that would honor a Christian prince, granting safe passage to Tripoli with her ladies and household goods. Five days later the proud city of Acre surrendered. The castle of Toron. Nablus. Sidon. Jebail. Beyrouth. Christianity oversea was falling.

His Holiness Urban chanced to be at Ferrara when he got the news.

By permission of God, Heraclius, miserable patriarch of the Church of the Holy Resurrection, sends greetings to the most holy father and lord, Urban, supreme pontiff. Our lamentation and sorrow we can but inadequately convey, Reverend Father. It is our misfortune to behold the calamitous subjugation of our people, to be present when all that we hold sacred is scattered to the dogs. The fury of the Lord has come against us and His fury drains our spirit. He has permitted the Cross, meant for our salvation, to be captured by Turks. His mercy has He withheld from the bishops of Lydda and Acre, one of whom is taken prisoner, the other slain. Our king and the Christian army has He abandoned, given up to Turks. Some have fallen beneath the sword, some led into vile captivity, a few have escaped. The cities and castles taken by these enemies of God include Tiberias, Sebastea, Nazareth, Lydda, Caesarea, Mirabel, Toron, Bethlehem, Nablus, and others. Alas, their inhabitants have fallen nearly all to the sword. Alas, the Lord has discarded His legacy. His anger surpasses His mercy and the magnitude of our grief knows no limit. The holy city of Jerusalem now lies imperiled, for Saracens have won the battle. Alas, Reverend Father, we despair of defending ourselves. We have no refuge apart from God. Therefore, unless compassion be stirred throughout the west, bringing aid speedily to the Holy Land, we in our grievous extremity will not prevail. The holy city of Jerusalem must fall. Saladin is near. Daily we anticipate his coming. He has subdued every bishopric and archbishopric of our patriarchate, excepting Tyre and Petra. He sweeps the earth.

deus lo volt!

Therefore, in the name of God, Holy Father, do we entreat your counsel and your protection.

Now over the horizon sailed a fleet commanded by Marquis Conrad de Montferrat approaching the fortress of Acre. No bells peeled in celebration, nor did a boat put out to greet them as was customary when Christian vessels arrived. For this reason the marquis ordered certain of his mariners to go ashore to find out why they did not hear the bell and get the latest news. They pulled close by the Tower of Flies and called out, asking who governed the city. People in the tower replied that it belonged to Saladin but they might safely land.

We will not, they answered, if it has been captured by enemies.

Sail away to Tyre! shouted some renegade in the tower. There will my lord Saladin take you, even as he has taken your holy cross and your wretched king and all your Christian host!

The men in the boat pulled away. No more did Conrad get this news than he ordered the fleet north to see what was happening at Tyre.

That may be how it was. Yet according to the chronicle of Geoffrey de Vinsauf, Conrad's galley dropped sail outside the port of Acre near sunset. And because a prevailing silence gave cause for suspicion he ordered all to remain aboard. They observed the sultan's banner at various quarters and Saracen galleys fast approaching, so the crew was full of alarm. But the marquis stood forth as spokesman to these infidels and declared, when asked who he might be, that he was master of a merchant ship devoted to Saladin. And he would wait on the sultan at break of day to display his excellent wares. However, during the night he took advantage of a strong breeze, hoisted sail and departed swiftly for Tyre.

There he learned to his dismay that the citizens were preparing to surrender. Already they had begun to negotiate with emissaries from Saladin. Indeed, from a watchtower floated the Muslim standard because they had lost heart and were terrified, but the arrival of Conrad hardened their spirit. When they saw how confidently he defied Saracen threats, when they saw him tear apart Muslim banners and fling them in a moat, the citizens of Tyre felt ashamed. They rebuked each other for cowardice and vowed to engage the Turks. Three and four times a day they would sally forth to attack those who were nearest, afterward retreating nimbly through the gates to avoid being chopped up.

No chronicle relates how Sancho Martín arrived at Tyre, nor from what Spanish city. Beyond doubt he felt moved to worship and serve our Lord. His weapons were enameled green and his helmet sprouted antlers like a stag. When he charged out the gate Saracens would dash up to marvel. They called him the Green Knight and his fine bearing gave them pause. It is said that the Muslim lord addressed this Green Knight, urging him to forsake Christianity and join the ranks of Islam. If he returned to Spain or perished in the Holy Land, God knows.

Marquis Conrad soon found out what little food remained in the city and no help imminent. He assembled the principal Franks, English, Pisans, and Genoese to consult. My lords, said he, we have not enough to keep our bodies alive. If any among you has an idea, by the love of God let him step forth.

A Genoese captain spoke up. We have with us many barges and galleys and other vessels, he said. I will take four galleys and embark just before dawn as though trying to escape. When the infidels catch sight of me they will not wait to arm themselves but will make haste to catch me. You and your men must be prepared to sail after them with great speed. When they are between us I will turn around and we will together fight them. If it please God to assist, He will send help.

This plan sounded good to the marquis and to others. Besides, if they did nothing they would starve.

The harbor by which vessels come and go lies within city walls, thus the Genoese and his crew were able to get under way before Saracens detected them. But at once the enemy ships, which numbered almost one hundred, gave chase. And when they had gotten out to sea the ships of Conrad followed, whereupon the Genoese turned about. So, caught between Christian forces, many unbelievers plunged shrieking into the bottomless pit. It is recorded that two Saracen galleys escaped. And Saladin who watched this battle from shore was lamenting, clawing his beard to see his people drowned or butchered. They say he cut off the tail of his favorite horse and rode around in view of his soldiers to disgrace himself.

Now he considered it best to let go of Tyre since his warships were taken or sunk, and when those inside the walls observed Saracen tents folded they stretched up their hands joyously to our compassionate Lord.

No sooner were the Turks out of sight than Archbishop Joscius boarded a galley whose sails had been painted black and sailed away to speak with His Holiness at Rome, pausing first at Sicily to plead with King William for help. King William grieved to learn the state of affairs. He put on sackcloth and hid himself for several days. Then he addressed letters to other monarchs beseeching them to call for a new expedition, a new pilgrimage.

Archbishop Joscius proceeded to Rome, escorted by Sicilian ambassadors. They found His Holiness Urban III old and sick. He could not endure the shock, expiring from grief on the twentieth day of October in that year of our Lord 1187. His successor Gregory, alarmed by such tidings from the Holy Land, despatched a circular letter recounting what had befallen Christ's kingdom oversea, offering plenary indulgence to all who took the cross, reminding the faithful how Edessa was lost forty years ago. Let true Christians lay up treasure in heaven, he advised. Let them enjoy eternal life in the hereafter by gathering to smite and crush Islam, meanwhile their property on earth would be ensured by the Holy See.

Saladin marched from Tyre to Ascalon where he showed important captives beneath the walls. King Guy of Jerusalem. Gérard de Ridfort, Grand Master of the Temple. Both entreated the citizens of Ascalon to lower the flag, but they would not. They replied with insults. Saladin therefore erected machines for hurling stones and began to attack the city. The inhabitants resisted, during which time they killed two emirs, but after a while they decided to capitulate and ask for mercy. Saladin granted them leave to depart with their goods and had them escorted to Alexandria and lodged under his protection until ships would convey them to Europe. It is reported that on the day he rode triumphantly into Ascalon a shadow passed over the sun, proof of divine supervision.

That same day here came ambassadors from Jerusalem to negotiate terms of surrender. Saladin greeted them in strange darkness, before the light returned. He insisted they must open the gates. They would not agree to this and went back proudly to that city where Jesus Christ gave up His life. Saladin vowed he would take it by the sword. Arabs say an astrologer once prophesied that he would lose an eye if he entered Jerusalem. He answered that he would give both eyes for it.

When these delegates got back to the city here was unexpected help. Balian d'Ibelin. By certain accounts he made his way to Jerusalem after escaping the battle on Mount Hattin. Or it may be that he was captured but asked leave to go and comfort his wife, Maria Comnena. And because Saladin looked indulgently upon princes and their consorts he allowed this distinguished noble to go, admonishing him to remain one night only. Nor should he take up arms. However, the citizens implored him to stay and prepare a defense. There were but fourteen knights inside Jerusalem, according to Geoffrey de Vinsauf. Balian stripped silver from the roof of the Holy Sepulcher and melted gold icons. With this money he recruited mercenaries. He knighted thirty members of the bourgeoisie as well as boys from aristocratic families and distributed swords to burghers as if they were fighting men. And because he had violated an oath he sent word to explain. Saladin, who behaved graciously to men he respected, forgave this breach.

On the twentieth day of September here came God's mortal enemies wailing and screeching. Hai! Hai! they called amid a clamor of trumpets.

deus lo volt!

Sepulcher of Christ! True and Holy Cross! shouted the Franks.

Saladin planned to attack the north wall but it was strongly defended and from that direction his soldiers looked up into the sun. After five days he decided to move his pavilion to the Mount of Olives where he could look down into the city. When people observed Saracen tents dismantled they began to celebrate, thinking he meant to withdraw. But when they understood the turn of it they wrung their hands.

Presently his miners set to work undermining the wall, busying themselves at the place where almost ninety years earlier Duke Godfrey broke through. Frightened citizens clustered about Queen Sibylla and the patriarch Heraclius, beseeching them to seek terms. Lord Balian therefore led a delegation to ask Saladin for a truce. But when they got to his pavilion he talked of how their ancestors ravaged Jerusalem. He declared they would be wise to surrender without argument.

If it please God, they answered, we will not.

I tell you now, Saladin replied. I consider Jerusalem to be the abode of God, whether Christian or Muslim. If I may have the city through peaceful agreement I will not besiege it nor attack the walls. This is what I desire. Here is what I will do. I will give you thirty thousand gold bezants to strengthen it. I will grant you an area two leagues in each direction where you may work and move about as you choose. I will see that you have provisions enough. If by Pentecost you have received no help from Christians oversea you will surrender Jerusalem.

To this offer the delegates replied that they could not give up the city where God's blood was shed.

Saladin then vowed that he would take it.

Lord Balian asked if his wife and children might be granted safe passage from Jerusalem to Tripoli. Saladin assented, despatching a Saracen knight to escort them.

Before the assault he notified the people once more of his conditions. Again they defied him. Then his soldiers moved against

Jerusalem between the Damascus Gate and the Tower of David. On the ramparts stood a cross erected in former times to commemorate the capture of Antioch. Saracens knocked it down with one blow and destroyed much of the wall. Miners dug tunnels that they packed with cloth, wood, and other materials and set ablaze. Petraries, trebuchets, and similar devices pursued their noisy work. Archers launched such flights of arrows that nobody could lift a finger. If the people of Jerusalem sallied forth to do battle they would be met by pagans carrying skins or bags that squirted dust into their eyes. So it became clear how God was determined to punish His recreant children.

In the city were two boys whose fathers chanced to be elsewhere. When these knights heard that Saladin had besieged Jerusalem they sent word asking for custody, explaining that as they themselves were free men it was not right for their children to be taken captive and led off to slavery. Saladin agreed. He directed Balian to let these children out of the city in order that he himself might watch over them. These were Thomassin d'Ibelin, who was a nephew of Lord Balian, and Guillemin de Jubail. And when they were delivered to Saladin he gave them jewels, clean robes, and food, after which he seated them on his knees and began to weep. The emirs asked why he felt sorrowful and he replied that everything is fleeting because whatever we hope to keep will be taken from us. Even now, he said, while I dispossess the children of other men, so will my children be destitute when I am gone. He said this because he did not trust his brother Malik al-Adil. Indeed, after his death Malik would seize control and disinherit Saladin's children, so the prophecy came to pass.

However that may be, when people in the city understood they could not prevail against these enemies of truth they took counsel, asking each other what to do. Some wanted to rush forth at night to challenge the Turks, thinking it better to fight than be trapped and miserably slaughtered. Heraclius the patriarch disagreed. For each man within these walls, he said, there are countless women and children. If we expend our lives then will the Saracens take our women and children and oblige them to renounce their belief in Jesus Christ. Hence they will be lost to God. But if we treat with Saladin and depart for Christian land, I think it would be better. One by one, next by dozens and hundreds, the people agreed with Heraclius. Lord Balian, seeing this was the case, rode out to consult with Saladin and make peace as best he could. But while they were talking together the Saracens once more attacked, put ladders against the walls and some got up on top and hoisted Muslim banners.

You wish to make peace now that my men have gained the wall, Saladin remarked. You are too late. Behold, the city is mine! And you should know how Godfrey de Bouillon slew thousands in the street, how they were slain while seeking refuge in the temple. I am hard pressed to respond with Christian blood.

Yet even as he spoke, such is the merciful nature of God, heathen banners were torn down and ladders thrust away from the wall. And when he observed this he grew furious. He directed Balian to leave, saying they would speak no further.

Nevertheless, Lord Balian rode out again next morning accompanied by various nobles. Saladin greeted them courteously. He said he would treat those inside the city neither better nor worse than Muslims were treated when Jerusalem was first conquered. Which is to say every man would be put to the sword, women and children sold into slavery. Thus would he exchange evil for evil.

Lord Balian answered rashly, saying that while those inside Jerusalem feared death and clung to life, if death should be inevitable they would kill their women and children and burn their property, leaving the Muslims not an écu. Not one woman would Saladin enslave. Not one man would be left alive to put in irons. The Chapel of the Sakkra and the Mosque al-Aqsa would be demolished, together with every other holy place. Muslims inside the walls, numbering five thousand, would be massacred. Nor would there be one animal left alive. And when we have finished this work, said Lord Balian, we will come out to fight you. We will die, but we will die free.

Saladin consulted his emirs. Then he said the Christians would be treated as captives who might ransom themselves. The price of liberty would be reckoned at ten gold bezants for a man. The value of a woman should be reckoned at five, that of a child at two. As soon as anyone paid this tribute he would be free to go, either to Antioch or under safe conduct to Alexandria for departure by sea. Those who ransomed themselves must leave Jerusalem afoot and take nothing concealed. Payment was expected within forty days, after which those who had not paid or could not pay would be enslaved for life.

So the people laid aside their weapons. And in our year of grace 1187, on the second day of October, the gates of the Holy City opened to Saladin.

By Muslim records this occurred on the twenty-seventh day of Rajab on which day centuries ago their Prophet visited Jerusalem while asleep. They say his winged steed Burac sprang from the rock in the Templum Domini, which they call Dome of the Rock, and carried the Prophet to heaven. There he spoke with Lord Jesus and with Abraham, thereupon descending safely to Mecca. This according to many pagans. Others think he was in Jerusalem that day and met Gabriel who escorted him up a ladder to celestial heights whence he gazed into hell at the dread punishment of sinners. But the faith of unbelievers is a vile repository gorged with misbelief. They argue that our Lord was born in the shade of a palm tree. Some argue that He was born in the mosque at Jerusalem and the Holy Virgin during labor gripped a pillar where the impress of her fingers may yet be seen. They believe a dark sun rising in the west will herald our last day and barbaric hordes led by Gog and Magog come to drink Lake Tiberias dry. And

deus lo volt!

Dajjal with his single eye, who is Antichrist, comes riding through Palestine on a donkey followed by seventy thousand Jews. They say he will enact mock miracles to ridicule our Lord. The sun will decline in the east while a trumpet sounds. All such malignity they imagine. Is it not evident how they would destroy the Holy Church? But those who behold the light of the world will see false counsel scattered.

The gates to Jerusalem opened wide that lamentable day because of Christian wickedness, because Christians strapped on the belt of knighthood and went strutting about with pride in their eye and created factions among themselves and perverted with knavery the Holy Church. Because of this Jerusalem fell. Christians weighted down by execrable sin grew blind to the sovereign light. We hear of a pilgrim wounded in this battle when an arrow struck his nose. The shaft broke off, the barb remained. Now, this arrow came as punishment, the barb embedded to remind him. Yet he lived, proof of our Lord's infinite mercy.

Once the city had been given up Saladin directed a crier of Islamic law to proceed to the summit of Calvary. And there, upon the rock, was the doctrine of Mahomet proclaimed. Nor was this enough. They pulled down a cross surmounting the church of the Hospital, spat upon it, kicked it with their feet and dragged it through excrement. Nor was this enough. They pulled down a gold cross adorning the Templum Domini to the accompaniment of loud cries, cries of rage from Christians, of joy from pagans. Three days they carried this gold cross through the streets and beat it with sticks. Infidel priests or bishops, which in their tongue Saracens call fakihs, marched rudely into the Temple of the Lord, which they call Beithhalla, and with ugly bellowings undertook to cleanse it, but defiled the Temple by shouting through impure lips. Allahu Akbar! Allahu Akbar!

One week after Saladin took Jerusalem his followers rejoiced in the mosque al-Aqsa. The qadi of Damascus spoke. They say that his voice was powerful but trembled slightly and he wore a black robe.

Glory to God, said he, who has granted Islam this triumph, who has returned Jerusalem to the fold after a century of proscription. Honor to this army chosen by God to effect the reconquest. Honor to Saladin, son of Ayub, by whose will the dignity of Islam is restored.

Now this Kurd from Mesopotamia, having got what he wanted, puffed with success, declared Mahomet's wisdom superior to that of Christ by virtue of victories on the field. All such vaunts he flung at Christian faces. Yet one true believer thought to answer wisely. God, having judged His children deserving of reproof, selected thee as agent. Likewise a father may pluck a cudgel from the mire to chastise an errant son but afterward throw it back.

As to what response the sultan offered, histories are mute.

He sent to Damascus for his sister, she whose caravan Reynauld de Chatillon imprudently seized, to come and worship with him. She loaded up twenty camels with rose water and rode to Jerusalem. These people believe that whoever eats the flesh of a pig is unfit to enter the house of God, hence she would not go into the temple, nor would he, until their priests washed it with rose water much as Christians purify churches that have been violated. Then he commanded Mahomet's erroneous law to be proclaimed from all four corners. So the Holy City that basked in the light of true believers was contaminated by filth.

Ambroise the jongleur relates that two very ancient men lived in the city, Robert de Coudre and Fulk Fiole. The first had served with Godfrey de Bouillon during the conquest. Fulk Fiole was born in Jerusalem not long afterward. Since both were feeble they asked Saladin to let them complete their lives in the city. This request he granted, directing that they be given whatever they needed as long as they lived. And he permitted ten brothers of the Hospital to remain for one year to attend any who were ill. He listened to the pleas of women whose husbands were slain, had them compensated from his treasury, wept as they wept. Therefore it should be remarked that the spirit of charity is not limited to Christians.

Lady Étienne de Kerak beseeched him to release her son Humphrey. Saladin agreed, provided she would surrender her two great castles of Kerak and Montréal. When she accepted this offer he brought Humphrey out of prison and sent the young lord to his mother. But the knights of Kerak and Montréal refused to obey Lady Étienne, declaring they would not surrender. Then because she was unable to keep her promise she ordered her son back into captivity. Such honorable conduct delighted Saladin who for a second time released Humphrey.

As for indigent captives unable to pay ransom, a multitude reckoned at fourteen thousand and more, Geoffrey de Vinsauf reports that all were enslaved. Malik al-Adil, troubled by this many bound for servitude, addressed his brother. I have helped you conquer this land and the city of Jerusalem, said he. I ask that you grant me one thousand from among the poor.

What would you do with them? Saladin asked.

How Malik replied is not known, but Saladin consented. Malik set these people free.

Now here came Lord Balian and the patriarch with similar requests in the name of God, for the sake of miserable paupers. Saladin gave up two thousand more. And it is said he gave ten thousand to the Hospitalers and Templars. But he wished to surpass the charity of his brother so he ordered a postern near Saint Lazarus to be opened and sent heralds to announce that those without money could leave through this gate. Among these was an Englishman carrying a stick across his shoulder and tied to the stick was a gourd, whereupon a Saracen monk cried out angrily. Look! The pig leaves with a gourd of wine! The monk smashed the gourd, which spewed forth gold coins. In this way Saladin heard about rich Christians trying to escape. Thenceforth nobody could leave without paying ransom.

Here came Lord Balian and the patriarch once again. Sire, they beseeched him, for love of God hold us captive until money is found to liberate the poor. But he was annoyed on account of the deceitful Englishman and would not discuss it.

By each gate stood a Saracen official to collect tribute, yet many of these pocketed what they were given. Also, here were citizens

187

hoping to keep their money who slid down the walls on ropes or escaped by other means, such as disguising themselves as soldiers or hiding in baggage carts. Hence there was confusion at every gate.

Things that deviate from their course fall back into order, albeit not as we expect. Margaret of Beverley was in Jerusalem when Saladin attacked. She carried water to men fighting on the ramparts and wore a cooking pot on her head for protection, all the same she was hurt when a stone from a Saracen catapult struck nearby. Afterward she bought her freedom and set out for Lachis. En route she was caught by Turks. They beat her with switches and forced her to gather wood until a pious man celebrating the birth of a son bought her freedom a second time. Again she set forth, one bread roll to eat and a ragged gown to hide her nakedness, dreading heathen no less than savage animals, her only comfort a psalter. She met a Turk who snatched away the psalter but came running back to fling himself at her feet in remorse, which proves the mighty arm of God. Close by Antioch the unbelievers caught her again and put her in a cell with others speaking parthica lingua, which is to say a language she could not understand. They condemned her to death because they thought she had stolen a knife. But the Turkish commandant listened to her praying, recognized the holy name of Mary and let her go. Anon she came to France where she found her brother who was a monk at Froimont. He did not know her until she spoke of their brother who died soon after baptism, their parents Hulnon and Sybil, and their home in northern England. To him she related her experience, which he put down in very fine verse. He persuaded her to enter a convent. Thus we see how due order is preserved by events.

As for those that went to Egypt, they traveled under Saladin's warrant. And when vessels from Italy put in at Alexandria the masters were compelled to take these refugees aboard. Still, not many got back to Europe, most being thrust ashore on some desolate coast by merchants from Pisa and Genoa who did not like the burden. How bleak the day when these exiles left Jerusalem for uncertain destiny, leaving the city reduced to servitude. Once the inheritance of our

Redeemer, defiled now by the ministration of God's enemies, Jerusalem was brought to low estate through the iniquitous behavior of her people.

What of Heraclius the patriarch? Saladin allowed him to sail for Europe taking as much as he liked, including gold plate from the Holy Sepulcher. In this way Saladin expected to earn the gratitude of Christians, undeniable proof that he misapprehended the western world. Many Turks were angered and shocked to learn how the patriarch ransomed himself for ten bezants like a common soldier and watched him leave Jerusalem all but staggering under his treasure, followed by carts heaped up with plate and jeweled icons.

He traveled first to Rome, thence to numerous capitals, dressing himself in black while he preached a new crusade. He described how Jerusalem suffered, displayed a painting of Jesus Christ bloodied by Mahomet striking Him. Look you! cried Heraclius. Behold how the Lord is beaten! Many who contemplated this fearful picture sobbed and wept, others swore vengeance. How should the calamity of so small a kingdom oversea afflict the people of rich and powerful countries? How could it not?

Anon came Saladin's brother, Malik al-Adil, and laid siege to Kerak. Those who defended the castle found themselves with less and less to eat. At length they turned out the women and children, thinking Saracens might feed their hapless families. Some were sold to the Bedouin. What became of the rest is not related. When the last horse was butchered and cooked and no help from any source, Kerak surrendered. Montréal held out longer, if not much.

Saladin himself, turgid with hate, wallowing in pride, stuffed with confidence, led his pagan horde against the city that previously defied him. Tyre. He fetched from Damascus the aged Marquis William de Montferrat, father of Conrad, who was captured during the battle on Mount Hattin. He exhibited this old marquis beneath the walls, telling Conrad that in exchange for the city his father would be released. Conrad answered that he would not give a stone in exchange for his father's life, declaring that his father was a wicked old man who had committed terrible crimes, whose hour was finished. Bind him to a stake, Conrad ordered, that I may shoot him. And with the aged marquis ushered close enough, guarded, shackled, Conrad let fly a shaft, obliquely, pretending careful aim.

When the unbeliever failed at his expectation of gaining the city by these means, cajoling and threatening, he tried his fortune another way, setting up engines to bombard the walls, attacking also by sea. But on the morning after Innocent's Day, which is the feast of blessed Thomas Becket, Christian vessels sailed forth to attack the Saracen galleys and scattered them, caused many to run aground. Then out the gate charged Lord Conrad and Hugh of Tiberias with a noble company and struck down many infidels. So it appeared to Saladin that he was opposed by fortune. He burnt the engines he had set up for casting missiles, burnt his few galleys, and ingloriously retreated.

Later, to show contempt for such a feckless monarch, he released King Guy without demanding a single écu, stipulating only that the king never again take up arms against Islam. Not many in the Holy Land cared, perhaps only Queen Sibylla who had prayed and beseeched Saladin to grant this favor. The Norman jongleur who recounted these affairs in verse sang of how King Guy was not a lucky man, in war neither terrible nor fierce, nor menacing to the sultan.

No more was Guy released than he found a cleric willing to invalidate his oath to Saladin. After all, had not the king been under duress? Besides, the promise was made to an infidel. Thus absolved, King Guy lusted to settle accounts. Fifty-two ships under command of Archbishop Ubaldo arrived during the month of April, so the king employed them. Now, his faint spirit replenished, he marched along the coast thinking he might storm the walls of Acre. Beside his feeble army sailed these Italians.

The news failed to alarm Saladin who was attacking the castle of Beaufort twenty leagues north. This castle stood on a cliff overlooking the river Litani and belonged to Reynald of Sidon, by repute a clever, charming lord fluent in Arabic. They say he more than once visited Saladin's court where he displayed knowledge of Islamic literature. And he seemed to indicate that he might one day forsake Christianity, embrace Islam, and move to Damascus. However, months went by as Lord Reynald did nothing but reinforce his castle walls and Saladin lost patience. After one visit he escorted Reynald under heavy guard to Beaufort and directed him to speak with the garrison commander. The gate must be opened. Reynald obeyed, telling the commander in Arabic to open the gate, but adding in French that he should not. Saladin or one of his counselors understood French well enough. Off went Lord Reynald to Damascus where he lodged in prison.

Saladin now considered the Franks under King Guy who had laid siege to Acre. They were camped east of the city along the little river Belus which provided fresh water. Also, they had access to the sea, which meant that vessels could unload troops and supplies. Indeed, more soldiers and militant pilgrims were arriving, by chance or through the exhortation of Heraclius preaching across Europe. Danes. Frisians. Genoese. Lombards. Flemings. Germans. Venetians. So by the end of that year a Christian city all but encircled Acre. One might see distinguished barons or knights such as James d'Avesnes as well as those of low estate who had felt moved to undertake the journey, tradesmen and peasants. Twenty or more languages could be heard. Ambroise composed and sang of how there were not women enough. Yet, as always, miraculously, they began to appear, ladies and whores. Some, disguised as men, took up arms on behalf of Christ despite their natural weakness, even as women once fought bravely to liberate Jerusalem. Three or more rode into battle astride horses, being revealed as women only when seized and stripped of armor. Beha al-Din speaks of one wearing a green mantle who used the longbow and wounded several Turks. When at last she was killed and her bow taken to Saladin he seemed astonished.

Counselors to Saladin had warned that Acre would continue to excite and tempt Christians, therefore he should raze it to the ground. Others argued that the city was too beautiful to destroy and he need only strengthen it. Accordingly he had brought from Egypt a renowned strategist, Emir Caracusch, who built the walls of Cairo. This emir set ranks of prisoners to do the work. They were thickening the walls and heightening towers when King Guy appeared. More Latins arrived led by nobles of Bar, Dreux, Brienne, Archbishop Gerard of Ravenna, Bishop Philip of Beauvais, the count of Guelders, as well as Margrave Louis of Thuringia and others.

We are told that Saladin thought Beaufort unimportant, and considering how many Christians threatened Acre he marched south with much of his army, leaving only a detachment to reduce the castle. Muslims say that his nephew Taqi got through Frankish lines to open a corridor, enabling those inside Acre to communicate with the Turkish host. Still, weeks and months passed, neither force able to dislodge the other. English vessels put in, but from south and east came other enemies of our Lord.

If those trapped behind the walls of Acre suffered, the soldiers of Christ fared no better. They got much they needed through access to the sea, but illness caused their skin to rot. Nor had they food enough. Germans constructed a mill for grinding wheat and corn, turned by horses, with the millstones grinding loudly, the first ever built oversea, which puzzled and alarmed the Turks. Most earnestly did they gaze toward it, says Geoffrey de Vinsauf, fearing it might be some fresh instrument for their destruction or was meant to storm the walls. Similarly, Franks contemplated the high walls before them like the walls of Troy and a multitude of Turks camped behind. Among these soldiers of Christ that streamed to the Holy Land, how many did not pray fervently?

Now up leapt the Devil. Ambroise sang of how on a certain Friday his disciples rushed yowling and screeching at pilgrims along the coast. Templars and Hospitalers rode forth to scatter them but the Devil caused a German to lose his horse. Then he pursued it, shouting at his comrades for help but none of them was able to catch the horse. Turks saw them galloping away from battle and thought they were routed and so gathered up courage to fight once more.

deus lo volt!

With truncheons, maces, and other weapons these iniquitous enemies left numbers of Christian dead beside the water, disemboweled, weltering. There was slain among others Andrew de Brienne, a valorous knight.

From that day the Saracen took heart, harrying and vexing. Saladin advanced from the north and got himself inside the city. He caused mangonels to be set up, petraries, and other machines. He was observed pacing the ramparts in ceaseless agitation. Some compared him to a lioness who had lost her young. He went three days with hardly any food, according to Beha al-Din who was there and joyously unleashed arrows toward the Christian host.

Franks on the hill of Toron saw a fleet of galleys bearing landward and thought they must be from Genoa or Venice or Marseille. But as they glided into the harbor they seized a transport full of men and victuals, took these captives inside Acre, slew them, dangled their mutilated bodies from walls to mock and defy the host. Yet is not our God a pillar of strength? Does He not hear and mercifully respond to the cries of His children? Down from Tyre with fifty vessels came Marquis Conrad de Montferrat. Saracens rowed out furiously to oppose him. Trumpets sounded. Greek fire was observed, Christian knights all ablaze hopping into the water. Others pierced by weapons tumbled overboard. Pagans climbed into one vessel and forced its mariners from the upper deck while those below sought to escape by rowing, hence the oars pulled different ways according to Franks below or Turks above. And here a Saracen galley was dragged to shore, assaulted by Christian women. Women grabbed Turks by their black locks, treated them shamefully, cut their throats with knives. Surely the Turks felt humiliated to be struck down by the weak hands of women.

Even so, like a multitude of insects here came more enemies, pagans of a different race, impetuous, hideous, savage heathen dark in aspect, of huge size and exceeding ferocity, abhorred by God and nature, showing crimson caps in lieu of helmets, wielding clubs notched with iron teeth, their standard a carved image of Mahomet.

193

Ambroise reckoned their number at five hundred thousand. He likened these tossing waves of crimson caps to a cherry orchard ripe with fruit.

During the feast of Saint James a great company of destitute pilgrims, ten thousand at least, rushed against Saladin's tents and unbelievers fled wildly in all directions. So the hungry pilgrims went about picking up food, whatever good things they could find. But the Turks, looking back, seeing them hampered, returned to hurl themselves at these foolish people. Seven thousand died. More would have perished except for certain knights who rode out to save them. Torel de Mesnil gave up the ghost that day and was sorely lamented. The Devil, who never sleeps, contrived this work which left the host diminished. Or it may be, as some think, our blessed Lord beckoned more martyrs to His kingdom. Similar affronts would trouble this army of God beneath the walls of Acre. Divers misadventures would the Lord suffer to befall His children, considering that He wished to try them with hardship even as He tried the saints, as gold itself must be tried in the furnace.

Atop a high rock adjoining the port looms the Tower of Flies, so called because in ancient days it was a place of sacrifice where swarms of flies settled on broken flesh. Acre was then situated at Mount Toron not far distant and was called Ptolmais. They say the ruins of Ptolmais exist to our day. Perhaps. There is a tower called Accursed that surmounts the wall enclosing the city, which earned its name because here were minted those thirty pieces of silver used to betray our Lord. There is a hill called the Mosque that is the sepulcher of Memnon, although no one can say how or why the husk of this great Ethiopian king came to be here. And the little river Belus flowing past Acre is enriched with glassy sand, for which reason Solinus named it a wonder of the world. Close by is a flat rock where Africa, Asia, and Europe meet, three divisions of the world. Now this is Acre toward which streamed eminent Christian princes to confront the tumultuous horde of Saladin. Here came Nargenot du Bourg, Otho de la Fosse, William Goez, Count Richard from Apulia, Engelram de Vienne, Theobald de Bar, Count John from Loegria, Hervey de Gien, Guy de Dampierre, Count Nicholas from Hungary, Count John from Seis with a nephew of the Danish king. Also, chiefs of the Danes and four hundred fighting men. Here came the bishop of Verona. Who does not perceive in this the hand of our Sovereign? Is not His mercy everpresent for those who defend His name?

Divers things indeed befell the host. As April gave place to May there was a pilgrim walking in the trench dug for protection, fitted like a sergeant with iron helmet and folded linen tunic. He had gone looking for weak parts of the wall or to strike an enemy with his sling. For what reason he stopped is not known, but some Turk shot through a loophole and struck him on the breast. They say the dart pierced his quilted doublet and rebounded, all twisted and bent. This was because he carried around his neck a parchment scroll inscribed with the holy names of God. Thus the dart plopped harmlessly to earth leaving him unhurt, which was attested by many that saw the miracle.

Or there was a certain knight hunched in the ditch attending to business when some Turk galloped at him with a lowered lance. Others perceiving his danger cried out for the knight to flee, but all unfastened he could not. Then he clutched a stone that he aimed and threw and struck this enemy on the temple. So the Turk dropped off his horse and broke his neck and died. Then the knight caught the horse, mounted, and rode back to camp. God directs the aim of those who believe.

Again. Ivo de Vipont embarked for Tyre with ten companions but a galley of Turkish pirates went gliding toward them. The mariners were frightened since they counted eighty or ninety Turks. O Lord God! O Lord God! they cried. We will be taken and murdered! But they were rebuked by Ivo de Vipont. Why should you fear those who are about to die? he asked. And when the galley was near to striking them with its beak he leapt on board and set about cutting down pirates with the axe he carried. So his friends gathered up their vitals when they saw his work prosper and clambered into the galley

195

beheading Turks right or left. These Christians proved victorious because they had faith in God who does not know how to be conquered. Muslims honor a faith that is counterfeit.

This also. Beha al-Din, unbeliever and historian, relates how a very great swimmer called Isa would dive under Christian vessels at night to come up on the opposite side where those who were besieged would greet him joyfully since he brought messages and money fastened to his belt. But one night while carrying letters Isa was caught by the Franks. Some days later his body washed ashore, the messages sealed with wax affixed to his belt. Had this Turk labored in the service of God his end would be different.

Or this. Christian fishermen throwing nets just before sunset happened to see a man swimming. They pursued him on their boats and saw he was a Turk who, alarmed by their shouts, tried to escape. But they rowed strongly, caught him in their net, and saw he was carrying a bottle of Greek fire suspended from his neck. So they landed their captive as though he were a fish and led him with his evil mixture through the army, scourging him, reviling him, after which they mangled his body and chopped him apart. Thus does the Lord scatter the counsel of heathen princes, undoing the obliquity they plan.

Now, because of frequent and unexpected sorties by these wicked enemies it was thought to bury foot-traps in the ground. And one day while certain Christians were tossing darts at a mark to amuse themselves here came Turks spurring toward them. Being unarmed and few in number the soldiers of Christ retreated. But one Turk outstripped the rest when his mount stopped short, caught by a trap. So the Turk, considering only his head, leapt off and ran away to his friends. That is how Count Robert de Dreux, whose instrument captured the animal, obtained a fine Saracen charger.

Yet again, while the season passed, divers and strange things befell the host. More than once those who defended Acre would flaunt holy relics or crosses from churches that they would insult, beat, and spit upon, because nothing in the world do they hate so much. One day here was a Turk skipping along the wall beating a wood cross he had found. For a long while he did this to spite the true faith. But he could not leave it at that, he let slip his drawers to defile the cross. Then a Christian arbalester set a bolt to the string, aimed well, and struck the pagan straight through the gut whereupon he sprang up dead with his feet in the air. So it is clear how malignant designs must fail.

And while the season passed, out from Acre sallied a company of Turks with an emir called Bellegemin who was of high lineage. Frankish knights rode forth to challenge these Turks and drove them back, all save Bellegemin who did not retreat. In one hand he carried a phial of Greek fire since he hoped to burn a petrary. But with one stroke a Christian knight laid Bellegemin to earth and emptied the fire on his genitals. Hence, what this Turk meant for others became the implement of his anguish.

Now as time went by certain pilgrims wearied of attacking the city while others never tired of collecting stones to fill up trenches so Christian engines might advance. The barons, too, brought stones on their chargers and helped to load sumpter beasts. Many women joined this task, rejoicing in service to the Lord. Among these a woman whose name is not remembered, struck in the belly with a Turkish arrow while discharging her burden, who fell down wounded to death. Pilgrims gathered around to lament while she lay writhing on the earth. Then her husband came running. Dearest lord, by your love for me, she said, by your piety as my husband and the faith of our marriage contract, allow my body to rest in this place. I pray and beseech you, since I can do no more, that a faggot be made of this poor flesh to complete the trench. So it was done and the Lord God tenderly embraced her soul.

Numerous engines did the barons construct and the archbishop provided a ram, a costly piece of goods. This ram was like a house, a sturdy mast inside bound at both ends with iron hoops. And those whose task it was to ram the wall did so eagerly. But from the parapet Turks threw liquid fire. Mangonels flung slabs of marble or freestone or beams of trees, buckets of sulfur, tar, pitch, tallow, logs, and then

197

again burning wood. All this and more did Mahomet's slaves heap on the ram to crush or burn it. They dropped missiles until they broke in the roof, crushed everything, left the archbishop's ram consumed. Whereupon they jeered and capered and whistled.

Soldiers of Christ next constructed a belfrois four stories in height to look down at the wall, using bronze, iron, wood, lead, and clay. This castle rolling toward Acre frightened the Turks who thought about surrender. But there was an enemy of God from Damascus who had studied naphtha and other fluids that would overcome the resistance of clay and vinegar, who explained his knowledge to the emir Caracusch. It is said Caracusch listened disrespectfully since many experiments had failed, but at length gave permission to do what he wished because Acre was imperiled. This Damascene threw pots of unlighted naphtha at the belfrois, producing no effect. Then the Franks took heart. Bold pilgrims climbed up in the castle to shout defiance. But with another substance thrown against it all at once the liquid burst into flame and these pilgrims burned horribly. Saladin wished to reward the Damascene yet he would not accept payment, telling the sultan that what he accomplished was done for love of Allah and to Allah would he look for gratitude. Infidels assert that all who believe Jesus Christ must burn in this world before burning eternally in the next. Such is the depth of Saracen turpitude.

And with the changing season rain deluged the Frankish camp. Illness spread. Knights, sergeants, common pilgrims, many sickened, teeth dropping out, features bloated. Each day a hundred lay down on their biers. But for herbs and seeds to make pottage nothing could have withstood the wasting. By certain reports Marquis Conrad hastily departed, vowing to send provisions but did not. Not one egg did he send. Rumor held that he forbade any ship to sail for Acre. Hence the pilgrims called him renegade, liar. So now, what with nothing or little to buy, famine loomed, nor the least vessel in sight. Never did bold knights reared among riches tolerate such distress, nor common soldiers, nor gentle ladies accustomed to tidbits. Some would gnaw bones already gnawed by dogs and sucked and licked after they could not find anything to gnaw, seeking the remembered taste of meat. Or, stripped of shame, ate garbage in view of others and called it delicious. And would drop on their knees to chew grass like grazing cattle. Yet this was pardonable since hunger urges men to do what otherwise they would not. God has created all for the use of men that they should not perish while subordinate creatures live. Hence these pilgrims slew good horses, ate meat or skin or brains ravenously, swallowed entrails, drank blood, licked their fingers in lieu of a napkin so nothing might be lost. Fine animals that once carried pilgrims on their backs now found themselves carried about in Frankish bellies.

And here was a merchant from Pisa who kept stacks of grain in his house and would not sell a measure except at monstrous profit. But our Lord knoweth. Fire consumed this house. And the people remarking God's wrath felt charitably toward one another. Those that had eaten flesh during Lent out of exigency confessed themselves, and three strokes of a stick upon his back did each get from the bishop of Salisbury who castigated them like a father. There can be no counsel against the Lord. He doeth as He will.

The knighthood of Christ found wine enough, yet without proportionate victual the body falters. Some thought to alleviate their pangs by drinking. Some crept humbly to Saladin's camp where food was abundant and denied their faith, denying it ever was true that God deigned to be born of a woman. Baptism and the cross these recreants abjured to preserve life on earth a few days longer. How pernicious the exchange, since the body is a fleeting servant.

And the archbishop of Canterbury when he observed these pilgrims grow hourly more dissolute, given up to wine, to dice, lascivious women, felt his spirit wither. O Lord God! he cried aloud. There is need of chastening and correction! Lord God, if it please Thy mercy, let me be removed from the turmoil of life for I have endured this army enough!

Chronicles relate how Almighty God answered his plea. Fifteen days later the archbishop arose to glory.

Turks allege that Conrad de Montferrat caused a diabolic picture to be carried throughout Europe by clerics who lamented and groaned while displaying it in the marketplace, calling upon Christians to avenge the shame. Here was a Turkish knight riding across the Holy Sepulcher, his destrier pissing on the tomb. So much do these misbelievers claim. Yet does our Lord keep count. One and all does He punish for malicious inventions of the heart.

Documents do not explain how Saladin escaped the beleaguered city but it is known that from his encampment he wrote to the caliph of Baghdad and to other Muslim lords, telling how Christians approached by land and sea. Behold, he wrote with anguish because he feared his men could not prevail against the mighty power of Jesus. Behold, our enemies subscribe together and submit to privation for the sake of misstatement. They vie for glory, yet are they devoted to their cause and believe that in this way they serve God. Thus they consecrate their lives and wealth. No king in Europe forbids his peasants or his subjects to join these marches. Let us defend the truth against error and with the help of Allah exterminate the Christians.

Messengers bearing this appeal rode away to princes of Sinjar, Gezira, Mosul, and others in Mesopotamia exhorting them to join the holy war. Not one refused.

Now as summer returned the sea grew calm. More vessels arrived from Europe, which caused ships from Egypt to withdraw. Nevertheless those inside Acre contrived to obtain what they needed. Good swimmers could be persuaded to bring valuable items in exchange for money. Also, the Turks despatched and received messages by using pigeons. So throughout the summer they resisted. They hurled stones, fire, and rotting corpses at Frankish tents. Saladin from his encampment launched sudden attacks. By his command dead pilgrims were flung into the river Belus to horrify their comrades and while decomposing pollute the water. A knight called Ferrand, left naked on the field and almost dead, hid himself under piles of bodies until dark when he crawled back to camp so disfigured, so crusted with blood he could not be recognized and was admitted reluctantly. Gérard de Ridfort, master of the Temple who ignominiously purchased freedom after being captured with King Guy, was caught again. This time the Saracens took his head.

All such news flowing toward Europe brought grave unease. Commoners and kings alike thought more passionately upon the Holy Land, distressed by reports of distant sacrilege, of suffering oversea. King Philip Augustus of France and King Henry Plantagenet of England with his son Richard Lionheart resolved to take the cross, as did the Holy Roman Emperor, Frederick Barbarossa.

So ardent grew this desire for pilgrimage that, as happened in the past, monks showed themselves devoted soldiers of Christ by quitting their libraries, exchanging cloaks for breastplates. Merchants abandoned their trade, countrymen their plows, bridegrooms their brides. Women complained that the frailty of their sex prevented them from leading armies. Wives scolded timid husbands, mothers denounced apprehensive sons. Those who hesitated might receive a distaff signifying cowardice. When these armies came into being the French adopted red crosses, the English white, the Flemings green.

At Mainz on the fourth Sunday of Lent, in the year of our Lord 1188, Emperor Frederick Barbarossa accepted the cross from the cardinal of Albano. Next he despatched a herald to Saladin ordering him to repent the injuries inflicted upon Christendom, challenging him to combat on the field, since it is usual for kings and emperors to give notice of war, to send word of defiance before attacking.

Frederick, by the grace of God emperor to the Romans, to Saladin, illustrious governor of the Saracens. Because you have profaned the Holy Land, which is our jurisdiction by authority of the

Eternal King, solicitude advises us to proceed with commensurate anger against your intolerable effrontery. Wherefore, unless you relinquish that land you have seized and give due satisfaction for such ruinous excess, toward which end we allot you twelve months from the first day of November, you shall experience the misfortune of war. We in our assurance can scarcely believe you ignorant of that which the most ancient writings confirm. Namely, that with inordinate cupidity you have occupied Armenia and other lands warranted to us by virtue of the Holy Cross. For this is well known to sovereigns who in times past have felt the Roman sword. Now shall you learn through sad experience the might of imperial eagles and be acquainted with the wrath of Germany which is the fountainhead of the Rhine. Now shall you meet the fierce Bavarian, the proud youth of Swabia, the Burgundian who does not savor peace, the Frison with his thong and javelin, the fiery sailor of Pisa, the resolute Tuscan, the wild Thuringian, the nimble mountaineer. Lastly, you shall meet and rue the strength of our right hand which you mistakenly suppose enfeebled by the passage of years, which can yet wield a sword on the day appointed for Christian triumph.

Saladin responded.

To the esteemed monarch and great leader of the Germans, Frederick, in the name of God who is merciful, by the grace of that one God encompassing us, of whose kingdom there can be no limit. Incessantly do we praise Him whose grace flowers across the earth that He may inspire the tongues of prophets, above all His messenger Mahomet from whom we have learned the law that is true above other laws. But we must make it known to the glorious king of Germans that we have a letter which was delivered to us by a certain envoy called Henry, professing to be from your hand. This letter we have caused to be read, we have listened to the words, and so it behooves us to reply. You enumerate those allies who will march with you against us. But if we should do the same, enumerating those who render us obeisance, who listen to our command, who are prepared to give up their lives in our service, we could not tally their numbers.

deus lo volt!

If you should count the names of Christians, the names of Saracens would be more numerous by ten, by fifty, by ten thousand. If there is a sea between you and us, between Saracens there is no impediment. Turkomans of themselves could annihilate our enemies. Bedouins alone would prove sufficient. With enjoyment Soldarii could despoil you of your riches, exterminate you. Even our peasants, should we bid them, would hunt for you where you assemble and thereby put an end to your presumption. Thus will we cast you back into the sea if you come against us. Nor will we content ourselves with these few lands we possess, for after the Lord has granted us victory there will be little for us to do but accept from His hands that which you call your own. More than once has the Christian faith marched against us, at Damietta, Alexandria, and elsewhere. More than once have Christians returned in misery, regretting the issue. Our people flourish in numerous realms, Babylon with its dependencies, Gesireh with its castles, India, others too numerous to mention. The limitless residue of Saracenic kings exalts us. The caliph of Baghdad, should we appeal to him, would rise from his throne and hasten to our aid. But if you have set your mind upon war, then will we meet and destroy you. If that letter which has come to us truly is by your hand, here is your answer. This have we caused to be written in the year of the prophet Mahomet 584, in praise of the one and only God. May God counsel and preserve Mahomet.

We are told that Emperor Frederick listened with contempt while this was read aloud. Angrily he consulted the princes of his empire at Mayence. As though of one voice they vowed to undertake the pilgrimage, for it seemed to them a noble work. Lords and vassals buckled on their armor, guided by the Holy Spirit.

Whether this army should travel by land or by sea to Jerusalem was much discussed. Some argued that any number of ships, however large, would be insufficient and therefore Frederick decided to march overland through Hungary. Or it may be that he asked his court astrologer what sort of death to expect. The astrologer requested time to calculate. Then he came back with troublesome news.

Your Majesty, said he, I have discovered the sign of drowning.

For this reason Frederick did not embark at Hamburg or another port but led his army overland. He is alleged to have been so considerate, virtuous, and humble that he regarded vagabonds and mendicants as his brothers. He provided carriages to accommodate those who might fall sick or prove unable to cross the deserts and mountains, a testament to the nobility of his enterprise since otherwise they would lag behind to perish. If a cart suffered damage while he was nearby he would not proceed until it had been fixed. By all accounts he was loved and respected.

King Bela of Hungary welcomed Frederick with a triumphant celebration and himself took the cross, followed by many of his subjects alight with eagerness to restore the Holy City. They feared nothing and looked forward to combat. Frederick's army crossed the Danube unmolested, but upon reaching the passes of Bulgaria they were attacked by Pincenates, Bulgarians, Alans, and other savages. From Bulgaria into Macedonia they encountered treacherous narrows, rocks and thorns, but overcame each obstacle and came to Philippopolis. The Greeks, who fear what they do not love, had run away. These people are perfidious and degenerate, gorging on ancient hatreds. Once the Greeks were proud, equally accomplished at war and the arts of peace, yet what once were fountains had diminished to trickles, or, as some assert, barren channels. The legacy of their virtue had turned to hollow pomp, their deceit surpassing that of Simon. They had grown more false than Ulysses, more diabolic than Atreus roasting the flesh of his nephew.

Frederick being anxious for peace sent ahead to Constantinople the bishop of Münster. Yet what did the double-minded Emperor Isaac do but cast him in prison, violating the regard that has obtained from antiquity, even among barbarians. Later, dreading Frederick's wrath, worried that Constantinople might be reduced to smoldering waste, Isaac set the bishop free. Many of Frederick's host asked why the emperor should go unpunished. And they learned of new mosques built in Constantinople with his consent. This malevolent sovereign, professed Christian, sought to ingratiate himself with Turks.

Now as Libra balanced days and nights toward equivalent lengths, the season ripening into autumn, Frederick took up quarters in Adrianople, there to await the passage of winter and the favorable climate of spring. His younger son, the duke of Swabia, looked about to find some employment for this maundering army, since enforced leisure might degenerate to sloth or malfeasance. He discovered a castle stuffed with Greeks who, proud of their strength, spun webs to catch and pillage Germans. Soon enough they were vanquished and shackled. Emperor Isaac, dreading tomorrow, offered to ferry this menacing host across the Arm of Saint George, thereby with God's help seeing every German off to Armenia.

In March of that year 1190 they crossed the narrow strait which divides the world between Europe and Asia, marking a fruitful limit.

So they approached Iconium, riding unaware toward pagan hostility. For the sultan had despatched messengers to Frederick while the army loitered in Greece, professing amity, urging Frederick to cross over, masking the venom in his heart while he longed for a cup of Christian blood. Indeed, the sultan accused Greeks of duplicity while proposing himself a devout and faithful servant, offering a market for Germans to buy what they needed en route to the Holy Land, vowing to set himself and all he owned at their disposal, pledging safe passage. Frederick, measuring others by himself, trusted the sultan.

With these Germans went one archbishop, two royal dukes, nineteen counts, three marquises. As to knights and common soldiers, Geoffrey de Vinsauf lists the former at three thousand, the latter at eighty thousand. To avoid disaffection in such a host Frederick divided them, making of his army a head, a trunk, and a tail. The duke of Swabia, his son, proceeded first. Next came those charged with the care of animals and baggage. Emperor Frederick himself came last. Hence all was judiciously arranged, pleasant to behold.

They entered Parthia, dominion of Turks, experiencing no difficulty save asperities of the road because the sultan wished to entice them. But he had populated the gorges, thickets, and mountain heights. His troops opposed Frederick with arrows and stones. Such was the safe passage promised, the promised market. During the night javelins pierced German tents, killing Jerusalemfarers while they slept. For six weeks these Germans did not remove their coats of mail. If a horse died they pounced on the flesh and drank the blood, pretending they dined on veal and swallowed good wine.

They came to a passage between high rocks. But here lay Turks in ambush and rushed from hiding once the duke of Swabia went through. When this news was brought forward the duke wheeled about red with rage and led his cavalry heedlessly into the defile, shouting his father's name. Turks knocked off his helmet and broke out most of his teeth, as could be seen later when he opened his mouth to talk. Yet his bare gums proved consolation of a sort, testifying to victory since the Turks retreated.

Whitsunday they got to Iconium. But the sultan, not anxious to meet Frederick Barbarossa, had shut the gates, so they were obliged to camp outside. Next morning here was God's enemy at every flank. What with shouting, whistling, thundering drums, the mighty blast of trumpets, and a clash of swords fit for purgatory, these Turks made noise enough to waken Antioch. The sultan meantime arranged himself comfortably in a barbican to enjoy the spectacle his cunning mind devised. So confident were these misbelievers that some carried chains in place of weapons. However, Frederick's troops quickly took the city. Heaps of dead infidels clogged the streets. Then the sultan, observing how matters stood, professing himself innocent, offered as much gold as Frederick wanted. The emperor, too lenient, took what was promised and let him go. It would have been more honorable to slay so great a villain.

Next to Armenia, rejoicing that a malevolent kingdom lay behind. Surely these pilgrims rejoiced to enter Armenia, a land where Christ our Lord was known to rule.

deus lo volt!

Anon they reached the fabled river Cydnus which long ago claimed the life of Alexander. And when they came to the water Frederick hesitated, mindful of that omen deduced by his astrologer. It is said he asked the guides how he might avoid crossing the bridge, if there might be a different road. They told him of a way, if he would ford the river. The ford is good, the water is not swift, they assured him. We will go ahead, they told him, and show you where to cross. So he went with them and watched while they crossed the Cydnus. When they had safely returned he ordered them to lead his son across, which they did, and again returned. Frederick now urged his mount into the river, following two knights. But when he was half across the animal stumbled, throwing him from the saddle. And the water being cold sucked away his strength, the veins of his body opened and he drowned. At this ford no other horse stumbled. How often things occur that amaze or confuse us, but there is meaning in our bewilderment since it encourages us to recognize and venerate the Author of every circumstance.

Frederick was old, near seventy, moderately tall, red hair turning gray, and the red beard that begot his sobriquet. His shoulders and chest were broad, as was his face, manly in all respects. His eyelids protruded above sparkling eyes, and about him was something both dreadful and distinguished, as was told of Socrates. His look denoted resolution undiluted by anger, sadness, or pleasure. If the heights of Gilboa where Saul was killed should be deprived of rain, why should the river Cydnus be deprived? It brought down a pillar from the temple of Christendom. All in his army felt afflicted, yet all agreed that Frederick Barbarossa gained admittance to heaven because he served worthily in the ranks of our Lord, pledged to retrieve the Holy Land. All gave thanks he did not expire in the realm of infidels. Some say that place where he drowned was marked with fatality. Here was an inscription from ancient times prophesying that a sovereign would come to grief.

Chronicles do not explain how Turks besieged at Acre learned of

Frederick's death, but they whistled with delight, beat madly upon timbrels, leapt about the ramparts while renegadoes cried out to dismay the Christians.

Your emperor is drowned! Your emperor is drowned!

The knighthood of Germany soon began to rot. Those Teutonic pilgrims felt the Savior cared little for them. Mourning occupied their hearts. Some, writhing between hope and dread, renounced the true faith to go and live among Turks. The wreath, they said, has faded from our brow. Some made their way to the siege of Acre. Some joined the garrison at Tyre. Others trudged toward Germany, broken, disconsolate, expiring as they walked. It is well known how Germans are fated never to reach the Holy Land.

Concerning Frederick, they soaked his corpse with vinegar. Perhaps, as many believe, the duke of Swabia carried what remained of his father toward Jerusalem, but it decomposed and was abandoned. Geoffrey de Vinsauf relates that Frederick was taken to Antioch where the flesh boiled from his bones was laid to rest in the church of the Apostolic see. His naked skeleton despatched to the city of Tyre, whence it should be conveyed to Jerusalem. If so, this must be a wonderful contrivance of God that the Holy Roman Emperor who contended gloriously for Christ might find repose in two paramount churches of Christendom, one rendered sacred by the burial of our Lord, one distinguished by the greatest of apostles.

Concerning Saladin, the drowning of Frederick seemed providential for it is widely understood that Germans without a leader have no idea what to do. Thus he might devote himself fully to the siege of Acre. And knowing how those inside the walls must be near death from starvation, he resorted to deceit. He ordered a huge vessel at the port of Beyrouth to be loaded with sheep, corn, onions, cheese, and other foods. The mariners he caused to shave their beards and outfit themselves like Franks. He directed that crosses be fixed to the mast and he caused a brood of pigs to be visible on deck. Thus disguised the Muslim ship went gliding among Christian galleys to the port of Acre where heathen troops greeted it with screams of joy.

deus lo volt!

So this was a fortuitous acquisition. Nonetheless, if oil is poured on the fire does it not bring forth a livelier flame? Of course. Does not the wheel, turning slowly at first, rise with increasing alacrity? Of course. So did word of Islamic success bring more and more to the cross, more and more who vowed to crush the serpent.

During the blessed year 1189, at Nonancourt in Normandy, King Philip Augustus and Richard Lionheart embraced like brothers. Richard now was king of England, his father Henry Plantagenet having lately surrendered the ghost. These monarchs intent on Jerusalem vowed to undertake the pilgrimage and live on cordial terms until at least forty days after they returned. They devised certain rules of conduct toward the prevention of disorder and gross turbulence. No man beneath the rank of knight should gamble for money since these games lead to quarrels and bloodshed. Nor were clerics, knights, or personal attendants of monarchs permitted to win or lose more than twenty shillings a day on pain of being whipped naked through the army. A pilgrim that struck another and drew blood should have his hand chopped off. Whoever slew another should be tied to the corpse and buried with it. If murder occurred at sea, the murderer drowned in the victim's embrace. For sailors guilty of crimes such as theft, boiling pitch was poured on their shaved heads so all might know them and at the next port they were cast ashore. In regard to women, none should accompany the host save washerwomen who had reached the age of fifty. Although it is known that many young women defied the prohibition to follow men of their choice.

These monarchs further agreed that a tax should be levied, which they called Saladin's Tithe, being the tenth part of each man's property, landed or personal, enforced throughout Christendom against all who could not or would not make the journey. The lord of each fief being charged to raise this tithe. However those who took the cross would enjoy lenience since they could not be oppressed for malfeasance of any sort, debt, thievery, murder.

King Philip Augustus accepted his pilgrim staff and wallet from the abbot of Saint Denys in June of the year 1190. Richard Lionheart accepted his at Tours, but when he leaned on the staff to measure its strength it cracked. If he made light of such an omen, no chronicle reports.

Now proceeding fruitfully in their knowledge of God these sovereigns traveled from Vézelay to Mulins, afterward to Mount Escot, and continued south to Lyons on the Rhône. They hesitated at this river because of its violence, but at length crossed over and erected their pavilions on the meadow not far apart. Pilgrims lodged here or there in the fields as best they could. It is said their number exceeded one hundred thousand with more arriving.

King Philip soon departed with all his men to cross the Alps, having contracted with Genoese, famous sailors, to carry him as far as Messina. King Richard bade him farewell amid protestations of mutual friendship. They agreed that whichever put in first at Messina should await the other.

No more was Philip out of sight than the Rhône bridge began to crumble and one hundred soldiers tumbled in, crying loudly for help. All were rescued save two, which must be counted a miracle. King Richard then had boats drawn up side by side, enabling the rest of his people to cross over. Three days afterward he marched away from Lyons and that very day the bridge dropped into the river.

He came next to Dompas near Avignon, thence by Salus and Marignan to Marseille where he encamped three weeks. Since billowing waves turned Richard's belly upside down he decided to proceed by land with a modest escort through Genoa, Pisa, and south along the coast, thinking he could endure a brief passage across the strait to Messina. Thus, on the day after the Assumption of Blessed Mary his army embarked for Messina without its king. They sailed between Corsica and Sardinia by means of a strait that those people call Bonifacio. They rowed and sailed by two burning mountains, Vulcano and Strango, and came in view of Messina where they cast anchor to await the sovereign.

Documents relate that Richard passed through the village of Mileto with but a single knight in his train. Soon thereafter he heard a falcon shriek. He turned aside and went into the house, expecting he would take this bird for himself. But here came peasants with staves and one drew a knife against the king. At this Richard smote him with the flat of his sword and broke it, overcame the others and got himself to the priory of La Bagnara. He did not stay long but crossed the strait and let himself down to rest beside a stone tower called Far or Pharos since it is a beacon. The king by incontinent desire for a peasant's falcon brought this trouble upon himself. Fittingly, the strait he crossed has been known from ancient days for two perils, Scylla and Carybdis, which may be called hauteur and greed.

Next day Richard came to his fleet, more than one hundred ships that included fourteen towering buzas. Some boasted three rudders, thirty oars, thirteen anchors, triple ropes of every sort. Each might transport forty destriers with riders, sergeants, mariners, and food to sustain all for eight or ten months. So when everything was arranged King Richard with the captains of his army and their attendants embarked on galleys to precede this noble fleet.

Messina, being first in Sicily for affluence, abounds with good things, but its citizens are wicked and cruel. Many claim descent from Saracens. They are insolent, hostile, pointing their fingers into their eyes to mock or threaten strangers, sneering, cutting throats, pushing victims into sewers. Hence they are called griffons.

Now if a sovereign is conspicuous for glory he exhibits his greatness to the admiration of all so that homage may be rendered. He does not by concealing himself tarnish the authority with which he has been invested. He understands the proverb. Such as I behold you, thus do I esteem you. Therefore when people heard that

Philip Augustus was sailing toward Messina they hurried to marvel at so famous a king. Yet this artless man, misliking the fulsome gaze of citizens, entered the port of the citadel privately. And they who had waited along the shore to writhe in the splendor of his coming interpreted this as miserable. They pointed at him with their mouths, cried to each other that a sovereign who slunk past like a timid dog was unfit to lead.

But here is King Richard. Again the citizens of Messina rush forth, crowd the shore, arrange themselves to watch. Faraway the water sparkles, helmets reflect the sun, swords flash fire. Distant and shrill a trumpet blast, booming drums, banners beyond counting. Now the sea mother gives birth to her swarm of galleys, each distinguished by singular painting on the bow, by the shields of valiant knights aboard. Pennons stream from the points of spears. The sea rages and shakes. Those on shore feel crushed by pounding drums, destroyed by the authority of imperial trumpets. King Richard is here. Richard of England. His galley splits the furious water. At the beaked prow he stands. Like a god he stands at the beaked prow. Waves rage beneath his foot. Those gathered along the shore clutch themselves in admiration. They touch one another. They say he is worthy. They say King Richard deserves to be set above nations, above kingdoms, for the majesty of which they heard is nothing compared to the truth of him.

Those of his equipage receive him at the landing, bring forth spirited chargers so the king with his attendants may ride to the hostel where they sleep. And the drums boom. Silver trumpets sound. And the griffons feel themselves checked by this English lion, knowing themselves inferior.

With the consent and goodwill of the kings of France, England, and Sicily a decree is promulgated as to lodging, gambling, borrowing, desertion and such like, down to the marketing of wine or making of bread. The price of wine shall not be raised after it is cried. Whoever buys corn shall have a profit limited to one terrin in each quarter and the bran. Other merchants, no matter what calling, shall have a profit of one penny in ten. Four Anjou pennies shall merit one English penny. Nor may any sound the king's money on which his stamp appears unless cracked within the circle.

But some pilgrim from Richard's army quarreled over a loaf of bread and would have it weighed. So the woman flew into a passion, abused him wickedly and meant to claw his hair. Griffons rushed forth, beat the Englishman half to death and trampled his body. Soon enough a complaint was listed. King Richard entreated all to relent, saying he had come to Messina amicably. For a time this matter rested, but all at once came back hotly to life. Both kings met with justiciaries and with respected citizens. Next a cry went up that griffons were attacking pilgrims. Others cried differently. It is reported that two merchants by name Luppin and Margarit excited the crowd for a purpose of their own. However it was, King Richard found himself subject to arrogant railings when he endeavored to make peace. Then he, who was not born temperate, offended to the depths by such mockery, took up arms. Then the people began to shout and seized what came to hand, javelin or stone, boasting of how they would resist. Some beseeched the French king for help against this English king, offering themselves, property and all, if he would help them. And Philip, thick with jealousy at Richard's fame, answered that he would aid the people of Messina sooner than he would the king of England. Thus two sovereign associates became adversary, vowing to fight on a loaf of bread.

Down from the walls showered rocks, darts, and javelins, sending three bold knights into the arms of Christ. Peter Tireprete. Matthew de Saulcy. Radulph de Roverei. Such an impetuous defense could not hold. In less time than required to chant the matin service Richard overwhelmed Messina and ten thousand Englishmen occupied the streets, robbed, took what women they liked. Sicilians fled here or there. Many leapt off house tops, thinking they could expect no mercy. And very soon the Plantagenet standard floated from a turret. Then the English king, mistrusting his Frankish ally and citizens alike, had a wooden castle built to overlook the walls and named it

Mategriffon, which is to say killer of Greeks. Those inside Messina now looked up at Englishmen forever watching.

But after long and stormy months when the season for travel approached these Franks and English became less churlish. They had loitered from the feast of Saint Michael until after Lent and all felt anxious to pursue the journey. Couriers brought news from Acre. Mahometans withstood the siege.

Both armies prepared to embark when news came of Richard's mother Queen Eleanor hastening toward Messina. She would bring his love Berengaria, daughter of King Sancho VI of Navarre. From the time he was count of Poictou he had loved the Spanish princess. She was his heart's desire.

King Philip, taking advantage of favorable wind, embarked on Saturday after the Annunciation of Blessed Mary. King Richard with his noblest peers accompanied the Franks some few leagues, but returned hastily to greet his love. Many think Queen Eleanor arranged this match. Who can look through centuries and be sure? After three days at Messina she sailed for England, charged by King Richard to administer the realm during his absence. And the king dallied with Berengaria, forgetful of all else, insensible to the fate of Jerusalem. Even so King Richard would linger beside his love, disdaining the journey.

Now there was a Cistercian abbot in Calabria, by name Joachim, who rushed to and fro with sword in hand, hair streaming, gibbering of Apocalypse, of seven heads of the dragon. Antichrist. Herod. Nero. Constantius. Mahomet. Melsemuth. Saladin. They say he was gifted with second sight and Richard summoned him to discuss futurity. To Messina came this prophet and they debated the substance of abomination, whether Antichrist would take up the guise of pontiff as Joachim declared, or Antiochene as Richard thought. Antichrist would emerge from the tribe of Dan to rule Jerusalem, Richard asserted, only to be hurled aside. He would cause persecution across the earth and by gifts, terror, and miracles would he elevate himself. Those who accepted Antichrist would be showered with gold. Those who rejected him would be conquered by horror, others led astray through malevolent signs.

But while they argued such matters a comet gleamed above Messina, signifying God's displeasure. King Richard, knowing himself to be the instrument, prepared for embarkation. Berengaria he quartered on a stout dromond with trusted knights and servants to assure her comfort, his sister for companionship.

Before leaving Sicily he presented to King Tancred that sword which Britons know as Caliburne, Excalibur as others say, that once belonged to Arthur.

Wednesday after Palm Sunday the fleet departed. Rowing and sailing with a fair breeze they came out into the deep, yet after a while it slacked off so between Calabria and Mount Gibello they lay at anchor. Then He who commands the wind of His treasuries sent forth a welcome gift on the day of the Lord's Supper. But soon enough the vessels met contrary wind. Waves beat together. Pilgrims dropped to their knees. Knights and sergeants felt much afflicted. Ships rocked back and forth on the restless face of the water and turned aside. Richard's fleet was cast apart. Toward evening the fury abated, a soft breeze arose that helped their confidence and all could see in advance a thick wax candle burning in a lanthorn at the stern of Richard's galley as was his habit in rough weather. So the vessels pressed ahead, not a sail lowered until they came to the harbor of Crete, equidistant from Messina and the Holy Land. Richard waited to count his ships. Twenty-five were gone. Because that dromond carrying his love Berengaria did not arrive he was much distraught.

Anon the wind rose high and with bending masts they put forth. They sailed across to Rhodes, city of Herod's birth, where they paused. Remnants of majestic buildings lay strewn about since this is an ancient city not unlike Rome. Once there had been numerous monasteries on the island and societies of monks. Now for the most part everything stands deserted, making it a gloomy place, the inhabitants few and poor. Richard being taken by some illness, the fleet waited upon his health. Meantime they searched the horizon. And the king inquired about the Greek emperor of Cyprus, Isaac Ducas Comnenus, who was said to be cruel, often detaining pilgrims en route to the Holy Land.

Ten days later they embarked and came into the gulf of Satalia where opposing currents meet and great waves collide, until at length shifting winds drove them ahead. Beneath a placid sky they observed a buza returning from Jerusalem. King Richard inquired about the siege of Acre. Mariners on the buza replied that the king of France was constructing machines to break down the walls. They said he had erected petraries near the tower called Maledictum where his army camped. This news pleased Richard.

Once more the spirit of the storm rushed against them. Much time was lost beating back and forth amid the waves. Again the fleet dispersed. Unknown to Richard, three small vessels got to Cyprus before him, if not as they wished. Driven by fierce wind against the rocks they broke apart. Many drowned. Others by clutching timbers or through providence were flung on the coast half dead. Among the drowned was Roger, surnamed Catulus, bearer of the king's signet. His body washed up before sunset on the vigil of Saint Mark the Evangelist.

Those who escaped the sea thought themselves fortunate and safe because Greeks on Cyprus were Christian. Instead, they were hauled before Isaac Ducas who ordered their heads forfeit, although they committed no wrong, but rather had journeyed in the name of God to cleanse the Holy Land. Yet through the grace of our Lord there was in Isaac's service a Norman knight who felt distressed by this cruelty of the emperor. He rode hastily to where the pilgrims would suffer death and in the name of Isaac Ducas Comnenus he commanded those charged with execution to sheathe their swords. And because they knew him to be in the emperor's service they obeyed. Then the knight addressed these pilgrims in French, bidding them hide themselves until the Messiah should come to their relief. And he begged them to pray for his soul because he knew Isaac Ducas would put him to death. Thus it happened. No more did Isaac learn of this perfidy than he ordered the knight's head severed, which was done at once, willingly, because Greeks regard Franks as heretic and think God is pleased if they kill a Latin.

Also, that dromond carrying Lady Berengaria arrived at Cyprus. The master thoughtfully did not make port at Limassol but cast anchor some distance offshore, not wishing to hand up King Richard's betrothed and his sister to the ruthless Greek who governed this island. Isaac Ducas sent gifts of ram's flesh, bread, and Cypriot wine, which is alleged to have no match for quality anywhere on earth, and he urged the noble ladies to come ashore. They would not, which was prudent. According to Geoffrey de Vinsauf, this Greek surpassed Judas at treachery, Guenelon at treason, and wantonly persecuted any who professed the faith of our Lord. They say he was a friend of Saladin whose blood he tasted, as Saladin tasted his. Hence the dromond carrying these ladies rocked in the swells and waited. All on board kept watch for a glimpse of King Richard and wondered at the condition of his fleet while the ladies resisted Isaac Ducas by keeping him in suspense, responding to his importunities with ambiguous answers.

On the festival of Saint John two vessels appeared. Those aboard the dromond saw them black as two crows riding the summit of curling water. Now here came others and it was Richard and he put in quickly at the port of Limassol before the Latin Gate. By some accounts he landed peacefully and established camp among nearby gardens after being told that Isaac Ducas had fled to the mountains. Others claim that Isaac Ducas with a large army surrounded the port to engage King Richard, blocking up the entrance with obstacles of every sort, benches, ladders, doors and windows from houses, timbers, casks, ancient galleys, whatever might impede the landing. Perhaps, as some relate, King Richard leapt from a barge, sword in hand, knights and sergeants after him baying like dogs because he had learned of Cypriot peasants looting his broken ships, taking half-dead mariners captive, plundering bodies. They speak of a peasant

217

who rifled the drowned body of Roger Catulus, found the royal signet and hoped to profit by selling it to the king. As to this peasant's fate, old narratives are silent.

It is known that Richard despatched three monks with a message to Isaac Ducas.

I do not understand why you have abandoned Limassol nor why you avoid me. I am a pilgrim in the service of our Lord and am keen to speak with you. Let us consult on matters to your advantage.

Isaac Ducas replied that he would come and speak with Richard provided he got safe conduct. Therefore a rich Norman, William de Préaux, rode up into the mountains where Isaac welcomed him and gave him presents and comfortable lodging. When this knight returned to Limassol he said that Isaac would bring his army and bivouac two leagues distant at the village of Kolossi. After which he would visit the king.

Richard chose a few men with dependable swords and tongues he trusted. Then out on the plain he rode, riding a mettlesome Spanish charger with high shoulders and pointed ears, long neck, matchless thighs, limbs so perfectly marked that no artist could imitate them. They say this animal would not be checked, by the alternate motions of its tense body seeming first to advance on hind feet, now on fore feet. Richard's saddle glistened with red and gold spangles intermingled, across the hinder part two rampant gold lions challenged one another, reaching toward each other, mouths opened wide to devour. The king himself was handsomely dressed, wearing a rose-red vest ornamented with silver crescents that winked in the sun. His spurs were gold. The handle of his sword was gold, the mouth of the scabbard latched with silver. On his head a scarlet hat adorned with needlework cleverly depicting sundry birds and beasts. Thus accoutred he bounded into the saddle. Out he went to the plain where his tent was pitched, there to await the Greek.

When he saw Isaac Ducas riding toward him he left his tent and walked as far as a man could throw a stone. Then the emperor of Cyprus dismounted and bowed numerous times. King Richard also bowed. So they went into the tent where they seated themselves on a bench draped with silk. Richard by means of an interpreter addressed Isaac Ducas.

I am astonished that you, a Christian who well knows how Turks desecrate the Holy Land, have sent neither aid nor counsel to your brethren. Even now, with Acre besieged, you fail to help. Your hostility seems apparent because you oppress and injure many who come to assist those in need. Therefore I require you on behalf of God to make amends. I require you to come in person to the siege of Acre, bringing as many knights and sergeants as possible. In this way you will honor yourself and put an end to complaints against you.

The Greek replied that if he should leave Cyprus he would not be able to come back. For, said he, the emperor at Constantinople disputes this land. The people would rise up against me if I do as you require. But most gladly will I send five hundred men until Acre is taken.

And it is related that he promised indemnity of three thousand five hundred marks to conciliate those who were abused and plundered. King Richard declared himself satisfied at this. They exchanged the kiss of peace. Isaac Ducas then returned to his luxurious pavilion where he ate and lay down to sleep. But a certain doublehearted knight, Pain de Caiffa, whispered that Richard meant to seize him. In darkness the Greek crept out, mounted a favorite charger and fled, leaving behind all of his tents and possessions. When he got safely to Famagusta he despatched a monk to Richard ordering him to quit Cyprus at once, saying that if he did not he would learn how little he was loved.

King Richard, not a patient man, marshaled his army for pursuit. Isaac Ducas left Famagusta and fled into the woods, which were difficult to search. Richard directed that the ports of Cyprus be strictly watched to prevent him getting off the island.

Now here came the bishop of Beauvais and a high noble, Drogo de Mirle, who were ambassadors from the king of France, who exhorted Richard to cross the sea at once, saying that he expended

219

himself on vainglorious duties while neglecting necessary matters, saying that by his campaign against Isaac Ducas he presumptuously harmed innocent Christians while the adjoining land bristled with more Turks than fleas, saying that King Philip Augustus waited on his arrival. To all of which Richard answered testily, saying he was busy enough punishing Greeks as they deserved and furthermore deemed it an obligation to subdue this island.

Then he marched toward Nicosia holding his army in close order, having learnt that Isaac Ducas waited in ambush. And here came a torrent of Cypriots shouting and growling like dogs, flinging javelins and darts. Isaac himself let fly two poisoned arrows at Richard, which so enraged the impetuous king that he laid spurs to his mount and tried to run through the emperor with a lance but could not because Isaac fled on a bay horse of such fleetness that no one ever saw its match. In a short time the ground where these Cypriots camped was strewn with swords, pennons, darts, and bloody coats of mail. Much fine stuff did Richard's soldiers pick up from the ground and pluck from the imperial tent. Isaac's bed and harness, silks, purple garments, silver plate. They took chargers that champed the foaming bit, splendid mules with embroidered cushions, agile and stubborn goats, ewes, rams, mares with foal. Not displeased at so much booty Richard moved on toward Nicosia whose citizens appeared to congratulate him as though he always had been their lord, a calculated piece of wisdom. To this he responded with grace but caused them to shave their beards in token of allegiance. And the emperor, when news was brought, mutilated every captive pilgrim to assuage his grief, scooped out eyes and cut off noses.

King Richard laid waste to Cyprus, nor hesitated nor shrank, but set about eradicating an evil root that he might plant a good strong seed of Roman Christianity. Every castle surrendered to him excepting those very difficult to attack such as Didemus, Bufevent, and Cherimes. He gathered up the spoil, golden cups, kettles, bowls, silver pots, scarlet robes, precious woven cloth with elaborate patterns, every manner of wealth. As much as Croesus possessed, Richard gathered.

deus lo volt!

At length he took the great fort of Cherimes. And here was the daughter of Isaac Ducas whom the Greek loved more than any living thing. They say Isaac howled and pulled his beard when told of her capture and thought to arrange peace, no matter what cost, for the pilgrim army had seized nearly all his forts and his people swore allegiance to the enemy with slight hope of resistance and they had got his daughter upon whom his soul depended. He sent word from the mountain where he hid, beseeching pity, vowing to keep aught for himself, not house nor land nor castle, pledging to lay all at Richard's throne but asking one grace, that he not be cast in iron shackles. To this King Richard agreed.

Down came the emperor of Cyprus out of hiding. And Richard Lionheart, turning to his chamberlain Ralph Fitz Godfrey, ordered the tyrant dressed with silver chains. Also, he took Isaac's magnificent horse Fauvel.

Some time after, having reflected upon Isaac's misfortune, Richard bade the miserable Greek sit beside him and permitted him to see his daughter, which made Isaac as joyous as if he touched the right foot of God. An hundred times or more Isaac Ducas kissed the sweet child and wept, after which they led him off to captivity.

In the chapel of Saint George at Limassol, on the twelfth of May in the year of our gracious Lord 1191, King Richard married his love Berengaria. There were present numerous high lords, as well as the archbishop and the bishops of Evreux and Baneria. On this occasion he proved cheerful and jocose. And his Spanish love Berengaria, sang the jongleur Ambroise, was the fairest, wisest lady on earth. Thus the king reveled in his glory.

But one day while he loitered by the shore at Famagusta here came a vessel from the east showing a flag with five black crosses on a white ground, envoys from the kingdom of Jerusalem. Philip Augustus wished to know why Richard dallied on Cyprus when troops were needed for the siege of Acre. Not long afterward Richard embarked, his men sailing and rowing as swiftly as they could since he had not traveled this far to be left without.

God defer the taking of Acre till I have gained the wall, said he.

That prize he sought is known to be among the oldest cities on earth, called Akka by some very ancient pharaoh. A while later Ptolemy named it Ptolemais to honor himself. Anon came Franks who christened it Saint Jean d'Acre. Save only Constantinople, no city boasted such wealth. Here was a very fine customs house where officers seated on handsome carpets dipped their pens into ebony inkwells. And on Sunday when church bells rang together the sound might be heard a league or more at sea.

What first met the gaze of Richard's men when they ploughed across the water was the fort of Margat, then Tortuosa, then Tripoli and Nephyn. Afterwards they saw the tower of Gibelath. And off Sayette they chanced upon a dromond packed with Saladin's Turks, eight hundred swarming over a solid vessel crowned by three tall masts. Nor was she an untidy piece of work but streaked across one side with green felt and yellow opposite until she resembled a fairy craft. She had meant to reach Acre but could not on account of the Christian army and now eased back and forth looking for another place to land, or glide into port by surprise. All stared in wonder, not knowing she was a Turk. No mark could be seen, Frank or otherwise, nor any Christian symbol. Then the king summoned Peter des Barres who commanded a galley, directing him to row speedily and find out who she was. Aboard the dromond was an interpreter who falsely cried out to Peter des Barres how they were Genoese bound for Tyre. But there was a galleyman with Richard who recognized the ship. Hang me or take my head, said he, if those are not Turks. And the king demanding if he was certain, he pledged his life.

King Richard sent galleys forward. Whereupon those aboard the dromond rose up shooting with Damascus bows and arbalests, shafts and bolts dropping thicker than hailstones. Richard swore an oath by the throat of God he would string up his oarsmen on gibbets if they idled or this Turk escaped. So they sprang to their work, plunging against the waves, and caught up to her because the wind carried her slowly. Geoffrey de Vinsauf, who was present, describes how they rowed more than once around the vessel to scrutinize her but found no point of attack, so large and stout she was and darts kept dropping on their heads. To meet the enemy on equal ground is enough, says he, whereas a dart thrown from above must tell on those below, considering how the iron point comes downward. All this Richard's men liked very little and their ardour slacked. Then the spirit of the king increased. He cast shame at the oarsmen, asked if they foundered, grew coistrel and timid from sloth. Therefore making virtue out of necessity because they cared no more for Richard's wit than iron darts, some hopped into the waves with rope to bind the Turk's rudders and slow her progress. Others got hold of cables and climbed up. All the same these pagans were no left-hand archers but skilled at combat and hewed off arms and legs as fast as Franks arrived, pitching bodies into the waves. And so King Richard's men thirsted after Turkish blood, crossed the bulwarks glowing with desire to thrust them back. Now up out of the hold rushed more, young and not afraid to die, thus both sides contributed to the bloody deck. Then the king, seeing how difficult it would be to take this stout ship, ordered galleys to attack with the iron beak that mariners call the spur. So they drew off far enough and reversing course propelled themselves with mighty strokes, rammed the dromond, skewered her. All at once this great ship cracked apart. Turks leapt howling overboard while the king and his men slashed right and left to kill as many as they could, and it is said Richard's lion shield dripped blood.

Some prisoners who could build or operate catapults he exempted from death, the rest slain, flung into the sea. Turks. Persians. Renegadoes. Had that dromond reached Acre, bringing seven emirs and all the means for defense she carried, Saladin's devils would have kept their grip. While at Beyrouth she brought on board one hundred camel loads of weapons, crossbows with winches, levers, darts, slings, racks, Greek fire in bottles, plus two hundred writhing gray serpents gorged with venom to hurl or drop from turrets into the living army of Christ. But through divine intercession the Turk was sunk, noxious vipers scattered across the waves.

Unbelievers on a hilltop witnessed this combat. They cursed the hour and wailed and brought the news to Saladin. He clawed his beard for grief, moaned that Acre was undone. Those attending him lamented the fate that brought them to Syria, ripped their garments, snipped their curly tresses because of so many emirs and slaves of Allah lost.

King Richard held course, passed by Candalion, by Casella Ymbrici, sailed within view of Acre's high tower. All about were the armies of Christ encamped. Beyond them Saladin's host covering hills and valleys. They saw his pavilion and the tent of his brother Malik al-Adil.

King Richard touched the strand at eventide in the week of Pentecost before the feast of Saint Barnabas while the ground shook with acclamation. Horns, drums, flutes, timbrels, pipes, harps, trumpets, shouts of welcome. Universal gladness reigned. Many recited the deeds of ancient heroes to express their delight at his coming, others sang familiar ballads. High and low, they gathered as one, dancing with jubilation. Wax torches illuminating the night made it appear the land was on fire. As for Turks who observed this celebration from a distance, they were alarmed and downcast, murmuring, tugging their beards.

King Philip met Richard at the shore, pretending friendship. It is said he embraced Queen Berengaria and graciously escorted her to dry land, hiding his fury. Once upon a time Richard paid court to Philip's sister. Before leaving England he had sworn an oath to marry her on the fortieth day after his return from Jerusalem. Instead, at Limassol, he pledged himself to the Spanish princess.

It is claimed that Philip might have taken Acre. When he first arrived he rode about to measure the defense. He set up iron screens,

having them tinned until they gleamed like silver to reflect sunlight,
as protection for crossbowmen, archers, and miners burrowing at the
wall. He directed that volleys of arrows and quarrels be launched until not a Turk dared show a finger. He put miners to work at the wall
where it abuts the Maudite Tower. Soldiers from Pisa rolled up a cat,
but Turks set this ablaze and threw down hams, oil, and fish to make
things worse so all beneath it met the Lord. However, a section of
the wall collapsed. Then a company of knights got through, albeit
they were driven back. Those inside Acre had flags for signaling and
a basket they raised above the church of Saint Lawrence, which they
had converted to a mosque. These signals appealed to Saladin for
help. Now they ran up their flags and the basket to say they felt hard
pressed. They struck timbrels, pounded on basins and platters to
alert Saladin. Thus, many argue that Philip would have taken the
city. But he decided to wait upon King Richard because they had
agreed to share the joy of conquest.

Ambroise sang high praise of Richard, singing of how he did not
shirk from carrying burdens on his shoulder half a league across the
sand as if he were not a king but a mule dripping sweat. By all accounts his strength was fearsome, a graceful man with long and flex-
ible arms, auburn hair, a taste for poetry and handsome looks gained
from his mother, from the house of Poictou. That he could be subject to quick or violent rage was no secret. It happened once outside
Messina that Richard and Philip had ridden together in friendly di-
version, each accompanied by his entourage. Along came some rustic
whose donkey was heaped high with reeds and various nobles to
amuse themselves took reeds for jousting. King Richard and a valiant
knight in the service of Philip, Guillaume des Barres, charged one another. Both reeds splintered. But the king's head-gear broke, at which
he set himself upon the French knight, seeking to overthrow him
without success. And the king's saddle slipped and he went down
quicker than he liked.

Get thee hence, said he to Guillaume des Barres. Take care not to appear in my presence, for I am from this moment an enemy to thee.

Now off went the Frank to his lord Philip for aid and counsel regarding what had fallen out, much aggrieved by this royal indignation. Then the king of France went to Richard, asking for peace and mercy. Richard would not listen. Next day here came the bishop of Chartres, the count of Nevers, the duke of Burgundy, and other nobles on behalf of Guillaume des Barres, casting themselves at Richard's knee. He would have none of it. Some time after, when they would embark for the Holy Land, here was the French king once more with his archbishops and bishops and counts and barons and beseeched King Richard. With much trouble they got him to consent, Richard undertaking to do this knight no harm nor proceed against him while both were busied in the service of Jesus Christ.

Or it may be, as the narrator of Reims declares, they were not at Messina but riding through the midst of Acre. Richard being thick with anger toward the Franks set himself against Guillaume to strike him out of the saddle with a truncheon. But on the passage Guillaume seized Richard by the neck, hauled him loose, flung him down grievously against the paving stones. There lay the mighty king of England in a swoon without pulse or breath while Guillaume rode at once to tell King Philip how it was. So the French king ordered his folk to arm themselves, that much did he mistrust Richard. Next here came Lionheart recovered from his stupor to assault the French. It is said they defended themselves sturdily. Now all at odds, they appointed a truce of three days during which the matter was accommodated.

Whatever the circumstance, this rowdy Plantagenet was at a single breath several men, cautious or bold, brutal or kind, crafty or generous with equal measure. Having learnt how Philip promised three gold pieces a month to any English knight that would enlist beneath the Frankish banner, Richard offered six to any Frank that fought beneath the lion standard. Nor was it secret how he could manage this extravagance. He had sold the ravaged island of Cyprus to knights of the Temple.

He was not long in Acre when he fell sick with what common people call arnoldia, which is produced when foreign climate despoils the blood, wasting the lips and face. Despite this illness he caused mangonels and petraries to be erected and built a fort. One mangonel flung stones so far they crashed into the marketplace or butchery. And he brought from Messina such a pebble as squashed eight Turks. Further, he set up a belfrois with steps, protected from top to bottom with hides and ropes against Greek fire. During this time he was languid and faint, almost unable to rise from his pallet. Saladin also had fallen ill, gruesome carbuncles circling his waist, and could hardly rest or sleep.

King Philip meanwhile busied himself with engines. He built a device that would creep forward and cling to the wall. And at great expense a cercleia, which is a hurdle of twigs protected with hides and clay. He himself would crouch beneath this hurdle to shoot at pagans who showed themselves. Or he would throw darts from a sling. But one day the enemy flung down blazing wood and poured so much fire that the valuable clay was burnt. So the king began to curse his own soldiers, those who ate his bread, because they did not wreak vengeance on the Turks. He had it cried throughout camp that on the morrow they would advance.

Near sunrise, having appointed men to guard the trench against Saladin, these Franks pressed forward. There were bright coats of ring-mail and many a glittering crest. So the Turks lifted a tumult, beating on timbrels and platters and metal basins and shouting to the sky and waving devilish banners to notify Saladin. Almost at once here came his army riding and yelping across the plain, howling in the pagan tongue, brandishing accursed standards, dismounting as they got near the trench. Some carried clubs equipped with spikes, or poignards, and when they got to the barricades there was bloody slaughter. Godfrey de Lusignan picking up an axe slew ten of

227

Mahomet's filthy disciples. Back and forth they struggled, more and more Turks appearing, until those Franks who went against the wall had to retreat and help their comrades defend the camp. It is said that King Philip became discouraged and confused and would not mount his horse. Without leadership the servants of God did not know what to do. They waited unhappily, wondering how to fight the Lord's battle. On that day the host suffered greatly.

Also, King Philip had brought from Europe a white falcon which he dearly loved. It escaped from his glove and flew across the wall into Muslim hands. This did not augur well. Philip offered one thousand dinars if they would give it back. They refused because they wished to present the bird to Saladin. Next the count of Flanders died, further disheartening the pilgrim host. Yet is not our Lord minded to be merciful? Here came welcome assistance, bishops and princes, each with his retinue. Jordan de Humez. Earl Robert of Leicester. Radulph Taisson. Gérard de Talebor. Henry fitz Nicholas. Here came William Martel and William Bloez, and Hugh de Fierte who served gallantly in Cyprus, and others. Which is to say, God succored the host while two kings lay indisposed.

Philip was first to regain his strength. He constructed a redoubtable perrier called the bad neighbor, Male Voisine, which struck night and day because the walls of Acre are such that carts may pass one another on the ramparts, making it no easy thing to breach. The duke of Burgundy set up a perrier that inflicted severe damage and made the slaves of Allah scurry about. There was one called Perrier of God because of a priest who stood beside it preaching, which shook the tower Maudite. Others manned by Templars and Hospitalers never ceased, never quit hurling, such as the Sling of God. Yet the Turks replied with a machine the Franks called Male Cousine, bad cousin to a bad neighbor. Philip directed miners to dig at the ground beneath Maudite, which already they had battered. But the Turks thought to confront them and obliged captives to dig a countermine held up with stanchions. Yet when these parties met in darkness beneath the tower they did not fight because the shackled captives were Christian who spoke to the Franks in their mutual language to such good effect that some got through the tunnel and escaped. This mightily annoyed the Saracens.

Next occurred a great deed. A Frank of prodigious size gained the ramparts. Others brought him stones to throw, and although he was wounded fifty times and drenched with blood the Turks could not drive him off or kill him until a bottle of naphtha exploded on him and made him a torch.

Here, too, was a very great deed performed by Aubry Clément, Marshal of France. If it please God, he was heard to cry, before sunset I will die or stand within the walls of Acre!

Then up the ladder he went and Turks rushing noisily against him. Franks who climbed up after him overburdened the ladder, which broke and tumbled them in a ditch, bruising some to death while others lay hapless, groaning and bleeding. Marshal Aubry, pierced a thousand times, ascended gloriously to the arms of Christ with Allah's subjects capering about the turrets, hooting, whistling. So did he verify himself, according to Geoffrey de Vinsauf. Others say he did not freely attack the wall but was caught and dragged to martyrdom by a Saracen grappling hook. Be that as it may, a chanson forever celebrates the name of Aubry Clément.

And now King Richard, very weak, wrapped in a silken quilt, caused himself to be carried forward because he wished to do what mischief he could. From the ditch, swaddled in his quilt, he let fly many a crossbow dart. They say he was skillful. A Turk dared show himself on the ramparts dressed in the armor of Marshal Clément, which proved his last boast. Richard shot a bolt through his heart. The Turk threw up his feet and died.

We are told that Saladin and Richard felt warmly toward each other. While the Christian monarch lay ill, wasted, fingernails loose on his fingers, hair dropping from his brow, and whispers of poison, he despatched an envoy to the sultan. King Richard wished to make it known that since kings are wont to exchange gifts, even during time of war, a gift would be delivered if it should please the sultan. Malik al-Adil answered for his brother that a gift would be welcome if something might be given in return.

We have with us falcons, said Richard's envoy, as well as other birds of prey, but on the voyage they suffered and are dying. If you will give us chickens to feed them we will offer them as homage to the sultan when they have been restored to health.

We give you what you ask, Malik answered, because we know that your king is ill and requires chickens for his health.

Subsequently, when Richard wanted fresh fruit he received it. And they say that once when his mount was slain, leaving him open to capture, the Muslim lord sent him a fresh mount. If so, a curious tale. How should Christians interpret this?

At length, seeing how violently they were bombarded, fearing Saladin would not help, the people of Acre took counsel and thought they had best surrender to the Franks because King Richard terrified them. They asked safe conduct for ambassadors, praying that Philip might lift his assault while they discussed the business. Having got this assurance they sent a deputation to speak with him in his tent. They told him the city would be delivered if those inside might leave with their families and goods. He answered that everything within Acre must be his, yet he would grant their lives.

King Richard, all unaware, thinking he would take the city for himself, doubled his attack. Now the Turks in King Philip's tent rebuked him. What safe conduct is this? they asked. We thought this must hold until we returned to Acre, but look you. The English king does much damage. Since you are not strong enough to bid him stop, we ask leave to depart.

I will punish the English for violating this truce, King Philip said. Chronicles relate that already he had buckled on leg armor when counselors persuaded him to let the matter drop. Otherwise great harm would have ensued.

Two winters and a summer the city lay besieged. Christian and heathen alike wearied of the struggle. Each came to know the face of his enemy. At times they would put aside their weapons to mingle peaceably. There would be dancing, singing, feasts, entertainment, much as happened in the days of Iftikhar and Duke Godfrey and Bohemond and Tancred while Jerusalem lay under siege. Children contested the field in mock battle, uttering shrill war cries, charging, retreating, little captives ransomed for a piece of gold. But on the twelfth of July in our year of grace 1191, those defending Acre knew they could not prevail. Caracois, who was in charge, agreed to Christian terms. Documents tell how a swimmer left the harbor to notify Saladin and he was horrified. They say that while he sat in front of his tent composing a message to the garrison forbidding surrender he saw Frankish banners unfurl. He moved away from Acre and camped along the road to Saphori, knowing he must wait to receive ambassadors whose faith he mistakenly thought untrue.

King Richard stipulated that all captives must be freed, whether held in the city or in Saladin's camp. As indemnity for Christian loss, two hundred thousand gold pieces, four hundred extra for the marquis of Tyre. Lastly, Saladin must deliver up the True Cross, which he captured during the battle of Hattin. If these terms were met, the lives of all who defended Acre would be spared. Until such time, for insurance, Richard imprisoned the garrison. He then took up lodging in the royal palace. King Philip lodged in what had been the Templar fortress.

Unseemly quarrels disturbed the Christian host. Archduke Leopold of Austria, wrapped in conceit, thinking himself equal to the kings of England and France, flew his standard from a tower, which so nettled King Richard that with his own hand he pulled down the standard, tramped across it and flung it in a cesspool. Next, some dispute opposed Guy de Lusignan to Conrad de Montferrat. This was in turn reflected by quarrels among lesser lords.

And now Philip Augustus, weary, desperate for the sight of France, resolved to quit this insalubrious land. Those who fought beneath his standard felt disconcerted and bewildered. Acre is a handsome prize, said they among themselves, yet does not the reconquest of Jerusalem matter more? Such was their resentment that many spoke of disavowing him as their lord. But he was ill and wished to go home. On the last day of July he departed, sailing to Brindisi, thence to France. In our year of grace 1223 he was at Mantes holding parliament during the feast of Saint Mary Magdalene when death saw fit to reach for him. He confessed, abjured past malfeasance, made his devises. To the Holy Land he bequeathed a third part of his treasure, to the indigent a third, to the Crown of France a final third in order that it might be governed and defended, whereupon he gave back his soul to God. Although he was blind in one eye, none that knew Philip considered him imperceptive. They thought him a skeptical monarch, shrewd enough. High barons and knights bore his remains to Saint Denys. At each resting place a cross was erected, the likeness of Philip carved in stone. Archbishop William Joinville himself laid King Philip away and chanted mass. The tomb is all gold and silver, very fine. On the four sides in relief stand forty-eight bishops with mitres on their heads, croziers in their hands.

After he had gone King Richard looked toward the restoration of Acre. It seemed advisable to fortify the walls and otherwise maintain the city as a lighthouse of Christianity, a beacon that would blind the Saracen eye, pierce and thwart the Saracen heart. He walked among the masons while they worked, exhorting them, since it was always his intent to recover God's inheritance. However, a plethora of women and Syrian wine proved inimical to his purpose, debauching soldiers, making them slothful, complacent, oblivious. Ambroise relates in verse how these women cast their spell, how lechery, gluttony, every sort of vice conspired to vitiate and spoil the aims of conquest. This was because the diabolic agent of discord through stratagem and tricks, allurement, persuasion, seeks always to multiply the army of the damned.

deus lo volt!

When three weeks were up, this being the term fixed by Richard for payment and restitution of the Holy Cross, it appeared that Saladin was a transgressor who did not stand to his word and covenant. Often enough he would despatch envoys with artful words and gifts, arguing that he did not have the Cross but would do everything to find it. By such duplicity he hoped to extract more lenient terms. Richard therefore took counsel with the lords of the Christian host and they resolved to punish Saladin for wanton arrogance. Turks garrisoned at Acre, numbering almost three thousand, were roped and led to a field beneath Tel Keisen where they would be visible to Saladin's army. Then at Richard's command his soldiers leapt on this mass of flesh, striking unbelievers with sword and lance, slicing away heads, which mightily upset the Turks. Geoffrey de Vinsauf reports that these hostages were not put to the sword but hanged, as they deserved in the sight of God and man, excepting some few nobles who might be ransomed or exchanged for Christian captives. However these dark spirits fled, King Richard aspired to vindicate his faith by decimating the satanic horde, negating the false doctrine of Mahomet. Many of those slain were disemboweled because gall of a Turk makes good ointment. Thus were they chastised on Friday after the Assumption of Blessed Mary.

Some argue that Saladin was not at fault, considering that he needed more than three weeks to levy so much gold. As for the Holy Cross, they say it was carried to Damascus where furious pagans hacked it to splinters.

How many Christian soldiers ascended to Paradise during the siege of Acre? Those obtaining martyrdom included six archbishops, twelve bishops, forty counts, five hundred lesser nobles, innumerable priests, clerics, and humble palmers. Through combat or pestilence one hundred thousand gave up the ghost. Which is to say, not more than one of every two in the host survived. Acre basked in the hands of our loving and gracious Lord for eighty-three years. Then it suffered beneath the infidel yoke. But at last His will could not be denied.

At this siege my grandfather Geoffrey fell asleep in God. Neither day nor circumstance could I cite, yet I have honored him to the best of my authority with a tablet set in the church of Saint Laurent at Joinville castle. May he rest eternally in Your arms, Lord God.

Pilgrims now yielded to luxury and sloth because the cellars of Acre boasted choice wine and women stood at the corner. Men did not want to leave. They felt reluctant to forsake such delights and cross the river.

August had well advanced when the reluctant host moved south. Women were prohibited save good old dames such as toil and wash for armies, deft as apes at picking fleas. King Richard himself took the van, his standard borne on a wheeled cart decorated with rose-red spots. The post stood erect like the mast of a ship, solid timber-work neatly joined, sheathed in iron so it could not be splintered or burnt. About it like a wall rode Normans famous for courage since if the banner were seized, or the cart toppled, men might believe their lord overwhelmed. Few soldiers have strength to confront the enemy when they do not see who leads them, but even the timid feel empowered if his banner flies. Those who have been wounded are brought near it for comfort, making it a refuge, a beacon of certainty, a post of command. Hence the king's emblem trundled down the road to Joppa, drawn by mules, able to pursue unbelievers or yield, according to necessity.

These pilgrims marching along the coast might look with enjoyment at the sea on their right, but on the left Saladin kept company. From mountainous heights the Turk watched over them. And at a narrow passage beneath a troubled sky here came Mahomet's disciples scuttling down like vermin upon carts and sumpter beasts, attacking, plundering, quickly vanishing. Some Turk cut off the right hand of Everard who belonged to the bishop of Salisbury. Everard with his left hand snatched up the sword to defend himself. Now all was confusion. John Fitz-Luke galloped forward to notify King Richard. And the king returned full speed to help those under attack, slashing at Turks on either side, routing these infidels who fled as did the Philistines from Maccabeus, albeit quite a few remained since they were deprived of their heads. Yet here were many devout palmers sprouting twenty Turkish arrows.

Each night when they encamped it was the custom to depute some pilgrim who cried aloud in a strong voice. Help! Help! Help for the Holy Sepulcher! Everyone took up his cry, stretching their hands heavenward, weeping, calling for mercy. This lament they repeated a second time, a third time, after which all seemed much refreshed. Brown spiders that are called Tarantulas crept out of the ground at night, feeding on them. Pilgrims bloated like toads and complained until a rich man offered theriac to counter the venom. At length, seeing how these pests disliked loud noise, the army would make a discord at nightfall, clashing shields, helmets, buckets, beating on casques, basins, kettles, flagons, caldrons, or any implement to raise a tumult, and by the clamor sent these creatures hustling back into the earth.

By day they marched slowly. Numbers perished in the heat. King Richard caused those who were sick or disheartened to be transported on barges and smacks and galleys that accompanied the host. Flies no bigger than sparks would attack, fiercely biting hands, neck, cheek, or any part exposed, making the soldiers resemble lepers. They arranged veils for themselves, so it is said they looked comical while trudging across the sand. Very long ago the Romans brought stone from nearby hills to make a road between Acre and Joppa in order that chariots might roll easily up or down the coast but time had almost buried this antique road so it was no more than a trace through thorny brush.

When they got to Caesarea, halfway to Joppa, they expected to bivouac in comfort but found that Turks had destroyed whatever might be useful and had broken some of the towers and did not retreat until the army approached. Our Lord with His disciples often visited this city and here performed miracles. Close by is a stream where two Flemings went to bathe and were swallowed by crocodiles, hence it is known as the River of Crocodiles.

From Caesarea they proceeded with caution because of Turks who rode up to whistle and scream insults and launch arrows. These unbelievers carried only a light spear, a bow, or a mace with sharp teeth and by the quickness of their motion would come very near the ranks. Also there were black Muslims from Nubia who carried little round shields and scimitars and could whirl and flee with the agility of ghosts.

Two days out from Caesarea adherents of the devil swept down like a storm but left stretched on the field an emir of stupendous girth who was called Ayas Estoï because that was the name of his famous lance, heavier than two Frankish lances. This emir was reputed to be of such strength that no one could topple him. Now the Turks seeing their champion fall, his brawny arm at rest, his proud head rolling across the sand, yelped with grief and cropped the tails of their horses.

God's army came next to the forest of Arsuf, which they thought infested with blackfaced misbelievers who would burn down the trees to roast them. In close order they marched through, prepared for battle, and marched by the mountain to open country, each expecting to lose his head because of Saracens rising on every flank. That day the Templars rode in front. Next came Angevins, Bretons, Normans, English, Hospitalers last. It is said the high lords rode so close packed that an apple could not be thrown without hitting man or beast. Those of a lineage rode together and the Christian host appeared so bound that no heathen force could rend it. Here was the count of Leicester who would not in any wise have been elsewhere. Alongside rode Huon de Gournai with others of equal renown, William Borriz who was raised in that land, and James d'Avesnes. They advanced almost at leisure, King Richard astride Fauvel, which he got on Cyprus, other valiants going before the host, in back, right or left, to watch for what the spirit of darkness might do.

Now all at once two thousand pagans came sweeping through the sunlit dusk launching arrows, others assigned no task but to pound drums or skip and screech. With these rode Duquedin, joined through blood to Saladin, whose astonishing standard flaunted a pair of breeches. Duquedin of all Turks most fiercely hated Christians. He rode up leading his squadrons trailing yellow banners, pennoncels of divers shape and color, with great speed and clattering hooves. And savage blackamoors, Saracens of the heath, hideous to face, blacker than soot, each with his bow and round buckler, nimble, swift, eager to strike those who believed in Jesus Christ. How thunderous were these pagan drums? One could not have heard God's own thunder, sang Ambroise the jongleur. To fend off this devil's pack the Hospitalers marched backward and shouted with clear voices to Saint George for help. Few in the host did not wish this journey ended, knowing how they stood on slippery points. Bearded Turks that dismounted to shoot would get their heads sliced off, so palmers and filthy Muslims bundled together on the hard ground thick as stooks at harvest. Banners falling down and the windrow of heathen dead stretched half a league. So many sharp swords could be gathered, so many darts, arrows, maces, bolts enough to load a score of wagons. And the misbelievers fled yelping, climbed trees to escape, screeched worse than goblins when Franks levied them out to chop off their heads. Many cast themselves shrieking from cliffs. Everywhere these misbegotten dogs that would not accept Jesus Christ fell wounded, groaned, lamented their fate, weltered in gore, expelled one last breath, which mightily pleased the Lord.

Yet among these bloody heaps was found the body of James d'Avesnes about whom they said he was superior to Nestor in counsel, to Achilles in valor, to Regulus in faith. Round about him fifteen slain Turks, though not until his face was bathed could he be recognized. And there narrowly grouped three from his household asleep in our Lord. On that day a mettlesome knight looked toward Paradise and chose a place beside Saint James the Apostle whom he held to be his patron. Never was heard more lament, such mourning, not on the death of any man since Adam bit the apple, for James d'Avesnes did serve his God right well.

And the sultan told of his choice troops scattered was wrathful. He summoned his emirs to upbraid them. Ho! said he, addressing

237

them with contempt. How splendid, how marvelous the feats of this army! Have my comrades profited from defiant boasting? Behold the Christian host wandering about Syria as it pleases. You found the battle you lusted for, but where is the victory you trumpeted? How low have we sunk beneath our noble ancestors, who waged such war against Christians, whose deeds will not be forgotten. Beside them we are not worth an egg.

At this reproach his emirs stood silent.

Now the host came down to Joppa and here was a port engorged with scabby women from Europe as though to divert them from the journey, to roil them, foment lust, multiply misdeeds. Whores established pavilions, beckoned stray birds to the nest, exchanged smooth bodies for gold, hoisted their ankles above their ears and caught with little screams the horns of butting rams. Ah! Ah, mercy! cries the jongleur. Should our Christian faith be reclaimed by such naked weaponry?

In November at Joppa it happened that King Richard wished to take the air with his falcons and went hawking. He meant also to note the proximity of Turks, should there be any, and seize them if he could. Anon he dismounted to rest awhile, as did those in his small company, and he went to sleep. Some Turks having learned of it came down at full speed, but did not know which he was. Then, to save Richard, William de Préaux called out in Saracenic that he himself was Melech, which is to say Rex. Turks laid hands on this bold knight and led him off captive, exulting that they had caught the king. During this engagement Reynier de Marun ascended to glory, as did his nephew Walter, and Alan and Luke de Stabulo. King Richard rebuked himself for what occurred. Yet the hand of providence had interceded on his behalf, preserving him for greater things.

238

Now as he saw that his army lived less in fear of pagans and with God's help could defeat them, Richard sent messengers to Saladin demanding the return of Syria and all that belonged to it, such as it was when last governed by the leper king. Also, he demanded tribute from Egypt together with dues and privileges that accrued to the kingdom of Jerusalem.

deus lo volt!

When this message had been read aloud Saladin was vexed. The bidding of your king, said he to the messengers, I find unreasonable. We cannot honorably consent. But I will agree, through my brother Malik al-Adil, to relinquish the land of Jerusalem from Jordan to the sea on condition that the city of Ascalon shall not be rebuilt, neither by Saracen nor Christian.

King Richard was bled only a little time previous when Malik al-Adil came to discuss this matter and did not feel strong enough. The business was postponed a day. At the king's order Stephen de Torneham entertained Malik and supplied delicacies for his table. Next day Malik sent to King Richard a luxurious tent and seven camels. And when he entered the king's presence, according to Ibn al-Athir, Richard announced his wish to hear the Muslim way of singing. Malik therefore caused a singer to perform, who accompanied herself on the guitar, all to the king's delight. When this pleasantry was finished Malik reiterated the offer. King Richard gave it much thought. Considering the uncertainties and disturbances attendant upon war, the inherent benefits of peace, as well as the departure of Philip Augustus, it seemed expedient to accept. Yet many high lords began to argue and complain against him for defaulting, so the king would talk no further with Malik. Almost at once Saladin's warriors rose up on every side and Richard went against them, taking pagan heads, twelve or twenty or thirty each day, depending on the number that fell in his path, to show how zealously he would persecute these monstrous enemies.

Soon enough, as expected, the rains of November came slanting down. Five leagues nearer Jerusalem the army halted. On the eve of Saint Thomas the Apostle it happened that Richard with a small retinue moved toward Blanchegarde, for what purpose is not known, perhaps to reconnoiter. Midway he paused, overcome with foreboding, and returned to camp. That same hour he learned that Saladin had despatched three hundred troops to Blanchegarde. What is this but divine intervention?

Now the earl of Leicester with a few knights essayed to punish an arrogant and boastful company of Turks passing by. The infidels fled, pursued by three knights on swift chargers. But in doing so the knights found themselves encircled. Then the earl of Leicester spurred forward to rescue them, followed by Henry de Mailoe and Saul de Bruil and others. Yet here came more Turks as though summoned by the Devil, flourishing reed lances tipped with steel. Garin Fitz-Gerald, toppled from his mount, was beaten almost to death with iron maces. Drogo de Fontenille Putrell was struck down, likewise Robert Nigel. The earl of Leicester was unhorsed, savagely beaten and came near drowning in the river. They say he was a little man, although not small in courage, for never did a man so slight perform such feats of bravery. Those at camp heard noise and charged toward the battle with King Richard in front, his gold crown flashing. Chronicles relate that some wished to dissuade him, fearing he would be killed, but he answered that he had sent the earl of Leicester forward and if these knights died alone he would not be called king again.

So the Turks, finding how unwise it could be to engage Richard Lionheart on the plain, retreated toward Jerusalem. The living host continued on its way. As they drew near the mountains it began to hail and rain fiercely. Horses drowned, tent pegs tore loose from the earth. Pork and biscuit spoiled, clothing rotted, armor rusted. Disconsolate pilgrims held up their hands. Yet in their hearts they felt joyous at the prospect of beholding Jerusalem and toward this end they comforted each other. Those on litters began to exalt God, praying only for a glimpse of the Sepulcher before they died. Turks lay in ambush for these caravans of the mortally sick, fell upon them like the wind, slaying those too weak to rise and all who carried them. Yet it is certain that our Lord, looking down, exchanged the brief agony of these pilgrims for eternal bliss.

Now began the Leap Year 1192, having D for its canonical letter.

deus lo volt!

On the third day after the circumcision of our Lord a company of Saracens attacked, slaying those Christians foremost in advance. Richard pursued God's enemies and they, recognizing his banner, took flight. Eighty rode toward Mirabel but he caught up with them and by himself despatched two before his knights arrived.

Meantime the Jerusalemfarers polished swords, helmets, and coats of mail lest some blemish discolor the brilliance when after so many trials they should approach the Holy City. They boasted that not all the strength of all the heathen could thwart them in their plighted vow. But those barons native to the land, wiser and less presumptuous, sought to dissuade Richard from proceeding. For, said they, a Turkish army in the hills could swoop down to pin us like flies against the wall as we besiege Jerusalem. Or should we take the city we must garrison it with experienced troops, which could hardly be done since many of the host wish nothing more than to complete the pilgrimage and return to France or England. King Richard hesitated five full days, then gave orders to withdraw. Hence the disgruntled army turned about, marched back the way it had come through sleet and mud. Sumpter beasts lurched and slipped beneath their loads. Pilgrims beat themselves on the breast with rage.

This to the English seemed God's will. But the Franks became indignant, and having got to Ramlah declared they would retreat still further to Joppa or to Acre. He urged them to stay a little longer, saying they would be provisioned at his expense if they would succor the Holy Land. They would not and demanded from Richard a safeguard. He assigned the Templars. He rode a while with the Franks, tears in his eyes, imploring them to stay, but they felt discontented. Certain of these pilgrims marched north as far as Tyre. Foolish people not understanding events therefore mocked the Franks, called them a pigeon-hearted race. But to whom did His Holiness Urban turn for help against the Turk?

Enough. Why invoke the past? Geoffrey tells how these recalcitrant knights succumbed to lewd song and debauchery, banqueted among harlots, girdled their waists with embroidered belts, fastened their sleeves with gold chain, hung jeweled collars around their necks, made for themselves pretty crowns of bright flowers. Not falchions did they carry but enameled goblets and exulted in dancing women. Being heated with lust they swaggered and lurched to the houses of prostitutes where they shouted oaths if the door should be closed against them and broke it down to have their way. Not all behaved in such wise. More than one expressed regret for the discord with Richard.

Meantime the Plantagenet brought his English host from Ramlah to Ascalon where he set them to work strengthening walls, for he knew well enough how soldiers need activity lest they provoke mischief. They worked throughout the winter and made Ascalon the sturdiest of castles. All engaged at this labor, princes, knights, squires, clerics, retainers, all joined to lug stone. In ancient days five turrets were named for those that constructed them. Criminals built the bloody turret, women that of the maidens, emirs another, Bedouin another. The strongest they called for the son of Noah, Ham, whose thirty-two sons built the city with help from subjugated people. At the direction of King Richard all were fortified.

Saladin elected to loiter about Jerusalem. Easter Eve he visited the Holy Sepulcher because of what he had been told, that divine fire would kindle the lamp. With his retinue he went and observed and listened to the devotion of captives beseeching God for mercy. And the flame descended. Turks scoffed, telling each other this was some fraudulent contrivance, but Christians rejoiced. Saladin ordered the lamp extinguished, which was done. Instantly the flame rekindled. Again the sultan had it put out. Again it lighted itself. A third time he ordered the lamp extinguished. But the patience of our Lord is everlasting, nor is there counsel against His wish. For a third time the flame descended. Saladin wondered and felt confused and declared by the spirit of prophecy that he must lose possession of Jerusalem or die, which prophecy came true since he would die the Lent following.

deus lo volt!

It was about this time that King Richard narrowly missed death. Not long after the feast of Saint Alphage he went riding and startled a boar. The monster having heard the noise of his party came forth to block the path, foaming, maddened, ears erect, hair bristling up. Nor would it move when the king shouted. And if he would circle it, then would the creature whirl about to menace him with tusks. So the king gripped his lance like a hunting spear and tried to pierce the animal but the cane lance broke. Then the boar, wounded to fury, a length of cane protruding from its breast, charged King Richard who laid spurs to his mount and fairly leapt over it. They say the hinder trappings of his horse were ripped away and only that length of cane in the animal's breast prevented it from closing. Again they charged one another and the king with his sword smote the boar when it passed and wheeling about slashed the sinews, after which he consigned it to his huntsmen. Thus by the grace of Providence he did not lose his life.

Presently came news of how the king's brother Earl John fomented unrest at home. Unless such disloyalty were checked the king stood in peril. Chancellor William by letter urged him to return, saying that he and others deputed to govern in Richard's absence were insolently expelled, some killed in riots. The king was astonished, but confided little while turning things over in his mind. He had traveled countless leagues and endured so much for the sake of Jerusalem. Now it appeared he should quit the journey if he would not have the heritage of his fathers wrested away. Therefore he summoned a council of barons, telling them he must leave and they should decide who ought to wear the crown of Jerusalem. Would they have Guy de Lusignan or Marquis Conrad de Montferrat? The barons had great respect for Conrad, small use for Guy. This being how it was, King Richard despatched his nephew Henry to notify Conrad in the city of Tyre.

When the marquis learned he would be king he stretched up his hands in prayer. O Lord God! he cried. Thou who infused this body with life, who art just and merciful, I pray Thee. If Thou thinkest me deserving, grant me to see myself crowned. Yet if it shall be otherwise, consent not to my promotion.

And when it became known across the city that he would be king there was extravagant rejoicing. Inhabitants got ready what they had. They borrowed money to buy new robes because they wished to make a splendid show at the ceremony, wishing to honor the dignity of their lord. They were seen burnishing rusted shields, polishing armor, rubbing lances, giving new edge to swords.

It seemed fitting that coronation should take place in the majestic city of Acre. Henry was therefore instructed to go and make arrangements.

However, the paths of men deviate from that of Almighty God. Conrad's wife, Isabella, decided one afternoon to visit the baths. At suppertime Conrad went to meet his wife but was told she wished to enjoy the bath a little longer. So he thought he would go and dine with Bishop Milo. When he got to the archbishopric he learned that the bishop had finished eating. Conrad turned homeward. Outside the gate by the exchange where the street narrows he came upon two men seated, one at either side. As he rode between them one held up a letter for him to read and when he leaned down to accept it a knife was thrust deep into his body. The second villain now leapt on the croup of his mount to stab him in the back. Marquis Conrad fell from his horse and rolled dying on the stones. Many people came running. They carried him to his palace. There he made confession and spoke privily with the marquise whose eyes were wet with tears, after which he gave up the ghost and was buried at the Hospital. As to the murderers, one being straightway slain, the other ran into a church for sanctuary but was caught and dragged through the streets until his black spirit fled groaning.

Some whispered that King Richard had brought about Conrad's death, a malevolent falsehood wrought by envious men seeking to augment themselves, hoping to diminish the luster of what they could not eclipse, such being the propensity of subordinates. In fact, when messengers from Tyre brought news of Conrad's death the king remained a long time quiet, very thoughtful.

Conrad de Montferrat was slain upon orders of the Old Man. Old Man of the Musse as some would call him. How he stood to profit is much debated. Like a peasant sowing grain in expectation of future harvest mayhap this lord of Assassins sowed turbulence and disorder. The truth is not known. Chronicles relate that a member of his brotherhood coming by ship from Saltelaya had been forced by high waves to put in at Tyre. Marquis Conrad arrested him, stole his money and took his life. The Old Man sent envoys demanding that the brotherhood be compensated, but the marquis would not. Next came a votary named Erwis to ask again, but Conrad, who was proud, threatened to drown Erwis in the harbor. This brought Assassins. They took up lodging and made themselves agreeable by pretending to be Christian while awaiting the moment.

Nor was Saladin himself exempt. More than once he narrowly escaped the brotherhood. In order to rid himself of these people he laid siege to their castle in the Nosairi mountains. And there on a hillside, as though prepared to enjoy the spectacle, sat the Old Man. Saladin directed a company of soldiers to go and capture him. But when these soldiers approached they began to feel weak, their legs would scarcely move, which horrified them, so they turned and fled, gathering strength as they ran. That night Saladin posted guards with torches around his tent and sprinkled ashes before the entrance, after which he lapsed into a troubled sleep. He awoke to find a shadowy figure gliding out of the tent. Now on his bed lay a dagger of the sort Assassins use, a poisoned cake, and a sheet of parchment with mysterious verse. He cried out to the guards, who swore they had seen nothing. Nor were there any footprints among the ashes. Next morning Saladin hurriedly returned to Damascus.

Such are the Assassins, those who tricked Conrad de Montferrat by offering him a letter to read, tumbled him bloody and dying on the streets of Tyre.

Those not witness to events have devised an egregious lie. They

245

claim the marquis was brought into the presence of Saladin with hands roped behind his back, for Saladin wished to meet this famous lord. Ah! Marquis! Marquis! Saladin cried softly. Where are those thousand knights you would bring against me? By Mahomet, has not your covetous nature betrayed you? If not, you shall have your stomach full this day! Whereupon he ordered molten gold and silver poured down Conrad's throat.

Such tales are false. Assassins took his life by order of the Old Man on the twenty-eighth day of April in our year of grace 1192.

Conrad was by all accounts a mighty man of war. And it may be argued that he proved himself no less so among the ladies, for when he married Isabella he had already two wives, both young and fair. One at Constantinople, the second in his native country, which was Piedmont. Nonetheless, defying God and reason, Bishop Milo married him to Isabella. Much did the archbishop of Canterbury murmur at this espousal, at threefold adultery, pronouncing the sentence of excommunication. Also, the pontiff at Rome disapproved. Many questioned if the Lord were present at such a wedding. I have heard that Conrad tampered with clerics by way of specious argument and gifts, sounding the effect of largesse, which happens enough. We, too, have seen the corrupt empowered.

Anon this steward of God's ministry, Bishop Milo, journeyed to Assisi where Saint Francis was born. While he was there some affliction lifted a monstrous swelling on his back from rump to shoulder. They say it gaped open as though struck by a cleaver. He lingered five days in agony before giving up the ghost, whereupon those who served him made havoc of all he owned. Thus does it fare with those who slight their calling.

Conrad being untimely dead, the Holy Land felt shaken. Grief superseded joy.

The lords of Tyre thought King Richard's nephew Henry should marry Isabella. Young Henry did not object since she was comely, although twice married and at the moment pregnant. Lady Isabella, however, shut herself inside the castle, nor would she give up the keys to her city. But a day or so having passed and she with time to reflect upon Henry's youth and handsome looks, and he rich enough for six or eight, she changed her mind, yielding her keys and self to Richard's nephew. Such is the nature of women, who delight at novelty, rejecting, forgiving, easily taught or led if subject to advice. They married one week after Conrad ascended to the embrace of our Savior.

King Richard invited the couple to Ascalon but Henry chose to loiter where he was, having at once fallen in love with his pregnant bride.

Now came news of Saladin distracted by revolt in Mesopotamia. Richard therefore thought to take advantage of the moment and attack Daron six or eight leagues down the coast. By sea and land he advanced toward Daron and of a Sunday pitched his tent. Saracens emerged from the fort shouting insults but prudently retired to bar the gates. In a little while English ships arrived with catapults and other engines, all disjointed. Richard and his lords did not shrink from carrying some piece of timber half a league. When this machinery was in place they undertook to destroy the fort.

After much pounding a gate broke apart. Many Turks fell groaning on the earth. Three vile misbelievers came out to sue for peace, offering to yield in exchange for their lives, but Richard would not. Defend yourselves, said he. And beneath heavy blows a tower fell, which brought forth God's enemies scrambling like mice in all directions. Some got away, but first cut the sinews of horses to render them useless. Now the living host entered Daron. First came Seguin Borret, followed by the equerry Ospiard who carried his armor. Next, a Gascon named Peter. As to the next, chronicles are silent. Turkish banners came down while that of Stephen de Longchamp unfurled, that belonging to the earl of Leicester, that of Andrew de Chavegui. Next the Pisans and Genoese lifted standards. Forty Christian captives were discovered languishing in shackles. Some three hundred enemies had sought refuge in the principal tower and Richard set close guard around them. Whitsuntide he ordered them out, hands strapped behind their backs so tight they roared with pain. Many tasted the sword, others hurled into the ditch.

S o quickly did Richard take this fort that his pilgrims were encouraged. They spoke of marching a second time against Jerusalem, English and Franks together. But there was disquieting news from England. A cleric arrived to say the king's brother fomented treason, abetted by Philip Augustus. Chancellor William was driven out of the realm into Normandy and the king's exchequer emptied, save what might be concealed in churches.

With the army bivouacked at Ybelin, near that valley where Anna the grandmother of Jesus was born, Richard took himself wearily to bed. And while he lay pensive in his tent, not knowing what course to follow, he noticed the chaplain William of Poictou. It appeared that the chaplain wept. And having asked the cause, King Richard was told that throughout camp were muttered rumors of his leaving.

Ah, Sire, may the day never come, said William. May never this reproach be charged against thee. On how many occasions hath God honored thee, since first I saw thee count of Poitiers. Dost recall the great emprises? The multitude of captives? Messina, which thou didst seize, and when thou overcame the Grecian rabble. But fifteen days it took to conquer Cyprus, which none other dared essay. Recall, too, the mighty Saracen vessel in Acre's harbor that thou took with little galleys, at which time the serpents drowned. How often hath God succored thee! Sire, dost understand why God spared thee the sickness which prevailed, that was named Leonardie, against which no physician helped, and other princes died? Recall these things, Richard, King of England, and so guard this holy land whereof thou hast been appointed guardian. For all did He commit to thee since the French king departed. Now do all that love thy honor say of one accord, great or small, that thou art wont to be father to Christendom. And do thou forsake this land, then is Christendom betrayed.

Thus the chaplain had his say and took the king to school, such a sermon was he preached. To it Richard answered not a word, nor did they that sat in his pavilion open their mouths unless to wonder. But the king thought hard against himself and his heart changed. He returned to Ascalon with his army, camping among the orchards. There he told the duke of Burgundy and other high lords that not for any need that would arise, nor any message or messenger, nor upon any quarrel, would he depart the land before Eastertide. He summoned Philip the herald, publisher of his bans, causing it to be cried throughout the city that all should prepare themselves, with all that God bestowed, for straightway against Jerusalem would they go and lay siege.

Pilgrims held up their hands while they listened to the herald. O God, they prayed, we adore Thee and thank Thee that we shall come to Jerusalem where the Turks have dwelt so long! Deserved have been our tribulations, our sufferings! Yet shall we be recompensed by the sight of the Holy City!

Such were the prayers they lifted to heaven. Each got himself ready for the campaign, humble pilgrims fastening bags of food about their necks. All seemed in harmony with their intent.

Sunday at dawn, Octave of the Holy Trinity, they went out from Ascalon, a chosen people nobly arrayed, issuing slowly because of the heat. Banners and pennons flew, men from varied nations bearing arms of different shape, crested helmets alight with jewels, gleaming mail, shields embossed with lions rampant, flying dragons. And sumpter beasts burned with indignation at being checked, so eager were they.

Richard's army crossed a river of sweet water, marched without obstacle to Blanchegarde and pitched their tents on the plain. Within a small space of ground that first night a soldier and his arms-bearer died of serpent bites. Yet the Lord in whose service they perished looked down with mercy, granting absolution to their souls.

On the ninth of June the living host arrived at Latrun and that night caught fourteen Parthians who crept out of the mountains to plunder. Next day the king with his escort rode ahead to Arnald castle, pitching his tent on the high side. Thence to Beit Nuba five leagues from the Holy City where they stayed a while expecting Count Henry. On the morrow of Saint Barnabas a spy informed King Richard that Turks lay in ambush on the mountains so at daybreak he went looking for them, surprised them by the fountain of Emaus, slew twenty, caught Saladin's herald, and put others to flight. His men captured three fine camels, mules, horses, beautiful Turcomans, various species of aloe, and similar costly things. Richard chased the fleeing infidels, striking them down right and left until he came into a valley where, having pierced another and cast the body aside, he looked up to behold shimmering at a distance the yellow walls of Jerusalem. Unable to contemplate the city of God, which he could not deliver, King Richard lifted his emblazoned tunic to hide his face.

Those inside Jerusalem were horrified when fugitives brought news of Richard's approach. None wished to challenge him. Muslim documents assert that if he had moved forward at once he could have taken the city because one and all had fled. Saladin himself demanded the swiftest charger to escape, not anxious to see close up that English visage.

However it may be, in Richard's army the lower order complained, as is their wont. Hitherto they had been ripe with eagerness, but now they muttered and spoke anxiously. O Lord God, what shall we do? How shall we hold out against Saladin? Lord God, how shall we accomplish the pilgrimage?

These doubts came to the notice of King Richard. Therefore he assembled the barons to discuss whether it would be expedient to go forward. If it please you to march toward Jerusalem, said he, I will not desert you. Yet that may be the height of imprudence, for Saladin's spies lurk behind every tent. He is conscious of our weakness. That we are distant from the seacoast he knows quite well. If, when we lay siege to Jerusalem, the enemy comes down in force out of the mountains to the plain of Ramlah and defeats those who bring provision from the sea, what should we do? Then, too late, we should repent. Moreover, the walls of Jerusalem are said to be very great in circuit and our few troops judiciously deployed might well prove inadequate to surround the city. If, then, a host of Turks should attack, we would be at a loss. Do I therefore command this hazardous enterprise while misfortune overwhelms the Christian army, then should I be held accountable for blind infatuation. Wherefore, on such a dubious issue, I think it may be rash to advance without precaution. Further, since we are ignorant of this ground, little knowing defiles and roads, if we hope to attain with joy and triumph that success we have long anticipated I think we should take counsel of the natives. I think also we should ask the Templars and Hospitalers their opinion whether we should proceed on this course to Babylon or Beyrouth or Damascus. By so doing, we will not, as now, divide ourselves into quarreling parties.

With mutual consent and the king's recommendation twenty men were sworn to advise. Five Templars, five Hospitalers, five nobles of France, five natives of Syria.

But while these twenty consulted and debated here came a spy born in Syria, Bernard, hastily returned from Egypt. He wore Saracen garments and with him two others in similar disguise who had no business except to keep watch on the Muslim host. None better resembled Saracens nor better spoke that tongue. To each King Richard had given three hundred silver marks when they departed. Now they mentioned caravans approaching Babylon and would lead him to them, which caused him to rejoice. He sent for the duke of Burgundy to bring the Franks and join him. To this the duke agreed, provided he might have one third part of the spoil. They mounted five hundred knights and with one thousand agile foot sergeants advanced to Castle Galatie. While they rested at this place a spy informed Richard of a caravan watering at the round cistern and he might capture it. However, Saladin learned of their intent and hurried up, so there were two thousand Saracen knights with the caravan, beside those afoot.

King Richard ordered barley given to the horses in the name of Saint George. And the men ate, after which they rode through moonlight until morning when they came to the round cistern and saw Turks fit for battle. The king was mounted on a tall charger conspicuous above the rest, we are told by musty parchment, and threw himself singly against these Turks, penetrating the foremost rank, pressing so hard that some fell aside with hardly a blow. And when his ashen lance shivered he drew his sword, cutting and hewing, splitting heads from skull to teeth. No sort of armor could withstand his blows. Very well also did the men of Poictou acquit themselves. Here were Angevins and Normans thrusting through eyes, through mouths, chopping off hands or feet, so many Turks dropping that pilgrims stumbled over heaps of bodies on the sand. Infidels scattered, saddles twisted, desperate for the mountains, leaving abandoned what they pledged to guard. Saracen herders now approached, stretching forth their hands in supplication, anxious to yield themselves captive, leading camels by the halter, mules and hinnies burdened with precious stuff, Greek textures, figured silk, samite from Damascus, quilted coats, pouches of money, divers weapons, gold cups, biscuit, wheat, conserves, wax, cumin, electuaries, medicaments in leathern bottles, goodly light armor, candlesticks, chess tables, cinnamon, bladders, sugar, wealth beyond counting. Pilgrims declared that never was such booty apprehended. They were much troubled to gather dromedaries and camels that got loose, God having made no other beast as swift. Neither stag nor hound can overtake these creatures have they a little start. In the end, with all together, counted by the help of sergeants, the number came to four thousand seven hundred, some animals larger than any Frank or Englishman had seen. As for Turks, seventeen hundred black souls putrefied, the sand everywhere moist with blood.

King Richard distributed these dromedaries and camels among his soldiers, a fine thing to do. They stuffed the flesh of young camels with lard before roasting so it was white and palatable. Nevertheless many pilgrims complained, saying the beasts ate too much grain and provender. Also they objected to the decision reached by twenty counselors that it would be unwise to besiege Jerusalem. Hitherto they felt alarmed by the power of Saladin. Yet now, but two leagues distant and learning they should not proceed, they raged and argued. Why have we traveled this far, they asked, if not to complete the journey? They cursed their leaders, claiming life itself mattered less than salvation of the Holy Land. Some mistook this world for the next, confusing earthly with heavenly Jerusalem.

Mistrust and jealousy of Richard caused many in the host to draw apart. Indeed the duke of Burgundy, provoked by malice, ordered a song trolled in public which was taken up by soldiers and lewd women. Yet the stream runs turbid or clear, according to its source. Those that mouthed vile poetry were not pilgrims of an earlier day who conquered Antioch, whose victories are even now recounted. Such were Bohemond, Tancred, Lord Joscelin, Godfrey de Bouillon, and their like, who held constant in the service of God, whose deeds jongleurs would forever extol.

Saladin rode to the summit of a hill so that he might watch these Christians retreat. What he thought or said, no chronicle reports. It is known that he despatched letters sealed by his own ring to Muslim princes, urging all to assemble at Jerusalem. And here came a multitude of unbelievers thick as locusts.

On Sunday that preceded the feast of Saint Peter, while Richard with his discontented army was in retreat to Acre, Saladin arrived at the gates of Joppa. Mangonels and petraries began to stroke the walls until those inside wept and held up their hands. After five days the gate opening on the road to Jerusalem broke apart, the wall crumbled. Pagans dashed about the city doing what they liked, slaughtering, robbing. They knocked holes in wine casks and wine trickled through the streets. Citizens rushed to the harbor, among them Alberic de Reims who had been charged with defense of the city, who would climb aboard ship to protect his skin. He was reproached for cowardice, forcibly brought back. They say he was thrust physically into a turret. Then seeing no help for it, danger all around, he gathered himself. Here shall we devote our lives to the service of God! he shouted.

However, the patriarch of Joppa decided to negotiate, proposing that a respite be granted until next day, hopeful King Richard might appear. In exchange, each man should pay ten bezants, each woman five, each child three. Further, he and other nobles would give up themselves hostage. Saladin felt agreeable. The patriarch surrendered, as did Theobald de Trèves, Osbert Waldin, Augustin de Londres, and others whose names are lost, all taken away captive to Damascus. Now when those in the turret paid ransom, once they delivered the gold their heads were cut off. Seven had been slain when this was found out. Whereupon the rest lifted their hands to God and confessed to each other because they could hope for nothing but salvation of their souls. Lamenting, weeping, they awaited the stroke of martyrdom.

King Richard was preparing to depart the Holy Land when news arrived from Joppa. Messengers came while he was in his tent discussing with his captains when they should embark. Joppa is taken, the messengers cried and tore their garments. All but the citadel where some few hold out. I will be with them! Richard swore. As God Lives!

He sought the lords of Acre to see if they would go. Aye, said they, for the good of Christendom. And it was decided he should go by sea with his fleet of galleys. The nobles would proceed by land, Hugh from Tiberias to lead, Balian d'Ibelin to command the rear guard.

Because of contrary wind Richard put in three days at Cayphas. Geoffrey relates that he was much vexed and exclaimed. Lord God, why dost Thou detain us? Consider, I pray, the urgency of our cause! And no more did he speak than a compelling breeze was felt, wafting the fleet toward Joppa.

Turks when they perceived these galleys rushed to oppose him at the harbor. They thronged the shore, launched clouds of arrows, screamed insults. Saracen cavalry spurred into the water with drawn swords, creating much anxiety throughout the fleet. Some argued it would be useless to land because the citizens by now were dead.

deus lo volt!

Therefore, they argued, why sacrifice ourselves? It is said that King Richard looked thoughtfully all around, when just at this moment he saw a priest from Joppa come swimming toward the royal galley. As the priest was helped on board he told about Christians still alive.

May it please God at whose direction we have come, said Richard, let us die with our brothers. A curse on him who hesitates.

With his shield hung at his neck the king of England grasped a Danish axe and hopped into the sea, followed by Geoffrey du Bois, Peter de Pratelles, and other brave knights. And now these Turks stood aghast when they saw King Richard rise out of the water with his axe. They retreated, blood and havoc claimed the shore. The king pursued them and gave no terms but despatched them groaning into hell. They say the haft of his Danish axe splintered and he defended himself with the mailed sleeve of his hauberk or his gauntlet, and whichever pagan he struck fell bloody. Not in the history of this world was any man born of woman who abhorred cowardice so much as he.

Saladin asked those flying into camp why they had returned and they said Richard was ashore. Malik al-Adil told them to point him out so they pointed at him where he stood on rising ground. Malik directed that a horse be sent to him, charging the ostler to say that a king should not fight on foot.

But the king looked shrewdly at this animal. Thank your lord in my name, said he to the ostler. It is not through affection that he sends a restive mount, since thereby he hopes to take me. Having said as much, Richard bade an ironsmith draw several of the horse's teeth. When this was accomplished he found the creature easy enough to rein.

Inside Joppa lay a vast quantity of slaughtered pigs, which Turks despise since they think Mahomet was devoured by swine. They say Mahomet was troubled by the falling sickness and his body shaken would fall to earth, eyes rolling, face twisting, mouth foaming, teeth grinding. This happens because the bodily frame trembles when God glides into the mind of a prophet, because weak flesh cannot endure the visitation of divine majesty. They say this overtook Mahomet while he walked by himself and as he writhed on the earth he was found by pigs who ate him, eating all of him except the heels.

Is it not fit that a Prophet of Filth should meet filthy death? Did he not loose the reins of wickedness to deceive uncertain minds? Every license permitted and no thought of rectitude. Christian morality condemned by a thousand reproofs, our Holy Gospel called harsh and cruel. Enough. Turks in Joppa threw the bodies of butchered Christians on the carcasses of swine to show contempt. But when Richard's men seized control of Joppa these martyrs were tenderly buried. Turkish corpses were left to rot and stink among slaughtered hogs.

Turks boast fraternities, Cordivi and Menelones. Certain of these took counsel because they were ashamed that Richard with such few men at his back could defeat them. They reproached themselves. They vowed to catch him while he slept and lead him fettered to Saladin who would reward them. Hence they rode toward the Christian camp by moonlight. Yet our merciful Lord through divers and wondrous method keeps watch over those who trust in Him. These Cordivi and Menelones became afflicted with the spirit of dissent. You proceed afoot to seize him, said the Cordivi, while we prevent others from escaping. Nay, you must go afoot, replied the Menelones, because your rank is less exalted. So they paused to quarrel and did not approach the enclave until near dawn. And a certain Genoese went out to empty his bowel in the field when he observed helmets glister against the first light and heard the sound of animals. Back to camp he flew as though streaking from Satan. Up leapt Richard off his pallet as did others who rushed from the tents, sword in hand, albeit some had not time enough to don their cuishes. Very quickly did the king mount. Ralph

deus lo volt!

de Mauléon, Gerald de Finival, Roger de Sacy, Count Henry of Leicester, and other valiants whose names are remembered by our Lord went with him as he spurred toward the enemy. Be it said that few in those days had greaves or bacinet, nor pointed coif nor helmet with a visor unless he were a prince or king. Most went lightly armored and if unhorsed might account himself very well afoot. Now, God be merciful, armor fits so tight and weighs so heavily that a knight tumbled from his mount is dead. But here was Richard Lionheart, more fierce than his sobriquet, pouncing on Cordivi, on Menelones, striking with such vigor that the skin of his right hand cracked and bled. He lopped off the head and arm of some iron-clad emir with a single stroke, despatched the vile spirit. Afterward they gave the king much room, sang Ambroise, albeit his mount and harness bristled enough with arrows that he looked the part of an hedgehog.

But here were more pagans to assault the Lion standard. Richard's men dug their heels in the sand, announced themselves over leveled lances. He set them two by two, an archer between. Ralph de Mauléon fell captive and Turks would lead him off until Richard cut a highway with his sword to bring back this knight. Chronicles tell how Saladin watched, lost in angry wonder, but those who covet the Lord know not how to be conquered. It is related that Saladin mocked his fearful men. Where are those who would bring Melech Richard before me in shackles? Who was first to seize him? Where is he? To which a Turk from the extremity of the empire responded. Melech Richard is unlike other men. He is first to attack, last to retreat. Truly we meant to seize him, all in vain. His onset is terrible. It is death to engage him.

Now filled with triumph Richard enjoined certain mameluks to go and address Saladin. Grant us peace, he charged these envoys to say. It is time for the war to end. I have heard of civil discord in England and wish to return. This war can be of no use to either of us. Then the king added that he would remain throughout that summer and the next winter if Saladin would not agree.

Saladin replied that he did not intend to yield. The English king might stay the winter if he wished, far from his family and his home, and that in the flower of manhood with all its pleasures. If so, continued Saladin, why should I be less valiant? I, in my own realm, with my wife and children, able to obtain whatever in life is sweet. Furthermore, I have reached the years of decline when one grows indifferent to gratification, weary of experience, and detests the world. And may the king of England know that in pursuit of this war I do what is pleasing to Allah. For these reasons I say to King Richard that I will not yield. Let Allah decide between him and me.

Some assert that Richard sought out the Muslim host, galloping along its ranks with his lance at rest but no infidel would measure his strength. Perhaps.

When I was a child very ancient men would speak of Richard Lionheart as if they had known him. On one occasion, they said, he went disguised as a Muslim beggar into the Holy City where Saladin gave him food. All such gaudy tales from the past I think resonant and strange.

However it was, Richard wearied of slaughter. He felt illness creep through his body. He asked Saladin's brother to seek a truce. Therefore, after speaking with the sultan, Malik returned. Ascalon should be razed to the ground and not rebuilt for three years, after which it might be occupied by Muslim or Christian, whichever gained hegemony. Joppa, together with the seacoast and mountains adjacent, should belong to Christians who might pursue their lives without molestation. Captives would be exchanged. Templars and Hospitalers would regain their franchise. Nor would tribute be exacted nor passage withheld from Christians on pilgrimage to the Holy Sepulcher.

This seemed good to Richard and he offered his youngest sister Joanna in marriage to the heathen Malik, if Malik would become Christian. Jointly they should rule as king and queen of Jerusalem. She would bring as her dowry those coastal lands. He would bring to this union the Holy City and such territories as Muslim armies had captured. Malik, when it was proposed that he renounce his fealty to Islam, asked for time to meditate, answering finally that he could not. Joanna, on her part, objected bitterly to such a marriage.

As for the rest, when all was put in writing and confirmed by oath King Richard betook himself to Cayphas by the edge of the sea to take medicine and improve his health.

Many pilgrims wished to complete the pilgrimage under Saladin's warrant. Hence they were organized in three companies. The first, led by Andrew de Chavegui, proceeded into Saracen land with letters from the king. When they got to Ramlah they despatched envoys to notify Saladin. But these men halted at the Tower of Soldiers, thinking it best to obtain safe conduct from Malik before going on. And while they loitered, wondering about their heads, they fell asleep until sunset, and waking up saw the pilgrims already had passed by and marched across the plain and were near the hills. Andrew de Chavegui and others now looked back to see their ambassadors hurrying forward and felt much alarmed because of Turks all around. So when these tardy couriers arrived they were showered with insults and told to make haste and do as they were instructed. Off they went to Jerusalem where two thousand Turks or more encamped around the city. They inquired for Malik and having found him explained the situation. He rebuked them smartly. Soon enough here came the pilgrims, ill at ease what with armed Turks everywhere grinning or frowning, by such looks indicating what enmity they nourished. That night it is said the pilgrims wished themselves anywhere else. Next day certain Turks gained audience with the sultan, asking leave to avenge the death of brothers, fathers, sons, and other relatives slain at Joppa, Acre, and elsewhere. Saladin took counsel with emirs such as Mestoc, Bedriden, and Doredin, together with Malik. They agreed the Latins should not be molested. For, said they, you would be disgraced if that treaty made with the king of England should be infringed. Ever afterward the good faith of Turks would be doubted. Saladin therefore directed that the pilgrims should not be harmed. Malik, at his own request, was deputed to escort them to the Sepulcher, after which they left Jerusalem and returned joyously to Acre.

These travelers may well have come upon enslaved Christians shackled in mournful groups, backs scourged, shoulders flayed, buttocks goaded, feet ulcerated, hopelessly bringing rock to masons fortifying the ramparts of Jerusalem. So much was reported by later pilgrims.

Geoffrey de Vinsauf marched to the Holy City with Ralph Teissun. He declares that when they got near enough to see Mount Olivet they knelt, giving humble thanks to God. Those with horses rode on ahead, says he, to gratify their desire as soon as possible, while we ourselves proceeded to Mount Calvary. We saw the stone in which the cross of our Lord was fixed and reverently kissed it. We proceeded to the church built on Mount Sion, from the left side of which Blessed Mary passed out of this world. We hastened to see the table at which Jesus condescended to eat bread and we fervently kissed the table. After this we left because Turks had strangled three pilgrims who wandered into the crypts. Uneasily we entered the vaulted room in which our Lord was held during the night preceding crucifixion. Our cheeks grew wet with tears. We departed on account of the Turks, grieving at how they used holy places for stables, and made our way to Acre.

Hubert Walter, bishop of Salisbury, led those other pilgrims who would complete the splendid journey. Saladin met him with honor and invited him to lodge at the palace but he refused, saying he was but one of many. Saladin gave him presents, after which they sat and talked a long while. Saladin inquired about Richard, what sort of man he was. Concerning my lord, said Bishop Hubert, he has no equal. In all things he is distinguished above every knight in the world. Were you and he taken together, bating your majesty's disbelief, no other two men on earth might compare. To these words Saladin listened courteously. Then he answered. I have long known how your king is honorable and brave, yet he is not prudent, often exposing himself to danger. For myself, I should sooner live reasonably and wisely than submit to immoderate zeal.

deus lo volt!

Saladin told Bishop Hubert to ask for whatever he wished and it would be given him. The bishop considered overnight. Next day he answered that because divine services were performed at the tomb of our Lord in the barbaric Syrian style, if it should please the sultan to grant his request, he would ask that two Latin priests with two deacons be retained. The same should hold true at Bethlehem and Nazareth, hence Christian rites might be conducted according to both traditions. Saladin assented with characteristic grace.

Under the sultan's license Bishop Hubert led his flock unmolested from Jerusalem to Acre. Having completed the pilgrimage they embarked for Europe but contrary winds drove them ruinously back and forth until great numbers ascended to heaven. Out of love for God and nothing else did they expose their weak flesh to suffering and martyrdom. Who can doubt that their souls found peace in the everlasting embrace of Jesus? Thus we see how the Savior cares for His children.

Be it said that pilgrims long ago met with precarious conditions and a multiplicity of dues. In our year of providence 870 the monk Bernard was imprisoned because he would not pay tax at the gate to Cairo, no matter that he displayed a pass issued by Saracens at Bari. Caliph Hakim ordered Christians to wear about their necks a copper cross ten pounds in weight. Jews should wear the wooden head of a calf. So it is clear how Saladin stood above previous monarchs.

On the ninth day of October, 1192, which is to say almost one hundred years since Peter the hermit called upon Christians to rescue the Holy Land, King Richard departed. However, before embarking he undertook to ransom William de Préaux who had cried out in Saracenic that he himself was Melech, saving Richard from captivity. Turks demanded ten of their nobles in exchange for William. King Richard gladly agreed.

And before embarking he counseled his nephew Henry, who was at times arrogant, to maintain good relations with Saladin. Soon enough Henry would join the celestial host. They say he called up sergeants and crossbowmen for the relief of Joppa and was leaning on a balcony rail to gaze down at them in the palace courtyard when the rail collapsed. More than once he had asked that the rail be fixed. Now he pitched headfirst to the cobbles. His dwarf Scarlet clutched at his leg, went tumbling after him and landed atop him, a bad day for the Holy Land since Henry was accounted wise and puissant, a young man of excellent character. Much benefit might have accrued had he not perished.

All night Richard's vessel sailed by the stars and next morning at dawn he looked back thoughtfully. He was heard to pray aloud. O Holy Land, in God's keeping I leave you. May He in His mercy grant me days enough to return with all the succor that is in my heart.

After which he bade his crew hoist sail and cross the sea with timely speed.

But the Lord grew wroth that King Richard elected to return while Jerusalem lay in shackles. He commanded a boiling tempest that scattered and destroyed Richard's fleet. Now who is able to count the dangers met at sea? Does the anchor break loose? A sailyard? Does the stern crack, fall asunder? Cables part? At night when clouds lock up the stars who shall steer a course? Or the vessel may grind against a rock. Not least that malaise which causes men to vomit, when the Body of Christ shall end up as bilge. Nevertheless we should not forget the Apostle Paul whose mariners let down a plummet to sound the depth and called it twenty fathoms. But a little further they cried out fifteen fathoms. Yet beside Paul stood the angel of God and they escaped to land. So did Richard, six weeks storm tossed, during which he sailed against his wish toward Barbary, at last make port on the island of Corfu. Knowing full well the courage of pirates he employed two pirate vessels with beaked prows to carry him north and he disguised as a Templar knight. With him went Philip his clerk, Anselm who was chaplain, Lord Baldwin de

Betun, and several Templars from whose lips the wretched story was learned.

When they had come to Zara he despatched a servant to the nearest castle, requesting of its lord safe passage. While in the Holy Land, mayhap at Joppa, he had bought three rubies at a cost of nine hundred bezants. One ruby he set into a gold ring. And this he offered as a gift. Now the servant, being asked for whom safe conduct was requested, answered that it was for pilgrims back from Jerusalem. The lord of the castle asked their names. One is called Baldwin de Betun, the servant replied. The other, who sends you this gift, is Hugh the merchant.

For a long time the castle lord did not speak. Nay, said he at last while fondling the ring. Nay, that is not Hugh the merchant. That is Richard of England.

Then he said he had vowed to take captive all pilgrims returning from Jerusalem. Yet by virtue of the nobility of this ring would he send it back to its owner with leave to proceed.

King Richard suspected betrayal. That night his men equipped the horses. Stealthily they rode away from Zara. But the castle lord had sent ahead to his brother, bidding him seize Hugh the merchant. The lord of that territory called for Roger d'Argenton who was a spy, a Norman by birth, and directed him to visit hostels where pilgrims lodged to unmask the king. By much routing and inquiring the spy found him. Now since he was himself Norman through ancestry he bade King Richard leave at once and provided a swift horse. Afterward, returning to his lord, Roger d'Argenton claimed such talk of King Richard passing through was falsehood. These pilgrims, said he, were Baldwin de Betun with several comrades. But the lord of this territory would not have it and gave orders for all to be arrested.

Three days and nights Richard traveled, accompanied only by some youth who could speak German and a certain William di Stagno about whom old documents reveal nothing. At length, pressed by hunger and weariness, they entered a village near the Danube in Austria. The German youth they sent to market but he flourished more bezants than he should and behaved with overmuch conceit, and being asked who he was, claimed to be employed by a very rich merchant. So he was looked at with suspicion. When he once more went to market he imprudently tucked Richard's gloves beneath his belt to swagger about and show his worth. The magistrates seized him, tortured him, and threatened to cut out his tongue unless he confessed where the king was hiding.

Archduke Leopold, being apprised, felt overcome with joy since at the conquest of Acre he was humiliated when Richard threw his banner in a cesspool and heard himself mocked by Norman jesters. Thus did he send people to take the haughty king. Richard, with no better idea what to do, slung a cloak about his shoulders, rushed to the kitchen of the hostel where he stayed and sat himself down to turn chickens on a spit. Even so, a king has not the demeanor of a cook. Leopold took him and imprisoned him, charged with murdering Conrad de Montferrat. He languished first at Dürnstein castle, later at Trifels, because Leopold and Emperor Henry VI both were relatives of Conrad. Tedious months he whiled away composing ballads and singing, the legacy of his grandfather Duke William of Aquitaine who was renowned as a troubadour.

Now the jongleur Blondel le Nesle had been much favored by Richard. At court they composed and sang together, for the king had a passing sweet voice. Blondel therefore took upon himself to go about strange lands until someone in a familiar way might speak of the king's presence. Accordingly he set out, singing as he journeyed. Not for two years did he catch the least tiding, not until he went into Germany to the castle where his sovereign was held. He found lodging nearby with an old woman and when he asked who might own such a fine castle she told him it belonged to the duke of Austria. Is there any prisoner? he asked.

Certes, the old woman answered. Yea, these four years past, albeit we know not who he is. They do guard him well. We think he must be some august lord.

Then it seemed to Blondel in his heart that he had found what he sought and he was joyous. He lay down to sleep until the watchman's horn, next to church and prayed to God for help. Then to the castle like any jongleur to make friends of the castellan, a merry young knight who bade him stay. So he went and fetched his viol and other instruments to serve the household. There he lived all winter but could not find out who the prisoner was. But one day in spring while he wandered through the garden adjoining the keep he thought of a song he and Richard had composed. He began to sing, loud and clear. Presently he heard from within a gloomy turret the voice of King Richard singing.

Now back to his chamber, took his viol and played a strain, rejoicing because he had found his lord. With the castellan he stayed until Pentecost, then declared he would go to his own country from which he was long absent.

Ah, Blondel, I do entreat thee! the castellan protested. Stay awhile! Abide with us!

But he would not. Seeing how it was, the castellan gave him his discharge, a new robe, and a sumpter horse. Many a day Blondel traveled until he got to England. There he told the barons he had found King Richard. They took counsel, debating who should go to beard the duke and redeem their king. Two wise and valiant knights were chosen.

Anon they greeted the duke. We have come on behalf of England's barons, said they. We have heard you hold King Richard prisoner. We beseech and pray you to accept ransom, so much as seems to you right and honorable.

Do you wish him, said Leopold, he will cost you two hundred thousand marks sterling. And speak no further, lest your journey be wasted.

The emissaries took their leave and when they got back to England the barons considered. Because they did not want Richard kept in bondage they went about collecting what Leopold wanted. And so the king returned. Still, on his account the realm was grievously impoverished. For a long time after Richard got his liberty, according to the narrative of Reims, mass was said with chalices made from wood or pewter because churches gave up jeweled chalices to help.

He was called an impetuous, violent lord. I am born of a rank that admits no superior save God, said he to Emperor Henry. Would any that knew him gainsay it? While oversea he put up gallows. Young or old, man or woman, native or stranger, no plea availed. Malefactors danced a desperate jig on air. So he was the Lion that let no mischief creep out of sight as King Philip was the Lamb that winked at wrongdoing. Once, from a rocky crag near Andelys, Richard flung three bound prisoners to horrible death. The castellan of Saint Michel, told of his return, dropped dead of fright. Yet here was a monarch eagerly served, as happens with imperious men. Troops winced beneath his fury and would hack their way through mountains or march to the Pillars of Hercules in blood if he should lower one eyebrow. At Messina he summoned the bishops and archbishops to the chapel of Reginald de Moyac, prostrated himself naked at their feet, conceded the foulness of his life and beseeched mercy. From these apprehensive clerics he received penance. Did the Lord God hear? According to Roger of Howden, thorns of lust had grown above Richard's head, nor was there any hand to root them up.

Are not the conceits and turns of men beyond compare? This chauncy lord sent back to England a Cocodrillus, an evil quadruped flourishing in rivers of the East that like a duck or goose lays eggs not in water but on land. It sports a jagged tail, weak claws, and has a stiff neck so it cannot look behind. No tongue does it have, but three rows of teeth and spiteful red eyes. When prepared to eat some animal or person who approaches the stream it opens wide its mouth to roar. The Cocodrillus that Richard consigned to England escaped its warden and vanished up the river Thames, so we are told. A marvelous queer tale.

Richard surrendered his soul to God not in combat with a Saracen host but through arrogance and sloth. At Chalus castle a peasant tilling the field unearthed a hoard of gold coins with a Roman shield from centuries past and Richard being overlord of Aquitaine would have it. The petty lord would not let go. Then came Richard Lionheart to subdue and punish such insolence. Now as he went riding back and forth to inspect Chalus castle, bereft of armor except shield and helmet because the day was hot, a bolt from an arbalest struck him at the bend of the right shoulder. Physicians drew out the iron and when they had searched the wound they said he need have no concern if he looked to himself. They cautioned him to rest, to eat little.

Once the castle had been taken every defender was hanged save Bertran de Gourdon who drew the mortal shot. Being hailed before the stricken king this vassal spoke defiantly. You slew my father and you have slain my two brothers. I will endure such torment as you devise.

Richard pardoned this upstart and gave him a handful of shillings on account of the wondrous shot. They say that Bertran, as he cocked the bow, shielded himself from English archers with a frying pan. Concerning the truth of that, I have no knowledge.

Richard ignored the wisdom of his leeches. He ate or drank as usual and lay with women. From the meritorious Consolation of Philosophy we learn that he is not master of himself who binds himself with shackles of lust. Accordingly the wound commenced to wax and burn. And now his mother, Queen Eleanor of Aquitaine, hurried to his bedside and held him in her arms. Thus it came about in the year of our gracious Lord 1199, less than seven years after quitting the Holy Land, Richard Lionheart gave up the ghost. His body they laid in Fontevrault Abbey next to the body of his father. His heart they buried in the cathedral at Rouen. His entrails lie buried at Charroux in Poitou.

As for his love, Queen Berengaria, why she did not hasten to visit while he lay dying, God knows. Long afterward, having taken the veil, she herself expired in the abbey of L'Espan.

Through the lawful covenant of things Saladin preceded King Richard in death. Beha al-Din, who understood him well, found him one day seated on a bench in the palace garden, his young children playing nearby. Saladin asked if there might be visitors outside expecting an audience. And being told of Frankish envoys, he ordered them admitted. But at sight of these foreigners with cropped hair and unfamiliar clothes one of his children began to cry. Saladin promptly dismissed the Franks, not waiting to hear what they wished to say. Next, writes Beha al-Din, he turned to me in his courteous fashion and inquired if I would eat, gesturing toward the food. As for Saladin himself, attendants brought milk-rice but he ate little, without pleasure, like one absorbed in a dream.

Bilious fever seized him. Day by day he weakened, complained of a bad memory and lassitude. On the fourth day his physicians drew blood, but the humors of his body were failing. On the sixth day Beha al-Din helped to lift him and place him on a chair with a cushion at his back. He was given some emollient to drink followed by a cup of warm water. He thought the water too hot so they prepared another, which he thought too cold. Great God, he said, does no one understand how to fix warm water? Yet he did not throw his cup at the slave who brought it.

At news of his illness the people of Damascus became alarmed. Merchants hid their property, not knowing what to expect when he should die.

On the ninth day he was unable to swallow. On the tenth day his limbs perspired copiously, seeping through mats. Twice the physicians administered enema, which seemed to relieve him and he sipped barley water. This news caused rejoicing. But when the physicians touched his body and felt it parched, withered, they gave up hope. The violence of his thirst surpassed belief. Now and again he would lose his wits. Sheikh Abu Jiafer, who remained at his bedside reading from the Koran, read aloud this passage.

deus lo volt!

He is a God beside whom there is no God. He knows both what is visible and what is invisible.

Saladin heard these words. It is truth, he answered.

He died at the hour of morning prayer, leaving one daughter and seventeen sons. Al-Daulai, a theologian, washed the corpse. Beha al-Din was invited to observe the ceremony but had not strength enough. Many citizens of Damascus came to express their grief. None but important scholars and emirs were permitted to meet with his eldest son, al-Afdal. Orators and poets were excluded. At the hour of evening prayer they buried him with his sword in the western pavilion. Muslims claim he took his sword to Paradise.

They say he charged one of his retinue to go abroad with a length of cloth fastened to a lance. Thou who carried my banner in war, carry now the banner of my death, said he. Thou shalt ride through Damascus and cry aloud. Naught does Saladin take from the treasury save three ells of cloth for his winding sheet!

In his treasury they counted forty-seven Nacerite dirhems, one Syrian gold piece. He left neither houses nor goods nor plowed land, no appurtenance, no estate. Having coveted nothing, he left nothing. When he captured the city of Menbij here were costly items inscribed with the name Yusef, this being the son of the defeated sheik. My name is Yusef, Saladin declared, which was true enough, and shall have what was kept for me. But then, after enjoying his little joke, Saladin distributed these valuables among the conquered women and children. What shall a Christian make of this? Had he wearied of turpitude and the habits of men? They say that in Egypt he consulted a Muslim Jew from Spain, Maimonides, renowned among these people as a philosopher, rabbi, and physician. To what purpose? Does any man elude the hand of God?

Turks report that after he subjugated Caucab in the year 584, as they account such things, he wished to visit Ascalon and other cities along the coast to prepare them for defense. With him went Beha al-Din. It was winter and the sea foamed angrily. This was the first time ever I saw it, writes Beha al-Din, and not for the world would I venture one league upon it. Indeed, I consider those who embark upon the sea for gold and silver to be mad. But while I occupied myself with such thoughts the sultan spoke.

I will tell you what is in my heart, he said. When God has placed in my hands all the other Christian cities I will divide them among my children. Then after I have bade my children goodby I will embark on the sea to go and reduce those countries of the West. Nor will I put down my arms until no Christian is left on earth, not unless death prevents me.

These words so astonished Beha al-Din that he forgot what he had been thinking. But then he recalled how the waves terrified him. Nothing could be more praiseworthy than to exterminate the Franks, he said. Yet it would be enough to send your armies. You, yourself, ought to stay here and not jeopard your life since you are the hope of Islam.

Which is more commendable? Saladin asked.

Beha replied that without doubt it would be more glorious to die in the service of God.

Then I am right to desire this, Saladin answered.

That he was devout, that he prayed assiduously and often, is attested by divers narratives. If he chanced to be ill, which happened frequently because he endured numerous afflictions, he would call for an imam and get up from the sickbed to join him at prayer. While traveling he would dismount to pray when the hour came round. He did not tire of hearing the Koran recited and would question the imam to make certain of the text. At night sometimes he would awaken to ask that three or four suras be recited and would sob while listening, or when told of some edifying parable. Tears flowed down his beard. Once he overheard a child reciting the Koran, which so gratified him that he gave the child some of his food. Heretics, philosophers, or those who opposed the Muslim faith he despised, for which reason he ordered a certain mystic of Aleppo to be arrested and crucified. He left the corpse suspended three days. Even so, he accepted the teaching of Scripture and believed in resurrection, that the virtuous would find a reward in heaven while sinners raged and frothed in hell.

Lord Baldwin, having been captured at the battle of Marj Ayun, thought to ransom himself. Saladin refused. Little use have I for money, he said. Besides, much honor accrues from holding captive so valiant a knight. And yet, following some argument, Saladin named a figure. Two hundred thousand bezants. By no means could I levy that much, Baldwin answered. Though I dispose of all the land I own I could not pay one tenth of it. Then I will pull out every tooth in your mouth, Saladin replied. You may do that, said Baldwin. However, with two teeth drawn out of his head he begged for mercy and said he would arrange the matter somehow. It is related that he went off to visit Emperor Manuel in Constantinople, the wealthiest sovereign on earth. Manuel greeted him with joy and agreed to pay the ransom. A chair was placed in the middle of the room and Baldwin sat on the chair while gold hyperpyra were heaped around him to the top of his head. Baldwin thus resolved the matter. Saladin felt much annoyed, thinking nobody could pay so much.

After Count Hugh of Tiberias was taken captive Saladin promised to let him go on one stipulation, that he should impart and demonstrate the ceremony by which a Frank is knighted. To this Count Hugh agreed. So he dressed the beard and hair of Saladin and brought him to the lavatorium. Here is the bath of courtesy and honor, said Hugh, which recalls the baptism of an infant, from which you shall emerge cleansed of sin as does the child from the font. Next he brought Saladin to his bed, signifying the tranquility of Paradise that a knight must seek to achieve. Next, raising him up, Hugh arrayed the sultan in a white tunic to represent bodily cleanliness, throwing over this a red cloak to remind him that a knight must be prepared to shed blood in defense of the church. Brown hosiery representing the earth to which he must return. A white belt to girdle the lust of his loins. Gold spurs to show that a knight must be swift as a charger to follow the commandments of God. Last, a

271

sword whose sharp edges bespeak chivalry, reminding the knight of his obligation to protect the helpless. Count Hugh then gave Saladin four precepts that bind a knight throughout his life. He must not conspire in false judgment, nor with treason. He must honor and come to the aid of women in adversity. He must, if possible, hear a mass each day. He must fast each Friday in remembrance of the Passion.

Forty-five Christians seized near Beyrouth were led into Saladin's presence, among them a very old man with wobbly teeth, shuffling, decrepit. The sultan was astonished, wondering whence he came and what he wanted. The ancient replied that he had marched from his country in order to worship at the Holy Sepulcher. Saladin pitied him, lifted him up to the saddle of a horse and directed him to the Christian camp. That very same day, Beha al-Din reports, the sultan's youngest children wished to behead a prisoner. The sultan would not consent. They are too young to know what is meant by infidel or faithful, said he. They are too young to trifle with other lives.

All who knew this strange prince agreed there was about him nothing low nor mean of spirit, nor was he tarnished with conceit. Throughout his life he exhibited that rare simplicity which marks those who do not feel compelled to inflate themselves. At some gathering of nobles he was overheard modestly asking for a sip of water, but no one troubled to fetch it. And not once during his life did he go on pilgrimage to Mecca, which seems unnatural since he was accounted most pious. Nor did fasting suit his temperament. How should such a riddle be chosen the instrument of God's wrath?

According to the chronicle of Reims, there was a pagan lord imprisoned at Acre who claimed to be Saladin's uncle, some old man with braided hair and a white beard hanging on his breast. King John ordered him up into the daylight and through an interpreter urged him to speak freely concerning the deeds of his nephew.

I will speak the truth, he answered. I will speak of a great marvel. My nephew pretended to be a Christian pilgrim with staff, wallet, and cloak that he might enter this hospital because he knew of its charity. Those who welcome sick folk laid him in bed, eased him, and asked what he would eat. Then did my nephew protest, saying that which he desired he could not have. Nay, ask boldly, replied the Hospitaler, for we have such commiseration that never did any man come short of his desire. The right forefoot of Morel is my wish, Saladin answered. I would see it cut off before mine eyes to make a bowl of soup. But that I cannot have since Morel is the Grand Master's favorite steed. Now have you listened to my folly.

Then went the Hospitaler to speak with the Grand Master, who pondered and turned things about in his mind. Go, said he at last. Fulfill this pilgrim's wish since it is better that mine horse should die than any man.

Straightway they led the animal to Saladin's bed, cast it to the ground, and there stood a knave with a sharp axe. Seeing it thus, Saladin lifted one hand. My desire turns to other flesh, said he. Now do I crave mutton to eat.

So the Grand Master felt right glad, for he dearly loved this horse Morel. They gave the sick man what he wanted. Three days after, he called for his staff and cloak and took leave. Back went he to our people, but did not forget the good things that were done. He caused a charter to be drawn, sealed with his seal, which decreed that one thousand gold bezants each year should be left to the hospital for sheets and coverings to cover the sick, which should be taken in perpetuity from the revenues of Babylon. And each year from that day forward did the hospital receive one thousand gold bezants on Saint John's Day.

More would I tell you of my nephew Yusuf, the old Saracen continued. One matter doth vex me. When he perceived that he must die he sent for a basin of water and asked that he be lifted until he was sitting. With his right hand he made the sign of the cross above the water. And having touched the basin in four places he spoke as follows. So far is it from this place unto this as from this unto this. After which he poured water on his head, uttering three words in the Frankish tongue that none of us understood. Thus he departed, the

273

finest prince of our land, who was my nephew, and lies next to his mother. Above them stands a tower wherein a lamp filled with olive oil doth burn night and day.

So much is told by Robert, chronicler of Reims. Just as the carbuncle shining in darkness throws light upon dark places, does this cast light upon counterfeit faith. Yet the supremacy of God shall determine the good, judge the wicked. I have heard that pilgrims across the Holy Land lamented Saladin's pagan birth and thought him almost worthy of conversion and wagged their heads and exclaimed. O God! What a Christian knight would he have made!

Saracens honor a custom not unlike our own whereby the patriarch of Jerusalem anoints and crowns each king. They appoint some high lord to march ahead of the man who will become sultan. He carries an embroidered saddlecloth that he displays, meanwhile instructing people to gaze upon their sovereign. That is what Malik did when Saladin was dead. Behold! Malik cried as he walked before the eldest son of Saladin, al-Afdal. Behold the sultan of Damascus!

Yet, as Saladin prophesied, Malik wished to acquire the kingdom for himself. So when he and al-Afdal returned to the palace he requested an apple. He took from his belt a knife with a poisoned tip and cut a slice for himself with the blade, and cut another that he held out to his nephew on the point. No more did al-Afdal eat what his uncle offered than he could feel poison lacerating his body and knew he would die. Then Malik rode away from Damascus as fast as he could and went to Tekrit in the land of Medes where he summoned a vast army of Kurds and others. When he reappeared with soldiers at his back he was hastily acclaimed by the citizens of Damascus. That is how he got what he wanted. Concerning Saladin's other children, I am told that al-Aziz who governed Egypt tumbled from his mount while chasing jackals near the pyramids and soon expired, a judgment proceeding from the severity of God. As to those others, our Lord by the ineffable strength of His hand brought to nothing the plans their malignity imagined.

Now when King Richard embarked for England he left behind a meager and threatened enclave along the shore. Still, it provided access to the sea. And soon enough here came merchants like dogs at the heels of war, sniffing the value of precious stuff. Traders from Genoa, Pisa, Venice, Marseille, and other cities, all intent on establishing principalities. Nor did the Church forget her mission. While decadent Romans gratified a taste for luxury in the mysterious lure of silk and took to bathing with aromatic oils as pagans do, His Holiness Innocent III renewed the urgent call. Some would charge that the pontiff slept, awakening to his obligation only because of a vulgar curate at Neuilly between Paris and Lagny-sur-Marne, by name Fulk. This curate spoke on God with assuredness, in a loud voice. Usury and lechery maddened him. Ardent, confident, he indicted clerics who kept whores in parish churches and pointed to strumpets in the crowd until those that listened to him preach did not know what to do. You must go and hear Fulk, they exclaimed. Listen to Fulk because he is another Paul! It is said he redeemed women as did Peter the hermit a hundred years before and got them settled at the convent of Saint Anthony, or got husbands for them, and dowries. Wherever he paused to storm at turpitude, penitents gathered. He gave sight to the blind, hearing to the deaf, movement to the lame. Those who were sick traveled long distances to wait in his path and touch his cloak, as happens today.

It was not always thus. Old histories say that Fulk had scant learning, was coarse and depraved, unfit to be curate. His parishioners at Neuilly jeered. He therefore enrolled at the University of Paris and was tutored by Peter le Chantre and with much effort got his degree. Yet when he came back to Neuilly he found the congregation rude. For two years they interrupted the sermons, hurled insults. Then all at once he received the gift of influencing souls. Like sharp arrows his words pierced the hearts of men, driving them to their knees, weeping, repentant. Peter le Chantre brought the university masters to hear him preach at Saint-Séverin. He was urged to speak not only in Paris but throughout Flanders, Brabant, Picardy, Champagne, or where the spirit moved him. He performed miraculous conversions. A certain usurer, repenting, confessed where his treasure was hidden, but when they went to the place of concealment here were snakes. Also, a rich man invited Fulk to supper but when the covers were lifted from dishes, platters of toads.

Once he undertook to upbraid King Richard, exhorting him to disinherit his three daughters. To which Richard answered that he had no daughters.

Nay, said Fulk. Thou hast three. Pride. Gluttony. Sensuality.

Ah, said Richard, whose tongue was quick. I bequeath pride to the Templars, gluttony to the Cistercians, sensuality to the clerics.

His Holiness Innocent, told of Franks clamoring for this curate's message, despatched an ambassador from Rome authorizing Fulk to preach a new crusade, authorizing him to enlist both white and black monks. Further, His Holiness provided an indulgence offering remission of sin for those who took the cross.

In the year of our Lord 1199, on the twenty-eighth of November, an illustrious crowd of nobles assembled at the tourney of Écri-sur-Aisne. They meant to exploit their courage in front of the ladies, to enjoy feasting, minstrelsy, and other delights. Tapestries draped the route of procession, standards unfurled in the breeze. Pennons fluttered from the tips of lances, argent, sable, purpure, vert, gules. Trumpets blared. But suddenly, with all prepared to joust, here came a priest into the lists and preached such a sermon that one by one the knights laid down their weapons, removed their helms of state. One by one they knelt before this curate Fulk and took the cross. Among these were Comte Tibald de Champagne, Comte Louis de Blois, and my father's brother, Geoffrey de Joinville. With such men of rank committed, enthusiasm mounted like waves heralding a storm.

Some felt reluctant to make the journey for lack of funds. Yet is it not better to follow Jesus Christ despoiled than go upon Satan's track with a mighty household? Some hesitated through precarious health, or fear. Some like domestic fowl preferred the roost at night. Some like fat palfreys wished to spend their lives at the stable. Others like Flemish cattle, each with a rope about its neck, would stand patiently beside the shed. Again, some were like river fish that turn back when they sniff the open sea, which is vast and fails to compromise. Yet be it said that each true knight looks toward the Holy Land as home, does not hesitate to leave wife and children for the sake of Christ. Is not His cross the wood of life?

All wondered how this expedition would face the sea. Lord Geoffrey de Villehardouin, Marshal of Champagne, was appointed to negotiate with Venice. So there he and his companions traveled by way of Mont Cenis pass, through the marquisate of Montferrat, through Piacenza, across the Lombard plain. During the first week of Lent they arrived to consult the venerable doge, Enrico Dandolo, who was by most accounts ninety years old and blind, or nearly so, requiring a groom to lead his horse. Some think he got his wound in a youthful brawl. Others say that when he visited Constantinople the Greeks put out his eyes with a burning glass. No matter that it happened fifty years ago, Venetians knew how Enrico Dandolo despised and hated Byzantium.

He greeted the Franks while seated on a throne draped with gold, a parasol overhead. The Franks offered letters of credence that authorized them to commit their principals. Enrico Dandolo instructed them to return in four days.

Anon the envoys stood before him and his Small Council, a council of six. My Lord, said the Franks, on behalf of those who have taken the cross, we come to you. In the name of God, consider the shame done to Jesus Christ in the land oversea. Whereupon they submitted to the doge and his council a request. Vessels adequate to transport four thousand five hundred knights with their chargers, nine thousand equerries, twenty thousand foot soldiers.

Enrico Dandolo replied that it was a serious matter needing much thought.

Eight days later he told them he would provide naves and usserii,

277

these being ships for transporting men and horses, as well as supplies for one year. In exchange, ninety-four thousand marks. Also, Venice would provide fifty war galleys in exchange for one-half of what the Franks and Venetians together should gain through conquest. The fleet would prepare to sail on the feast of Saints Peter and Paul. These conditions seemed reasonable to the Franks.

Then, as was customary, Doge Enrico summoned the popular assembly of ten thousand citizens. He spoke to them inside Saint Mark's, explaining how this agreement would honor and benefit Venice. Next he invited the envoys to address the citizens. Lord Geoffrey spoke, saying the powerful barons of France had sent him and his colleagues to Venice because no other city on earth so thoroughly governed the sea. He implored Venetians to think upon Jerusalem, to recall how it was desecrated, violated. He fell on his knees, weeping miserably, joined by his comrades, and all vowed they would not get up unless their supplication was granted. Enrico Dandolo wept, as did others. Many stretched up their hands. And toward heaven went such a roar as shook the church.

We consent! We consent!

Although this agreement did not specify where the fleet should drop anchor it was assumed to be Alexandria at the mouth of the Nile, or perhaps Damietta, whence the Holy Land might be invaded. For good reason was Alexandria called the marketplace of two worlds and if Christians gained control of that port they might thrust a stake through the vitals of Islam. No longer would Babylon communicate by sea with Turks. Next, Jerusalem would fall.

Yet there was discord from the start. Many preferred to embark at Marseille. And when the barons gathered at Venice they had not money enough to pay for the ships. Common pilgrims and sergeants contributed. Still there was not enough. Then, said the Venetians, you must capture the port of Zara, which was wrongly taken from us by the king of Hungary. So after much consultation the barons agreed, albeit some did not think this right.

deus lo volt!

Doge Enrico Dandolo again spoke to a vast assembly in the church of Saint Mark. He praised the Franks, saying they were to embark upon the greatest conquest in the history of the world and if in their hearts they wished him to take the cross to guide and govern them, that would he do. With a single voice they beseeched Enrico Dandolo to lead, to guide and direct. Down he came from his reading desk and he went before the altar where he knelt, weeping through sightless eyes. They sewed a cross to the doge's cotton hat because he wished all men to see it.

His Holiness Innocent, who thought they would assault Damietta or Alexandria, grew furious when he learned their destination and excommunicated them. It is related that he acted like a wild beast struck with an arrow that claws and bites the wound. Numerous pilgrims, too, felt troubled and quarreled among themselves. Robert de Clari speaks of this proposal to attack Zara as cruel and iniquitous because the inhabitants were Christian, also because the king of Hungary himself had taken the cross and made his land subservient to the pontiff. Thus, some who objected to pillaging and slaughtering fellow Christians decided to go home.

In October of that year 1202 the fleet departed. Forty Venetian naves for the transport of Jerusalemfarers. One hundred usserii for conveyance of animals. Sixty-two galleys. This according to the author of Devastatio, whose name is lost, perhaps a German or Italian in the service of Marquis Boniface. Nicetas Choniates, who would observe this fleet from a turret of Constantinople, counted more.

Each lord equipped his galley to please himself. All were light and swift and sleek, propelled by sixty benches of oarsmen, directed by two oars at the stern. Each carried forty to fifty armed sergeants, apart from oarsmen who themselves went armed. From the yard depended an iron spike to drop on enemy vessels and bilge them, while a pointed ram extended from the bow. Thus, each would cause the bravest man's teeth to clatter. It is said that once upon a time galleys were constructed with three, four, five banks of oars one above another, stroking the sea at greater or lesser distance. When Augustus fought Antony during the battle of Actium here came galleys with six banks of oars, called liburnae since they were built at Liburnia in Dalmatia. But such mightiness has passed away.

Doge Enrico's galley from beak to stern was painted vermilion and a vermilion canopy to protect him from rain or sunlight. Cymbals clashed, drums rattled, four trumpeters stood before him playing silver instruments, and here was the banner of Saint Mark fluttering. Priests and clerics stood on the high afterdecks chanting Veni Creator Spiritus. So there was great rejoicing, albeit many wept, unable to staunch their tears. In the eyes of Robert de Clari there could be no finer spectacle since the beginning of the world. Yet that famous nave assigned to Stephen de Perche, which was called Violet, listed and sank, as if our Lord would strike these pilgrims in their pride. Thus we see how the King of Kings holds all things unto Himself, how His nets are stretched across mountaintops and beneath the waves.

Now the brass and silver trumpets brayed, producing majestic noise. Now urged by clashing cymbals and pounding drums these two hundred vessels slid through Venetian lagoons. At sea they hoisted bright ensigns and opened sail until the water trembling with color might have been afire.

Anon they came to the city of Pola where they made port to refresh themselves, to secure provisions. The citizens of Pola were astonished by such a noble fleet.

Next to Zara and came in view on the eve of the feast of Saint Martin. At once these people closed the city gates and raised a chain across the harbor mouth. And because they knew Venetians hated them, they had obtained a letter from His Holiness Innocent stating that whoever made war against them would be anathema.

How shall we take Zara, asked the pilgrims, since it is guarded by formidable ramparts. How shall we subdue and pillage this ancient city, which is very rich, unless with divine help? After consulting together they rowed straightway toward the chain and broke it. Other vessels came gliding into the harbor, knights and sergeants waded ashore, blindfolded chargers walked down the ramps. Siege engines were quickly mounted, pavilions organized.

In a little while here came a deputation of citizens to the scarlet tent of Enrico Dandolo, offering to surrender Zara if the people would be spared. The doge answered that he would speak with his allies. But the Franks were bitterly divided. Many set their faces against this conquest of a Christian city, seeing how they must explain to God. Abbot Guy of Vaux-de-Cernay, Lord Enguerrand de Boves, and Count Simon de Montfort all objected, which angered the doge. Zara lay within his palm. These Franks had vowed to help. Yet they refused. He demanded that the barons keep their word, whether all should be excommunicate or not.

Then the abbot of Vaux got up to speak. My lords, said he, on behalf of the pontiff at Rome I forbid you to assault the city of Zara, for within are Christians and you are pilgrims.

You have covenanted to help me conquer Zara, the doge responded. Therefore I summon you.

The high lords all began to speak at once. Many condemned Abbot Guy for wishing to dissuade the host, arguing that they would feel shamed if they did not take Zara, and told the doge they would help him. Lord Enguerrand and Count Simon, however, set their tents apart to disengage themselves from a sinful act.

Frankish mangonels, petraries, and other engines undertook a bombardment. Venetian ships attacked from Val di Maestro to the Porta Terraferma. Abbot Martin relates how they went about this sadly yet vigorously in order to complete the hateful business. Before long the terrified inhabitants understood that the body of Saint Chrysogonus, which lay within the walls, could not protect them and they tried once more to surrender. This time the proposal was accepted. The gates of Zara opened. Jerusalemfarers rushed through the streets stealing what they wanted, sacked churches, spoiled what they could not use, murdered as it pleased them. Citizens who angered Doge Enrico were decapitated. Many fled to the hills, sought refuge in Arbe or Belgrade. Some few reached a monastery, Saint Damien of the Mountain. According to Archdeacon Thomas of Spalato, in Zara not enough remained alive to bury the dead.

These pilgrims full of virtue had left home to prosecute a war against unbelievers. Now, sick with guilt, helped Venetian merchants to strip and gut a Christian city. And so, despising themselves, turned about to fight Venetians and claimed the merchants responsible. What is this but a record of present days? What is this but a palimpsest? Men in their blindness do not know where to find the wealth they seek.

These shameless pilgrims, troubled by the anathema laid upon any who would attack Zara, sought absolution. Robert de Boves and the bishop of Soissons were delegated to visit the pontiff at Rome. Also, Doge Enrico addressed a letter to His Holiness explaining how cold weather was imminent and they must winter at Zara whose people had long been intractable, hence it was no impiety to wreak vengeance.

That winter many pilgrims deserted, mistrusting not only Venetians but their own Frankish lords who seemed more adept at lining their pockets than consummating the journey. We have not come to battle other Christians, said they, but to fight on behalf of Christ. Reluctantly, therefore, the barons authorized some to go and fulfill their vows however they might. But then, with so many preparing to depart, the barons announced that no more might leave. Still the pilgrim host dwindled. Some marched away to vanish in Sclavonia, starved, murdered. Those with money enough bought passage on merchant ships, yet one such vessel carrying five hundred pilgrims overturned so they drowned. God who orders things from their beginning as He sees fit brings all to conclusion. It is not for us to question His intent.

282

In spring when snows began to melt the barons contemplated their army and knew they could not stay month after month at Zara. My lords, said Enrico Dandolo, who boiled with fury at the Greeks, Greece is a rich country overflowing with useful and valuable products. If we go there we can obtain what we need to see us toward the Holy Land.

Marquis Boniface de Montferrat arose to speak. My lords, I have been to the court of Emperor Philip of Swabia and there I met a youth who claims for himself the throne of Constantinople. He is Alexius, the son of Emperor Isaac Angelus who was treacherously deposed by his own brother. We might justifiably enter the territory of Constantinople if we take this young prince with us, because he is the legitimate heir.

Abbot Guy arose to speak for those who objected. They had not left their homes, said he, nor journeyed this far to attack Christians. Nor would they consent, but would of themselves proceed to Syria.

The abbot of Loos, who was famous and very holy, declared that for the sake of God and compassion they should keep the living host intact and proceed to Constantinople, by which the land oversea might be reclaimed.

This sounded good to most. Accordingly, messengers were despatched and the Greek youth was overjoyed to hear what they said. He replied that he must consult his brother-in-law, Emperor Philip. The emperor approved, saying that Alexius would get nothing of his heritage but for the help of these Franks. Alexius now told the envoys he would pay two hundred thousand silver marks if he were seated on the throne of Constantinople. He would join the Christian host at Zara.

He had escaped from Constantinople not long after his father was imprisoned. How he did so is partly known. When his uncle marched off to crush a rebellion in Damokraneia he accompanied the expedition but slipped away and fled to Athyra. There lay a Pisan merchant vessel pretending to load ballast. And there lay a skiff awaiting this young prince. Then his uncle ordered every ship in the port of Athyra to be searched. Alexius could not be found. It may be that he quickly snipped off his long hair, clothed himself like a mariner, and mingled with the crew. Or it may be as the Novgorod chronicle relates that he got inside a water cask with a false bottom. Greek soldiers drew out the plug because they suspected he might be hiding in one, but water spurted from the bunghole and they were deceived. Whatever the truth, Alexius got to Ancona, thence to the Swabian court of his brother-in-law.

Many Frankish barons felt uncomfortable when they thought of how they had been persuaded to support this claimant to a Greek throne. In their hearts and minds they envisioned the Holy City of Jerusalem. Instead, the ramparts of Constantinople loomed. Therefore when the fleet paused at Corfu these dissidents camped by themselves amid the odor of mutiny. Marquis Boniface and the doge took Alexius with them to assuage these malcontents. All three knelt on the grass, pleaded and wept, claiming they would not get up off their knees until unity was restored. Also, Frankish bishops testified that invading Greece would not contravene the wishes of God. On the contrary, it would be no sin but a righteous deed since the young prince thereby would gain his natural inheritance. Yet quite a few of the host were unconvinced. To proceed toward Greece and meddle in distant affairs seemed at once foolish and perilous. Why should we go to Constantinople? they asked. Why purchase that city with our blood?

Even so the fleet pressed on. At Cape Malea they encountered two vessels filled with pilgrims returning from the Holy Land. These pilgrims spoke of plague at Acre, which made them debate the wisdom of their course.

Anon they entered that sound which is called the Arm of Saint George. They glided north propelled by oar and billowing sail, galleys in the lead, bows swaggered with carved and gilded faces, stern quarters enhanced by painted scrolls, rubbing strakes resplendent with gold. From bulwarks hung the shields of knights on board, each testifying to the valor of his lineage. Chronicles relate that now and again some galley master struck the gong, raising or lowering his stroke to keep pace with others. Behind them wallowed merchant ships, huissiers, palanders. And in their wake dipped white lateen sails for here came pirates, traders, Jews.

deus lo volt!

Near the abbey of Saint Stephen they cast anchor, whence they could marvel at shimmering walls and formidable towers of the most fabulous city on earth. Those who had not seen Constantinople looked with amazement, and none so bold or sated by experience that he did not feel his heart contract. In centuries past numerous fleets and armies had tried to vanquish Constantinople. All had withdrawn, bloodily defeated. Twice the Bulgars laid siege, but the Greek emperor Basil slew so many he was named Bulgaroktonos, and sent home fifteen thousand enemies blinded to serve as warning.

Early next day the living host overtook fishing boats, which they showered with arrows and bolts from crossbows. Where, they wondered, would Greek warships emerge to challenge them? But not one appeared. This tyrant had usurped a throne carved from wormy wood, an empire in decay. Innumerable functionaries bore titles and pocketed stipends while doing nothing. Once the Greeks could launch five hundred armed galleys and twice that many transports. Now there were as many admirals as fish in a lake, captains beyond counting. Indeed, Lord Admiral Stryphnos sold the very ships of his command like some alchemist transmuting iron anchors to gold. Also, the keeper of imperial forests did not authorize wood for building new ships because of his great affection for trees. Nor did the emperor investigate. According to Nicetas Choniates this emperor knew as little about the empire as if he inhabited Ultima Thule. He spent the days traveling through his estates on the Sea of Marmora, designing flowerbeds, gathering blossoms, embraced by sycophants of a thousand hue, knaves, vipers, whelps, jackdaws. Some painful disease hobbled him and little would he undertake without consulting astrologers. The empress Euphrosyne deceived him with such contempt that citizens laughed. It is said he could not forget how he had mutilated his brother and lived in terror of retribution even while asleep.

Athwart the Golden Horn, from Constantinople to Galata, the protective chain was lifted and stretched taut, iron links so huge they measured in cubits. Secure beyond this chain fat merchant vessels lay at anchor, stuffed with goods. Shops and houses of traders, Jews, Venetians, Genoese, could be seen on the slopes of Galata. Many in that quarter felt less allegiance to Byzantium than to Europe. Over-all, from Galata across the Golden Horn where palaces and church domes gleamed through smoky haze, the immensity of Constantino-ple humbled these Franks, so radiant, so majestic, so invulnerable did it seem. As for the Greeks, they appeared on rooftops to stare with dumb astonishment at this fleet. And that night a thousand lamps il-luminated the vast dome of Sancta Sophia while torches were seen moving along the battlements.

Next day brought an emissary, Nicholas Roux, a Lombard cho-sen because he spoke the language, who asked why this fleet arrived to menace Constantinople. The citizens and Emperor Alexius him-self are Christian, said he. And you, are you not en route to the Holy Land? Why not go on your way? The emperor will give you what supplies you need. He is reluctant to harm you, although he is capa-ble of this if you do not proceed to Jerusalem.

Lord Conan de Béthune responded. We have with us the nephew of a traitor who has usurped the throne. It is our intent to restore him to his legacy. We intend to see this youth crowned emperor.

On the following day ten galleys rowed along the walls under a flag of truce. Aboard was the young prince, Doge Enrico Dandolo, and many famous knights. A herald cried to the people looking down that this was their natural emperor whom they should ac-knowledge, else Constantinople would be pounded to ruin. But they shouted back defiantly that they did not know him.

Therefore the pilgrims disembarked at Galata. This happened on the fifth day of July in our year of grace 1203. Greeks sallying from the tower to repulse the Frankish host quickly lost heart and tried to escape. Some dashed into the water and drew themselves hand over hand along the chain as if they might travel like apes to Constantino-ple. Others ran up and down the shore, running faster than arrows launched at them. So the pilgrims gained admittance to the tower that housed a great windlass controlling the chain. By certain accounts they unshackled the chain, which sank to the harbor bed. Others speak of how the powerful ship Aquila drove its iron prow against the chain and snapped it. Galleys that had waited outside, backing and filling with beaks raised to attack, all at once came gliding forward, propelled by slaves bent to the loom of oars. And so next morning at sunrise here was the Golden Horn thick as a forest with Venetian ships.

Day after day the knighthood of Christ prepared. Cattle hides were lashed across forward decks and over the prows to fend off burning oil. Petraries, mangonels, and other machines assembled. Greeks now and again rushed out to molest the Frankish encampment. Once with Burgundians on guard here came the Greeks. They were repelled, forced backward to the gate, but on this occasion Guillaume de Champlitte, a gallant knight, got his arm smashed by a stone from the ramparts. Other sorties followed. Many Jerusalem-farers went to sleep in Christ.

Anon the living host stood ready. For each Latin outside the wall, according to Geoffrey de Villehardouin, two hundred Greeks stood inside. When have so few besieged so many?

It was agreed that Venetian ships would attack the walls overlooking the harbor while Frankish knights and sergeants would strike Blachernae palace. Long ago this palace stood outside the walls and here the emperors chose to live because it gave access to hunting grounds, away from city noise and dirt and smoke. Chronicles do not say just when the walls of Constantinople extended to Blachernae, but very long ago. Here lodged goldsmiths, weavers, craftsmen who carved ivory and wood, those who worked in mosaic or illuminated manuscript. And the Greeks thought Blachernae could not be taken since here was preserved the uncorrupted robe of Our Lady, which was seized at Capernaum. Princess Anna Comnena relates how each Friday worshippers rejoiced in the presence and sweet aroma of this hallowed garment.

On the seventeenth of July came word that Doge Enrico and his Venetians would advance. They glided close to the city and

287

unleashed showers of arrows. Old narratives make no mention of Greek fire, perhaps because there are few outlets in walls overlooking the harbor. Still, those Greeks had trumps through which they might have funneled the liquid. It is known that for at least five centuries Greeks and Arabs have employed this unnatural mixture to horrify and confound enemies. Also, a fleet of Christian warships going to the relief of Jerusalem was met by Saracen dromonds vomiting fire through the gaping mouths of brass serpents, lions, and dragons. As to how this fire is mixed, they keep the secret. In Constantinople are said to be metal tubes, casks, and porcelain vessels of curious shape, but no one is allowed to see how the instruments conjoin. Some Russian prince once sailed down the Black Sea with a mighty host but when his ships got near the wall they were spattered with flame out of long tubes. Many Russians leapt into the sea weighted down by armor, electing to drown rather than burn to death. I have heard that the substance is able to follow swimmers and ignite fires impossible to quench, but that is doubtful. Vinegar extinguishes it. Sprinkling sand subdues it. Most difficult to understand is how flame, which by nature ascends, can be made to fall downward. This appears contrary to the essence of its being, thus indifferent to the will of God. Men experienced at warfare, chemicals, and the like, when asked how this might come to pass, give differing answers.

Venetian galleys nearing the ramparts approached with caution, not certain what to expect. Then the blind, feeble doge stood erect beneath the banner of Saint Mark and called for his men to drive on. And when he felt the prow grind against land he leapt from the galley, so others followed. Overhead the ladder bridges swung forth, enabling Venetian soldiers to jump atop the wall. In this way several towers were captured and it seemed that Constantinople would be taken. But the emperor brought up increasing numbers of troops, which caused the Venetians to retreat. Ladies from the imperial court were seen on distant bulwarks avidly watching, discussing the struggle.

Latins established themselves in a fortified abbey known as the

deus lo volt!

Castle of Bohemond to honor this famous knight. From behind palisades they set catapults to work throwing stones at Blachernae palace. From inside the walls Greeks likewise cast stones at pilgrim tents
and often sallied from one gate or another to destroy Frankish instruments, but each time were driven back. Thus, while Venetians
attacked by sea, these Franks prepared to move against Blachernae.
There were but seven hundred knights, asserts Robert de Clari, of
whom at least fifty were afoot. They grouped themselves to advance
with sergeants following. Being this few, they conscripted grooms or
cooks or anybody who could stand upright and fitted them with
quilts and saddle cloths and copper pots for helmets, pestles or
maces for weapons, so they looked very hideous. It may be supposed
that Greek soldiers would jeer and laugh, but on the contrary these
mudlarks, ostlers, gullies, scullions, and God knows what else sporting buckets on their heads with kitchen tools for weapons inspired
such terror that the Latin camp proved safe enough.

Frankish knights long ago wore helmets like a cone. Now they
were like a barrel, flat on top, slits through which the knight looked
out, and a mailed cap underneath. Chain mail they laced up in back,
over this a white linen jupon embroidered with a cross. Inhabitants
of Constantinople appeared greatly frightened by such a spectacle,
alarmed by pounding drums, the blast of oliphants. And here were
Latin chargers dressed in cloaks that almost swept the earth while
the ground shook beneath their hooves.

Near the seaward gate two ladders went up. This gate was held by
the imperial guard, Varangians, blue-eyed men with red or flaxen hair
and long mustaches, descended from Anglo-Saxons conquered by
William the Norman at Hastings. Odoric Vitalis reports how a
multitude of these people left their country rather than submit to
Norman law. Many went to King Sven of Denmark, urging him to
reclaim the land of his grandfather Canute. Others exiled themselves
to foreign places, some as distant as Constantinople. Hence these
blond Varangians, thinking of defeated ancestors, hated Franks and
savagely assaulted them with axes when they tried to climb the wall.

Villehardouin asserts that fifteen mounted the wall and fought at arm's length, swinging swords as best they could. Most went down bloodily under Danish axes, limbs crushed. Two were led captive to Emperor Alexius who expressed delight. So the Greeks plucked up courage.

Now there was confused battling under the ramparts. Here came the emperor himself out the Roman gate, arranging his people for combat. The count of Flanders went riding to challenge him, each animal sumptuous in silk or another cloth displaying his master's coat of arms. But the count did not press his charge. Two captains, Eustace de Canteleux and Pierre d'Amiens, a giant, called out they should advance. In God's name! they cried. All at a trot! Then the count of Flanders to redeem his honor spurred forward.

Court ladies appeared at palace windows to observe and criticize. Alexius, not much caring for the look of things, withdrew. So his ladies gathered at the windows harshly berated him.

Late at night the emperor decided to escape. His cowardly behavior has been much argued. Latin chronicles mention civil unrest, people threatening to welcome young Alexius and make him their lord. Nicetas Choniates, a man of noble birth and well acquainted at court, describes the emperor as soft, weak in spirit, devoid of pride, fearful and anxious since he blinded his own brother, so what he did was but a natural expression of his character. They say this man exuded poison, animals could smell it. His mount reared frantically on the day he was crowned, almost unseating him, throwing his crown into the street. Now at midnight he fled, deserting his empress and their children, excepting the princess Irene whom he favored. Some think he recalled how David fled before Absalom and lived to reclaim the throne. That he forsook his empress is no mystery since she had betrayed him often enough. Indeed, a brother of the empress accused her of disgracing the imperial bed like a whore. Alexius abandoned her to the wind and like Moses escaping Egypt took as many pearls and jewels as he could, ten thousand gold pieces, and choice concubines to grease his loins. Where he went is argued. To a village called Develtos near the Black Sea, according to some. To the Sea of Marmora, say others.

Ministers of state when they learned he was gone did not know what to do. Outside the gate camped a host of Venetians and Franks. It seemed they must have a new emperor, but they could not decide whom to nominate. The imperial treasurer, a eunuch, proposed to restore Isaac Angelus. No matter that he languished sightless in prison, half bereft of sense. If he were set on the throne would not Constantinople have its rightful lord? How should the Franks deny him? How might they claim the youthful prince held jurisdiction above his father?

So here came a delegation of Greeks to the Frankish camp. They inquired for the son of Isaac Angelus and were directed to his protector, Marquis Boniface. And when they met the young prince they flattered him, rejoiced over him, profusely thanked the barons who delivered him, invited Frankish nobles to come and visit.

Geoffrey de Villehardouin, Mathieu de Montmorency, and two Venetian lords rode to the gate of Blachernae, not quite trusting these Greeks. They dismounted when the gate opened and entered the palace, walking past members of the Varangian guard who stood as usual with axes in hand. There on a golden throne they saw Isaac Angelus dressed in costly robes, old and blind. There at his side a most beautiful woman, his wife, sister to the king of Hungary. Around them such a press of nobles and ladies that it was difficult to move. Here were mosaics depicting famous heroes, Ulysses, Alexander the Great, Achilles, Agamemnon. The ceiling glowed with luminous tesserae, water spouted from bronze fountains.

After these envoys talked with the emperor they felt reassured. They mounted their horses and rode back to camp. Then the young prince was escorted to the palace where his aged father embraced him, weeping for joy. Another throne was brought so he might sit beside his father until by the grace of God he alone should rule.

Isaac Angelus pointed out that if Latins bivouacked on the far side of the Golden Horn there would be less chance of dangerous quarrels. The barons admitted this was true so they moved across to Galata. Nevertheless, Constantinople drew many pilgrims to visit. They admired churches and palaces, gazed at stupendous wealth and holy relics. They looked toward the distant heliograph winking messages from a hill in Asia, messages that could be understood from a balcony in front of the senate. They visited the gate known as the Mantle of God, surmounted by a golden globe that protected the city from thunderbolts. They wondered at the triumphal gate with two elephants cast in copper. This gate was not opened except when the emperor returned in triumph after subjugating foreign lands. They saw a marble column fifty toises in height, wrapped in copper, bound with iron hoops. Atop this column an estrade holding a great copper horse, some emperor from ages past astride the animal, holding out one hand as if to chastise unbelievers. This might be Heraclius, some thought. Others thought Justinian. There was writing on the pedestal which declared that the Saracen would find no truce. Moreover, Constantinople was home to twenty thousand eunuchs. Pilgrims contemplated such remarkable sights and nudged one another. They looked up at two enormously high columns, each with a hut on top where a hermit lived. Each column had a little door through which one might enter and climb a staircase in order to watch the hermit. On the outside of these columns were prophecies that could not be understood until they had been fulfilled. Here were carvings that depicted strange ships, ladders, assailants with cropped hair who dressed in chain mail.

It happened that one day when certain Frankish lords went to the palace to visit Isaac Angelus they encountered a man with black skin and a cross burned on the middle of his forehead. They were astonished because they had not ever seen a man whose skin was black, nor any man with a cross burnt on his forehead. Interpreters asked if they knew who this man was. They replied that they did not. They were told that he was the king of Nubia who had come on pilgrimage to Constantinople and was lodged at a very rich abbey. The Franks talked to him through interpreters and asked where his country was. He answered that his country lay one hundred days' travel below Jerusalem and sixty of his subjects accompanied him, but when they reached Jerusalem only ten were alive. And by the time they reached Constantinople there were only two. He said he would go on pilgrimage to Rome, thence to Santiago de Compostela in Spain because he wished to view the uncorrupted body of Saint James, miraculously transported there after martyrdom in Judea. Then, said this black king, from Santiago de Compostela he would return to Jerusalem and there would he die, if he should live so long. He said furthermore that all of his people in Nubia were Christian and when a child was baptized a cross was imprinted on its forehead with a hot iron. The Frankish lords, hearing this, wondered greatly.

In the cathedral of Sancta Sophia, on the first day of August in that year of our gracious Lord 1203, young Prince Alexius and his aged father were simultaneously crowned. Yet the people seemed indifferent, as if the ceremony had lost meaning. And each day brought quarrels between citizens and Latin soldiers because the people did not like armed foreigners dressed in chain mail who swaggered about the streets cursing, drinking wine, and staring rudely. Also, they began to dislike the youthful emperor who was propped on his throne by Franks and Venetians. They watched him go to the foreign encampment where he gambled and otherwise debauched himself. Nicetas Choniates asserts that he let drunken Franks wear the imperial crown. So the Franks, having no respect for one who demeaned himself, treated him with contempt. They snatched off his crown, replaced it with a wool cap. Young Alexius vainly sought to ingratiate himself by imitating his drunken hosts. Such was the heir to Constantine, Justinian, and Basil.

He confessed to Enrico Dandolo that his people despised him. They show a pleasant countenance, he admitted, yet they do not love me. If the Franks should leave Constantinople and proceed to the Holy Land, he said, he would lose his empire and his life. He implored them to stay, at least until spring, vowing to provide whatever the army required.

293

Presently, upon the advice of counselors, he set out with a huge following to establish peace throughout the realm and confirm his authority. While he was absent certain people set fire to Constantinople. It may be this was done for malice. Flames swept from the Gate of Charisius to Sancta Sophia near the lighthouse. Churches burned, consuming priceless relics. Shops and houses fell to ashes. This mighty wall of flame seemed half a league in width. For eight days the city burned. Franks across the harbor felt sick with grief but could do nothing.

Enmity between Greek and Latin could no longer be assuaged. Foreigners in the city gathered up their goods and crossed the Golden Horn to seek lodging in Galata, or joined the pilgrim camp.

They say Alexius was gone a very long time on his tour and did not get back until Saint Martin's Day. The people welcomed him affectionately, which they had not done before, thinking that now he had learned to manage affairs. And he for his part, feeling more confident, grew haughty toward the Frankish barons who put him on the throne. He became less grateful to his benefactors, less submissive, no longer came to visit them in camp. And they on their side despised the youth because he had not paid two hundred thousand silver marks as promised. The old emperor Isaac Angelus counseled his son to honor the debt, but he would not listen, nor would members of his court.

Isaac Angelus began to decline, ill, wasting, and spent his days among astrologers. They advised him to remove the ancient statue of the Calydonian Boar from the hippodrome. In legendary days this famous boar had ravaged Anatolia. Now the astrologers persuaded Isaac Angelus to drag it to Boukoleon palace. With help from the boar, they said, we will vanquish the Latin host even as the boar once rent its enemies. Such prophets and monks fed the emperor's senile fancy, Nicetus wrote, while stuffing themselves on fish and good wine at his table. Have we not seen the like?

Influential at court was a noble wretch untimely let out of prison, by name Murzuphulus. His first name in fact was Ducas, but Murzuphulus they called him because like an ape his tufted eyebrows grew together above his nose. Seven years he languished in the dark for some conspiracy but young Alexius let him go since he was descended from the house of Comneni, from Constantine X and Michael VII. At once this villain insinuated himself and gained the title of Protovestiarius, which means steward of the imperial wardrobe, and with unseemly pride wore the green buskins of office.

Ah, Sire, he whispered to the youth, already you have treated these Franks too generously. Already you have given too much. Would you mortgage your palace? Dismiss them from our land.

Milon le Brébant de Provins, Conan de Béthune, Geoffrey de Villehardouin, and three Venetian counselors rode to Blachernae, swords at their sides. They dismounted by the gate to enter the palace. They found Alexius with his blind old father seated on thrones, Greeks of noble rank all around. Conan de Béthune spoke, saying that he and his companions had come on behalf of the Frankish lords and the doge of Venice, and he presented his argument. It was heard with displeasure by Alexius and the nobility, as was evident from unsmiling faces. It seemed to the Greeks they had been threatened. Some who were present say angry murmurs filled the hall. Others say this affront was met with gracious words but perceptible hatred. Be that as it may, the envoys walked out of Blachernae palace unmolested, thankful to pass through the gate and mount their horses.

Doge Enrico Dandolo had himself rowed across the harbor to consult the arrogant youth. They met on some islet or perhaps along the shore. Chronicles disagree. Yet there is much accord that Enrico Dandolo asked why Alexius behaved with vulgar ingratitude. We have obtained for you the throne of Constantinople, he said, and you should respect the agreement we made. Alexius replied that he would not. Already he had paid enough, he said, asserting that he did not fear the Franks. Indeed, they must vacate the land. If they did not leave he would do them harm. To this the doge replied. We plucked you from shit, miserable boy. We will cast you back.

nrico Dandolo went away thick with loathing. Presently the high lords gathered but could not agree on what to do. Venetians argued that it would be difficult to operate catapults in cold weather, this being the season between All Hallows and Christmas. And while they occupied themselves with discussion the Greeks packed seventeen ships full of greasy fat, dry wood, shavings, pitch, tow, and other combustibles. At night when a breeze came up they unfurled the sails and set the cargo afire and these vessels began drifting toward the Latin fleet. It is on record that many brave Venetians leapt into galleys and barges, caught these blazing ships with grappling hooks and drew them into the current so they floated out to sea. Otherwise the living army of God would have been imperiled. Had their ships caught fire they would have been stranded on the peninsula. As it happened, only one vessel of the Latin fleet, a merchantman from Pisa, took fire and sank.

Murzuphulus began to plot and whisper against Alexius, whispering that Greece deserved an emperor who could rid the land of Frankish invaders. He sought to frighten Alexius. The great statue of Athena carved by Phidias had stood for centuries in the forum, but Murzuphulus caused a demonstration and pointed out that Athena was facing west as though beseeching the Franks for help. Consequently the statue was attacked, mutilated, arms broken off, head shattered. And Murzuphulus entered Blachernae palace late at night telling the Varangian guard that conspirators had arrived to kill the young emperor and they should hurry outside to put down the revolt. He wakened Alexius and said they must escape because a crowd marched upon the palace to murder him. So they crept out, Alexius hiding his face beneath a cloak. Now the villain led Alexius to a tent where conspirators seized him, stripped off his clothing and shackled him. Murzuphulus, who proudly wore the green buskins of Protovestiarius, took for himself the scarlet buskins of imperial office.

This usurper was crowned in the church of Sancta Sophia, anointed with consecrated oil by the patriarch of Constantinople, hailed by citizens as vice regent of our Lord on earth. Human flesh shudders. Yet it is not for mortals to debate His mighty scheme.

What of Alexius? More than once conspirators poisoned the food, even while he sat at table with his captor, but it was not God's intent for him to die that way. During the sixth month of a wicked administration Murzuphulus entered the room where Alexius slept, accompanied by sergeants. They cracked his ribs with a metal instrument, looped a bowstring about his neck and drew it taut. Murzuphulus then declared him dead from natural reasons and had him buried with ostentatious ceremony. Next he shot an arrow into the pilgrim camp bearing news that Alexius was no more. Frankish barons were indifferent. A curse on those who care, said they.

What of Isaac Angelus? Some few days later he died of grief. He had reveled in good things, a sea of wine, savory meat. Never would he wear the same garment twice and every second day he bathed. Yet when he gave up the ghost few spoke of it, he meant so little.

Round about Candlemass, being grievously short of victual and other things, certain pilgrims learned of a prosperous town called Philia ten leagues distant. Off went thirty mounted knights plus a company of mounted sergeants. They rode until dawn, captured the town and many citizens. They helped themselves to cattle, weapons, food, clothing, and other valuables. There they spent two days. But as they started back to Galata they found themselves encircled by Murzuphulus with a thousand Greeks. Then the Franks cried out to God and Our Lady and did not know which way to turn. However they thought they should die fighting. So when the Greeks rushed forward they dropped their lances and struck in all directions with knives, swords, and daggers. The patriarch Samson accompanied these Greeks and had brought a jeweled icon of Our Lady. Pierre de Bracieux struck him on the helmet so hard that he dropped the icon and Pierre dismounted to pick it up. Also with the Greeks was a Spaniard who rode unhelmed, around his head a cleverly wrought gold band. Henry, brother to the count of Flanders, dealt this Spaniard a blow that sliced through the ringlet, the sword going two fingers deep into his skull. Concerning Murzuphulus, he lurched wounded across the neck of his mount and escaped galloping away so fast that he dropped his shield. Then the other Greeks, seeing how it was, flew out of sight. Pierre Bracieux brought back to camp the jeweled icon, entrusting it to the bishop of Troyes. Some say this was a triumphal cross embellished with a tooth of Infant Jesus. Others call it a portrait of Mary painted by Saint Luke. Whatever the truth, all repaired to church amid much rejoicing and the bishops chanted service. God willing, said the barons, this holy image should be delivered to Cîteaux. If it got there, I do not know.

Now here came Murzuphulus to Constantinople pretending he had destroyed the Franks, but many citizens felt suspicious because he did not have the icon or the imperial standard. He pretended he had put them away. However this news went up and down until the Franks heard it, so they manned a galley and went rowing along the walls holding aloft the icon and the standard. Ah, said Murzuphulus when people jeered at him, those Franks will pay dearly. And he sent word that they must vacate his lands within a week or he would slay them, one and all.

What? said the Franks to each other. Let Murzuphulus beware. And they sent word they would not continue on the road to Jerusalem until they secured full payment for what Alexius promised. But it appeared they could not get what they were owed unless they captured the city.

Murzuphulus hearing of such talk ordered the battlements strengthened. He compelled citizens to work on the walls and he levied taxes. Yet it is said that life in Constantinople did not change very much. Despite a Latin fleet that controlled the harbor there was food enough. Charcoal braziers glowed in the street. There was cinnamon, ginger, dates, sugar, olives, heaps of fish pulled from the sea. Forcemeat turned on spits. Tanners pursued their trade, emptied vats of foul residue into the drains. Hammers clanked through the district occupied by coppersmiths and iron workers. Jewelers and those who worked in enamel continued to produce exquisite art, the silence of their quarters undisturbed save for the tiny click of mallets or the buzzing of drills. Garment stalls overflowed with embroidered silk. Precious stones winked in the smoky light. All because no other city could boast such wealth. Lords of Constantinople wore slippers and gloves studded with pearls. So much and more had envious Franks observed while wandering the streets.

Now the tyrant Murzuphulus suspended three captives from hooks, burnt them to death in view of the host. Alberic de Trois-Fontaines relates how all watched in dismay because nothing could be done.

On the ninth of April in our year of grace 1204, just after sunrise, here came Venetian palanders and galleys with the living host. They landed on mud flats beneath the walls. Petraries, mangonels, rams, tortoises, all had been readied. Knights and sergeants led horses ashore. Companies of miners dashed forward to dig at the foundations. Scaling bridges were hoisted by tackle. These Franks and Venetians attacked Constantinople at more than one hundred places while the morning resounded with battle cries. They were able to see the tent of Murzuphulus on the summit of a hill, whence he might look down at ships and moving soldiers and direct his people this way or that. Huge stones began falling on ships in the harbor, on Frankish catapults. Miners gnawing at the fundament quit their work and ran away, so the Greeks whistled and hooted, jumped up on ramparts to drop their clouts and show their buttocks. Murzuphulus had his timbrels sounded, and his silver trumpets, and cried out to his army. See the dogs run! Have I not done well? Tomorrow I, Murzuphulus, will capture the Franks and hang them!

The discouraged army of Christ sailed back across the Golden Horn, having left numerous bodies in the mud, unburied and unblessed. It seemed they had been chastised by God. Yet the clergy declared they had performed a righteous deed, since at one time Constantinople was obedient to the laws of Rome but now had become disobedient. The bishop of Troyes, the bishop of Soissons, the bishop of Halberstadt, the abbot of Loos, Chancellor John Faicette who was most eloquent, and others preached throughout camp on the following Sunday. They proved how the Greeks were disloyal traitors who murdered their sovereign, hence more accountable and reprehensible than Jews. By authority of God and in the name of His Holiness, they declared, those who fought the Greeks would be absolved. They ordered pilgrims to confess, to receive communion, to renew the assault. They sought out light women who infested the camp, ordered them put aboard ship and sent away.

Doge Enrico assembled the barons to devise another plan. Some argued for attacking close to the harbor mouth because Murzuphulus had not fortified those walls. But the Venetians understood why he had not. Because at that point the current swept dangerously over rocks and shoals and the walls rose sheer, without purchase, so they could not hope to land. Anchors would not hold. Ships would break loose and be carried off. They explained that Franks, Lombards, and Belgians might be excellent horsemen, but the sea was different. With such logic they convinced the others. According to Villehardouin, some would have been happy to go sweeping down the straits to anyplace on earth if it meant escaping this country.

Those who climbed scaling ladders during the first assault were forced back on account of so many Greeks. Now the barons thought to put twice as many Franks ashore by lashing two vessels abreast. And while they debated such ideas the living host rested. Clerics went about reminding all that Greeks were heretics who denied the authority of Rome.

Once more Venetian ships came sliding across the harbor. Church bells warned of their approach so thousands of Greeks hurried to the walls. Greek catapults flung stones at the fleet, stones so heavy that no man on earth could lift one, but each vessel was protected by grapevine, hides, and planks. Murzuphulus was seen outside his tent encouraging his officers, directing them. Timbrels shook and silver trumpets rang before the monastery of Christ Pantepoptos. The Greeks, puffed with conceit, thought they would be victorious. Yet all events are decided by God. Here was a strong wind

Boreas hurtling down from the north, which lifted the vessels. Two that were lashed abreast struck a tower. These were Peregrina, which belonged to the bishop of Troyes, and Paradisus, which belonged to the bishop of Soissons. For a moment the flying bridge of Peregrina touched the wall and some Venetian laid hold of the tower with hands and feet, clung, and pulled himself up but straightway got hacked apart with battle axes, so it is thought Varangians killed him. Here came another gust of wind and a huge wave, allowing André d'Ureboise to climb in the tower. Greeks struck at him and were amazed because he withstood their blows. He drew his sword and drove them back enough for other pilgrims to secure the bridge. They could be heard shouting praise of the Holy Sepulcher.

Now those on the beach understood what happened and lifted scaling ladders. Some assaulted the gate with rams or pickaxes even as boiling pitch fell on them. Other servants of Christ hastily disembarked, each wishing to take the van. Pierre de Bracieux, wounded, leaking blood, brought a company to force an old postern that had been walled up. They battered it with pikes, rods, axes and swords, and broke through. But when they looked inside they saw half the Greeks on earth. Now here was a doughty cleric pressing forward, Aleaume, brother to Robert de Clari. Robert contested him, saying that he should not go through the opening or he would be killed. Aleaume vowed to his brother that he would and dropped down on hands and knees to wriggle through. Robert got him by one foot, but Aleaume kicked loose and crawled inside. Greeks came rushing toward him. This cleric pulled a dagger and ran at them and the Greeks scurried away quicker than geese. Aleaume shouted to those outside, so Lord Pierre urged his people to scramble through the opening. Now there were ten knights and sixty footmen inside Constantinople. Murzuphulus came riding down from his tent on the hill and made a show of spurring toward them.

Lord Pierre cried out to encourage his men. We shall have battle enough! Here is the emperor! Let us acquit ourselves!

Murzuphulus, observing that the Franks had no wish to escape, decided he would do better commanding his army and galloped away.

Lord Pierre despatched sergeants to force the gate. They hacked and struck with axes and swords at iron bolts until they contrived to swing it open. At once a column of knights rode in and galloped toward the emperor's vermilion tent. When Murzuphulus saw them he ordered his gongs and trumpets to sound, which made a huge clarion noise, after which he ran through the streets to join a crowd of merchants driving wagons out of the city. They say Murzuphulus escaped westward to Thrace. Documents assert that raging pilgrims butchered camels, horses, mules, whatever lived, whatever moved. Almighty God knows how many Byzantines gave up the ghost. By reason of perfidious behavior they deserved what they got.

That evening about six o'clock the knighthood of Christ sheathed bloody weapons and agreed to rest because it would take a while to subdue this great city. Doge Enrico camped beside his fleet, which had performed such gallant service. Count Baldwin took for himself the tent of Murzuphulus. The marquis of Montferrat lodged near the disputed quarter. Thus it happened on the anniversary of Saint Basil that for the first time in nine centuries Constantinople was taken. No relic availed the Queen City. Not the holy icon at Blachernae, which housed a portrait of Our Lady and a shred of her robe, nor bones of apostles, martyrs, saints, nor even the head of John the Baptist.

That night Count Bernard of Katzenellenbogen, frightened by shadows, dreading attack in the darkness, set fire to certain buildings. Flames once again took hold. Until vespers next day the city burned. More houses burned than could be found in three of the largest cities in France. This according to Geoffrey de Villehardouin.

Now the marquis of Montferrat rode through smouldering ruins to the imperial palace, Boukoleon, which he understood to be the governing seat and spiritual heart of Constantinople. He expected strong resistance and was followed by knights in armor, but no one opposed him. The palace surrendered on condition that the lives of those inside be spared. Many noble ladies had gathered within, among them Empress Marie who was sister to the king of Hungary. So the marquis took Boukoleon for himself. Henri, brother to the count of Flanders, took Blachernae. Other lords occupied lesser palaces and abbeys.

What was Boukoleon in its glory? Old men used to speak of what their fathers knew. Beside the imperial throne stood two gold lions that could open their mouths to roar. Mechanical birds in golden trees would trill and flap their wings. The palace contained five hundred rooms conjoined and blazoned with gold mosaic. Here were thirty chapels, the Holy Chapel so rich that hinges and latchets were silver, every column porphyry or jasper, the pavement of marble glistening like crystal. Here were enshrined two fragments of the Cross upon which He suffered. Two of the nails that pierced His body. Here was the tunic He wore and that crown of reeds with thorns more cruel than dagger points. Here were famous relics such as that image of Saint Demetrius painted on a panel, exuding so much oil it could not be wiped away as quickly as it flowed, which Emperor Manuel selfishly took from the sarcophagus of the saint at Thessalonika. Was this Boukoleon? Or the faded dream that old men dream? Years later a Greek from Nicaea, Michael Palaeologus, would subjugate Constantinople, by which time the palace lay in hopeless disrepair. They say the last Frankish emperor stripped lead from the roof to pay his debts.

However it was, Robert de Clari asserts that important lords secured fine accommodations, each according to rank, but did not mention this to lower nobility, much less to common folk. Thus, when pilgrims heard of the barons in opulent quarters they felt justified in doing what they pleased. So began the sack of the wealthiest city on earth. Never had such treasure been accumulated, not in the days of Alexander, not in the days of Charlemagne. Greeks themselves claimed proudly that two-thirds of the world's valuables reposed at Constantinople. Monasteries, churches, shops, homes, all were looted. Some have said these pilgrims behaved like infidels, disciples of Satan, raping children and nuns, murdering, spoiling, pausing often enough to break open wine cellars. Into the cathedral of Sancta Sophia, sanctuary of divine wisdom, they spurred their horses and stripped vestments from priests. They took gold reliquaries preserving gifts the Magi brought to Lord Jesus. Here lay tablets of the Law that Moses once held, which they took. Here stood an image of Our Lady whose eyes dripped tears, which they took. Slender trumpets played at Jericho. These and more. Vessels that might be melted, converted to coin. Gemstones, chalices, enameled boxes, patens, icons, manuscripts, whatever richness they found. The altar had been made like a church spire of solid silver and the table of gold with precious jewels mixed. And the place where these Byzantines read the Gospel exceeded description. An hundred chandeliers hung down, each hanging by a silver chain thicker than a man's arm, each chandelier with twenty lamps. In the choir stood twelve silver columns, which they broke. On the altar twelve crosses in the shape of trees, the largest taller than a man, all broken. Forty chalices encrusted with gems. Censers of pure gold. Whatever was gold or silver or studded with jewels they took. Did one among them gaze into that dark alcove where the guardian angel dwelt?

Columns held up the dome of Sancta Sophia and not one but failed to work miraculous cures. One healed sickness of the kidney if rubbed against, another sickness of the side, and so forth. And from a bolt on one of the silver doors hung a tube like the pipe that shepherds play, which possessed marvelous virtue. If any sick man put this tube in his mouth his eyes would roll up and down while venom dribbled from his lips and he could not get free until the sickness had been sucked out. But the pilgrims dismantled these silver doors because corruption prevailed in their hearts. Nor was gold and silver enough. On the throne of the patriarch they seated a harlot who bawled lewd songs dishonoring the name of Jesus Christ and danced lasciviously to flaunt her private parts. Thus did Constantinople fall into the hands of men led astray through wicked error and ignorance. Wisely does Boethius inform us that it is natural for other living things to be ignorant of themselves, but for man this is a defect.

How much was melted, plundered, bartered for gold? The bronze image Lysippus made of Hercules, reputed to be so large that the waist of a living man was smaller than his thumb. Bellerophon astride Pegasus, of such size that herons built a nest on the animal's croup. Beneath the innermost nail on the left rear hoof was a mysterious emblem. What it signified could not be learned. Vanished in the melting pot. That prodigious statue of Juno that stood in the forum of Constantine, so huge that four horses struggled to drag away the head. Nor was this enough. Anemodoulion atop a revolving sphere who faced the prevalent wind. Franks scaled the obelisk with axes and levers and descending left the pedestal empty. Or the famous bronze ass with its driver, cast by Emperor Augustus following the battle of Actium where he questioned some ass-driver to find out the position of Antony. This much did servants of Christ take and melt because they were in need of funds to continue the arduous journey. Yet who shall debate the need? Did they remember our Lord's redemptive act? Did they contemplate the debt they owed to a spring so bounteous?

Lord God, is there not a great difference between things temporal and things eternal? Surely. That which is temporal we value most when we do not have it, but seems less valuable when we acquire it. Why? Because it fails to satisfy the soul. On the other hand, that which is eternal cannot be diminished through possession. Why? Because no one can set a value on it that is not its own.

Some that pillaged Constantinople did so out of fright, dreading excommunication when they returned unless they might give the church a martyr's knuckle or shin, mayhap silver enough to smooth the abbot's palm. Only the Venetians acted with much restraint, albeit they scoured churches and homes and public buildings for what might grace their handsome city. As for merchants from Pisa and Genoa who took up residence in Galata, once Constantinople lay in

Frankish hands they streamed toward it avidly, feeling they were dispossessed of shops and trade. Gunther the monk alleges that they murdered two thousand citizens. So reduced was Constantinople that Greeks knelt in the street if pilgrims rode by and laid one finger behind another to form a cross, signifying their mutual faith.

Abbot Martin of Elsass, who did not want to return with nothing to show for the expedition, considered what he might carry off. Because it did not seem virtuous to search for worldly objects he thought of relics. Accompanied by a chaplain he went to the church of Pantokrator, which held the sarcophagus of Emperor Manuel's mother, Irene. There in the church he saw Jerusalemfarers eagerly helping themselves to gold and silver and precious stones. But as he thought it sacrilegious to rifle a church except in pursuit of some holy cause he ventured deeper. And he encountered an old man with a long beard, a priest, yet not dressed like a priest. Abbot Martin therefore mistook him for a layman and spoke roughly. Come now, said he. Show me your most puissant relics or you shall die! This terrified the old man and with a few words of Romana lingua he sought to pacify the abbot. He unlocked a coffer bound with iron hoops to show the treasure. Abbot Martin thrust both hands into the coffer to help himself and he filled up the arms of his chaplain, whereupon they departed. As they hastened away from the church they were asked by others if they had stolen anything or not, for if not how could they be so loaded down as they walked. To which Abbot Martin responded that they had done well. Thanks be to God! the others answered. Gunther the monk saw fit to note what this abbot delivered to his church in upper Elsass. One foot of Saint Cosmas the martyr. A tooth of Saint Lawrence. An arm of Saint James. A piece of the skull of Saint Cyprian. A splinter from the Holy Cross. And among other items a trace of His precious blood, shed for our redemption. In these gifts the church exulted.

Chronicles report that Dalmatius de Sergy took the mummified head of Saint Clement from the church of Saint Theodosia and presented it to the monks at Cluny. The bishop of Soissons returned with one arm of John the Baptist, the skull of Saint Stephen, and the questing finger Doubting Thomas thrust into the side of our Lord. As for Robert de Clari, they say he collected numerous relics, which he gave to the church of Saint Peter at Corbie, including thorns from the Crown, a shred of the loincloth He wore on the cross, an arm of Saint Mark, a finger of Saint Helena, and Veronica's holy sudarium. I have no knowledge of the rest.

King Andrew of Hungary some time afterward took from the Holy Land a length of Aaron's rod, a water jug used at the marriage feast of Cana, the head of Saint Margaret, the right hand of Saint Thomas, the right hand of Saint Bartholomew. Yet is not simony a doubtful act? Lord, if it please Thee, lighten the darkness of our understanding.

These Latins swore on Holy Gospels to pass through Christian land without spilling blood, looking neither right nor left because they had vowed to oppose Saracens and would spill the blood of Saracens only. They vowed to keep themselves chaste as befits servants of God, but used the inhabitants of Constantinople worse than Saracens. Images that should be adored were trampled underfoot, altars overturned, reliquaries stripped, sacred vessels used for drinking cups as if these Latins might be the vanguard of Antichrist. They brought mules to the doors of churches because they could not by themselves carry off so much. Should a sumpter beast slip on bloody cobblestones, what did they do but stab it. All around took place the most brutal acts. Shrieks, cries, laments, groans from every quarter. Nicetas declares that when he escaped the blazing city he saw the patriarch on a donkey like a follower of Jesus Christ, yet unlike those apostles of old he was very far from entering Jerusalem. Indeed, such hatred did the sack of

307

Constantinople engender that Greeks for a century afterward preferred Islamic falsehood to the Church of Rome. How can it be that God does not prevent what He foresees? How is it that through love of evil we proceed to sin?

Now with Constantinople subject at their feet, with Murzuphulus in exile, the barons resolved to crown a new emperor. They summoned a parliament. However, so many wished to speak that not until next day could twelve electors be chosen. These were the bishops of Soissons, Troyes, Halberstadt, and Bethlehem, the abbot of Lucedio, and the bishop-elect of Acre. Six excellent Venetians were selected. Twelve honorable men. All vowed on the Holy Gospel to be faithful to their appointment, to elect him most fit to rule.

On the ninth of May in that year of our grace 1204 these twelve secluded themselves in a rich chapel at Boukoleon palace. At midnight, the hour of God's birth, Bishop Nevelon of Soissons appeared. Lords, said he to the barons, we have agreed. And you have sworn that whomever we elect will be your emperor and you will not oppose him, nor in any way help another to oppose him. We have elected a man of gentle birth, Baldwin, count of Flanders and Hainault. Cries of joy met this announcement since Baldwin was descended from Charlemagne, although some who admired Marquis Boniface of Montferrat were dissatisfied. The date set for Baldwin's coronation was three weeks from Easter.

On that day the high lords, bishops, and abbots, Frankish and Venetian, rode to Boukoleon palace. From there Count Baldwin was borne aloft on his shield in the ancient manner to the church of Sancta Sophia. He was divested of outer garments and they put on him long hose of vermilion samite and slippers encrusted with gems. They clothed him in a tunic sewn with gold buttons, front and back. Over this they placed the ecclesiastic mantle, which hung down in front to his ankles, so long in back that according to tradition it wrapped around his waist and draped over his left arm like the maniple of a priest. The pallium sparkled with valuable stones. They put on him a garment embroidered with eagles, bedizened with so many pearls, emeralds, rubies, sapphires, and diamonds that it seemed to have caught fire. And when he had been thus vested they escorted him to the altar. The count of Saint-Pol carried his sword. The count of Blois carried his imperial standard. Marquis Boniface bore the crown. All the lords attendant were richly arrayed in samite and fine silk.

At the altar Count Baldwin knelt. They removed his mantle, next the pallium. They unfastened the gold buttons of his tunic to expose his breast so they might anoint him. Then he was dressed as before. The bishops laid hands on the crown to bless it, making the sign of the cross, and together placed it on his head. About his neck they hung a ruby the size of an apple, which long ago had cost Emperor Manuel Comnenus sixty-two thousand marks. Emperor Manuel had worn this gigantic ruby on a green purple robe encrusted with red garnet and pearl in the year 1161 when he entertained Kilij Arslan. Be that as it may, the new emperor ascended to a high throne where he remained while mass was sung, holding the scepter with one hand, in his other hand a golden globe surmounted by a cross.

Afterward he mounted a white charger and was led from Sancta Sophia to Boukoleon where he sat on the great throne of Constantine. There all did homage and those Greeks who were present bowed down. Then they feasted. Now the bishops, abbots, and Latin barons returned to their lodging while Emperor Baldwin remained at his palace. Thus was inaugurated the Latin empire of Constantinople.

In good time the emperor wrote with extreme joy to His Holiness Innocent, boasting of the splendor God had wrought. His Holiness responded in kind that he, too, rejoiced at this work of the Lord.

It may be that none felt more joyous than clerics in Europe when treasure arrived to enrich the churches. Gold candelabra, relics, jeweled icons. They joined voices in godly hymns, praising the fall of a decadent capital, Constantinopolitana Civitas diu profana.

What became of those Greeks that ruled the city? What of Alexius who blinded his own brother and usurped a throne? What of Murzuphulus who strangled the young pretender, proclaimed himself sovereign and escaped through bloody streets? Their wicked lives intertwined as if they were mating serpents. Both sought refuge in Thrace and Murzuphulus made overtures to the treacherous knave who preceded him. Alexius answered that he welcomed Murzuphulus as he might welcome his own son. Indeed, he would give his daughter to Murzuphulus in marriage so they might be truly united. So they conferred, it was done, and the fugitive emperors declared themselves inseparable. Presently here came a gracious invitation. Alexius would have Murzuphulus dine with him, after which they should visit the baths. Murzuphulus accepted. But all things obey their ancient law. No more did this tyrant arrive expecting a pleasant interlude than he was hurled to the floor of a private room and both eyes torn from his head.

What happened next, I do not know. Robert de Clari asserts that a brother to the count of Loos, Thierri, one day went riding to look over his land and while passing through a defile who did he see but the blinded villain followed by numerous ladies, all riding daintily. So my lord Thierri rushed straight at Murzuphulus and caught him and returned him to Constantinople clanking with shackles. Emperor Baldwin thrust him in prison and asked what punishment a man of such evil deserved. One thought he should be hanged. Another thought he should be dragged through the streets until he fell apart. But a venerable scholar mentioned an ancient prophet, the basileus Kyr Leo, who in times past erected a high column with a prophecy on the basement declaring that here a faithless emperor should meet death.

The words of Kyr Leo may come to pass, the scholar said. And the nobles listening to him were astonished.

They went to look at the column. Doge Enrico Dandolo now spoke up, saying that for a tall man such as Murzuphulus there should be high justice. Nor did anyone disagree.

On the day scheduled for execution a mighty crowd gathered to enjoy the spectacle. So there was Murzuphulus hoisted to the top of this pillar and forced to jump. They say every bone in his body shattered and demons swarmed on the mangled flesh to capture his soul.

deus lo volt!

As for Alexius who blinded his compassionate brother Isaac Angelus for love of a crown, he ended his days at peace in a Nicaean monastery. How mysterious the gaits and forms of providence. Yet we understand that God, Author of all things, is good.

Soon enough His Holiness Innocent found out more of what happened at Constantinople. Blasphemy. Rape. Murder. Theft. It is said he recalled the intent of Venetian merchants. He wrote again to Emperor Baldwin, his fury undisguised.

You undertook to liberate Jerusalem from bondage. You were forbidden under pain of excommunication from molesting Christians unless they refused you passage through their land. You were under the most solemn obligation, but disregarded your vows. You drew your sword not against infidels but against your own. You did not capture Jerusalem, but Constantinople. Your minds were set on earthly riches. But more than this, you held nothing sacred. You gave up yourselves to debauchery. You have violated married women, widows, virgins, even those whose lives were dedicated to Christ. You have stolen from the Emperor. You have stolen from citizens, rich and poor. You have desecrated sanctuaries of the Holy Church. You have stolen sacred icons. You have destroyed images and relics. Therefore it is no surprise that the Church of Greece, however lamentable, rejects obedience to the Holy See. Nor are we surprised that it perceives in you nothing but malevolence and the primacy of Satan.

The rage of His Holiness did not abate. He demanded to know why swords honed to shed pagan blood now dripped with the blood of Greeks. How was it that instead of seeking the purpose of Jesus Christ they had sought ends of their own? Had they not committed incest, adultery, fornication? Had they not plundered the treasuries of princes and churches? Had they not taken silver plates from altars and hacked and melted them? Had they not violated sacrosanct places? Had they not carried off inestimable relics? Furthermore, under what guise might the Church now beseech others to aid Jerusalem? For surely these Franks and Venetians deviated from their purpose by returning laden with booty, guiltless, absolved.

As for the Greeks, they sent word privily to the king of Vlachs and Bulgars, Johanitza, avowing they would make him emperor if he would rid Constantinople of these Latins. Johanitza had reason to hate the Franks. When he was young he was called John the Vlach and tended horses at the Greek court. If sixty animals were needed, or an hundred, he brought them. One day, according to Robert de Clari, a court eunuch struck him across the face with a whip. Nicetas Choniates asserts that it was not John but his older brother whom the eunuch punished. Whatever the fact, John left court burning with humiliation and returned to Vlachia. There he got a Coman wife and presently made himself lord of these Comans. He began conducting raids as far as the gates of Constantinople and the Greeks were afraid of him. And when the Franks besieged Constantinople he sent word that he would bring one hundred thousand warriors to help them take the city if they would make him king of Vlachia. The barons were surprised. After discussing it they sent word that they needed no help from Johanitza, nor did they care much for him. Further, they would cause him much harm if they could.

Johanitza appealed to His Holiness Innocent. And the pontiff reflected that he might gather these distant Vlachs, Comans, and Bulgars to the Latin church. Therefore he despatched Cardinal Leo with a diadem and scepter, with authority to crown Johanitza and to confer the dignity of primate on Basil, archbishop of Trnovo. All this according to papal missives dated the twenty-fifth of February in the year of our Lord 1204. Thus a provincial youth who had been a sergeant combing horses acquired a throne. He did not forget the court eunuch, nor the insult delivered by Frankish barons.

Now because a Latin empire had been inaugurated, and a Frank wore the crown of Greek emperors, there was tumult. The city of Adrianople revolted. Emperor Baldwin marched away to besiege the city when all at once here came Johanitza with a multitude of Coman warriors. These savages drink milk and live in tents and do not worship anything except the first animal they see in the morning. Each warrior has eight or ten well-trained horses, which enables him to travel a huge distance without stopping by riding one horse after another. And wherever these people go they take captives. It is said the Franks laughed because the Comans wore sheepskin and resembled sheep, and joked that an army of sheep was threatening them. However, three hundred Frankish knights went to sleep in Christ while others retreated to the safety of Constantinople, Doge Enrico Dandolo among them, leaving the earth around Adrianople wet with Frankish blood. Thus did the Lord God castigate these arrogant pilgrims, chastise them, remind them of bad faith and pride.

As for Baldwin, Johanitza led him captive to the city of Trnovo and chopped off his feet and threw him into a deep gorge.

Before long a Coman army trapped Marquis Boniface outside the city of Mosynopolis, took his head and delivered it to Johanitza. Nevertheless, all things are embraced by a certain and perfect order. Johanitza some time afterward rode to the gates of Thessalonika where he put up siege engines. But here lay the corpse of Saint Demetrius who would not allow Thessalonika to be captured. Saint Demetrius climbed out of his sarcophagus, walked to the tent of King Johanitza and thrust a lance through him.

As to Doge Enrico Dandolo who diverted these Christians from the Holy Land, he gave up the ghost comfortably at a very old age in the palace of Boukoleon and was buried with full rites in the church of Sancta Sophia. Some have called this inappropriate, a fortuitous harvest. Yet we know how the Lord God cannot be mistaken since He foresees all things.

It may be argued that in Constantinople the heretic troubadours of France were born. Princess Anna relates how during the reign of her father Alexius an unfamiliar and noxious cloud appeared. Sectarians. A monk, Basil, guided them, with twelve followers misnamed Apostles, which is blasphemy. They spewed poison, infected Christian souls, and derelict women trafficked at their heels

313

much as happens in our day. Bogomil they styled themselves after some unclean priest, hiding their wickedness beneath cowl and cloak. Even so, the emperor lured them into daylight as cleverly as one draws a serpent from its crevice. He invited Basil to the palace and when this ape of darkness arrived Alexius courteously got up from his throne and otherwise pretended he would like nothing more than to hear the doctrine of Bogomil. My one desire, said he, is salvation of my soul. I pray you help me understand your teaching since the dogma of our Christian church is not conducive to virtue, he continued with a look of supplication, smearing the cup with honey. Now was the excessive pride of Basil puffed up. And like Renard coaxing that raven to sing in order to snatch the cheese, Alexius urgently flattered him. And the ape of darkness, hearing this, vomited forth his foul belief. Holy churches he described as temples of demons. At the divine nature of our Lord he looked askance. Other hideous blasphemies did he utter, proudly. But when the emperor had heard enough he gestured, a curtain flew apart and here was a scribe copying down each loathsome falsehood.

Alexius now rooted out those thought to be apostate and brought them together on the polo field where two funeral pyres were blazing. Some denied the charge of heresy while others hugged the corruption to their breast. All must burn, Alexius said, and he gestured for a cross to be set beside one fire. Go to that of your choice, he said, yet surely it is better to seek the loving embrace of God than plunge downward to hell cloaked with flame. True Christians then marched joyously toward the cross while Bogomil disdained it. And when he saw how these Christians would accept martyrdom for the Lord he turned them loose. The followers of Basil he cast in prison where they were visited and instructed by church elders. Some would die wrapped in the filthy rags of misbelief, others freed after comprehending their mistake.

As to the false monk Basil, Emperor Alexius gathered his Senate, his generals, and his church penitentiaries including Patriarch Nicolas Grammaticus. The diabolic teaching was read aloud. Basil neither denied nor refuted, clinging obstinately to Satan. Therefore, while deciding what to do, Alexius had him kept under guard in a little house close to the palace. And that first night, after the meeting of the synod, stones plummeted from a cloudless sky under a bright moon, pelting and rattling the roof-tiles. This was the work of demons furious at Basil for disclosing secrets.

Now the emperor ordered a trench to be dug at the hippodrome and filled with burning logs. Documents relate that when Basil came in sight of this roaring inferno, sparks soaring above the obelisk, he laughed and boasted that angels would save him.

It shall not come nigh thee, chanted the profane monk. Only with thine eyes shalt thou behold.

Yet he was devoid of sense, darting glances this way or that. He clapped his hands, beat his thighs, crowed wildly of miracles. So the executioners threw his cloak at the fire. Let us see if that will burn, said they.

Look! Look! Basil shrieked. My cloak flies up to the sky!

And they would toss him in, clothes and shoes and all. But now the flame bent forward to swallow him because the elements of earth do not tolerate impiety. And he was consumed. And nothing more was seen of Basil except one filament of smoke. And the excited crowd would throw other Bogomil in the trench, but Emperor Alexius refused.

Of that false monk no particle survived. Even so, flame did not extinguish the pernicious doctrine of Bogomil. When I was a child I frightened myself at night by imagining that Boulgres had gained the castle wall. How is it that unholy faith endures? I do not know.

Nor could I say if heretic troubadours descend from apostate Greeks. Some think them born of Manichees arguing that good and evil dwell side by side, beans in a pod. Whatever the fact, at Lau Ragais, Minervois, and elsewhere, versemongers pointed sharp fingers. Guyot de Provins, demanding to know why Christians marched against Constantinople, accused the papacy of avarice.

Huon de Saint Quentin sang blasphemy. The river, the Sepulcher, the Holy Cross, all speak with a single voice. All claim Rome plays at false dice!

So did the minstrel and tailor Figueira spew harsh words. Insidious Rome, grasping, you clip the sheep too close. May the Holy Ghost hear my prayer and snap your beak. What truce have I with you? For Greeks a sword, for Saracens a wink. Let your office roast in the fire of hell!

None sang more defiance than troubadours of Languedoc who thought their bountiful land exempt, singing ridicule at a distance. Like all who do not know themselves imperiled, they made keen use of levity to make light of sacred matters. Here was Raimon Jordan caroling sweet words to praise a night with his beloved. Far better, sang he, than celestial paradise. Bertran d'Alamanon rejoiced at the shadow of Antichrist whose power enabled him to seduce a reluctant maiden. Guillem Adémar delighted at cuckold husbands absent on crusade. Yet what is this but empty joy? What is lust if not the den of anxiety? What is gratification but a nest of remorse?

Now the language of Provence owes more to Aragon than to muddy Parisian streets. And so these provincial Franks speaking almost like Spaniards, isolated, corrupted by the seductive music of ardent misbelievers, corrupted Catholic belief, threatened Catholic unity. For is not apostasy a presumption that contradicts Holy Scripture? Can it not be demonstrated of apostates, Jews, and lepers, that all copulate voraciously, that from their bodies emanates a fearful stench, that all cherish links to the Devil? With what sweet grace and strength did that noble lady Gormonda de Montpellier defend the Christian faith. Truly did she sing. A Saracen heart is far less false than that of a heretic. Whoever would earn salvation should march against the infidels of France. Guillem Figueira merited torture and death for slandering the Holy Church.

316

Dissenters clustered about the town of Albi, for which reason they acquired that name. Albigenses. Much was quickly established concerning their ungodly dogma. Lucifer was perhaps a son of God, said they, and highest among angels. Yet he grew stiff with pride, descending from the spirit realm to create this visible world. Man and woman did Lucifer make from clay, albeit the wretched creatures had no soul until our Lord God took pity on them. And the woman lured the man to lie with her and from that moment their souls were caught within their flesh. Lord Jesus, said they, is but a vain illusion who did not suffer on the cross. We do not venerate the cross, said they, because it is evil as are all things material. What truths the Lord revealed have been falsified, said they, and misinterpreted by the Church, which is but some handiwork of Lucifer.

Nor was this enough. Albigenses would have none of the sacrament. Further, they maintained a sacerdotal college whose initiates essayed to slip the bonds of temporal life and so believed themselves pure, Cathari, which in Greek means purity. Nevertheless they celebrated unspeakable rites, defiled chalices under the approving gaze of bishops out of disrespect to the body and blood of Christ, such depravities being recorded. Nor did these Albigenses practice in secret but preached widely, persuading fools to conform, which is abominable. No theologian had they, no counselor, no text, therefore the strangeness of such malpractice could not be understood. Domingo de Guzmán, who would in time be venerated as Santo Domingo, disputed with some heretic claiming that the Holy Church is Babylon, mother of fornication, drunk on the blood of martyrs. Why should not fiery death reward those who imperil the salvation of others? Only through belief in eternal truths taught by the Church shall men be saved, only by accepting the sacrament. Therefore much happiness is not to be expected. Only through submission may one anticipate the blessed life. Only thus shall men tread the path to redemption. Whosoever would deny this, who would repudiate the sacrament, he is anathema, a weak and vain murderer who would slay the immortal soul.

Wicked peasants at Bucy-le-Long called mouths of priests the mouth of hell. Heretic discourse they called the word of God. That divine dispensation we are granted they called delusion. Baptism of children below the age of understanding they considered void. If ever

317

they took the sacrament to disguise their misbelief, no more would they eat that day. By candlelight they gathered in cellars and a young woman exposed her buttocks. So they would offer candles to her ass. And with light extinguished they copulated madly in darkness, men upon men, women upon women. Chaos! they would shout. Chaos! Chaos!

His Holiness Innocent, grieved by the spread of devilish liturgy, issued interdicts against princes that favored it. In a letter to King Philip Augustus he wrote that heretics were more threatening than Saracens, for certainly it is wiser to defend the faith at home than oversea. And is not failure to combat heterodoxy as wicked as the sin itself? He urged King Philip to lead an army south, pointing out that crusaders stood more to gain than spiritual benefit since they might expropriate the land and goods of occidental barons who tolerate ungodliness.

He directed his legate, Pierre de Castelnau, to go and confront Count Raymond VI of Toulouse. All knew how Raymond indulged and patronized recreant Albigenses. All knew he wallowed in luxury, engaged at incest with his sister, seduced the mistresses of his father, and had five wives. It is said he listened avidly to the chansons of Raimon de Miravel on the art of seduction. He mocked the Old Testament, invited the bishop of Toulouse to hear Cathari preach at midnight, withheld punishment from one who urinated on the altar, attributed creation of the world to Satan, kept at his side a heretic priest to administer the consolamentum if he should fall ill. It was alleged that like Saracens he believed in portents derived from the flight and cries of birds. If all such charges might be proven, God knows. They were so avouched by the Cistercian, Pierre of Vaux-de-Cernay. Should these prove inadequate, it could be shown that misbelievers practiced their unspeakable faith with impunity in twenty-six towns of Count Raymond's private demesne.

His Holiness chafed at news of infidelity in Languedoc. Papal documents refer to the Lord's flock menaced by wolves, plague, malignant canker. He would attend to it himself, charged with the sword of God, but could not, since he would need a month to journey from Rome to southern France. Therefore he must rely on legates. Through excommunication and interdict they might enforce his wishes. They should have jurisdiction over heresy, which had been the prerogative of bishops. And whatever cleric the legate deemed unsuitable might be removed from office without notice, nor right of appeal. Thus did the pontiff consider himself and style himself Vicar of Christ.

Narratives from those days preserve little of that first meeting between Pierre de Castelnau and Count Raymond. But it is certain that the legate denounced him for want of zeal and grew indignant when Count Raymond would not consent to a slaughter of Albigenses. The legate denounced him at his own court, excommunicated him, and went away. Not until after dusk did Pierre de Castelnau with his attendants come to the banks of the Rhône just north of Arles and so they camped, not wanting to tempt this river in darkness. Next morning, the fourteenth of January in that year of our Lord 1208, they celebrated mass before dawn and were approaching the river when a horseman came up behind the legate and drove a lance into his back. He looked round at this assailant. God forgive you as I forgive you, he said before tumbling from the mule. He repeated these words at the point of death, ignoring the bitter anguish of his wound, until at last he slept joyfully in Christ. They carried him five leagues to the abbey of Saint Gilles where he was buried in the cloister by monks holding lighted candles. As to the murderer, this was a lackey in the service of Count Raymond.

News got to Rome some weeks later. According to the ambassador from Navarre, His Holiness Innocent dropped his face into his hands. Then he retired to pray at the high altar of the Vatican basilica.

Presently here came bishops of Toulouse and Couserans and the abbot of Cîteaux with a full report. There seemed no doubt of Raymond's guilt.

Thus, with twelve cardinals encircling him, His Holiness excom-

municated Raymond anew and extinguished a lighted taper as tradition demanded. The pontiff then addressed a missive to Frankish
nobility, to prelates and princes, enjoining true Christians to pick up
the cross, to lay hands on Count Raymond, to expropriate all he
owned. By authority of the apostolic see would all who fought
against heretics have indulgence equal to that of crusaders in the
Holy Land. Whoever helped to extirpate and crush them would, like
all who visited the Holy Sepulcher, be shielded from attack upon
property or person. Wealth and honor in this world awaited those
who would burn and void the noxious stench of heresy in Languedoc. Such was the pontiff's address.

Go forth! Soldiers of Christ! Go forth! Go with our cry of anguish in your ears! Avenge the insult to our Lord! Fill your souls with
holy rage!

And the message was preached as it was first preached by His Holiness Urban at Clermont in the year of our Lord 1095. At Lyons
immense crowds gathered beneath the standard of Amalric, abbot
of Cîteaux. A multitude that exceeded belief, according to Roger of
Wendover. Knights from Burgundy were everywhere present, silk
crosses on their breast.

Documents relate that Count Raymond lacked courage to oppose this army, but delivered up his fortress and submitted himself to
public flogging in the abbey of Saint Gilles. When he had been
stripped naked to the waist he was led into the presence of three
archbishops and nineteen bishops. He abjured his indulgence of heretics and Jews, abjured his employment of mercenaries, admitted
himself suspect in the murder of Pierre de Castelnau. Milo, who was
papal secretary, placed his stole around Raymond's neck and drew
him into the abbey while flogging him with a switch. In front of the
altar Count Raymond was granted absolution. So many spectators
pushed into the abbey that he was taken out by way of the crypt, past
the sarcophagus of the murdered legate.

Now the papal secretary wrote to His Holiness concerning Raymond. Mistrust his dextrous tongue, which is skilled at the distilla-
tion of lies and moral obliquity.

deus lo volt!

Raymond Roger Trencavel, viscount of Béziers and Carcassonne, likewise submitted to the church yet did not merit exculpation. He summoned his most faithful vassals to defend these cities, abandoning villages of no consequence. He himself retreated to Carcassonne since it was remote and strongly fortified, which little pleased the citizens of Béziers. All the same, Béziers in its pride decided to resist. Anon the living host marched into view and sent forward Bishop Renaud de Montpeyroux riding on a mule to negotiate. He brought with him a list of heretics which they should turn over for punishment. If not, the people of Béziers themselves should be excommunicate and blood upon their heads. The citizens replied with scorn. The barons in hope of saving Catholic lives made overtures. But all at once here came citizens riding through the gate flaunting white pennants and shouting insults and with arrows cut down a member of the host who had ventured upon the bridge. So the orderlies who had been setting up tents were infuriated and rushed against the city with clubs and poles and started digging at the walls. Others smashed at the gate with wooden beams while armored knights and sergeants gaped in astonishment.

Now from the ramparts citizens threw down the Holy Gospel. Behold! they shrieked. Here is your law! We have no need of it!

The army of Christ then crossed the fosse, quickly scaled the ramparts and rushed through churches and homes, murdering priests, children and women hugging reliquaries or crosses, searching out wealth because these Franks tolerated Jews and were rich beyond measure. The abbot of Cîteaux, when asked how Catholics might be distinguished from heretics, replied that all should be slain since God would recognize His own. By certain accounts every inhabitant of Béziers met the sword, twenty thousand or more. Others state that few Catholics were slain. However it was, people throughout the countryside left their homes and fled in panic toward the mountains. Did they once look up at the vault of heaven?

Next to be invested, Carcassonne, a populous city glorying in wickedness. On the feast of Saint Peter the living host arrived and quickly succeeded in crossing the entrenchment. Suburbs were taken, much of Carcassonne subdued after a week. However the abbot wearied of obstinate resistance and proposed to negotiate with Viscount Raymond Roger, offering safe conduct sanctioned by his oath and that of the barons. Therefore the viscount with three hundred men came to the abbot's tent. But why should faith be kept with the faithless? The abbot dressed them all in chains. Three months the viscount lodged in prison before expiring. It may be that God received his soul. As for the inhabitants, when Carcassonne was subjugated a number contrived to escape. Many more embraced the stake or mounted the scaffold on account of their infidelity since the inquisitors proved rigorous. So much has been reported. Others say that in accordance with terms of capitulation every citizen departed, including sectaries, but all had left their property as spoil and Carcassonne was plundered in orderly fashion.

Lord Simon de Montfort, trustworthy and zealous, was chosen viscount of Béziers and Carcassonne. Tall, having a thick bush of hair and strong as any ox, albeit an old man near fifty. Heretics he loathed and considered his elevation to viscount a thread in the tapestry of God. Think you I am afraid? he replied to a Cistercian who would encourage him. My work is Christ's work. We cannot be defeated.

Yet the air stank of rebellion. These Provenceaux grew less submissive. And the army dwindled because many in the host had little appetite for such a crusade. Faithless as southern Franks might be, they had no link to Saracens, Frankish blood ran through their veins. The count of Nevers made up his mind to go home. The duke of Burgundy followed. Thus it came about that Simon de Montfort commanded a fistful of knights and mercenaries. Winter and early spring went well enough. Albi surrendered. Limoux surrendered. Lesser towns opened their gates when he approached. Still, the passing of time caused those who had been terrified to question themselves. What are we? they said to one another. They began, cautiously, to strike. A soldier would be ambushed and killed, another seized. Now the count of Foix, observing how matters stood, took back one of his castles.

deus lo volt!

Simon addressed a plaintive appeal to His Holiness Innocent. I am left almost alone. Enemies of Christ occupy the mountains and hills. The land is impoverished. Heretics destroy or give up weak castles while strengthening others they expect to defend. I have been obliged to double the wages of my soldiers lest they depart. Without help I cannot govern much longer.

To what degree His Holiness responded is not known. But the wife of Simon de Montfort, Alice, brought a few hundred soldiers from Île-de-France. They were not many, but enough. He took the castle of Bram, sliced away the upper lip and nose of every defender and scooped out their eyes, all save one, granting this recreant a single eye that he might lead his mutilated comrades to the defiant fortress of Cabaret. It is related how some time afterward Bishop Folquet during a sermon compared heretics to wolves, the faithful to sheep, but was interrupted by one who displayed his wounds and asked if ever a wolf was so abused by a sheep. The Holy Church keeps dogs to guard its flock, Bishop Folquet replied. A loyal dog has bitten you. In this response we hear the guiding voice of our Lord, a mighty fortress against which advocates of Satan dash themselves in vain.

After a siege lasting seven weeks the garrison at Minerve chose to negotiate. Three Cathar women who thought themselves perfect now abjured a perfidious faith to save their skin. Others clinging stubbornly to the devil's bosom were burnt, a number that exceeded one hundred and forty. Some hopped eagerly into the flame.

Termes resisted nine months but opened to Simon de Montfort on the twenty-third of November in that year of our Lord 1210.

Many succumbed, felt the whip. Alayrac. Pennautier. Coustaussa. Gaillac. Montaigu. La Grave. Still, a rank odor emanated from Languedoc.

Viscount Simon marched against Lavour. After two months of battering, the walls crumbled. Simon hanged Aimery de Montréal, who was commandant, with eighty of his knights. Yet by God's design the gibbet broke, hence many that had expected a rope got their

323

throats slit. Four hundred Cathari were rounded up, men and women both, and marched into a meadow where all burned rejoicing, such was their obduracy. Lady Guiraude de Laurac, chatelaine of Lavaur, after being dragged outside the gate was thrown into a well, stones dropped on top to bury her. A very great loss and sin, according to a chanson of those days, for never did a living soul depart hungry from the castle. However that may be, all were anathema to God and so this was not homicide but malicide. Truly did blessed Saint Augustine remark that precepts of forbearance should be kept by a wary heart.

Viscount Simon crossed the Rhône thinking to chastise other sectarians, unwisely marching away from the center of his strength. He attacked the proud city of Toulouse. Several times he was repulsed and the legate began to grumble. Why did he not subjugate this nest of vipers? Had he engaged in some evil that brought about God's wrath?

During the ninth month a powerful chatte was built that could be rolled close to the ramparts and look across the city. But the men of Toulouse made a dawn sortie. Simon was hearing mass when he learned they had breached his camp. After concluding devotions he hurried to the battle, but just then Guy de Montfort was struck by an arrow. Simon rushed toward him, lamenting bitterly, and was hit by a stone in such wise that eyeballs, teeth, brains, and skull flew all to pieces and down he dropped stark dead and bloody. Now the city and the very paving rang with the sound of horns, trumpets, church bells, gongs, drums, bugles, ringing and hammering gladly since this took place where anyone could see. Up from Toulouse went a huge clamor of relief that Simon de Montfort was dead, murmurs of consternation from the Catholic camp. It is told in the chanson that young girls served the catapult that destroyed him. What could be the purport of this? When a thing deviates from our expectation there must be some error in our thought.

Straightway they bore him to burial in Carcassone, celebrated the service at Saint-Nazaire. And those who know how to read may learn from his epitaph that he is a saint, a martyr destined to rise again, to flourish in unparalleled felicity, to have his place in the Kingdom. This according to the Canzon de la Crozada.

Montfort es mort! they sang in Toulouse. Es mort! Es mort!

Soon enough old Count Raymond followed his enemy, yet being excommunicate was denied the succor of religion. Forbidden burial in consecrated earth, he lay neglected outside the cemetery and was eaten by rats. Hospitalers some time later got his skull.

Anon, Honorius became pontiff, and it seemed to him that foxes were creeping into vineyards of the Lord. Thus he despatched Cardinal Romanus to France and the cardinal vigorously preached his message. All who were able to carry weapons should march against the tainted city of Toulouse. Prelates and laity responded. King Louis himself assumed the cross. However, King Louis would not proceed until he got letters from the pontiff that forbade the English under pain of excommunication to annoy his realm while he was absent on crusade. Then would he march against defiant Provenceaux.

The army assembled at Bourges on Ascension Day. Roger of Wendover declares that as it moved south along the Rhône it could have been taken for an army of castles in motion what with fifty thousand mounted knights and more sergeants than could be counted, all with glittering shields, accompanied by archbishops and bishops holding innumerable banners.

Whitsunday Eve they came to Avignon. King Louis requested leave to shorten their march by passing through, but the citizens would not open up. They said the king meant treachery. Then he was provoked and swore not to depart until Avignon lay subject at his feet. So with mangonels and crossbows and other devices he launched a furious assault. But the city was well defended, well equipped, giving back stone for stone, dart for dart, inflicting griev-ous damage. Numerous Franks went to sleep in Christ.

Moreover, the people of Avignon had stripped the countryside of grain, fruit, horses, swine, cattle, everything serviceable, and

325

ploughed up their fields. Hence the Franks were obliged to look for nutriment. Pilgrims, sergeants, knights, God knows how many gave up the ghost for lack of sustenance to fill their bellies. If this were not enough, black flies crept through tents, pavilions, crept over spoons, plates, cups, and bloody flux tormented the living host. King Louis fretted with good reason because if he failed at his purpose he would be mocked. Therefore a huge attack was ordered. Now such a multitude of armored men crossed the bridge that, either from their weight or because these treacherous people undermined the arches, the bridge crumbled. Franks plunged groaning into the tumultuous stream, dozens, hundreds, bringing shouts of joy from the besieged.

And one day with the Franks at table, unprepared to fight, these watchful citizens sallied from the gate, rushed around killing as many as possible before scuttling back to the city. King Louis ordered bodies flung into the river on account of the smell. He ordered a trench dug between Avignon and the Frankish camp to prevent this happening again. Now the assembled prelates, having no better idea, declared excommunicate the citizens of Avignon. By this time good weather was nearly used up. Few in the army looked forward to cold winter rain.

King Louis thought to escape this unhappy condition with pestilence all around, so betook himself to the monastery at Montpensier. But here came Henry, count of Champagne, who had served forty days at the siege and therefore, by Frankish custom, asked leave to go home. King Louis would not give permission. Then said the count, having served those forty days he meant to go home if the king would like it or not. This roused King Louis to swear an oath that should the count go away in such fashion his territory would be ravaged by sword and fire. Whereupon the count, bursting with lust for the king's wife, caused poison to be administered and in a little while Louis took sick as the potion worked through his vitals. So he died. Cardinal Romanus and his advisers thought it best to dissimulate. King Louis, said they, had fallen ill but in the judgment of physicians would recover. They preserved the husk of King Louis with salt, wrapped it in waxed linen that they tucked within the hide of a bull. His entrails they buried in the convent. Thus, experienced at cunning, they sought to reassure the army.

But finding themselves with no advantage and a dead sovereign on their hands, plus other hindrance, Cardinal Romanus despatched a message to Avignon requesting that twelve elders be sent out to discuss peace under guarantee of safe conduct. Twelve citizens emerged. Cardinal Romanus earnestly advised them to surrender, by which they could save their lives, properties, and liberties. They answered that they would not consent to live under Frankish dominion whose insolence and pride they had endured more than once. Cardinal Romanus requested leave to enter Avignon with his prelates so they might test the faith of inhabitants, vowing that he had pressed the siege merely for the benefit of their souls. Therefore, when oaths had been sworn on both sides, the cardinal with his prelates entered. But while the gates were open, as had been secretly arranged, Frankish soldiers rushed forward and got inside to capture the city.

Priests carted off the skin and bones of King Louis to Paris so he might be interred among his ancestors. As for soldiers who followed the king on this journey, Roger of Wendover asserts that twenty-two thousand perished, considering all slain or drowned, counting those who died from plague or starvation, bringing grief and tears to numerous households. Yet these soldiers of Christ achieved martyrdom no less gloriously than their brethren in the Holy Land since extirpation of heresy at home or oversea does great honor to the Lord.

Guillem Figueira, tailor and troubadour, again sang out. Rome! Little do you hurt the Saracen but murder Greek and Latin! Deadlock and hellfire be your throne! Grant me no share of your indulgence nor pilgrimage to Avignon!

Much on the track of apostasy His Holiness charged Archbishop Stephen de Burnin with the particular task of quenching misbelief in Languedoc. The archbishop approved two Dominicans, Peter Seila and William Arnald, the first Inquisitors, whose authority was confirmed. They were deputed to proceed without obligation to episcopal or civil justice in the dioceses of Toulouse and Albi. Soon enough they laid hold of a false theologist, Vigoros de Baconia, who was tried, condemned, straightway executed. Thus were the Cathari deprived of an energetic leader.

Peter Seila remained at Toulouse while his associate toured the province, visiting Laurac, Villefranche, La Bessède, Saint-Félix, Fanjeaux, all predisposed to concealment. The count of Toulouse objected to His Holiness that these Dominicans ignored legal process, denied counsel to the accused, heard testimony behind locked doors, as is common to this day, and otherwise trampled on the subjects' heads. It was claimed that as a result of such methods people used these interrogations to charge private enemies with heretic theology. In this way the trials guided witnesses toward error, not in the direction of truth, creating turmoil, rousing citizens against the clergy and monastic alike. Therefore His Holiness advised the Inquisitors to proceed with circumspection. Also, he wrote to Archbishop Stephen and to various bishops, suggesting they intercede if necessary.

This did not curb zealous pursuit. In Toulouse lived a certain Jean Tisseyre, a workman, who took it upon himself to go about the streets haranguing people. Listen to me, citizens! he would shout. I have a wife and sleep with her. Like everybody else I curse and lie and eat meat. I am a good Christian. Do not pay attention if these Dominicans call me atheist because they want to punish innocent folk. They will be after you before you know it.

That this man Tisseyre got acquainted with Cathari who had been rounded up by the bailiff Denense is a fact. He converted to their faith with such ardor that he received the consolamentum at their hands. He professed allegiance to these wicked people and declared a wish to share their fate. Justifiably he went to the stake alongside them.

For two years Peter Seila and William Arnald questioned suspects in Toulouse and the provinces. Betimes they decreed a period of grace, a week or fortnight, during which those who lapsed from godliness might admit to error without coercion. This brought out

328

many citizens eager to accuse themselves, hoping thus to elude the stake or dungeon, hoping for canonical penance such as going on pilgrimage or paying a fine or carrying a cross. It is related that during mass confessions a suspect named Doumenge omitted to step forth. Being threatened with death, he saved himself by disclosing where ten Cathari hid themselves at Cassès. Three of these ten escaped, seven were caught and met the stake since they had gone astray. Thus did our Heavenly Father see to their conclusion.

Brothers Seila and Arnald traveled to the district of Quercy. More than two hundred seculars did they find at Moissac and burnt every one. Also, they conducted posthumous investigations, exhumed and burnt numerous corpses.

In Toulouse a singular occurrence was noted. Just as Bishop Raymond du Fauga washed his hands before entering the refectory he learned of an old woman nearby who had accepted the consolamentum. He went at once to the address, followed by the convent prior and others, to interrogate this dying old woman on matters of faith. And she, being told the lord bishop had arrived, mistakenly thought him a Cathar bishop and spewed forth the odious dogma. Then said Bishop Raymond, encouraging this misapprehension, not even fear of death should make you confess to other than that you hold most firmly. To which the old woman answered that so long as life remained she would not deny Catharism. So now Bishop Raymond disclosed himself for what he was, not Cathar but Catholic, and he implored her to recant. She would not. In front of witnesses she persevered ever more stubbornly. Then she was carried in her bed as far as Pré-du-Comte since she was too feeble to walk, put to the stake and burnt forthwith. After which the bishop with his entourage went back to the refectory, gave thanks to God and fell cheerfully upon the food. Anon the prior delivered a sermon likening the fire that consumed her to that which Elijah called down from heaven to confound the priests of Baal.

More interrogations came about. A certain perfectus, by name Raymond Gros, having seen the light of Jesus Christ, denounced

large numbers of dead citizens. Graves were opened, bones and carcasses dragged on hurdles through Toulouse and a public crier announcing their names to warn the living. Qui atal fara, atal pendra.
Which is to say, whosoever does the like, so will he suffer.

Behold! Behold! warned the Inquisitor. Behold a greedy fire swallow thy companions! See how the people surge close to watch eager
flames lick thy flesh! Shalt thou burn or shalt thou conform? Answer
at once!

Little refuge existed but at Montségur five leagues from Foix. On
a pinnacle the castle stood secure, none thought it could be taken.
They say it was built in our year of grace 1204 by Ramón de Perella
who sympathized with Cathars and gave lodging to notorious re-
cusants. So they resolved to make this a permanent home whence
they might descend on quick tours of their frightened laity. They
strengthened the keep. Being succored by villagers they put up huge
stores of grain to withstand a siege, and like worms burrowed cells to
accommodate the rising population. Soon enough came four Inquisitors from Toulouse who took quarters in the village of Avignonet to
conduct their work. Pierre-Roger, who was commandant of Montségur, led eighty-five knights with axes and swords to the citadel
where these examiners slept, slashed and chopped them all to death,
so much hatred did persecution hatch. Old narratives relate that Inquisitor Guillaume Arnaud died with the Te Deum on his lips, run
through the body numerous times, his head smashed against flag-
stones.

Do not those in God's service go armed with inimitable authority? Hugh d'Arcis brought soldiers to encamp beneath Montségur
but on account of the terrain he could not surround it. During the
winter Bishop Durand arrived with soldiers from his diocese and
erected a powerful trebuchet that severely damaged the east tower.
Commandant Pierre-Roger thought the escarpment would protect
them on that side, so he withdrew his men from the outworks. But
there were some Basques who knew the slope. They climbed it,
knifed the sentinels, and got control of the barbican. These Basques

could not penetrate the central keep, nevertheless Montségur would fall. Those inside, like trapped garrisons everywhere, took to reading the breeze for news, telling one another fabulous tales of armies hastening to their aid. The count of Toulouse is en route, they said. The emperor of Germany marches to save us.

After nine months of resistance Montségur capitulated. All were permitted to leave, accepting light penance for their sin, generous terms indeed. All were allowed to depart excepting those who would not abjure perfidious belief. Some openly received the consolamentum, thus defiantly condemning themselves to the stake. These were led from the castle in chains. Beneath Montségur on a pyre of blazing wood these obdurate sectarians gave up the ghost, more than two hundred, including the daughter of Ramón de Perella, Escalaramonde, together with Bertrand de Marty, the last heretic bishop.

Catharism thenceforth ceased to be a church. Congregations declined because they had no cleric to lead the wicked service. Some few persisted yet when hailed before Inquisitors did not know what they believed. Some had not heard the faith preached for years before they were arrested.

While this happened in the south there occurred in the north an event that caused men to bite their lips and wag their heads. Children resolved to do what kings and princes could not. They would march oversea to liberate the Holy Sepulcher. In the province of Orléannais a shepherd boy named Stephen from the village of Cloyes began to preach a doctrine never before heard. He declared that while tending his flock near Cloyes he was approached by a stranger, a pilgrim returning from the Holy Land, who asked for something to eat. And when Stephen shared his food the pilgrim revealed himself to be Jesus Christ, saying that the innocents of France would succeed where kings had failed. He appointed this boy Stephen to lead the march and gave him a letter addressed to King Philip Augustus who was spending that summer at Saint Denys, burial place of Frankish kings since the time of Dagobert. Here, too, was the Oriflamme kept, holy standard of the realm. Concerning the identity of this stranger who claimed to be our Lord, chronicles report little. Mayhap some heretic thinking to reach the king. By himself he could not gain audience, but it is known how children work marvels and by means of an artless shepherd boy he thought to reach court with his diabolic argument.

Some think the boy's wits addled by Saint Mark's Day when church altars are draped in black, when citizens parade through the streets chanting and waving crosses swathed in black to commemorate those who died for the Holy Land, to implore mercy on those enslaved. Groans, shrieks, laments, dolorous chants, seizures, black crosses nodding in the street, all this might afflict the orderly process of thought, arouse a feverish desire to expel Saracens from Christ's kingdom oversea. Without question those who are inexperienced may be seduced by charming the senses.

Might it be Satan's work? We are told that Stephen witnessed the Feast of Asses, which insults Blessed Mary as well as God since the choir follows the Introit, or Kyrie, or whatever part is chanted, by imitating the dreadful song of the ass. And a sermon devoted to praise of the ass is preached with Latin and French intermingled, hence many in the congregation feel bewildered. And this farce being ended, the priest brays three times, whereupon the congregate responds not with Deo Gratias but with abominable noise. Hin-hawm! Hin-hawm! Hin-hawm!

Further, at the time of Epiphany certain Christians having lost all sense of duty celebrate the Feast of Fools. Eudes de Sully when he was minister tried to suppress the vile charade, in vain. Clerics select an archbishop and a bishop who are escorted to the cathedral by mock prelates gowned with utmost pomp. Masked, disguised as buffoons, sporting animal hides or garments meant for women they leap and gesticulate, dance through the holy edifice, bawl monstrous songs. They gamble at dice on the altar, burn leather sandals for incense, perform and strut with hideous vulgarity to defile the church as though to express what most weighs upon their souls, that Christianity is a fable, their obligations but deceitful acts from a counterfeit drama. Could such pageantry rattle the wit of a witless boy?

However it was, the young shepherd set out for Saint Denys and preached while he walked, exhorting other children. He likened himself to Moses, subserving a new crusade, pausing at castles and villages. Thus he gathered children out of their homes and led them off and it is said no lock or bolt could prevent them. Neither pleas nor threats dissuaded them. Chanting in the common tongue, singing, joyously they marched at his heels and listened with delight to his every word.

To Saint Denys, therefore, he walked to see the king. And at the sepulcher of martyred Dionysius, garbed as though he were yet in the field near Cloyes, crook in hand, this child apostle spoke of suffering in Jerusalem, Christians enslaved. Many who listened thought they could hear groans, cries for help, clanking chains. He pointed to the shrine of Dionysius thronged with pilgrims and compared it to the tomb of Jesus vilified by Saracens. He likened Jesus to a banished king, Jerusalem to a captive queen. He spoke of a dream in which the sea rolled apart for him and for those who followed him. He displayed the letter to King Philip Augustus. He said that one day he was unable to find his sheep because they had left the pasture, but discovered them in a field of grain. He began beating them to drive them out, at which they dropped on their knees to beg forgiveness, and by this sign he knew he was appointed to liberate the Holy City. Documents from those days testify that outside the sepulcher of Dionysius he performed miracles.

If this boy Stephen gained audience with the king has been debated. But it is known that on account of the children Philip Augustus consulted his advisors and learned men at the University of

333

Paris, after which he ordered the children to disperse. They refused. Instead, like thistle on the breeze they gathered at Vendôme, high and low, descending from castles on the mountain, emerging from wretched mud hovels, singing while they marched, holding wax tapers, waving perfumed censers, bringing copies of the red silk Oriflamme with gold flames scattered. And if asked how they would accomplish what grown men could not, they replied that they were equal to the will of God and whatever He might wish for them, that would they humbly and gladly accept.

News of these crusading children got to Germany and Lotharingia quick as a storm. The Benedictine William at his monastery near Guines wrote of it. The monk Reiner at Liège wrote of it. And in Cologne the monk Godfrey wrote that a child called Nicholas began to preach outside the Byzantine cathedral where bones of the Magi rest in a golden casket. They say Archbishop Raynuldus brought back these inestimable relics from the sack of Milan. Whatever the fact, thousands came to worship. Nicholas preached to all who approached, holding up a metal cross in the form of Tau. But he did not preach the slaughter of Muslims, saying the holy word of God would illuminate their lives, would convert them, would cause them to abhor the wicked faith of Mahomet and worship Jesus.

They set forth about the time of Pentecost, according to the annal of Cologne, and left behind their plows and carts, abandoned the animals they pastured. Many took up pilgrim costume, wide-brimmed hat, palmer's staff, gray coat and a cross sewn to the breast. By repute they numbered twenty thousand. Some leapt or danced like storks prepared to migrate. Thus wrapped in mighty delusion they walked from Cologne to Basle, to Geneva, traversed the Alps near Mount Cenis, by which time half were lost, murdered, starved, frozen, drowned in raging mountain streams, devoured by famished wolves.

334

In August they reached the gates of Genoa, but three thousand more had disappeared. Nicholas petitioned the Senate, begging hospitality for one night, explaining that the sea would divide next morning as it divided for Moses and they would march on to Jerusalem. His petition was granted. But at dawn the waves broke without remission. Therefore the children marched to Pisa, thinking they had missed their appointment. How many perished on this journey is not known. The Senones chronicle states that two shiploads of children sailed from Pisa to the Holy Land. What became of them is not recorded. Others wandered uncertainly toward Arezzo, Firenze, Perugia. It may be that a few walked to Rome where they met the pontiff. Without doubt some reached the port of Brindisi where a Norwegian called Friso sold the boys into slavery, the girls into brothels. Illi de Brundusio virgines stuprantur. Et in arcum pessimum passim venumdantur.

Concerning Nicholas, one document from those days asserts that he came at length to the Holy Land where he fought bravely at Acre, later at Damietta, returning unharmed. Perhaps. But when the citizens of Cologne learned what happened to their children they hanged his father.

As for Stephen, thirty thousand innocents gathered beneath his standard, a woolen cross affixed to the right shoulder of each. When they set out they were accompanied by animals and birds, overhead a cloud of butterflies, which are bearers of the soul. They leapt and shouted as did the German children, and sang for joy. O Jerusalem! O Jerusalem! Our feet shall stand within thy walls!

Through the fruitful heart of France they marched south to Lyons, beside the Rhône to Valence, Avignon, Marseille. Stephen traveled at his leisure in a chariot fitted with carpets and a decorated canopy protecting him from the August sun. Twelve youths from noble families surrounded him, forming the honor guard, each handsomely mounted, each holding a lance. It is said that while Stephen was a child in years, ten or twelve, he was adept at vice, lecherous, quick to benefit from his role as saint and prophet. If he stood up to address the multitude thousands pressed forward. On such

335

occasions many were trampled or suffocated. Those nearest him would reach out to pluck a thread from his coat, a splinter from the cart, a hair from the mane of the horse that drew him, much as it was with Peter the hermit.

At Marseille they found the sea unyielding. Waves curled and broke, adamant. Now two agents of Satan slipped out of the darkness. William Porcus. Hugo Ferreus. Concerning the first, some have called him a merchant of Marseille while others think he was a Genoese sea captain of high repute. Yet again, he is called William de Posquères who fought at the siege of Acre with Guy de Lusignan. As to Hugo Ferreus, most think him viguier of Marseille, which is to say the viscount's representative and traded in the Holy Land. No matter. Without cost, for love of God, absque pretio, causa Dei, so these knaves declared, would they charter what vessels were required, enabling a fervent army of Christ to reach Jerusalem. Seven vessels these traffickers obtained. What sort is not known. Gulafres. Dromonds. Buzas.

For eighteen years Europe did not learn the fate of these children, not until a priest who had accompanied them returned. Of all who embarked at Marseille he alone came back to say what happened. West of Sardinia rises a deserted islet, Accipitrum, referring to falcons that nest among the cliffs. Three days out from Marseille a furious storm drove two vessels against this rocky islet. All aboard were lost. The remaining vessels bore south to Africa and the slave market at Bujeiah. Here the Frankish children were sold. Some vanished in Bujeiah. Others went to Alexandria where the governor, Maschemuth, put them to work cultivating his fields. Sultan Malek Kamel bought seven hundred. Some few did set foot in the Holy Land but were carried away to Damascus or Baghdad where they were decapitated or drowned or shot by archers if they would not renounce our Lord.

Was this done by instinct of the devil? Cloyed with the blood of martyred men, did Satan in his blackness desire a cordial of childish blood to slake his thirst? Gregory, who was pontiff in those days, groaned with despair when he learned how these children suffered and died. Have they not put us to shame? he wondered aloud. Have not these innocents perished while we slept?

He thought to raise a monument in their honor. That islet called Accipitrum where two ships foundered was deemed appropriate. Many small corpses had washed ashore during the storm and fishermen who sometimes visited the place had buried them. His Holiness directed that a church should be constructed, the bodies of these children exhumed and reburied within. If they were found wondrously uncorrupted or not has long been argued. The church is named Ecclesia Novorum Innocentium, which recalls the murdered children of Bethlehem, and was so endowed that twelve prebends live nearby, praying incessantly. All things flow constantly from God as water flows from a spring, tending ever to return.

Belgicum, Albericus, Thomas de Champré, and others make some mention of these innocents, none at length. The foolish little army had quickly come and gone. Besides, in those days the Church was bent on purifying Languedoc.

What of Stephen? An English monk, Thomas of Sherborne, while traveling through France long after the children vanished was held captive for eight days by a militant host of shepherds. This monk spoke of an old man commanding the shepherds who had been a slave in Egypt and promised the sultan he would lead an army of Christians into bondage just as he had led Frankish children into slavery when he was a child. So he journeyed here or there preaching with no authority or license, claiming Our Lady had empowered him to conscript herdsmen and ploughmen by virtue of their simplicity to recover the Holy Land, claiming to hold a mandate from the Virgin in his clenched fist, braying that the Lord was not pleased with Frankish pride in arms. Country folk left their flocks and herds to follow this old man. For, said they, God Almighty hath chosen the weak to confound the strong. And they cut themselves banners whose insignia was a lamb bearing a flag in token of humility. Exiles, thieves, rogues, excommunicates, all came swarming. Spears, axes, knives, and poniards they carried. And whoever challenged their passage they would attack. And when their master preached, what did he do but condemn various orders, calling Franciscans and Dominicans hypocrites, calling Cistercians greedy, Benedictines gluttonous. He preached unspeakable filth about the Roman curia. He raved, cursed, deviated madly from acknowledged tenets of Christian faith. People who heard such things spoken in hatred applauded loudly.

To the city of Orléans did he lead his flock, whereupon the bishop forbade clerics to listen or consort with them since it was the devil's snare. But the citizens would hear what was preached. And the old man blasphemed, hurled insults, at which a scholar strode up close, denouncing him as a liar, heretic, enemy of truth. So a shepherd with a pointed axe split the scholar's head to silence him. Then this army went about smashing doors, pillaging, murdering, burning books, and drowned priests in the Loire while terrified citizens pretended not to see. Next to Bourges. A curious throng assembled when this old man announced he would preach and perform miracles. But his assertions the crowd perceived as foolish, his miracles fraudulent. Some butcher cleaved his skull with a hatchet, after which they dragged his carcass to the crossroads for animals to eat. So the wicked army flew apart, each loutish soldier anxious to save his nuts. Most were caught, slain like dogs that foam at the mouth. All this did Thomas of Sherborne set down in writing after he escaped these pastouraux who got no closer to Jerusalem than Bourges.

If the furious old man who led them was Stephen of Cloyes has been much debated. Myself, I think not. If he surrendered the ghost in boiling surf at Accipitrum, lost his head at Damascus, mayhap lived out his years in Muslim slavery, or if he declined to board the Judas ships and turned back to Cloyes, who shall decide? He with all who followed him had put their trust in Almighty God, expecting to win by faith what mounted knights could not through force of arms. They had gone armed with belief in lieu of steel. For love of our Lord they undertook the voyage, not for wealth or high repute. Those who devote their lives to Him, will they ever be disappointed at His reward?

338

*N*ow six hundred, threescore and six years were almost up, a number allotted to Antichrist, whose name is the Beast. Was not Mahomet conceived that long ago? Surely an hour had turned. From northern Thule to southernmost Sicily, from east to west, Europe rejoiced at a marvelous awakening, the resurrection of hope, of faith, of urgent desire. Indeed, His Holiness wrote to Sultan al-Adil about wrath to come.

Six days before Whitsuntide, that high feast which men so richly keep, here were signs and portents. Bishop Oliverius of Paderborn wrote to the count of Naumr that while in the diocese of Münster, accompanied by abbots of the Cluniac and Cistercian orders, thousands gathered to hear him speak. All seated themselves in a quiet meadow outside Bedum. No leaves rustled. Anon, from a luminous white cloud in the north a cross emerged, another manifesting in the south. Above and between these two appeared a majestic cross upon which a human figure was suspended, that of a naked man, his head leaning on his shoulder. Nails could be seen penetrating his hands and feet just as they are skillfully pictured in church. A girl of eleven pointed this out to her mother and grandmother and to other people nearby. They became lost in adoration. More than one hundred people witnessed this miracle.

Further, in a different part of the country a cross like a rainbow was noted by the abbot of Heisterbach. And above the Frisian port of Dokkum where Blessed Bonifacius achieved martyrdom a cross traveled through the sky as if drawn by a cord, as if to summon and direct pilgrims.

Bishop James of Acre, in those days visiting Gaul, preached a new sermon. He imagined Christ as a lord robbed of patrimony who calls upon his vassals. The Lord would know if His vassals were faithful. For by the loss of patrimony is He much afflicted, said Bishop James. We read in the book of Kings how the priest Eli, hearing that the Ark of the Lord was taken, fell off his stool and died from excessive grief. Who is not moved that the Holy Land is trodden underfoot?

339

Enemies of Christ stretch forth sacrilegious hands toward her most intimate parts, oppressing the city of our salvation. She has been made the habitat of dragons, the pasture of ostriches. Which among you is not consumed by zeal for the house of the Lord? Where is the anxiety of Mattathias? Where is the dagger of Phinehas? Where is the sharp blade of Ehud? Although it is true that none is bound to our Lord by feudal law, He offers inestimable remuneration. He offers remission of sin and sheaves of joy. He offers eternal life. Therefore should we hurry to Him.

In cities and villages everywhere people awakened from a long and thoughtless slumber. Forty thousand in England began to equip themselves for the journey. The cleric Humbert asserts that he alone set down that many on his rolls. Nor did there come an end to portents. On the eve of the nativity of John the Baptist a glowing crucifix was observed from which hung the body of Jesus Christ spattered with blood and His side pierced by a lance. A trader hauling fish to Uxbridge saw this. He stood lost in ecstasy, awed by the immanent brightness. Next day at Uxbridge he related this miracle. Many believed. Others laughed until persuaded to change their opinion because the Lord materialized elsewhere to convert the incredulous through His glory. Bishops Peter of Winchester and William of Exeter made ready to join the expedition. They, like all the rest, praised God for having condescended to touch their lives. Emperor Frederick of Hohenstaufen felt moved to take the vow. Countless thousands in Germany followed his example.

Bishop James considered that in order to welcome and comfort this multitude when it reached the Holy Land he should return to the diocese of Acre. Thus he set out for Genoa on a mule, but was assaulted by the devil. There is extant a letter he wrote from Genoa in October of the year 1216.

No sooner did I come to Lombardy than Satan cast my weapons into the stream. That is to say, my books, with which I meant to fight him. Because of melting snow the stream was greatly swollen. Bridges and rocks had been carried off. One of my trunks filled with books was swept away, but a second trunk that contained a finger of my mother, Marie d'Oignies, buoyed the mule and saved it from drowning. The first trunk I found caught in the branches of a tree. Although my books were somewhat spoilt, one might yet make out the words.

Is it not clear how Satan rouses volatile passions against us? A nun in the Abbaye-aux-Dames at Caen devoted herself not to the Lord but to venery, nor would she be persuaded to confess. No matter that she was admonished on her deathbed, she chose to expire obstinate, admitting nothing that would do her any good. Not long afterward a sister slept in the cell where this nun died and dreamt of a fire on the hearth and the wicked nun burning, all the while beaten with hammers by two black spirits on either side. Then at the stroke of a hammer a spark darted into the eye of the dreaming sister, which caused her to wake up. Now she understood the vision, and there was a stinging pain in her eye to verify it.

We are told of a monk who requested tutelage in the black arts from Satan. That I could not do, replied this ancient enemy of mankind, except you deny your faith and make a sacrifice. Then the foolish monk asked what sacrifice he should make. That which is delectable, said the adversary. You shall make a libation of your seed for me to drink, but you shall taste it first. The monk did as instructed, by this horrible act declaring his renunciation of God. We are informed that he made unscrupulous use of a nun if the brother who shared his cell was absent. But one day the brother returned sooner than expected so the monk called upon the black magic he acquired from Satan, changing his lascivious nun into a dog. This matter came to the notice of Anselm who was abbot of Bec, later archbishop of Canterbury. Through Anselm's judgment the monk was cast out from administering divine mysteries. Yet so long as he lived he thought he would someday become bishop. This proud idea he got from Satan, who tells lies perpetually, since when the monk died he

341

was no more a bishop than a goat, but an unfrocked priest forever. Are we not privileged to observe how the Creator guides us, how He confronts and vanquishes Satan at every turn?

How should we recognize our antagonist? Some think his head remarkably small, like a green fruit, his shoulders extremely broad. All at once he may show himself in a whirlwind. Anon, he will take up the guise of a querulous bitch that spins about and bites and snaps. His manifestations defy us. Devils are known to appear en masse, garbed as pilgrims, wallets slung against their haunches in the manner of Scots. Or like badgers, as reported from the district of Vexin. Guibert de Nogent declares that our enemy takes the guise of a little man who wears an orange-yellow tunic, a defiant sparrowhawk riding on his hand. Guibert when he was young awoke during the night to a clamor of voices and saw a man who earlier had died in the baths. Then, says he, I leapt screaming from my bed. I saw the lamp extinguished and saw a hideous shape, the devil's outline.

Some time ago a priest of benign temperament devoted himself to the monastic life at Saint Germer, but managed to rouse a devil. With this good priest hunched over making a noisy stink the evil one appeared, having taken the guise of a cowled monk, shuffling his sandals on the floor as monks do when requesting permission to visit the stall at night, evoking such terror that the kindly priest leapt up and struck his head on the lintel of the door. Thus the devil contrived to wound his body, whose soul he could not harm, thereby disclosing his own poverty of spirit.

We hear of an excellent woman who lay down on a narrow bench to rest after Sunday matins but fell asleep. Then it seemed she was led through a colonnade to the mouth of a well. And up from the depths sprang human shapes with hair eaten by worms, who sought to draw her by the hand down into the well. But a voice cried out. Therefore the ugly phantoms plunged back into the depths. She had been saved because while walking through the colonnade she prayed to God for one thing, that she might be restored to the bench where her body rested.

deus lo volt!

Also, the monk Suger on his deathbed was approached by the devil carrying a book. Take this book and read it, said the devil. Jupiter sends it to you. The monk was horrified by the sound of this atrocious name. After relating what had occurred he lost his senses and was chained to his bed, but died in peace after making a good confession.

Thus we see how our Nemesis would lead us through circles of hell by the bridle of iniquity. Even so must he fly in terror from the inimitable light of God. Once we have known Jesus Christ we need not fear the stench of Satan. Therefore we lift our voices in praise, our hands in gratitude.

Bishop James, having reserved quarters for himself and his companions aboard a newly built ship, took passage from Genoa. He writes that he meant throughout the voyage to study his precious books, those arms that enabled him to combat the devil. And when he got to Acre he would preach the word of God in his diocese while awaiting the knighthood of Christ.

Anon, this host assembled. Teutonic knights with the duke of Austria. Templars. Hospitalers. Bishops of Nicosia and Bethlehem. King John of Jerusalem to lead the army. Here, too, the patriarch of Jerusalem. All being persuaded of their cause, wrapped in hope, on Ascension Day at the Castle of Pilgrims they set sail with a north wind rising, sailing toward Egypt, vault of infidel wealth and power.

Three days out they sighted Damietta. But a few leagues up the Nile stood Babylon, Cairo, tongue of the serpent, head of the Beast, poisonous tooth of authority.

With God's help they were able to make port and establish camp on the west bank. All understood that since Damietta governed the waterway to Cairo it must be taken. Bishop Oliverius reports an eclipse of the moon not long after they landed, which pilgrims interpreted to the disfavor of Egypt, considering how there shall be signs in the moon and sun and stars and on the earth distress of nations. When that hammer of the ancient world, Alexander, set forth against Darius and Porus in Asia there occurred a similar eclipse, which he pointed out to his men. They felt encouraged and went on to defeat the Medes and Persians. So did the living host feel encouraged since Egyptians impute the moon to themselves, they rely much on its waxing and waning. Hence a fading orb signified the outcome.

These pagans had built a castle on an island near the west bank in order to supervise and regulate what might travel upstream or downstream. King John attacked with seventy barques sheathed in leather as protection against flaming naphtha, but did not succeed. The duke of Austria and Hospitalers of Saint John fixed ladders aboard two ships, but Egyptians shattered that of the Hospitalers so it crashed together with the mast, hurling people headlong. That of the duke broke under the weight of armed men in chain mail and they disappeared in the river. Many vigorous Christian soldiers thus achieved martyrdom to the advantage of their souls. Egyptians who remarked what happened began to make a loud noise with sackbuts and drums.

Bishop Oliverius now explained how two vessels might be joined with ropes and planks until they resembled one, having four masts and a balustrade of poles and nets covered with hide. So it was done. Under the balustrade, suspended from ropes, a ladder extended thirty cubits beyond the prow. High barons were invited to look over this vessel to see if anything might be lacking, but they marveled and declared that such a work had not been imagined since the beginning of the world. Men from every nation were assigned to it so there could be no empty boasting.

On the feast of Saint Bartholomew as clerics walked barefoot along the shore and the patriarch of Jerusalem lay prostrate in the dust before the cross this vessel eased forth. Now came a shower of stones from the ramparts of Damietta. And as the vessel got closer those who defended the castle thrust out lances. They threw oil and fire, which caused the wood to burst into flame. Soldiers attempting to quench the fire with gravel and sour liquid fell into the Nile, including the standard bearer of the duke. The Babylonians shouted with joy, thinking themselves victorious. However a young knight from the diocese of Liège got into the castle. After him a Frisian soldier carrying a flail of the sort used in threshing grain, equipped with chains for combat, who lashed out right and left and knocked down the infidel bearing Sultan al-Kamil's standard. God's enemies seeing this grew alarmed and retreated to where they could not escape. At last, seeing no help, they wished to discuss things. When it was agreed their lives would be spared they gave up their weapons to the duke, excepting some who during the night had thrown themselves from windows to drown or swim ashore. Pilgrims now controlled the waterway to Cairo. Many brave knights and sergeants here ascended to glory, delivered from human woe. Lord Ithier de Toucy. Lord Hervé de Vierzon. Brother William from Chartres. Oliver, bastard son of John Lackland. Their names will not be forgotten.

On the feast of Saint Denys here came armed galleys rowing against the pilgrim camp but they were repulsed. Few escaped Christian blades and treacherous currents of the Nile. As was learned afterward, nearly one thousand perished. Almighty God is a wall of strength to those who trust in Him.

On the feast of Saint Demetrius, alleged to be the uterine brother of Blessed Denys, here came Saracens once more, at dawn, to invade the Templar camp but were again driven back. On this occasion five hundred plunged shrieking into hell.

Anon a Templar vessel carried by the powerful stream drifted near Damietta. Pagans assaulted it with stones, fire, and grappling hooks and swarmed aboard. And since the hull was pierced it sank quickly leaving only the mast above water, drowning many from both camps. Even as valiant Samson claimed more when he died than he killed in life, so did these Templars draw into a watery grave more than they despatched with swords. Thus hostilities raged while the living host sought to encompass Damietta, Saracens arriving unexpectedly from every direction to harass and trouble them.

345

During the vigil of Saint Andrew the Nile began to rise, advancing into camp. Tents floated away, fish came squirming up where they could be seized by hand. This storm did not abate for three days.

Excepting our Lord's infinite compassion all would have been sucked into the river or the sea. Next came plague. Blackness developed on the shins, legs afflicted with sudden pain, flesh in the mouth corrupted so the victim was unable to chew. Physicians despaired. During this trial many ascended to Christ.

How often men lapse from the counsel of our Lord. These pilgrims, having subdued the castle on the island, slipped downward into boasting indolence and revelry. Three months they loitered, gambling at dice, fornicating, drinking. Where, they asked themselves, was this Emperor Frederick of Hohenstaufen with his Teutonic legions?

As to Saracens locked inside the walls of Damietta, during this time they lost their governor on account of illness and had no one to direct them. Therefore they addressed a message to Sultan Malik al-Kamil at Cairo, beseeching him to provide a governor with knowledge enough and strength to rule. This message they fixed to a pigeon beneath her right wing and straightway let her go. She lifted herself up into the air, looked about, and sped away to the dovecote in Cairo where she was hatched. And the keeper took her to Sultan al-Kamil who plucked the message from her and caused it to be read. Then he felt alarmed because Damietta was the key to his land.

After consultation with his advisors he ordered an ox-hide to be folded four times in the shape of an egg, tightly sewn, daubed with pitch, and a cork belt around the middle so it would not overturn or sink. Inside this egg they put the sultan's nephew, a hole cut in the top of it for him to breathe. According to the chronicle of Reims they lowered this egg into the Nile after dark, not much could be seen above water, and away went al-Kamil's nephew on the current. But the Christians had stretched a net for whatever might chance to come, so at dawn they spied an object fetched against it and paddled out to investigate. They pulled the egg ashore with hooks, carried it to King John's tent where he ordered the ox-hide cut apart and here was a young Babylonian miserable and famished and damp with a letter in his tunic announcing who he was. So the king clapped him in

346

irons and had him right well guarded because he would be useful to exchange. How long he languished in shackles the chronicle does not report. Late one night his guards drank themselves to sleep whereupon the sultan's nephew thought this a good chance and went running among the tents looking for some way out. Now his guards woke up. Hoy! Hoy! they cried aloud and went seeking him. Already he had gotten among the hindermost tents and surely would escape but some bakers kneading dough for next day heard the rattle of his irons with men crying stop the prisoner. Hence the bakers ran after him and one who carried a rolling pin hailed him a mighty thump on the skull so he fell dead. At this news King John grew wroth because he had thought to trade the sultan's nephew for a Christian of gentle birth.

Al-Kamil himself came down the river to settle at Fariskur not three leagues from Damietta. Thus, Christians found themselves encamped between the sultan and the city, arguing bitterly whether they should tighten the siege or attack the sultan. Near the end of August a horde of discontented pilgrims took it upon themselves to decide and went rushing leaderless against him. The Saracens feigned alarm, retreating, but all at once turned about. Were it not for Hospitalers, Templars, and skillful barons come to their aid these audacious servants of God would have spread their bones along the river bank.

It is said that Brother Francis of Assisi observed the battle with dismay. Now in hopes of arranging a truce he sought permission to go and talk to al-Kamil. Reluctantly, after some debate, he with his companion Brother Illuminato were granted leave to do as they wished. Under a white flag they approached the pagan army bearing no weapon save their faith. And because al-Kamil had issued orders to lop off Christian heads it may be that mameluks who watched these two plodding through the brush considered them mad or otherwise afflicted. However it was, they came into the sultan's presence unharmed. Brother Francis undertook to preach. Sultan al-Kamil listened. For several days he preached to this Saracen host and was offered numerous gifts, all of which he refused. Take them and distribute them among your Christian paupers, advised the sultan of Egypt. Brother Francis replied that divine providence would comfort the poor. And he offered to walk through fire accompanied by a Saracen priest in order to validate the teaching of Christ. Al-Kamil answered that he should not, nor did the sultan think any Muslim would consent to such a trial. The steadfast devotion of Brother Francis disturbed this heathen lord. Fearing that his soldiers might be converted if they heard much else, he had these friars escorted back to the Christian camp. Yet as they departed he spoke these words to Brother Francis.

Pray for me. Pray that God may disclose the law and the faith that is most true.

All know how deeply Brother Francis felt attracted to the sacred Manger, how he reconstructed it for the devout at Greccio. Perhaps this fervent love summoned him to the Holy Land. Perhaps his journey marked one step toward comprehending the significance of the Cross. While praying at Mount La Verna not long after his return he experienced the stigmata, wounds on his body corresponding to those endured by our merciful Lord. I am told they could be seen to the day of his death, albeit he kept them hidden. Shortly after ascending to Paradise this humble, unwashed servant of God would be canonized by His Holiness Gregory in the year 1228. Beyond doubt the law and the faith that is most true were disclosed to him.

Chronicles from those days assert that al-Kamil longed for peace, feeling much oppressed by the siege of Damietta, which he could ill afford to lose. Olives, grain, fabric, goods of every description from half the world flowed through this port. He therefore assembled the princes of his realm to consult. He reminded them how the Nile was lower than usual and famine threatened. He suggested terms for peace. Christian prisoners would be freed, those newly caught as well as those who had languished so long they forgot their names. What land the Christians had lost would be restored, save the castles of Montréal and Kerak for which Egypt would pay each year as much as these castles might be worth. There should be a truce lasting twenty years. All this would Sultan al-Kamil guarantee if Christians would lift the siege of Damietta.

His counselors did not object. Now the captives were told, which delighted them. They chose Lord Andrew of Nanteuil and John of Arcis to carry the message. Meanwhile the rest stood surety under pain of losing their heads.

These nobles traveled to King John's tent. The barons assembled to hear what al-Kamil had said. Also present was Cardinal Pelagius Galvani. Two cardinals had accompanied the host, Robert of Courson who was English and this Galvani who came from Portugal. Cardinal Robert soon expired but Pelagius lived, which some thought a great pity since he caused much evil. While Brother Francis preached to Saracens in their camp this legate argued that he had gone over to their misbelief, had converted to Islam. Other clerics agreed. Bishop James wrote from Damietta that the unlettered little mendicant friar was dangerous.

Cardinal Pelagius had no wish to share the earth with any but Christians. He dreamt of subjugating Cairo in order to exterminate Islam throughout the world, to Damascus and beyond. He argued that the sultan's offer must be deceptive since pagans did not keep their word. Milo, bishop-elect of Beauvais, agreed. Concerning Milo, they say he had more pride than Nebuchadnezzar, which was enough. Together they prevailed.

Back went Andrew of Nanteuil and John of Arcis with dolorous faces to explain that, on advice of Cardinal Pelagius, King John would by no means retreat from Damietta.

Thus matters stood until a November night when certain Franks venturing close to the wall did not hear a sound, not a voice nor anything, not in the turrets, not by any gate. To the king they hurried.

349

Sire, it may be that all have died, they said. We hear naught but silence.

To the ladders! cried King John. And that man who is first to enter Damietta, he shall have one thousand bezants!

Ladders were made fast and up they scurried quick as mice, each for himself, but were not opposed. They ran to the gates and cut the bars and swung the gates apart for King John's host. A familiar stench pervaded Damietta. Once there had been sixty thousand inhabitants. Now, by some accounts, three thousand remained alive. Christians rushing through the city saw how the dead had slain the living. Dead husbands and dead wives lay on their beds, wasted away, corrupting their own homes. Starved infants with open mouths hung in the embrace of dead mothers. Avaricious merchants blue and cold among stacks of wheat, so there was food, yet not what they required. Fruit, herbs, garlic, vegetables, butter, olives, fish, none of it slipped the Christian noose. Courtyards, public houses, streets, temples, everywhere corpses rotted. By order of King John these bodies were dragged outside the walls for burning. King John and Cardinal Pelagius saw fit to enter when Damietta had been cleansed. They found gold, silver, weapons, handsome armor, corn and wine enough, whatever belongs in a good city.

As to the living inhabitants, most soon expired. Others went into captivity, others baptized. Some few notable citizens were kept to barter.

How often it is said that men are made into thieves by concupiscence of their eyes. Here was Babylonian luxury. Pearls of varied color. Silken stuff. Fringes with golden threads. Apples cunningly whittled from amber. Soft pillows. Bodkins, necklaces, silver chains for the ankle. Little moons and ornaments for shoes. Sweet tablets to suck. Jewels to hang on the forehead. Cloaks. Looking-glasses. Veils. Lawns. Crisping pins. Now was the army of Christ debauched, given to adultery and drunken chambering. And that summer while they loitered here came fourteen galleys from Venice wondrously appointed. And merchant ships wallowing with provision. But a fleet of

Saracen galleys kept watch and swept in to capture these supplies. Also, the pagans made for a great vessel bringing Henry, called the Lion, who was duke of Saxony. Through the grace of providence these unbelievers were repulsed. Still, they burnt and sank a ship belonging to the Teutonic House that was loaded with barley. Also during that summer Count Diether resolved to sail for Thessalonika, no matter if the legate objected. Stubbornly he would do as he pleased, hence the legate excommunicated his renegade ship with all aboard. Off the coast of Cyprus he fell among pirates and his ship burnt. Count Diether narrowly escaped death by swimming away. Again we remark how the Lord adjudicates and punishes those who disregard His wishes.

Emperor Frederick did not yet show his face. The principal barons asked one another. What is to be? Shall we sit closed up in this place? Have we not come to conquer Egypt? Then off they went to ask questions of King John and Cardinal Pelagius.

Their desire to attack Babylon gratified the legate, but King John demurred. The Saracens are full of anger, said he, but wise enough to discern what advantage they hold. This is their ground. For my part, I think we should wait until the flooding of the river is past.

Nay, said Cardinal Pelagius, we are better going now.

Nay verily, answered King John, it would be far worse. Nevertheless, I will not halt the plan.

Then let us move ourselves, said Pelagius. We will go to Babylon, assault it and take it.

How many Templars, Hospitalers, and valiant knights gave up the ghost at Damietta? Among others the noble Count Milo of Bar-sur-Seine with both of his sons, delivered from human grief in the shadow of these walls. This I know because my father Simon battled at their side for glory, as once he fought to crush faithless Albigenses at Béziers and Carcassonne.

Here also departed from life Barzella Merxadrus, ordinary soldier, citizen of Bologna. On the twenty-third day of December in the year 1219, feeling mortally ill, he dictated terms for burial and disbursement of his goods. Five bezants he left for the repose of his soul. Weapons, armor, and hauberk he bequeathed to the Hospital of Germans where he wished to be interred. One bezant to James of Ungine, notary. One bezant to the army common chest. To his companions in the tent, three bezants. To his wife Guiletta, rights and benefits of office oversea in this army and his share in the city of Damietta, or spoil therefrom, which in any form might accrue. To his wife, aforesaid Guiletta, his part in the tent with furnishings that she might enjoy fully and peacefully as she had heretofore. Such was the testament of Barzella Merxadrus, humble pilgrim, drawn up beside the walls. Some little note writ on parchment, a register of light account, nothing to inscribe on stone. And yet, what our Lord has created in His image, that does He embrace.

From Damietta to Cairo requires three days. Without bloodshed a route was found through Saramsah, which boasts a magnificent palace. Inhabitants who fled in terror from the mighty visage of God had scorched their fields. Still, the pilgrim host found vegetables, barley, straw, fruit hanging in the gardens.

Anon to that church where Blessed Mary paused with the child Jesus when she fled into Egypt and heathen idols toppled. From here is but half a league to that balsam garden where she drew water from a spring to wash the clothing of the Holy Infant. They say this garden is like a vineyard with plants growing after the fashion of willow. Sirobalsam is the name of this plant, which has a sparse leaf pointed like the licorice leaf. If a branch is cut or scratched a fragrant liquid seeps out and is caught in dishes. Afterward the balsam is poured into bottles that the sultan distributes as gifts to important princes. And in those days when God's army marched against Cairo the master of the garden was Christian with infidel and Christian servants.

Throughout this demonic realm are Christians. Beyond Leemannia extends the broad land of Ethiopia, which is governed partly by devilish kings, partly by Christians. Here live the people of Nubia who signify the Cross with only one finger, arguing that two natures

352

unite in the universal nature of Christ. Prester John, long thought to live in uttermost Asia, now rules as Negus, patiently waiting to deliver a blow for Christendom.

Soon enough the living host got sight of infidel Cairo, the vast extent of it, after which the lords took counsel with King John and Cardinal Pelagius and all agreed they should advance no further. Indeed, all thought it prudent to turn back at once. Now the sultan, who was full of wrath and exceeding shrewd, caused the river to be dammed and forced out of its bed. So it overflowed the isle where the pilgrims had encamped and near midnight they found themselves half afloat. The sultan could have drowned them, but did not. If he drowned them he would gain little because they had left Damietta strongly garrisoned. Therefore, keeping them in constraint, he made known they must withdraw and render up his port, else he would have the river submerge them to the last knight and mule and garbage rat. So the differing lords and Cardinal Pelagius and King John being overcome with distress, esteeming themselves fools, seeing what their case had become, fearful that none would survive this accursed land, reminded Sultan al-Kamil that both he and they might profit from the inestimable benefits of peace. And they made such agreement as they could, which altogether reflected the sultan's will. Then he let loose those prisoners he held, requiring the presence of King John as hostage until his chastised army withdrew.

Thus, on the eighth day of September in that year 1221, Sultan al-Kamil got back Damietta while the Christian host embarked, gnawing their thumbs. Straightway did King John make for the city of Acre. Concerning the haughty and disagreeable legate, he fed himself with angry dreams, traveling north to carry out some directive from Honorius who was pontiff. Later he embarked to Europe. Honorius made use of him on various occasions. What the pontiff thought of this expedition I could not say, nor do chronicles report.

Guillaume le Clerc, a jongleur more adept at malice than craft, assaulted the Church with ugly verse. Because of Pelagius was Damietta lost through wicked folly! Let clerics recite psalms while knights give

353

battle! Let the cleric pray for the knight, let him shrive the sinner! Ought not Rome be reproached for losing Damietta?

In Provence, drenched by heretic blood, Guillem Figueira sang out. Rome! False beyond compare, do you govern for aught but silver? Damietta was lost because of you! Child of an evil mother, privy to evil covenant! Rome! God punish you!

Yet here was Lady Gormonda de Montpellier defending the legate, charging the humiliation at Damietta to indiscreet and venal men. Peirol, troubadour and pilgrim, one of few that laid aside his instrument to confront unbelievers, sang furiously that Emperor Frederick was responsible for this defeat by virtue of hollow promises.

How shall crested men be checked? Frederick seemed reluctant to fulfill his vow. Albeit he took the cross in 1215, this grandson of Frederick Barbarossa found other matters more engaging. Nine years elapsed. Anon the balding little man with crooked back and sparse red hair saw fit to augment his empire through marriage to Princess Yolanda, age fourteen, heiress to Jerusalem's throne. He sent her costly fabrics and jewels, handsome gifts to her uncles and other relatives. To the city of Tyre she was delivered in regal splendor where Archbishop Simon married her by proxy to Frederick and set the crown on her childish head. There ensued fifteen days of dances, tourneys, and feasting. This according to Philip de Novare.

That summer the tiny empress would embark for Brindisi, escorted by innumerable galleys. She was accompanied to shore by the queen of Cyprus and other highborn ladies, all weeping because they did not expect to see her again. Nor did they. One last moment she gazed upon the land and was heard to murmur. I commend you to God, beloved Syria.

At Brindisi the vows were celebrated afresh. However, Frederick soon took to bed a cousin of his bride. What grievance he held against Yolanda is not reported, but some time afterward he committed her to the harem he kept at Palermo. Here she gave birth to a son, Conrad, and one week later ascended to glory.

Frederick was by most accounts disposed to corpulence, solidly built, despite a skewed back by no means monstrous, with sensual lips and cold green eyes. What few hairs embellished his skull at age thirty was that distinctive reddish hair of the Hohenstaufen. They say he was fluent at Latin, French, Greek, Italian, and Arabic, his mind ravenous for knowledge, whether medical art, theology, science, music, or news of distant lands. For all this he could number his friends on the fingers of one hand since he was cruel, sly, selfish, vindictive, lascivious beyond understanding, and of such conceit he thought himself appointed viceroy to our Lord. Half-German, half-Norman, he sought the company of minnesingers and troubadours. He was himself a poet to some degree, artist, scientist who wrote at length on the anatomy of birds and the art of hawking. De arte venandi cum avibus. Stupor Mundi, so called by Matthew Paris. Indeed, who would not be astonished at a Christian emperor entranced by the wicked dogma of Islam? That he was born in Sicily might account for this. He spent much time there, child of an island half-Greek, half-Arab, compounded of West and East.

Al-Kamil directed Emir Fakhr al-Din to find out what sort of man this sovereign encyclopedia could be. So to Palermo came the emir and everything said about Frederick was true. He despised the barbaric West that was his home and legacy. He spoke Arabic to perfection. His palace guard consisted of Arabs who bowed toward Mecca at times of prayer. The call of the muezzin sounded across his island.

Al-Kamil and this uncommon emperor began to exchange letters in which they considered such topics as immortality of the soul, the origin of the universe, and the logic of Aristotle. And when the sultan discovered that Frederick enjoyed studying the behavior of animals he shipped apes, bears, dromedaries, and elephants to Sicily. He felt greatly pleased to learn that Frederick disliked the persistent war between Muslim and Christian.

In our year of grace 1226 Frederick embarked for the promised land, taking but six hundred knights and not many sergeants as if he thought the expedition meaningless. Three days at sea Landgrave

Louis of Thuringia succumbed to plague. Frederick quickly changed course to Otranto where he disembarked and hurried off to bathe in the springs of Pozzuoli. There he lingered until His Holiness Gregory excommunicated him. Such harsh treatment seemed to him unjust. He argued that he felt ill and vowed he would continue the journey. It is said the pontiff cursed him, accused him of poisoning Landgrave Louis. And those palmers in the expedition felt dismayed, thinking the emperor's conduct disgraceful.

Once more he embarked for the Holy Land, accompanied now by seventy galleys as well as transports stuffed with knights and footmen. He put in at Cyprus, at Limassol where Richard Lionheart disembarked four decades earlier. To the lord of Arsuf, Jean d'Ibelin, who was then at Nicosia, he sent a courier.

I pray you and request you to come and dine with me, bringing your children and your friends, for I would honor and reward you.

Jean d'Ibelin willingly complied, traveling at once to Limassol where Frederick greeted him with every appearance of respect and called him Uncle. One favor was asked, that he with his retinue take off the black robes they wore in memory of Jean's brother Philip who recently had died. Your pleasure at my arrival, said the emperor, ought to exceed the sorrow of your loss.

Jean d'Ibelin cheerfully acceded, whereupon Frederick gave him a scarlet cloak and some fine jewels. Jean responded with grace for he was half-French, half-Greek, assured in the labyrinth of diplomacy. My body, my heart, and my worldly goods I place at the disposition of the emperor, said he.

You shall be rewarded, Frederick answered. You shall be repaid amply and richly.

That night he ordered a postern in the wall adjoining the garden to be opened. Three thousand of his men were admitted through this gate, sergeants, arbalesters, mariners, who quartered themselves in stables, bedrooms, and elsewhere.

Next morning Frederick insisted that Jean d'Ibelin sit beside him at table and Jean's two sons would serve, one with the cup, another

356

with the bowl. Sir Anceau de Brie should carve, a muscular youth
whose blotched skin, flat nose, and fierce expression made everyone
think of a leopard. At Frederick's table sat the king of Cyprus, the
king of Salonika, the marquis of Lancia, and various high barons, all
seated in such a way that they might watch the emperor when he
spoke. Not until they had almost finished eating did Frederick announce the presence of his men. Here came almost an hundred, each
gripping a dagger or a sword.

I require of you two things, said the emperor to his guest. First,
you shall hand over to me the city of Beyrouth. Second, you have for
ten years acted as bailiff of Cyprus since the death of King Hugh,
therefore you must pay me what it is worth. That is, ten years of rent,
which is my right according to German usage.

Sire, Jean d'Ibelin answered, I believe you mock me. Or it may be
that some who hate me have counseled you to demand this.

Frederick touched himself on the head. I will have my way, said
he. By this head, which often has worn the crown, I will have my way
concerning these things I ask, else you are prisoners.

The lord of Arsuf stood up and spoke with great pride. Beyrouth
do I have and hold as my rightful fief, since it was given to me by
Queen Isabella, who was my sister on my mother's side and a daughter of King Amalric. By the alms of Christendom and my own labor
have I maintained and strengthened it. As for the regency and governance of Cyprus, I received no rent. Nor will I deny what I have said
upon fear of death or threat of prison.

Your words are fine, the emperor said. But I will show you how
subtlety of thought will not prevail.

Jean d'Ibelin answered. When I arranged to come here I was told
by my council that you would do what you are now doing. I refused to
believe it, yet I came fully aware. I should rather meet prison or death
at your hands than have it thought or said that the worth of our Lord
and the conquest of the Holy Land were neglected by me or by those
of my lineage. I am prepared to endure all that might happen because
of the love I bear our Lord who suffered death for us and who will

357

deliver us. If it shall be His wish or design that I suffer death or imprisonment, then do I thank Him for it. In every way do I submit to Him.

Having said as much, Jean d'Ibelin sat down. Those at the table were astounded and afraid. They looked from him to the emperor. It is said that clerics intervened. So at last all agreed that the court of Jerusalem should decide. Meanwhile twenty Cypriot lords would be delivered up as hostage. By their selves, their goods, and their estates would they pledge Jean d'Ibelin to serve the emperor and warrant he should appear at court to prove his rights. Also, Frederick demanded his sons for hostage. These were Baldwin and Balian. The emperor had them trussed to iron crosses so they could not bend their arms or legs.

Afterward two lords came privately to speak with Jean d'Ibelin. Let us go with you to the emperor, they said. We will carry knives in our hose. We will stab him and our people will be on horseback at the door.

Jean d'Ibelin threatened to strike them, telling them that by such an act they would be disgraced. Throughout Christendom it would be said that traitors oversea had slain the Lord Emperor. Then must our right become wrong, the truth of our cause discredited. He is my lord, said Jean d'Ibelin to those who would assassinate Frederick, and I will keep my faith and honor.

After forty-three days on Cyprus the emperor embarked, whence he sailed to Acre and put ashore during the feast of Our Lady. Templars and Hospitalers dropped to the earth when he arrived and kissed his knees, thinking his appearance foretold the salvation of Israel. Citizens and clergy greeted him with respect but since he was excommunicate they did not confer on him the kiss of peace nor wish to join him at table. Most bitterly did Frederick rage against the pontiff, complaining that anathema was unjust.

Straightway he began cajoling and flattering Sultan al-Kamil because he coveted the throne of Jerusalem. He despatched ambassadors with fine gifts to Nablus where the sultan had encamped. Al-Kamil responded with gold, silver, jewels, racing camels, many

358

wondrous things made of silk, and so forth. Anon they reached accord, which gave Frederick what he wanted. For a period of ten years, five months, and forty days there should be a truce enabling pilgrims to visit the Holy City. Nazareth, Bethlehem, Emmaus, Ramlah, Lydda, all would be restored to the kingdom. The road from Joppa would be secure. In exchange, Frederick vowed that his army would not threaten Egypt.

From Acre he marched south with eight hundred red knights and ten thousand foot soldiers to Joppa where it had been arranged for ships to victual the army. Now it may be the Lord God was furious because a storm blew up. Yet through His vast mercy, which permits no man to be tried beyond endurance, the wind abated, the sea abated. Then came a fleet to anchor with necessities. Rumors of this host gathering strength at Joppa disturbed the Saracens.

On the seventeenth day of March, in our year of grace 1229, Frederick entered Jerusalem. He requested the archbishops of Capua and Palermo to celebrate a coronation mass, but they would not, fearing the pontiff's wrath. Nor would the patriarch of Jerusalem attend. Frederick went to the Holy Sepulcher on Sunday, lifted the crown from the altar and crowned himself. Hermann of Salza, Grand Master of Teutonic knights, read first in German, next in French, a proclamation justifying this arrogance.

Patriarch Gerold wrote in a missive to the faithful that it should be known how astonishing and deplorable was the conduct of this emperor to the great detriment of our Lord and Christianity, there being no common sense in him from the sole of his foot to the summit of his head. He came oversea excommunicate, impoverished, attended by not enough knights. He came first to Cyprus where most discourteously he seized Jean d'Ibelin and his sons who were invited to his table under pretext of discussion. And the king of Cyprus he retained almost captive. Thus through violence and fraud he got possession. Then to Syria, promising marvels, boasting loudly. Thither to Jerusalem on Sunday eve when Oculi mei is sung, which is the third Sunday of Lent. Without due ceremony he went next day to the chapel of the

Holy Sepulcher, and to the manifest prejudice of honor and imperial dignity placed the diadem upon his own forehead. All this to the chagrin and bewilderment of pilgrims.

Once there had been cordial interchange, such as existed between King Fulk and the emir Mu'in al-Din. Or between Richard Lionheart and Saladin's brother Malik al-Adil. But there lurked in the soul of this German some perverse and wicked taste for Mahometry. All knew he did not scruple to employ eunuchs as though he were a Muslim prince. All knew he bought Islamic girls for the harem. Yet he was not embraced by Saracen lords. He could not win their hearts. It was written in the Collar of Pearls that this balding emperor with weak eyes, smooth cheeks, and reddish body hair would not fetch two hundred dirhems at the slave market, did not in the least resemble those Christian paladins from long ago. Nor did Muslims think him religious in any way but an atheist, a skeptic who pretended.

During his first night in Jerusalem no muezzins called. Next day he consulted Shams al-Din, the qadi who guided him. Why did they not call the prayer? he asked.

Out of respect for your visit, said the qadi.

I am not pleased, said the emperor. If I spent this night in Jerusalem it was to hear the muezzins call.

Yet those he sought to flatter through egregious blasphemy mistrusted him. That he could disparage the faith to which he was born disquieted them. Christ, Mahomet, and Moses, said he to the Muslims, all three were imposters. And so they considered him void of faith.

He wished to see the mosque of Omar. When he had climbed the steps he saw a Christian priest seated beside the footprint of Mahomet, Bible in hand, begging alms. Frederick threatened him with death, struck him, cursed him for a pig. Going round the Dome of the Rock he stopped to read a mosaic scription placed there by Saladin after every trace of the Father, Son, and Holy Ghost had been expunged. With a smile he asked who these polytheists might have been. He wondered about gratings over the windows and learned they kept out sparrows. Now, said he, instead of sparrows God Almighty has sent you pigs. By which he meant Christians.

He did not stay long, less than two days before returning to Joppa, thence to Acre. Perhaps for no reason but to demonstrate authority he launched an attack upon the Templar fortress of Chastel-Pelèrin. So he roused up enemies like scorpions on every side, Templar, Hospitaler, Venetian, Genoese, baron, knight, merchants at their stalls. It was known that he would soon quit the Holy Land, yet all knew he would exercise power from a distance.

Before sunrise on the first of May he went furtively and quickly to the port of Acre. What tumult played within his soul, no chronicle relates. But the citizens had learned he would depart and stored up pails of slop, filth, sheep guts, and other garbage, which they flung at his head. Butchers shouted insults, chased him, pelted him with entrails and shit. Constable Odo de Montbéliard, hearing such a racket, came and arrested those who abused the emperor and called out to him, commending him to God. Frederick's voice was heard across the water although he could not be understood. Thus did he embark, scorned, repudiated. Who could believe this deformation of spirit? How is it that when we see the beginning of things we do not guess their end? Yet not fortuitously but designedly does each achieve its goal, as a stone once hurled must drop to earth.

God is just. On that December day in our year of grace 1244 when King Louis took the cross, on that day was the spirit of Jesus Christ reborn.

I knew King Louis well. When his younger brother Alphonse was knighted I served at table carving meat, the first time ever I stood next to his majesty. I was seventeen. Thenceforth, excluding residence at Joinville, I attended court.

Forty years afterward I testified on the matter of his canonization. And in the year of our Lord 1298, thanks to almighty providence, I was present at the exhumation of his body.

I have heard it said that King Louis, withal the excellence of his heart, lacked that strength of understanding which becomes a useful sovereign. He was no more than thirteen when his father Louis VIII gave up the ghost. Thus he knew as regent during his minority the inflexible hand of his mother, Queen Blanche of Castille, virtuous, godly, ardent, with an uncommon taste for politics. Frankish nobility liked her not much, calling her Dame Hersent after that she-wolf in the fable of Renard. I believe she nurtured Louis none too gently, as though he were destined for the Church. Perhaps such filial devotion exceeded the limit proposed by nature and exposed the king to mockery. That he passively accepted her restraint cannot be doubted. As to his weakness, I do not presume to know, unless it be called faith or trust.

His first counselors were experienced, wise and prudent, veterans from the court of his grandfather Philip Augustus. Later, as though to sound the depth of spirituality, he brought to advise him such clerics as Eude Rigaud, archbishop of Rouen, and Bishop William of Paris. I think his preoccupation with the salvation of souls conformed easily, as the glove conforms to the hand, to his concept of sovereign power. Now since what is not true cannot be beautiful, the truth that our sainted king sought in all things must be the measure of his worth. Otherwise no enduring likeness of him could be traced.

He seemed to live for God alone. Not once did I hear him address the devil by name. Countless hours day and night he devoted to prayer, oppressed by the knowledge that our Lord was neither adequately served nor loved, grieved by the existence of infidels, certain that he himself did not honor God deeply enough. Offices he had read in the king's chapel as though it were the chapel of a monastery. There also he had the Hours sung. By his request was the Office for the Dead included. He would hear two masses, at times three. Very little would he study but Scripture and the Fathers. He would ask that a candle as high as his waist be lighted and while it burned he would read the Bible. So long did he remain on his knees at prayer that sight and wit intermingled and he would rise up dazed, murmuring, not certain where he was, unable to find his bed. At midnight he was up to hear matins sung by his chaplain, rising so quietly that equerries failed to note or got up late and chased after him barefoot. Each Friday he made confession after which his confessor must apply the discipline with five iron chains his majesty carried in an ivory box. Similar boxes he ordered, with similar little chains, giving them to his children and to friends, and counseled them to make good use of scourging. Should the confessor strike him gently he would demand harder blows. One such did strike with force enough to lacerate his majesty's sensitive flesh, yet the king held his peace, nor afterward mentioned it save with amusement. Most were less tenacious. Indeed, they reproved him for austerities that imperiled his health, persuading him to give up a hair shirt he wore during Advent and Lent and on the vigil of numerous feasts. In its place he adopted a horsehair girdle. Good Friday he walked to church barefoot. Which is to say, he wore shoes for the sake of appearance but had the soles removed. Before approaching the cross he took off his upper garments excepting vest and coat. On his knees he would advance a short distance, stopping to pray, advancing further. Beneath the cross he would prostrate himself as though crucified, arms outflung, weeping. And if during litanies he heard that verse appealing for a fountain of tears he would respond.

O Lord, I dare not ask so much, but a few drops to water my parched and sterile heart.

I do not doubt that he hoped to achieve a state of ecstasy. He took visible pleasure from sermons, and liked discussing nuances of morality with theologians whose minds he valued. In that respect he differed from his pious cousin Henry who felt quite content to hear

363

sundry masses. Chaste, temperate in appetite, mystic, opposed to deceit, such was our sainted King Louis. Few men in any age have discerned so clearly the principles of our faith.

Who could be more avid for relics? He seemed possessed by the need, as lesser men vanish into their need of extravagant fabric or the bodies of women. He acquired a vial of our Lord's precious blood, His swaddling clothes, the Virgin's blue mantle together with a bottle of her milk, the Holy Sponge, a fragment of the Shroud, three Holy Nails. Surely this testifies to a mind perfecting itself.

Rigorous of speech, averse to coarse and equivocal language, such constraint bespoke purity within. Every sense he held in strictest bondage. Licentious poetry trumpeted on the street filled him with loathing. Popular songs he despised. Should some thoughtless menial give voice to a ballad of the day King Louis would advise him to sing Ave Maris Stella. I think this hardness hung like chain mail about his presence, mayhap an unwonted gift from his grandfather Philip who counseled the boy to abjure familiarity. Nonetheless, high or low, all that knew Louis the king succumbed to his gracious manner.

I am told he was a virtuous, unshadowed youth, and marriage to the affectionate princess Marguerite but lifted his chastity into high relief, albeit they would have eleven children. He appeared little touched by his wife, nor had she much influence. She struggled to obey him and I think made life happy enough, so much as a saint might understand it. She would have him dress more elegantly until he, tiring of this complaint, agreed to do so, considering that the law of marriage urges a man to please his wife. Yet she, in exchange, must wear humble robes. And very quickly Marguerite let the subject wither. She feared him somewhat. When their first child was born she dared not tell him he had a daughter but called in Bishop William of Paris to break the news. Throughout his life he sought to avoid temptations of the flesh. When he tired of work he used to sit with her and the children, but she observed that he would avoid looking at her while they talked and thought he must be offended or displeased. She asked if that were true. No, said he, adding that a man should not gaze upon what he could not possess. It may be that he detested every soft thing in life.

He was lean, tall enough, his countenance sweet. Yet toward the end when he undertook that last mad journey to convert the emir Mustansir from which none could dissuade him, thinking to light a flame on the invidious coast of Barbary, I saw not the king whose trusted seneschal I was but a bent old man in quest of martyrdom.

Scribes illuminate pages of their books with azure, gold, red, and other glorious colors. So did King Louis illuminate the Frankish kingdom with glorious abbeys, such as that of Sainte Chapelle, which he built to house relics purchased from Emperor Baldwin. When he despatched aid to provinces in need, or himself attended the feeble and sick, comforting those pocked with fulsome disease, abasing his office for the sake of ministration, then certainly did he illuminate the greatest of Christian precepts. I have watched him at hospital tend the putrefying and like a nurse carry out pails of excrement. God help me, I myself could not.

Some faulted him for lavish spending on benefactions. Sooner would I give alms for the love of God, said he, than waste a sou on empty vanities. He built Quinze-Vingts, that asylum for the blind. He built that establishment for common whores, Maison des Filles-Dieu, allotting four hundred livres a year to maintain it. He built the nunnery of Franciscan sisters at Saint-Cloud, which my lady Isabel had founded by his sanction. Throughout the realm he built houses for lay sisters who took no vows, béguines, stipulating that they live chaste. Liberal as he might be with alms, he was not less so with food. Each day six score decrepit old men were summoned to eat what he ate. During Lent and Advent he summoned yet more to be fed. At great vigils here were two hundred ravenous beggars. Wednesday and Friday throughout the year he brought thirteen into his own room to feed them by his own hand, without disgust at their filth. Often did I watch him cut bread for the starving. If any was blind King Louis would put bread into one hand, guiding the other toward the bowl that held his portion. Should it be fish, King Louis would remove the bones and dip it into sauce and place a morsel in the blind man's open mouth. Saturday he would choose three of the worst afflicted and lead them to his quarters in which towels and basins of water had been readied so he might wash their feet. Reverently would he bathe and dry and kiss those feet, however coarsened by usage, however deformed. He knelt to offer these odious vagrants water to clean their hands. He kissed those hands, gave forty deniers to each.

Seneschal, he once said to me, do you wash the feet of the poor on Maundy Thursday?

Nay, said I, for I think it indecorous.

Whereupon he rebuked me, pointing out that our Lord had done so. Then he continued, wondering if I would follow the example of the king of England who washed and kissed the feet of lepers. Some faint trace of levity I discerned in his voice, albeit none in his eye.

I am told that when he first assumed his father's crown he would disguise himself as a squire and go out early each morning, followed by a servant carrying a sack of pennies. With his own hand he would distribute pennies to miserable beggars who waited in the palace court, taking care to give the most to the neediest. Now it is usual for serfs to pay a four-penny tribute each year to their lord, and it is usual for serfs of a church to place this money atop their heads before depositing it on the altar. So each year on the feast of Saint Denys the king betook himself to the abbey, and on his knees, bereft of the crown, he laid four gold coins atop his head before depositing them on the altar. In this way he declared himself bound to Saint Denys. Such gestures of humility were, I think, but half intelligible to less devout monarchs.

The preoccupation of his mind was to lead and guide men heavenward. He charged Vincent de Beauvais, author of Speculum, to provide moral and religious instruction for princes, knights, ministers, and others resident at court. He himself composed Enseignement, that pious text regarding the duty of a Christian king. Each

366

night he summoned his children before they went to bed and spoke with them about good emperors and good kings. He caused them to memorize the Hours of Our Lady.

He caused Muslim children from the Orient to be educated at Royaumont abbey. Similarly, with gifts he persuaded many Jews to accept baptism. Little enough did he like Jews. Their very presence on earth disturbed him. With much difficulty did counselors persuade him to let Jews go about their affairs because they were shrewd at commerce, thus benefiting the realm. He once told me how a debate was scheduled between Christians and Jews at the monastery of Cluny. There was present some injured knight who asked permission to speak. So he got up, leaning on his crutch, and asked to confront the wisest Jew. To this Jew he put one question.

Do you believe that Blessed Mary, who was virgin, bore God in her womb and gave birth to Him?

The Jew answered that he believed no such thing. Then said the knight, you are a fool to enter her church and her house since you neither love her nor believe in her. Whereat he lifted his crutch and fetched the Jew a blow on the skull so he dropped to the floor. Then did all the Jews run away. Now came the abbot to reproach this knight and said he had been foolish. Nay, it had been foolish of you to hatch this, replied the knight, for if it continued there would be many good Christians deceived by the wicked argument of Jews.

His majesty told me he agreed with the knight, and none but a learned cleric should presume to argue with Jews.

Persecution of Cathari and Albigenses, which marked his father's reign, had much abated when he came to manhood. Nevertheless, when His Holiness Gregory proposed to root them out through inquisition King Louis thought it advisable. With his mother Queen Blanche, zealous as himself, they defrayed the cost. And the king with his mother provided guards for these inquisitors, who were much hated. Heretic, apostate, recreant Catholic, no matter. Few escaped the net. It is good, his majesty said, to thrust a sword as far as it will go into the belly of whosoever vilifies or abandons the faith of

367

our Lord. Nor would any at court dispute him since confiscation of heretic property tended to the king's advantage.

He told me how certain men of Albi approached the count of Montfort, requesting him to come see the body of our Lord that manifested itself as flesh and blood. You that are faithless, the count replied, you go and see it. For myself, I believe in what the Holy Church teaches us concerning the Sacrament. And do you know my reward for accepting the word of God and His saints? I shall wear a finer crown in heaven than any I might have worn on earth. King Louis thought this a very fine reply.

As surely as did Godfrey de Bouillon he considered himself God's advocate. Nor would he hesitate to punish unruly tongues. A goldsmith was heard to use vile words, so the king had him bound to a ladder in drawers and shirt, pig guts and harslet wound round and round his neck up to his nose. And here a blasphemous Parisian whose lips the king ordered seared with glowing red iron. He said he would quite willingly have himself branded if every oath were banished from the realm. I never did hear him swear by God, by the mother of Christ, nor by any saint. Never did he cite the devil, unless that name could rightfully be mentioned. Devil take it! How often we hear such turn of speech, which is sinful because we have no right to maledict what the Lord God has created. On my faith and deed, foul words at Joinville castle merited a blow. Yet that is by the way.

During summer his majesty liked to go and sit in the forest of Vincennes. There, resting his back against an oak, he would listen to complaints or whatever related to his subjects. They would come and talk without hindrance. Or he might enter the gardens of Paris wearing a plain wool tunic and sleeveless surcoat, his hair neatly combed but without a quoif, and white swansdown hat, black taffeta cape about his shoulders. There on a carpet we would seat ourselves around him. And he would pat the ground, addressing me. Seneschal, you sit here. At first I equivocated. My lord, I said, I dare not sit so close. But he would have it no other way and my garment touching his.

deus lo volt!

Sickness followed him like a tiresome guest. Fever, chills, his skin mottled red. While battling the English in a noxious marsh near Saintonge he contracted some disease that almost cost his life. Mortification he inflicted upon himself for the sake of our Lord further weakened him. When news came of Muslim victory at Gaza he lay ill, so near death that one of two ladies attending him made as if to draw the sheet across his face. Another who was present intervened, objecting that the king's soul hovered within his body. He could hear them while they talked. And the Lord caused him to regain his power of speech, whereas until that moment he could not whisper a word. He asked for the Cross, which was given him. When the queen mother Blanche learned that he had spoken she was overcome with joy. But when she learned that he had vowed to go on pilgrimage she wept as though he were dead.

His three brothers took the cross, followed by the duke of Burgundy, the count of Flanders, Count Hugh of Saint-Pol and his nephew Gautier, to say nothing of other high lords. Yet nearly four years would pass before they embarked. There was reason. Our king left little to chance. He did not think any port acceptable, hence he ordered the building of Aigues-Mortes, by which is meant dead waters.

I myself took the cross with our beloved king. But since I did not know how long I would be oversea, the enterprise attending with danger, I wished to make a settlement of my affairs before I left Joinville. It seemed to me that I should leave everyone satisfied with my conduct so that I might honorably enjoy the fruits and pardons merited by crusaders through concessions of the sovereign pontiff. Therefore I gathered neighbors and friends, giving all to understand that if any felt censorious or the least misemployed I stood ready to make amends. Afterward I traveled to Metz in Lorraine to mortgage my estates because at that time my mother Béatrice was alive and enjoying the great part of my fortune as her dower.

Anon, the king summoned his barons to Paris.

As I was entering the city I noticed a tumbrel holding the bodies

369

of three men, sergeants from the Châtelet who had been robbing citizens and were slain by a cleric. They had robbed this cleric of all save his shirt, whereupon he rushed back to his lodging and got his crossbow and a child to carry his sword and went after them shouting he meant to kill them. He fixed his crossbow and shot one through the heart whereat the others lifted their heels to the moonlight. He got his sword from the child and ran after them. One thought to escape by wriggling through a hedge and the cleric hacked off his leg. Both pieces of this rogue lay in the tumbrel, his leg wearing a boot. The last robber was begging admittance to a house when the cleric arrived and split his head open to the teeth. So the provost was carting off these villains to show King Louis, along with the cleric who had surrendered, in order to find out what the king wished to do. I heard some time after that his majesty came out from chapel and paused on the steps to consider the dead thieves. He told the cleric that what he had done had lost him all chance to become a priest. However, his majesty said, I will take you into my service and you shall go with me oversea. King Louis did this because the young man was courageous but also to let people know he would not approve misconduct. Then his subjects called upon God to grant the king a long and fruitful life because they understood the wisdom of what he said.

His majesty wanted the barons to swear fealty, promising that if anything happened to him oversea they would remain loyal to his children. I refused. I told him I could not take the oath because I was not his vassal. Soon afterward I returned to Joinville. My cousins, the count of Sarrebruck and his brother Gobert d'Apremont, had joined with me to make up a party of twenty knights. We arranged that our baggage should be sent by cart to Auxonne, thence by way of the Saône and the Rhône to Marseille where we had engaged a ship. Therefore we would not embark with the king at Aigues-Mortes but some leagues distant at Roche-de-Marseille.

On the day of my departure I summoned the abbot of Cheminon, a most worthy white monk. I am told that one night as he slept in his dormitory he felt warm and threw aside the cover, whereupon the Holy Virgin approached and drew it across his chest so the night wind would not make him ill. If the story be true, God knows. From this monk I got my wallet and pilgrim staff. I then left Joinville castle afoot, in my shirt, with legs bare, to visit Blécourt and Saint-Urbain, which has many fine relics. Not once did I look back, fearing that my heart might wither away if I glimpsed my children.

My companions and I paused to eat at Fontaine-l'Archevêque where the abbot presented us with a quantity of jewels. Thence to Auxonne, downstream on boats with our equipment while the horses were led along the bank. We passed the ruin of a castle that was called Roche-de-Glun, destroyed by his majesty because the lord of this castle had robbed pilgrims and merchants. So in due time to Marseille and prepared for the voyage.

Horses were admitted to our vessel by means of a door in the side, which was then shut and tightly caulked because it would be submerged when we were loaded just as the bottom of a floating barrel is submerged. When this was done and all in readiness the master mariner told priests and clerics to advance, bidding them sing Veni Creator Spiritus. Once they finished singing he cried aloud to his people. In God's name, unfurl the sails!

Thus, on the twenty-seventh day of August in that year of our Lord 1248, we cast off.

Presently the wind took us. Behind us the land receded. Each day the wind took us further from the place where we were born. Each night we slept not knowing if morning would find us drowned on the bed of the sea.

Now it is good to organize body and soul and mind for a voyage. Indeed it is wise to put the miserable flesh in order. Greffen Affagart recommends that each traveler carry a straw mat since the beams of a vessel are coated with pitch. Also, two jars. One for Saint Nicholas water, which remains sweet at sea, another for Padua wine, which is beneficial to drink in hot climates. Also, one should take a flask of preserved rose syrup to fortify the bowel. Little cooking pots, to be sure. Concerning food, salted ox tongue or ham, biscuit, cheese, almonds, figs, raisins, and sugar. We ourselves were less comfortably equipped. As to mind and soul, they must be at rest because infinite peril lurks above and beneath the surface. We are told of stupendous fish that gnaw ships apart and will not be dissuaded except by a man's angry visage, hence one must confront them at water level with a countenance equally bold and horrific. There was some mariner, whose name I know not, who let himself down on a rope to affright the terrible fish but growing alarmed forgot his scowl and was snapped in half.

Be that as it may, one evening off the Barbary coast we observed a mountain formed strangely like an egg. All night we sailed, yet at dawn here was the mountain, unmoved. Again this happened so we felt uneasy. A priest said we should make three processions round the masts of our ship. I myself was at this time very ill and weak but found men to carry me in their arms. After a short while, thanks to the intercession of our gracious Lord, we passed by this mountain.

When we came to Cyprus we found King Louis already there, having sailed aboard his ship Montjoie and disembarked at Limassol two weeks before the feast of Saint Rémy. We saw in profusion the granaries and cellarage he had ordered, casks of wine heaped atop one another until they resembled barns. Here were stacks of barley and wheat that had begun to sprout because of rain falling on them so they might have been grassy mounds. Yet as we loaded grain aboard ship for transport to Egypt we saw that underneath the lush growth it was as good as if newly threshed.

372

Because many troops had not arrived we loitered on Cyprus until Ascension. We heard that a battle impended between the king of Armenia and the richest pagan on earth, the sultan of Iconium. They say he poured melted gold into jars of the sort used to hold wine, each large enough to contain three or four hogsheads, and smashed

the jars so these enormous gold forms stood upright to the astonishment and delight of visitors. It is said that twelve strong men could
not topple one. Now since we had little to do while awaiting rein-
forcements a number of sergeants crossed over to Armenia with the
idea of enriching themselves, but not one came back. In a paltry desire for wealth they forgot the Savior.

Also during this period the sultan of Cairo thought to wage war
against the prince of Homs. Away he went and besieged the city. But
the prince of Homs learned through spies about a canker on the sultan's leg and bribed a ferrais, who is a valet, to administer poison.
The ferrais smeared poison on a mat where his lord was accustomed
to sit while playing chess and as the sultan moved his leg this venom
worked into the canker and impinged upon his heart. For two days
he could not eat or drink or speak. Without leadership the Babylonians felt confused. They retreated to Cairo, leaving the city of
Homs at peace. This shows how each man is subject to his body,
an inconstant and wretched master. But the Lord God remains un-
changeable.

Also while we loitered on Cyprus here came two Nestorians,
Mark and David, envoys from the great khan of the Tartars. They
brought a letter professing sympathy for our cause and said the khan
would help us free Jerusalem from the infidel grip. Many at court
heard this with grave surprise. King Louis, however, expressed delight. He responded by despatching two friars from the Order of
Predicants, entrusting them to deliver a costly tent of vermilion
cloth for use as a chapel. Included were small stone effigies to illus-
trate Christian theology. Annunciation, Nativity, Baptism of our
Lord, stages of His suffering, Ascension, arrival of the Holy Ghost,
and so forth. In addition his majesty sent cups and books and whatever else would be required for the Predicants to celebrate mass. All
this he did in hopes of making our faith attractive to these Tartars.

373

With God's help our people assembled. We were two thousand
five hundred knights plus five thousand archers, as well as a great
many armed pilgrims. King Louis ordered us to the vessels and sent
each captain a letter with instructions that it should not be opened

until we had cleared port. Then the seals were broken and we learned
that we should follow his majesty to Damietta at the mouth of the
Nile. How many ships followed in the king's wake I do not know. If
little boats were counted, perhaps two thousand. It was a fair thing
to see, more beautiful than a picture made with stained glass.

Whitmonday the wind slackened. Thursday we came in view of
Damietta. There were the sultan's forces drawn up, kettledrums
booming, cymbals clashing, Saracen horns screeching, all contribut-
ing a fearful noise while the armor of these pagans winked gold in
the sun.

His majesty ordered the fleet to anchor well offshore and summoned the barons to speak with him aboard Montjoie. There at
council we agreed to land next day, whereupon the king addressed us.
Loyal friends, said he, if we hold steadfast in our love we shall prove
invincible. Without permission of Christ our Lord we would not
have ventured into a realm so powerfully guarded. I, Louis, king of
France, am but a man whose life will end as do the lives of other men
on a day it pleases God. All is for the best, whatever we meet, whatever befalls us. If we are vanquished, so be it. If we succeed in our
quest, surely we exalt the glory of God, the glory of France, and the
glory of Christendom.

We confessed our sins. Each man readied himself for the morrow
and organized his affairs, knowing he should die if it so pleased our
Lord.

Very early the king heard mass as it is said at sea. Then, having
armed himself, he ordered everyone to do likewise and go aboard the
small boats. He himself boarded a Normandy coche, as did the legate who was holding the True Cross. Into a longboat went Geoffrey
de Sargines, Jean de Beaumont, and Matthew of Marly with the banner of Saint Denys. While I was looking to the conveyance of my
people one of Érard de Brienne's knights called Plonquet attempted
to jump into a boat as it was pulling away but fell in the water and
drowned. We set our course toward land where a large party of Saracens awaited us, fully six thousand. At our approach they spurred

hotly forward. When we got ashore we thrust the points of our shields in the sand and fixed lances. At the last moment these unbelievers wheeled aside, none anxious to have his belly punctured.

Soon thereafter came a message from Baoudoin de Reims. He asked if I would hold up for him, which I did quite readily since he was a valiant knight bringing hundreds more. I saw the Comte de Joppa, his galley surging through the waves like a thunderbolt amid the screech of horns and drums booming. His galley looked very fine, what with painted escutcheons that bore his arms and three hundred men at the sweeps. Alongside each hung a targe displaying the arms of Joppa, which are gold with a cross of gules patée, and from each fluttered a pennon. When this galley came ashore his knights leapt out and hurried to join us. About the distance of a crossbow shot to our right here came the banner of Saint Denys. A Saracen boldly galloped toward it thinking others would follow, or because he was unable to control his mount, and went galloping straightway to hell.

As for his majesty, the legate and others urged him to remain on board until the landing was decided for if he were slain the expedition must fail. But when he learned the banner of Saint Denys was ashore he would not be separate from the emblem of his sovereignty. He set his feet together, slung his shield about his neck and all at once leapt into the water, which came up to his waist. Now others shouted Montjoie! They flung themselves into the sea, a rare and splendid thing to behold what with pagan arrows glancing like sparks off their helmets. So the Babylonians drew together, excitedly speaking in their tongue, and came toward us. We advanced with the spirit of Christ while the legate held overhead the True and Holy Cross.

Our Lord proved merciful. By noon the unbelievers had enough and retreated to the city. I think they lost quite five hundred, including four emirs. All plunged shrieking into eternal fire. Then his majesty sent for the legate and the bishops. Loudly we chanted Te Deum Laudamus.

Next morning came emissaries to speak with the king. They said the fighting men had gone away and the city was deserted, excepting old people and the sick. They said the king should hang them if they did not speak the truth. His majesty detained them until we could find out. Presently we learned that certain of our knights were inside and our standard flew from a turret. We gave thanks and praised the Lord because Damietta was very strong, with moats and palisades, barbicans, weapons of every sort. We could have taken it only after a siege reduced the people to starvation, as King John took Damietta more than a generation earlier. Our enemies had sent pigeon messengers to Cairo but heard nothing, so they thought the sultan was dead. That is why they quit the city. In fact, the sultan had not recovered from the poison he got while playing chess at Homs.

We learned that he punished his soldiers for giving up Damietta and had fifty officers strangled. I am told that one of these officers, condemned along with his son, requested the favor being executed first. But the sultan denied this indulgence. On the contrary, the officer was forced to watch his son strangled. Such is the cruelty of Egyptians.

We released a good fifty Christians who told us they had been enslaved at Damietta for twenty-two years. They told his majesty how the unbelievers called us pigs. The pigs have come, said they. Also there were Syrians who had been subservient to these infidels, who displayed crosses when we entered the city. They were permitted to keep their houses and goods.

We thought we could not leave Damietta until the feast of All Saints because each year the Nile spreads across Egypt, preventing much travel by land. However we did not feel threatened. King Louis with his queen took up lodging in the palace. The legate and each high baron took a beautiful house appropriate to his rank inside the walls. The army camped outside. Bedouin now and again would approach but rode away if crossbowmen went to shoot at them. During the night they returned to steal horses. They would cut off the heads of sleeping pilgrims or dig up corpses of hanged men in order to collect heads because Sultan Ayub paid ten gold bezants for a Christian head. Thus it became necessary to keep watch. At times they got into camp after the guards rode past, which is how they killed my lord of Courtenay's sentinel whom they found asleep. They left his body on a table but took his head to show the sultan. As a result his majesty posted crossbowmen and directed the guards to patrol on foot, walking so close together they almost formed a palisade, which made us rest easier at night.

During this time Gautier d'Autrèche surrendered his soul to God. When he perceived cavalry not far away he was overcome by rage. He armed himself, mounted his charger and had the flap of his pavilion lifted. Then he spurred out to meet the enemy but lost control and fell off. This happened because some of the enemy horses were mares and Gautier's stallion was attracted to them. People who observed this said that four Saracens rushed toward Gautier while he lay on the ground and struck him heavily with maces. Constable Imbert de Beaujeu with several of his majesty's sergeants picked up Gautier and brought him back. He was unable to speak. Physicians examined him and bled both arms. That night Aubert de Narcy thought we should find out if he had improved. The chamberlain met us when we entered, saying Gautier was asleep. We approached quietly. He lay on a pallet draped with miniver. He was dead. King Louis, being informed, remarked that he cared little for such men in his army because the knight had gone out unattended.

We discovered later that many soldiers visited harlots while we were encamped and would engage them in the very shadow of the palace. Of bodily pleasure what can be said? Men seek happiness outside themselves when it may be met only within.

The feast of Saint Remigius having passed and no news of Comte Alfonse de Poitiers, who was his majesty's brother, we began to worry. At length he appeared, delayed for a reason I do not know, which was fortunate or he would have sailed through the vortex of a storm outside Damietta. More than two hundred vessels, counting little boats, were flung about, smashed, nearly all on board drowned.

377

In truth it is not for us to comprehend the multitudinous paths of His divine work, nor expound upon them. We should live content in the knowledge that He embodies all things and maintains the universe.

Anon, King Louis assembled us to discuss a means of conquering Egypt, whether we should besiege Alexandria or march against Cairo. Most thought we should lay siege to Alexandria because of its good harbor where ships could land provisions. A second brother of the king, Comte Robert d'Artois, dissented. Cairo is the principal city of Egypt, said he, and if you would kill a viper you must crush its head. His majesty agreed.

Now the river that flows through the heart of Egypt, past Cairo to Damietta, originates in Paradise. The rivers Pison, Hiddekel, and Euphrates also descend from Paradise, each differing from the rest. But this mighty river partitions itself in order to become several streams. Then once a year it seeks to unite itself by overflowing the land, hence the water grows murky. Whoever wishes to drink it must draw a bucket at sundown, adding a handful of beans or almonds so that by morning the water will have clarified. Peasants till their fields when this flood recedes. They harvest rich crops of wheat, cumin, barley, rice, and I know not what else. How these floods arise is a mystery to all save God. Fishermen who live far to the south cast their nets in the Nile at dusk and each morning harvest the produce of heavenly trees such as rhubarb, aloe, cinnamon, and ginger. This happens because strong winds topple dry wood in Paradise just as they do on earth.

The sultan of Cairo a long time past, desiring to learn the source of this river, despatched an expedition to find out. These men subsisted on a kind of bread that is twice baked, so is called biscuit. When they got back they reported divers marvels. Elephants, lions, serpents that walked or crawled to the river bank to gaze at them while they traveled. At last they came to the base of a cliff so huge and steep they were unable to climb up, from which the Nile fell streaming down. They were able to discern at the summit a foison of green trees, therefore they told the sultan they had glimpsed Paradise on earth.

As to practical matters, we learned that if water from the Nile is poured into white earthenware jugs made by Egyptians it becomes as cold as water drawn from a well. We suspended jugs of it from the cords of our pavilions. And we learned to our dismay that these accursed unbelievers had dug more canals than might be seen in all of France. Thus, travel was no easy march. I do not know how many streams the Nile makes of itself. Some say four, one proceeding to Damietta, another to Alexandria, another to Tanis, another to Rexi. We encamped by the stream of Rexi while opposite our tents a host of Saracens prepared to dispute the crossing.

His majesty ordered the construction of a mud embankment or causeway. Hence we built two chats-châteaux, which are small turrets, donjons for cats, to shelter the men on guard. We also built covered ways to protect those who were transporting earth. Meanwhile we flung stones at the enemy. They likewise flung stones at us. That was how matters stood when we came to the week before Christmas. And I, God forgive me, too often caught myself remembering Joinville castle.

Presently we observed how the Babylonians hindered us by digging trenches that filled up with water. That is, while we extended the embankment on our side they on their side proceeded to widen the stream. Thus they undid in a day what had cost us three weeks. Also, one night they brought up a petrary and hurled Greek fire. The noise was thunderous, night became day when a horrible burning mass with a long flaming tail soared into our camp. By chance I was on watch with Lord Gautier d'Écurey when they did this. My friends, we are in grave peril, he said, for if the turrets burn we are lost. Yet if we abandon our post we will be dishonored. Therefore my counsel is that each time they hurl fire we should fling ourselves down on knees and elbows and pray the Lord to keep us. So that is what we did. Three times during the night here came Greek fire from the sling of a petrary. Lesser amounts they shot at us from swivel

379

crossbows. I was told that whenever King Louis heard the roaring flame he lifted himself half out of bed and wept. Then he would direct a chamberlain to find out if any were killed or burnt.

On the eve of Shrove Tuesday we buried Hugues de Landricourt, a knight-banneret. While his corpse lay on a bier in my chapel I happened to enter and found the priest much annoyed because half a dozen knights were loitering on sacks of barley chattering as they might in a tavern. I told them to be quiet. I said it was not proper to talk while mass was sung but they laughed and said they were discussing the widow of Hugues. I said this was neither decent nor appropriate, that they seemed already to have forgotten their comrade. Our Lord was listening to them jest and He was angered because next day all were killed or mortally stricken, leaving the wives of all six free to marry.

Thanks to divine providence we learned of a Bedouin who would take us to a ford at the canal of Achmoum in exchange for five hundred bezants. Some people think this man was a Copt, which is to say Christian. However it may be, King Louis agreed so the money was paid.

The Templars were selected to lead. Comte Robert d'Artois with his men should come next.

Shrove Tuesday at dawn we rode into the stream where the Bedouin indicated and our horses began to swim. No sooner did we get to the middle than our horses felt bottom and were happy about not having to swim anymore. Many slipped and some fell on the riders while trying to climb out because the bank was steep and soft. It was here that Jean d'Orléans ascended to glory. I called to those with me that we should continue upstream until we found a better place. When at last we climbed out we could see Egyptians flying away pursued by Comte Robert, which should not have happened because the Templars were chosen to lead. They, much affronted, feeling dishonored, sent word for him to check his people. He did not get this message because a knight in his service, Foucaud de Merle, a gallant knight but also quite deaf, did not hear what the Templar said and continued shouting at the top of his voice that everybody should pursue the Babylonians. After them! After them! he shouted. Because of so much confusion the Templars set spurs to their mounts and galloped forward.

I have heard that the Grand Master tried to stop Comte Robert, saying they were in danger of being surrounded. God's mercy, he cried. Let us await the king who must get here soon.

They say Comte Robert pretended to laugh and told the Grand Master that among Templars would always be found some hair of the wolf, by which he implied treachery.

Ride as you will, the Master retorted. Nor ever, please God, shall you impeach a Templar for cowardice. Yet will Christendom suffer this day, even as my heart forebodes.

Whereupon both struck spurs to their mounts and rode straightway through the village of Mansourah into fields beyond as if they would chase Egyptians all the way to Cairo. How far they went into the fields I do not know, but as they returned through Mansourah the rooftops thronged with citizens anxious to hurt or kill them, dropping sharpened stakes, hot water, stones, timbers, throwing down all manner of objects, and these Christians pressed so tight in the narrow streets of destruction they lost themselves. Three hundred gave up the ghost, among them Raoul de Coucy and his majesty's brother, Comte Robert d'Artois. And round about this time here came a strong force of mameluk Turks.

I myself saw none of what occurred at Mansourah because I resolved to attack some enemies of God who were collecting equipment in their camp. When I rode among the tents I saw an unbeliever with hands on the saddle of his mount getting ready to draw himself up. I thrust my lance in his side and he fell dead. We saw a great many who had retreated into the fields. They, after consultation, came charging toward us and killed Hugues de Trichâtel, lord of Conflans, who rode beside me holding a banner. I saw Raoul de Wanou struck down and went to his aid. Egyptians thrust at me with lances and drove my horse to its knees so I pitched forward and shook the earth but got up as best I could with sword in hand. Érard de Silverey, a bold knight, pointed to the ruin of a house, saying we ought to take refuge behind the walls until his majesty arrived. As we went toward it, some afoot, others on horseback, Egyptians charged again and rode over me so I lost my shield. Érard helped me to the ruin. Frédéric de Loupey, Renaud de Menoncourt, Hugues d'Écot, and others whose names I do not recall joined us. From everywhere Egyptians appeared like wasps, some climbing the walls to thrust down lances and prick us, cursing hideously in their language. Hugues d'Écot got three lance wounds in the face. Frédéric took a lance deep in the back, which brought his blood spouting like wine from a barrel. Érard took a sword cut on the face that left his nose dangling over his lips. I thought of Saint James and prayed aloud. Érard heard me. He spoke through the blood streaming down his face and said if I thought neither he nor his heirs would incur reproach for it he would go to fetch help from the Comte d'Anjou in a field close by. I answered that he would earn great honor if he went for help to save us, adding that I thought his life in jeopardy from his wound, which in fact was true since later he died of it. He took counsel with other knights and having listened to them asked me for his horse, which I held by the bridle. I gave it to him and he rode furiously out of the ruin. We saw him approach the Comte d'Anjou. There was some argument, but presently the Comte looked in our direction. Now his sergeants laid spurs to their mounts whereupon the pagans who bedeviled us took flight. I saw Pierre d'Auberive riding toward us with his sword clenched in his fist and could not but think Saint James heard my plea.

I stood there all bloody since I had got a lance thrust between my shoulders when King Louis appeared with his battalions and screeching trumpets and clashing cymbals and kettledrums like thunder, which was the most welcome music on earth. He drew himself up on a raised causeway to look across the field. He wore a gilded helm and carried a long sword of German steel. I never saw a more perfect knight.

deus lo volt!

When I next saw him he was close to the river. His men had been forced backward by Egyptians attacking with maces and swords. Some of his men thought to swim across to join the duke of Burgundy, but the animals were tired and the day had got very hot so as we moved downstream we saw lances and shields everywhere with horses and men drowning. King Louis was almost captured. Lord Jean de Saillenay told me that some Turks grasped the bridle of his horse but he freed himself with vigorous sword strokes. Then his people gathered up courage and rallied about him.

We were guarding a little bridge when Pierre de Bretagne came toward us and such a cut face that his mouth was full of blood. He rode a stout pony and had dropped the reins in order to grip the pommel with both hands since he did not want to be jostled by the men crowding him. He cursed and spat blood while the pony trotted. Ha! said he. God's head! Did ever you see worse dregs! By which oath he meant his own people. Directly after him was Pierre de Neuville, whom they called Caier, and the Comte de Soissons, both leaking blood, followed by Egyptians attempting to finish them off. I told the Comte de Soissons, who was my wife's cousin, that we ought to hold this bridge since otherwise the enemy would attack our king from both sides. He said he would stay if I remained. I assured him I would. So we faced them, I mounted on a sturdy cob, Pierre to our left. From behind us out of nowhere came an Egyptian who struck Lord Pierre on the head with a mace, laying him across the withers of his pony, and got away before we could do anything.

These accursed unbelievers had brought with them a mob of peasants who flung clots of earth at two of his majesty's sergeants, Guillaume de Boon and Jean de Gamaches. One threw a pot of Greek fire at Guillaume who stopped it on his shield or he would have turned to ashes. We were now all of us abristle with darts. By good luck I had found a padded Saracen tunic and used it like a buckler. The Comte de Soissons now thought fit to jest. Seneschal! cried he. Let the dogs howl! By God's bonnet we shall one day speak of this, you and I, at home with our ladies!

Near sunset a company of his majesty's crossbowmen formed ranks ahead of us, an agreeable sight. When these good men set foot to the stirrup of their bows the enemy did not much care for it, vanishing quick as roaches.

The constable said I should go to King Louis and remain at his side, which I did. As we went riding along I persuaded the king to take off his helm and put on my steel cap so he might get some air. Soon afterward Henri de Ronnay, who was provost of the Hospital, came up and kissed his gauntlet. The king asked if there were news of Comte Robert, to which the provost answered that his majesty's brother was in Paradise.

Ah, Sire, the provost continued, find solace in the knowledge that no king of France has earned such glory as you, for you have crossed a river to defeat the enemy and have captured their tents. You will sleep at peace tonight.

To this King Louis answered that we should thank God for every blessing. Then he sighed. As he spoke I saw his eyes fill with tears. If, said he, my brother lies dead, God grant him forgiveness of his sins, both him and all the rest.

During the battle certain of our men shamefully quit the field, vitals drained. No argument would make them stay. How unlike the courage and dignity of our sainted king.

We had no more put the infidel troops to flight than Bedouin rushed forward to pillage their empty camp. These wretched nomads who would not expose their bellies to danger now felt entitled to the spoil. What can be said of the Bedouin? It is widely known how they descend like birds of prey to feast on what is vulnerable. I am told they do not obey the precepts of Mahomet but follow the teaching of his uncle, Ali. They do not sleep in castles or villages but in open fields. If the weather is bad they construct little huts with poles and hoops over which they drape sheepskin so they resemble the covered litters in which Frankish ladies travel. The men wear long hairy mantles or cloaks and after it rains they spread these on the ground and apply a dressing of alum. In good weather they wear a tunic like the surplice of a priest and tie up their heads with cloth going underneath the chin. They are very ugly, what with black beards and black hair. They carry no weapons except spears and swords and do not put on armor because they think no man dies until his appointed day, at which time his soul enters a different body. Should they wish to rebuke or shame a child they call him accursed like a Frank who dons armor in hope of cheating death. How many Bedouin exist is not known because they travel constantly through the kingdoms of Egypt and Jerusalem and other lands. Their belief that a man does not die until his appointed day is most offensive, implying that our Lord has no power to assist us when we beseech His aid. We know the opposite is true. Christians rest secure in the knowledge of His omnipotence.

That night we took up lodging in the enemy camp. I myself had need of a peaceful sleep, considering the blows I had taken. It was not to be. At daybreak the infidels came back. My chamberlain, who slept at the foot of my pallet and whom I sent outside at the alarm, returned quaking with fright and said the king's sergeants were up against the ropes of our pavilion. I gathered my knights and we rushed out, albeit few of us put on hauberks because of our wounds. After we routed the pagans I sent to King Louis for aid. In a little while here came Gautier de Châtillon to establish a position between ourselves and a strong force of the enemy. However, eight of them took shelter behind a stone bulwark from which they let loose flights of arrows. Then a priest in my service, Jean de Voysey, left camp wearing a steel cap and quilted tunic and walked toward them, trailing his spear so they might not see it. They, finding him alone, behaved contemptuously. But when he got close he gripped the spear and ran at them, whereupon they fled.

Ever afterward my priest was well known. Look you, said one to another, there goes Joinville's priest who took the measure of eight Saracens.

The first Thursday in Lent we were told by his majesty's spies that a very brave Egyptian who had been elected leader held up the shield belonging to Comte Robert. He did this to encourage his people. He pretended it was the shield of King Louis. Behold the royal coat of arms, said he. A body without a head can do no harm, nor an army without its king.

When his majesty got word of this he told us to make ready because the enemy would attack. He gave instructions that our men should be deployed between the tents and a surrounding palisade of stakes. Next morning at sunrise here they came, a good four thousand cavalry with thousands more on foot. Seeing how our forces had been arranged they stopped to consider. About midday they advanced with a huge noise of kettledrums, which they call nacaires. During this assault the Comte d'Anjou was almost taken because he dismounted to fight alongside his knights. King Louis at this news spurred directly into battle and rode so deep among the enemy they burnt the crupper of his mount with Greek fire. Guillaume de Sennac, who was master of the Temple, lost an eye, which injury caused his death. He had lost the other eye during the battle on Shrove Tuesday. God comfort him. The Comte de Poitiers was dragged from his mount and would have been led off to captivity but for some butchers and women selling provisions who began to shout, so he was rescued. After him went Josserand de Brancion with twenty knights afoot, of whom twelve perished. Josserand himself was handled so roughly that he could not stand up and later died of these wounds. During his life he fought thirty-six battles. I met him once before we came oversea. He approached me and my brother on a Good Friday and requested our help because some Germans were desecrating a church. We accompanied him and rushed at the Germans with our swords drawn and forced them away. He then dropped on his knees in front of the altar and prayed aloud. Lord, be merciful to me, he prayed. Release me from these battles among Christians. Allow me to die in Thy service that I may come to Thee in Paradise. Surely his words reached up to the Lord on high.

King Louis assembled his barons and spoke to them when the fighting ended. Many thanks do we owe our Savior, he said, for on Shrove Tuesday we caused the enemy to abandon this camp where we are quartered. And on the day just finished our Lord has enabled us to defend ourselves. His majesty also thanked the barons, graciously and charitably, as was his habit.

Nine days afterward we noticed bodies rising to the surface of the water. Putrefied gall may account for this. Whatever the reason, they floated downstream toward a bridge between our camps, but since the Nile was high they could not float under the arches. There they collected, bumping together, glistening with snakes, nudging each other like swimmers in a current. Now and again a bird would settle on a head or a shoulder. King Louis employed a good many wretches to throw pagan bodies over the bridge so they would float away. Pagans could be identified because they were circumcised. Christians were buried in trenches, which took all of a week. I saw quite a few pilgrims looking for comrades among the dead.

In consequence of my wounds I fell victim to a malady that afflicted legs and head and caused rheum to drip from my nostrils, so during the middle of Lent I took to bed very ill. The priest who came to sing mass was similarly afflicted and at the moment of consecration he turned pale. I got up as best I could and held him in my arms and told him to proceed if he felt able. At length he managed to complete the sacrament but I think he never again sang mass. During this period we had no fish to eat except eels, loathsome creatures that had been gorging on corpses. Because of such hazardous food, I believe, together with the unhealthful climate, many fell sick. Arms and legs withered, bloomed with brown or purple spots that one might find on a mouldy boot or saddle. Teeth loosened in the mouth and whoever was stricken by this malady could not hope to recover. When he bled from the nostrils he understood that he was finished.

387

One thing we did not know was that Sultan Ayub died at Mansourah. Indeed this was kept secret from his own people. He reigned ten years, but suffered a fistula in the lung. They say it was Ayub who gave dignity to the slaves by organizing them into a militia. Thus, inadvertently, by conferring status he prepared them to seize control of government. How often we see the beginning but cannot imagine the consequence. Now when Ayub died his favorite wife Chegeret ordered everyone to keep quiet until Prince Turanshah arrived from Syria. She may have been so counseled by a most powerful emir, Fakhr al-Din, upon whom she depended for advice. This emir twenty years previous had gone to Sicily at the request of Sultan al-Kamil to acquaint himself with Emperor Frederick and learn about Christians. I am told that from Mansourah he despatched a letter to Cairo saying the people must be ready to sacrifice their lives. His letter was read out loud in a mosque, which brought forth groans and sighs. Many decided to leave Cairo, thinking they could not withstand us, but those with more courage resolved to join the army at Mansourah. Fakhr al-Din was himself a brave man. On Shrove Tuesday when we crossed the ford and charged the infidel camp he was enjoying a bath while an attendant dyed his beard with henna. He at once mounted a horse and came flying against us, albeit his mount had neither saddle nor bridle. I believe some Templars despatched him.

As if we had not trouble enough, the Saracens anchored galleys between our camp and Damietta so that no one dared sail up the river with provisions. We knew nothing of this and were puzzled until a ship belonging to the Comte de Flandre by good luck slipped the blockade. We then learned something else. Several of our galleys had been captured as they came upriver and all aboard murdered. Thus our supplies dwindled and we had no idea what to do. His majesty after consultation with the barons said we must retreat downstream. Yet as we began to make preparations these Babylonians gave us no rest. They used every means to find out our condition, being especially anxious to take prisoners. One of them who was a very powerful swimmer scooped out a melon and fitted this over his head. Then he swam slowly past our camp and a sergeant leapt into the Nile to seize the melon. But the Egyptian caught hold of him and carried him off. We did not see him again.

Our situation growing more perilous by the day, we thought to arrange a truce. We proposed this agreement. If we might have the kingdom of Jerusalem we would surrender Damietta. The sultan should look after Christians in Damietta who were too sick to travel and he would not destroy the salt meat we had stored. He might hold all property belonging to us until it could be retrieved. Such terms seemed reasonable to us. Emissaries from the sultan wished to know what security we would give. We offered to leave as hostage either of his majesty's brothers, the Comte d'Anjou or the Comte de Poitiers. But the emissaries said they would come to no agreement unless King Louis himself were left as pledge. Upon hearing this, Lord Geoffrey de Sargines declared he would sooner these misbelievers finished us or took us captive than be reproached throughout eternity for having pawned our king.

While we debated these terms, beseeching God for wisdom, more of our people sickened, racked by wasting of the gums so they could not chew or swallow. Barbers cut away the rotted flesh. While this was done one could hear pitiful moans as though women in labor cried out.

Now it was evident that we should die if we remained at this place. Common lackeys wore breastplates and stood guard because so many knights and sergeants lay ill or had given up the ghost. Therefore his majesty decided to strike camp on Tuesday after the octave of Easter and retrace the Nile to Damietta. Sick and wounded should go aboard galleys. At this time his majesty was gravely weakened by flux. I do not know how often he fainted. He appeared pale unto death. More than once he had been lifted from his mount and the seat of his drawers snipped open, his bowel a putrid stream.

Those attending him could scarcely draw breath on account of the stench. Yet he would not board a galley to escape. Please God, he said, he would not desert his people.

Late in the afternoon I embarked with two knights and my servants, expecting to go downstream on the current. But our mariners objected. The sultan's galleys are between us and Damietta, they said, so we will be caught and put to death. While I argued with them I saw the Babylonians approach. We had lighted fires in camp to attract the sick or wounded and now as it grew dark I could see the heartless pagans murdering these unfortunates by firelight. When my sailors observed this it occurred to them we might be better off anyplace else and quickly weighed anchor. Next we heard men shout from the bank ordering us to wait for the king, and they let fly bolts from crossbows. So we held up. But then, I do not know why, they told us to continue.

About sunrise we came in view of the sultan's galleys and could see all around them Christian vessels that had been captured. Egyptians were stealing property and murdering people and throwing bodies overboard. We were noticed by mounted Saracens on the bank who began discharging arrows tipped with Greek fire that dropped from the sky like comets. I was given a jousting hauberk to wear for protection. But now I learned the crew wanted to set me ashore, hoping thereby to save themselves. I got one of my men to lift me up by the arms since I felt very weak and with sword in hand told the crew if they pulled over to the bank I would kill them. We argued some time, they behaving with utmost insolence. Shortly after this here came four Egyptian galleys pulling toward us with at least one thousand men aboard. I thought we might surrender to those ashore or to those on the galleys but we could not by any means reach Damietta. I consulted my knights. We agreed that if we surrendered to those on land we would be separated and sold to Bedouin, whereas if we gave ourselves up to the sultan's galleys we might stay together. Yet one of my people, a steward from Doulevant, began to complain. When I asked what he thought we should do he replied that we should let ourselves be killed so we might ascend to Paradise. However, no one else liked this idea. Realizing that we must forfeit our liberty, I gathered up my jewels and holy relics and tossed them in the water.

One of the crew asked if I would permit them to say I was his majesty's cousin. For if you do not, he explained, they will certainly butcher all of us, including yourself. He seemed convinced of this. I did not know what good it might do, but told him to say whatever he pleased. He therefore took it upon himself to make this announcement. When the closest galley was about to ram us and send us to the bottom he shouted that I was blood relative to King Louis. And they, instead of splintering our craft, dropped anchor alongside.

Almost at once a Saracen clad in linen breeches came swimming toward us. Later I found out he could speak more than one language because the emperor of Germany governed the place of his birth. No sooner did he climb up on our ship than he grasped me about the waist and said I must act quickly or I was lost. He explained that Egyptians swarming aboard were looking for plunder and would not at first notice me so I must jump on the galley. With God's help I managed to do as he instructed but would have fallen back into the river if he had not leapt after me. He kept his arms about me when I was flung to the deck, even as I felt a knife at my throat. He cried out again and again that I was the king's relative. Why he chose to endanger his life for my sake I do not know. In any event, I was led to a castle aboard the galley where Saracen knights were housed. They took off my hauberk and gave me a scarlet wrap lined with miniver that in fact belonged to me, having been a gift from my mother, and a hood to cover my head. A fit of trembling overcame me on account of my illness and because I was terrified. I asked for a drink so they fetched a jug. However, I could not swallow. The water came spurting out my nostrils. I asked to speak with my people and when they appeared I told them I was dying. They asked why I thought so and I replied that I had a growth in my throat, which I showed them. They began to weep. The Saracens asked the man who had saved me what was wrong. He told them I could not hope to recover because of this growth. But one of them said he would give me a potion that would cure me in two days, which is what happened.

The emir in charge of this galley asked if I was indeed related to King Louis. I answered that I was not and I explained the situation. He said I had been shrewdly advised, otherwise I would have lost my head. He also inquired if I might be related to the emperor of Germany. I answered that I believed my mother was a cousin, which was true, and he seemed gratified.

While we were dining together he had a citizen of Paris brought to the table and this man noticed with astonishment that I was eating meat. My lord, he exclaimed, what are you doing? Well, said I, what do you think I am doing? In God's name, said he, it is Friday! I had not been aware of this so I put the bowl aside. The emir asked my savior why I had pushed away the meat, and being told the reason said he doubted God would hold this against me.

One of my people, Raoul de Wanou, had been hamstrung during the battle on Shrove Tuesday and there was aboard the galley an old Saracen knight who carried Raoul on his back to the latrine whenever necessary, a little act of kindness at which I never ceased to wonder. It may be there exists some universal understanding of the mind.

Those taken captive were put ashore near Mansourah. My good priest Jean fainted while being led from the hold so they killed him and threw his body in the Nile. His cleric also fainted because of sickness. He too was murdered, the corpse tossed overboard. Saracens with drawn swords watched us, prepared to kill any who fell and could not get up. I protested to the emir that I thought this very wrong, contrary to the teaching of Saladin who said one does not kill a man after sharing bread and salt with him. The emir replied that those too feeble to help themselves were unimportant. He brought forth my crew, assembling them in front of me, and said every one had renounced the Christian faith. I said he should not trust them, since as quickly as they renounced our Lord, just as quickly would they renounce Islam. He admitted this was true, for as Saladin ob-

served, never did a good Christian make a good Saracen, nor vice
versa.

I was given a palfrey to ride and traveled with the emir. We
crossed a bridge constructed of boats and presently got to Mansourah. Scribes at the entrance to a pavilion took down my name.
And here the courageous infidel who saved my life, who translated
for me, who befriended me, explained that he could not go any further. He advised me to keep hold of the hand of a boy who accompanied us, otherwise the child would be taken away. This was Ami de
Montbéliard's bastard son.

When my name had been inscribed the emir led me to a pavilion
where the barons were held, along with thousands of captive knights
and sergeants. The barons exclaimed because they thought I was lost.
After some time the principals among us were led to a different enclosure. What happened to the knights and sergeants I did not find
out until later. One by one they were asked if they abjured Christianity. If not, their heads were lopped off.

The sultan's counselors came to speak with us, accompanied by
dragomen, which is to say, men who could interpret. Since we had
appointed Comte Pierre de Bretagne to speak on our behalf, they addressed their questions to him. My lord, said they, the sultan in-
quires if you wish to obtain deliverance. If so, what are you prepared
to give? Lord Pierre responded that we would give whatever we
could, provided it seemed reasonable. Would you give, said they, any
castles belonging to the barons of Outremer? Lord Pierre answered
that he held no jurisdiction over these. Then, said they, would you
give castles of the Temple or the Hospital? This could not be done,
said he, for the castellans of such fellowships have sworn on holy relics that they will not give up the castles to procure any man's freedom. Then, said they, if we had no wish to be delivered they would
let soldiers play games with our heads. Having said as much, they
departed.

Straightway into the enclosure came a horde of young infidels
with drawn swords and a little old man leaning on a crutch who had

a long beard and white hair. They said he was one of their holiest
men and he wished to question us. Was it true that we believed in a
God who was put to death on our behalf, who came back to life?
That is true, we said. Then, said he, we should not mislike our persecution considering that we had yet to die for him as he had died for
us. And if our God had strength enough to lift himself out of the
grave, most certainly would he be able to deliver us. With that he
took leave and the crowd of young soldiers as well, which relieved us
beyond words.

Presently we were told that King Louis had negotiated ransom.
Baudouin d'Ibelin, Guy d'Ibelin, Jean de Valéry, and Philippe de
Montfort went to learn the conditions. Very much that we had not
known was made clear when they returned. Muslim counselors had
approached his majesty as they approached us, to find out if he
would give up castles belonging to the Templars or Hospitalers or to
the barons of Outremer. His majesty replied as we replied. They
threatened him. They vowed to place him in the bernicle, which is a
cruel method of torture. Two lengths of wood notched with teeth
are bound together with oxhide straps and they put a man's legs inside these jaws and pile weight on top until the bone is crushed. After three days the legs are red as a crab so they put him in the bernicle
again and again crush the bone. King Louis responded to this threat
by saying he was their captive and they might do as they wished.

When they found out they could not intimidate his majesty they
demanded to know what he would pay for his deliverance and if he
would give up Damietta. He replied that if the sultan would accept a
fair amount he would advertise his consort Queen Marguerite to
levy it. They asked why the king himself did not guarantee ransom,
to which he answered that Queen Marguerite was mistress of herself.

Now they conferred with Turanshah who had returned from
Syria and became sultan after his father's death. Turanshah set a price
of one million gold bezants, which is to say half a million French livres. King Louis agreed to this in exchange for the release of his people. And he agreed to surrender Damietta in exchange for his own

release, since it would be inappropriate for one of his rank to purchase freedom with money. Then the king's brothers visited Sultan Turanshah to receive his oath and a truce of ten years was proclaimed.

When last I saw his majesty on Tuesday after the octave of Easter he looked near death. I was told that next day while he stood leaning against his saddle those around him separately and then in unison urged him to embark on the river in hope of escaping, but again he refused. Then his brother, the Comte d'Anjou, admonished him. Sire, you do no one good service by scorning us, for by waiting on you because of your infirmity the march is delayed. By refusing to take ship you do endanger us to the last man. At these words the king turned wrathfully on his brother. If I am a burden to you, he said, be rid of me. But I will not rid myself of my people.

Thus he was taken captive. He had ridden with Geoffrey de Sargines to the rear guard and was riding a stout little cob with silk housing but grew very weak. Lord Geoffrey took him to a nearby hamlet. He was carried more dead than alive into the house of a woman who by chance had been born in Paris. None thought he could live till sunrise. His teeth clattered, his skin like a winding sheet, flux having drained his body so every bone poked out. With him at this extremity was a single attendant, Isambart, the rest having succumbed to disease. Isambart cooked for his majesty and baked bread, dressed and undressed him, carried him outside to void his bowel. According to what Isambart later said, King Louis endured each humiliation with noble patience and was steadily at prayer.

During the illness he was protected by a most courageous knight, Gautier de Châtillon. There was but one road through this hamlet and if enemies appeared either way the knight would charge furiously. I was informed by Jean Fouinon that as he himself was led captive to Mansourah he noticed a Turk riding Gautier's horse, the crupper smeared with blood. Jean inquired how the Turk came by it and was told that he had cut the owner's throat.

I learnt also what happened to Jacques de Castel, bishop of Soissons. When he saw our people in retreat he rode forth by himself

395

against these villains and was slashed to death. I believe he had no wish to see France again. The saintly man had but one desire, which was to be with God. Beyond doubt he joined an illustrious company of martyrs.

At this time his majesty's consort Queen Marguerite lay abed in Damietta prepared to give birth. Three days before the event she learnt of our defeat. Then she summoned a venerable knight of eighty who by custom slept at the foot of her bed, for it appeared that Egyptians would take the city. By the troth you have plighted, said Queen Marguerite, if Saracens enter Damietta I beg you to grant my wish. When they come for me you must cut off my head. My Lady, responded this good old knight, be assured. Already I had decided they should never take you.

No more was she delivered of a son, Jean, called Jean Tristram owing to the sadness of those days, when she found out that merchants from Pisa and Genoa and other cities were making ready to depart. She summoned the most influential merchants and beseeched them to have pity, if not upon her, then upon the weak creature at her breast. How should we stay? they answered. We are dying of hunger. The queen replied that she would purchase food at the king's expense to keep them all from starvation. And they, smelling profit, informed her majesty that they would remain. Thus do men consummate their office.

King Louis knew nothing of such matters while he languished near death in a house menaced by the sultan's army. Philippe de Montfort arrived to say he had talked with an emir concerning a truce and if the king so wished he would again consult the emir. Through negotiation they might agree on terms. King Louis said he was willing. Some agreement was reached, whereupon the emir pulled off his turban and a ring from his finger to signify that it would be honored. But all at once a sergeant rode around camp shouting that the king had surrendered. It may be that terror stripped his wits or Egyptians bribed him to do what he did. However this came about, our people laid aside their weapons. Now the emir told Lord Philippe there would be no truce because already we were surrendering. Hence the army was rounded up, all taken captive. Was this the will of God? If so, how mightily we must have sinned. I think we were not far from that place where Sultan al-Kamil nearly drowned King John and his army in the year of our Lord 1221.

Muslim chronicles relate that when Turanshah knew we were defeated he camped along the Nile and devoted himself to lechery. Being anxious to acquaint the world with his triumph he wrote to Emir Djemal Edden who was governor of Damascus, claiming in this letter to have slaughtered thirty thousand Christians, apart from those who leapt into the river, apart from innumerable prisoners slain whose bodies joined the current. And like some noisy ass Turanshah brayed how the king of the Franks implored clemency. Further, Turanshah sent to Damascus his majesty's cap, which was scarlet and lined with soft fur. They say the governor decided to wear this cap while reading Turanshah's letter in public. Also, a Muslim poet wrote a verse declaring the cap of the Frank to be white as paper, which changed to red when dyed with Christian blood by the sword of Islam.

These infidels believe our king retreated ignominiously to a hillock and there surrendered to the eunuch Djemaddelin on condition that his life be spared. They believe he was taken to Mansourah in shackles. They believe that Muslim soldiers felt embarrassed by the abject submission of countless Franks. I do not know how many lies were told about us. I have heard that each night Turanshah had three hundred Christians beheaded, their corpses thrown into the Nile. God knows. What can scarcely be doubted is that he disgusted his own people. Upon ascending the throne he strangled his brother. And he commanded Sultana Chegeret to render up accounts of his late father's wealth because he could not get enough. It is said also that Muslims detested his sullen, gloomy nature.

Be that as it may, when conditions of the truce had been resolved King Louis, his brothers, and the principal barons proceeded downstream on four galleys. Imbert who was High Constable, that most worthy knight Guillaume de Flandre, Comte Pierre de Bretagne, and the brothers Ibelin accompanied me. One week before Ascension we anchored in sight of a wooden tower draped with blue canvas that marked the entrance to a huge encampment. Inside was a pavilion where knives, swords, and other weapons were deposited by nobles who came to visit Turanshah. Beyond this, a second tower giving access to the pavilion where this despicable monarch held court. A third tower, very high, gave access to his private chambers. They say he climbed up here if he wished to observe his camp or meditate upon the scenery. There was yet another pavilion beside the river to insure privacy when he wished to bathe.

It had been arranged that Damietta would be given up on Saturday before Ascension. However the Egyptians suddenly took to quarreling among themselves with such excitement that we were astonished. We did not know the cause, nor would they answer questions, but it seemed we might be slain at any instant. I am told that King Louis, fearing the worst, ordered the Office of the Cross to be sung, together with that of the Holy Ghost and that of the Requiem. We did not learn until afterward what happened. Sultan Turanshah had dismissed from his counsel several emirs he mistrusted. So, feeling insulted and shamed, those who had been deposed consulted one another. The sultan has stripped us of the high office to which we were appointed by his father, said one. Therefore when he gains control of Damietta he will arrest us. We will die in prison.

These emirs approached the Halca, which is to say the imperial bodyguard, and demanded that Turanshah be assassinated following a banquet to which they themselves were invited. So at the appointed moment one of the Halca, said to have been the royal sword-bearer, struck a blow with that very sword at Turanshah's hand, splitting it between the fingers all the way through the wrist up to the arm. Turanshah cried to his emirs for help, but they did nothing. The bodyguards shouted that they would kill him because otherwise he would do the same to them and kettledrums were beaten, which was a signal to divert the army to Mansourah. And so Turanshah, being young and nimble, dashed away from the banquet, got inside the highest tower and climbed to the top. The bodyguard wrecked his pavilions and crowded about the tower shouting for him to come down. He replied that he would not unless they spared his life. They shouted again for him to come down and set about burning the tower. Those of us aboard the galley could see flames licking up the planks. Turanshah cried out that he would abdicate his throne and return to Huns-Keifa, which is on the banks of the Tigris very far from Egypt, but they paid no attention. As the fire got close he leapt from the tower. His garment caught on a pole and for a few moments he hung suspended. Then he fell to the ground, jumped up and ran toward the Nile with conspirators after him. One of them thrust a lance into his side but he continued running and the lance dangling from his ribs. He plunged into the Nile but they waded after him and caught him and murdered him a short distance from our galley. A blue-eyed Turk called Baibars, who was leader of the Halca, is said to have finished him off. I have heard also that a knight called Faris al-Din Octai cut open Turanshah's breast and pulled out the heart, which he brought to King Louis. What will you give me? asked the Saracen knight whose hands were slick with blood. What will you give, now that I have killed the sultan? To this our noble king answered not a word.

According to these people, fire, water, and iron put an end to the life of Turanshah. They left his corpse on the bank of the Nile for three days. Such are the Egyptians. God affright them.

Concerning the bodyguard, they feel no allegiance to anyone because they are poor youths brought from distant lands and sold at high prices. The emblem they wear is that of a sultan except that they add red roses, crooks, or another device. If one proves himself in battle he will be made emir, given command of two or three hundred knights. Yet as they become famous and powerful the sultan wonders if they might dethrone or kill him, so he may put them to death.

That is how Sultan Bondocdar punished some who approached while he was hunting. We have troubled the king of Armenia, they said, and come to you for a fine reward. I salute you not, answered Bondocdar, since you have disturbed the chase. Whereupon these Halca lost their heads.

Now having murdered Turanshah the guards did not know what to do. After consultation they decided to place Sultana Chegeret on the throne. She, like them, was of lowly birth. She had been a slave, Armenian or Turk, until Sultan Ayub bought her and fell desperately in love with her and took her with him wherever he went and would not let her be separated from him. Muslims called this woman Shajar al-Durr, which is said to mean Tree of Pearls. So in love was Ayub that he stamped her name on a coin. However that may be, when this woman was enthroned after Turanshah's murder she respected the treaty made with our king, which is much to her credit.

Mahometans say this Tree of Pearls later married a mameluk chief called Aybeg and conferred upon him the title of sultan. For seven years they governed together. But one day in the bath she rebuked him for having taken a juvenile concubine. Do I no longer please you? she asked. She is young, Aybeg unwisely answered, whereas you are not. At this she blinded him with soap and stabbed him. By chance one of Aybeg's sons observed water flowing through a drain streaked with blood so he rushed into the room and found Chegeret almost naked and a dagger in her hand. We are told that she dashed wildly through the palace corridors but slipped, struck her head against a marble post and died. God castigate such people. May all plunge downward to the dolorous house of hell.

No more was Turanshah put to death like a screaming pig than here came thirty Saracens with Danish axes slung around their necks clambering aboard our galley. Baudouin, who understood their language, told me they had come to take our heads. Many of our people gathered about Jean, a monk of the Holy Trinity, to confess their sins. As for myself, I was too frightened to recall any sins and could think of nothing except that if I tried to escape or defend myself they would make it all the worse for me. Since I could not imagine any way out I crossed myself and knelt before a Saracen who was gripping an axe of the sort carpenters use. In this manner, I thought, Saint Agnes died. Guy d'Ibelin knelt beside me and confessed himself. I absolve you, I said, with such power as God allots me.

The Saracens told us to get up. At this my senses returned and it occurred to me that I could not recall a single word of Guy d'Ibelin's confession.

We were led into the hold of the galley and spent the night packed tight as fish in a keg. Comte Pierre's feet against my face, mine against his. In great misery we speculated that we might be plucked out one after another and beheaded like chickens.

Next day we were brought on deck. The emirs wished to speak with us concerning the truce arranged by Turanshah. Those who could walk were led ashore. I myself, Comte Pierre, High Constable Imbert, and others in very poor shape did not attempt to go. By the grace of God our people and theirs came to agreement. King Louis and the nobles would be released when Damietta surrendered. Concerning ransom, his majesty would pay half before embarkation, the second half when we reached Acre. Saracens would look after the sick in Damietta. Also, they would attend to our equipment, engines of war, and provisions such as salt meat until his majesty sent for them. All this was put in writing and the emirs swore that if they did not keep their covenant they would be utterly dishonored. Further, should they break faith with King Louis they would be as disgraced as a Muslim who eats pork. Nicole d'Acre, being a priest who understood these people, assured his majesty that there could be no avouchment more binding.

But the emirs had an oath drawn up that they wanted our king to sign. This on the advice of certain renegade priests who had forsaken Christ to join the enemy. Should King Louis fail to keep his covenant he would be stigmatized as one who denied our Lord and Blessed Mary, hence outcast from the community of apostles. Should the king break faith he would be stigmatized as one who denied God and in contempt of God spat upon and trampled the Holy Cross.

When this was explained to King Louis he declared that never would he take such an oath.

The emirs spoke to Nicole d'Acre and bade him give the king this message. We take it badly that, while we have bound ourselves to keep faith, you on your part refuse. Be it known that if you do not accept this oath your head will be forfeit, as will the heads of your people.

King Louis replied that the emirs might do as they liked. For himself, he would sooner die in the arms of Christ than live opposed to our Lord and His blessed mother.

The emirs charged that King Louis had been so advised by the patriarch of Jerusalem. This patriarch, being eighty years old and greatly esteemed, was given leave by Turanshah to visit the king. However, amongst both pagans and Christians it is understood that a sovereign's warrant of safe passage becomes invalid if he dies. Thus, Turanshah no longer sultan, the patriarch had been roughly seized. Let us send his head flying into the lap of King Louis, said one emir. Others would not consent. Whereupon they tied this good old cleric to a post in the royal pavilion, hands lashed behind his back, which made them swell up like gourds and blood seeped under his fingernails. The patriarch implored King Louis to swear what the Saracens demanded, saying he would take upon his own soul any sin there might be.

I think to some degree his majesty swore an oath, enough to mollify these accursed people. And the Saracens called him the most steadfast Christian in the world, citing as proof that whenever he issued from his tent he prostrated himself and made the sign of the cross over all his body. If Mahomet subjected Muslims to such abuse, they said, their belief would not survive.

Thus, matters having improved, we proceeded downstream and cast anchor above the Damietta bridge.

At sunrise of the appointed day Lord Geoffrey de Sargines entered Damietta, charged with its surrender. Muslim banners soon went up and infidel knights wandered the streets drinking wine until all were drunk. One got aboard our galley to show his sword dripping blood and boast that he had slain six of our people. We gave perpetual thanks to God that Queen Marguerite with her newborn son Jean Tristram had sailed to Acre some days before.

We looked to our release the morning Damietta surrendered, but were kept aboard. Nor did we get a thing to eat. The emirs passed this time quarreling, unable to decide if we should be killed. One argued that King Louis and all of us should taste the sword because our children were young and could not seek vengeance for many years. Another, by name Sevrici who was born in Mauretania, protested that already they killed the sultan and if now they murdered King Louis it would be said that Egyptians were the most wicked people on earth. Others admitted that indeed they had done wrong to kill the sultan because Mahomet commanded them to venerate their lord. Yet, said they, something else was written in the Book of Mahomet. And one of them turned over a page of their holy book where it was written that to safeguard their faith they must slay enemies of the Law. Hence, if they did violate the precept of Mahomet by murdering Turanshah, they would sin more deeply if they neglected to kill the lord of Christians. And one of those we knew to be set against us pulled off his turban, waving it as a signal, whereupon the galleys weighed anchor and took us back upstream a league or more in the direction of Cairo. At this we commended our souls to God.

What changed their hearts I do not know. Near sunset our vessels returned downstream and drew up alongside the bank. Since

403

Damietta now belonged to them we demanded our release according to agreement, but they would not let us go until we had eaten, saying the emir would be chagrined if we should leave hungry. They brought us some little cheese cakes baked hard in the sun to keep them free of maggots and boiled eggs with the shells colorfully painted to honor us.

By the time we got ashore his majesty was being escorted to a Genoese galley. It looked as if twenty thousand Saracens with swords in their belts were following him. A plank was lowered so he might board the galley. With him went his brother, the Comte d'Anjou, and various nobles including Henri du Mez, Philippe de Nemours, and myself. The Comte de Poitiers had been detained as security until half the ransom was paid. Everyone had left Damietta excepting the very old and sick whom the Egyptians had vowed to protect. Instead, the villains murdered one and all. They knocked apart our catapults, heaped the bodies of slain citizens between layers of salt pork and wood and set everything ablaze. The fire burned Friday, Saturday, and Sunday. May the Lord God punish Babylon. We are hard put at such times to grasp the manner of His Divinity. Withal, how should we doubt or question His intent?

Mahometans say the negotiators harshly lectured our beloved king. They asked how a wise and vigilant sovereign could embark on a voyage to a land populated by servants of Allah. According to our law, said they, a man who would do this could not testify at court. Why not? asked King Louis. Because, said they, it would be assumed that he had lost his faculties. Concerning the truth of this exchange, I, Jean, have no knowledge.

Two days were needed to count the ransom, which was reckoned on scales by weight. During this time a Saracen of pleasing aspect brought his majesty a bouquet of divers color and jars filled with milk and he addressed the king in French. Upon being asked how he had learnt our language this man replied that he was himself French, born in Provins, but years ago came to Egypt, married one of their women, and now by his own estimate was a gentleman of conse-

quence. Being asked if he did not understand that he would be forever damned if he should die in this circumstance, he answered that
he did. He explained that he dared not return to Christianity because
poverty and shame would be his lot. He preferred instead his life of
wealth and ease among infidels. When it was pointed out that on
Judgment Day the magnitude of his sin would be exposed, he seemed
indifferent. Soon thereafter he went away. In due time this rogue
must face the Lord.

The king's men who were counting money sent to tell him they
had not enough by thirty thousand livres. I suggested that his majesty borrow this amount from the Templars. He approved and
instructed me to consult them. I therefore spoke to Étienne d'Otri-
court who was Commander of the Temple, but our discussion went
badly. My lord of Joinville, said he, your advice to his majesty does
you little credit since you know that money entrusted to us cannot
be lent. I then said to the Templar several things that are best forgotten. At this point Renaud de Vichiers, who was Marshal, spoke up.
We cannot violate our oath, said he, but if King Louis thinks fit to
take the money we would not be surprised. If that should be the case,
his majesty demanding what belongs to us in Egypt, why then, we
should requite ourselves with what belongs to him in Acre.

Seeing how matters stood I told the king that, if he so wished, I
would go and take the money. He directed me to proceed.

Marshal Renaud accompanied me into the hold of the treasure
galley and when we got to a massive chest I asked the Treasurer for
his key. But as I appeared more dead than alive from sickness and imprisonment and he not knowing I was sent by the king, he gazed at
me in stupefaction. After some moments he replied that he would
not. I thereupon picked up a hatchet and said it might serve as his
majesty's key. Marshal Renaud however clutched my wrist and ordered the Treasurer to comply. When the chest was opened I threw
out all the money and had it carried to the boat that brought me and
watched while it was handed down.

As we drew near the king's galley I became excited and started to

405

shout. My lord! My lord! I exclaimed. See how I am provided! He for his part looked at me with delight.

After this was reckoned and our debt paid, Lord Philippe confided that ten thousand livres had been withheld. I saw King Louis grow dark in the face. I now stepped on Philippe's toe and said it must not be true, considering how Saracens are the shrewdest bargainers on earth and not readily deceived. Philippe wisely agreed, saying it was meant in jest. Nonetheless his majesty frowned. He remarked that he thought such a jest unwarranted. If by chance the full amount was not paid, he said, by the fealty you owe me as my vassal I command you to redress that error.

Now with all in place and his oath acquitted King Louis ordered the galley to leave Damietta and carry him to sea where a ship awaited us. I think we traveled a good league before anyone spoke, so concerned were we at leaving the Comte de Poitiers hostage. Indeed, while negotiations were under way certain counselors advised his majesty to refrain from paying the Egyptians until they let his brother go. Our saintly king would have none of this. He would honor his pledge, expecting enemies to do likewise.

Presently a galleon drew alongside and Lord Philippe de Montfort cried out for the king to greet his brother. Then the king crossed over to his brother's ship, as did I, and they embraced. So the apprehension we felt was replaced by joy.

When at length we got to the ship that would take us to Acre we found those aboard unprepared for his majesty's arrival. Neither bed nor clothing had been readied. Therefore he was obliged to sleep six nights on a wretched pallet and wear clothes the sultan had made for him, a black samite ensemble lined with miniver and gray squirrel pelt, all decorated with gold buttons. I spent those days seated beside him and not many days have I felt worse. He told me in detail about his capture and he seemed much interested to learn of my various misadventures. He said I should thank the Lord for deliverance. Also, he complained that his brother the Comte d'Anjou seldom bothered to visit but chose to spend the time amusing himself with friends.

One day while the Comte d'Anjou was at dice with Gautier de Nemours and others King Louis got unsteadily to his feet, tottered across to the gamblers, snatched up dice and boards and flung them into the sea. He then castigated his brother for unseemliness. I think Gautier fared well enough, tipping what was on the table into his lap.

Citizens and clergy welcomed us by the shore amid great rejoicing and there King Louis happily met his queen.

I was offered a palfrey to ride yet no sooner did I mount than I all but fell off. The man who brought the palfrey held me upright. Later he assisted me in climbing steps to the king's hall where I rested by a window. Ami de Montbéliard's young bastard, called Barthélemy, stood not far away. He was at that time perhaps ten years old. While I sat there very weak and faint I was approached by a lackey wearing a scarlet tunic with yellow stripes. He bowed and asked if I remembered him. I did not. He said he was Guillemin. He came from the castle of my uncle at Oiselay and being at the moment unattached he would serve me if I wished. I was pleased to engage him, so he combed my hair and found me a white cap.

Now his majesty sent word that I should dine with him. During my imprisonment the Saracens had given me an old coverlet and from this my people fashioned a short tunic. What remained of this cloth I bestowed upon young Barthélemy along with some ells of camlet. My new servant Guillemin accompanied me to carve the meat and he obtained a little food for the child. King Louis with unfailing grace did not comment on my appearance while we ate.

Guillemin quickly proved his worth, finding rooms for me near the baths. That night I went to wash away my prison filth, but while seated in the bath was again overcome by dizziness and do not know how I could have managed without his help. Some few days later, having clothed myself more suitably, I paid a visit to the king who reproached me for my absence, saying he had expected to see me sooner. He commanded me to eat with him morning and evening. He was then much in doubt whether he should stay oversea or go back to France.

Anon the bishop of Acre let me use a dwelling that belonged to a priest, yet I had no more settled myself than fever attacked. To make things worse, beside my bed was an entrance to the church and not a day passed without at least twenty corpses delivered. Thus, feeling sick beyond repair, I lay stretched out on my pallet hearing a constant refrain. Libera me, Domine. Each time I heard this I wept and praised God. I thanked Him for my suffering because I often had succumbed to pride when I lay down to sleep or when I awoke. And I prayed Him to cast off the bonds of my infirmity.

When it seemed I had got back my faculties I asked Guillemin to account for money spent and discovered he had nipped me of ten livres tournois, so I dismissed him. Afterward I was told by certain Burgundians who brought him oversea that he was the most courteous thief in the realm. If a thing was needed, strap or knife or gloves, no matter what, Guillemin would slip out to steal it.

Of a Sunday the king sent for his two brothers and other lords, myself included. He said he had neither peace nor truce with England and the Frankish domain stood in peril. The Queen Mother implores me to return, he said, but many protest that all would be forfeit if I depart. I pray you, then, consider and give me your thoughts. Eight days from this day I would know your counsel.

Guy Mauvoisin spoke on our behalf when we returned to advise his majesty. Sire, in concert your brothers and the high barons have disclosed their thoughts. We believe you cannot stay without prejudice to your honor. Of two thousand eight hundred knights you led to Cyprus no more than one hundred may be found in Acre. Hence it is our judgment that you should depart. In France you will be able to levy troops and money so that you may with good speed return to the Holy Land to avenge yourself on the enemies of God.

When Guy Mauvoisin had finished speaking King Louis addressed himself to individual knights, asking if they agreed. All did, save the count of Joppa who begged to be excused. For, as he explained, his castle stood on the frontier and if he counseled the king to remain it would be whispered that he looked to his own advantage. As it came my turn I told his majesty that I agreed with the count of Joppa. His majesty in very poor temper asked how he might abuse the Saracen with so few knights. I replied that, while I did not know if it were true, people said the king spent revenue from the church but not his own. Therefore, said I, let the king obtain knights from Morea and other parts with his own resources. Knights will arrive in good number if they hear the king pays generously. Thus we may hold the field. And should it please God, we may liberate those despairing captives who must otherwise languish without hope of freedom.

Silence fell when I spoke these words. Not one in that room but had a friend held captive. Many began to weep. The legate asked Marshal Guillaume de Beaumont what he thought and he replied that I had spoken very well. At this Lord Jean de Beaumont, who was his uncle and nourished a great desire to see France again, cried out sharply. The king admonished Lord Jean, saying he should let his nephew speak. Certes, I will not! Lord Jean replied. Guillaume kept silent. Nor did others speak on my behalf, excepting Lord Châtenai. The king said he would reflect upon our advice and tell us by the end of the week what he meant to do.

At supper he bade me sit beside him as he customarily did if his brothers were absent, but throughout the meal he said not a word to me. I thought he must be annoyed so while he was hearing grace I got up and walked to an embrasure near his bed and thrust my arms through the bars of the window. I stood there considering what I might do if he returned to France. I thought I would approach the prince of Antioch, to whom I was related, who had asked me to join him. I would be able to stay there until another expedition came oversea. Then by the grace of God we might deliver those unfortunates from bondage. While I stood there contemplating the future someone leaned against me and put both hands atop my head.

409

Philippe de Nemours had plagued me because of the counsel I offered so I thought it must be he.

Philippe, I said with little grace, I beg you leave me. Feeling vexed, I turned my head. At this a hand slipped across my face and I saw an emerald ring worn by the king of France.

Calm yourself, his majesty said. I want to ask you something. How is it that you, who are young, dare counsel me to stay when the wisest men of France advise me to depart?

I replied that if there had been wickedness in my heart I would not have spoken as I did. He asked if I thought it would be wrong for him to leave. I said I did. If I should stay, he asked, would you also? I answered that I would stay if possible, either at my own expense or at the expense of someone else. Do not trouble yourself on that account, he said, adding that he was well pleased with my advice. And he bade me not speak of our conversation till the week was up.

During that week I heard from Pierre d'Avallon who lived in Tyre, who sent word that I was ridiculed for having urged his majesty to remain. I was mocked as a colt, which is a name given to peasants of that region. Pierre suggested I defend myself by saying it was better to be a colt than a weary draft horse.

Sunday, which was Saint John's Day, we assembled. King Louis invoked the Holy Spirit by making the sign of the cross upon his mouth, after which he thanked those who had counseled him to return to France as well as those who urged him to remain. Then he said that on no account would he abandon the kingdom of Jerusalem, which he had come to liberate and protect. He said he would offer such generous terms to the nobles and to other knights that if they did not choose to stay in the Holy Land the fault must be their own. At his words some appeared struck dumb with amazement. Others wept.

I now took it upon myself to visit the shrine of Saint James.

Soon after I returned from this pilgrimage his majesty summoned the members of his council and began to complain in a loud voice. My lords, he said, a month has passed and I have not heard of

410

any knights retained in my service. At this meeting, along with myself, were Lord Geoffrey de Sargines, Gilles le Brun whom he had made Constable after Imbert de Beaujeu ascended to glory, and the chamberlain. The others, I think, had set sail. To his majesty's complaint these nobles replied that all of the knights seemed anxious to go home and thus laid a high price on their service. Who could be got most cheaply? he asked. The lord of Joinville, said they, yet even he insists on quite a lot. So the king turned to me. Seneschal, come here, he said. I went and knelt before him. He bade me take a seat. You know I am fond of you, he said, but people tell me you are difficult. Why is this?

I answered that it was not my fault since I had lost everything while I was held captive on the river. He asked how much I would need. I told him that two hundred thousand livres would keep me till Easter. Then he asked if I had bargained with any of my people. I said I had spoken with a knight-banneret, Pierre de Pontmolain, who demanded four hundred livres, as did two other knights-banneret.

Twelve hundred livres, said the king, reckoning on his fingers.

Do not forget, I said, that horse and armor for myself will cost at least eight hundred. Further, the expense of food must be counted since I doubt you would invite all of us to your table. His majesty after some reflection said he did not consider my demand excessive.

His brothers, the Comte d'Anjou and the Comte de Poitiers, were at that time preparing to depart. If he ordered them to France, mayhap to supervise the realm during his absence, or if he gave permission at their request, I do not know. However it was, both admonished me to watch over the king, saying he put much faith in my judgment. When they were ready to go aboard ship the Comte de Poitiers distributed a number of jewels to those of us who remained. As for the Comte d'Anjou, when it came time to embark he lamented and wept so passionately that all were amazed. Still, he did not change his mind.

Soon thereafter came envoys from the sultan of Damascus seeking his majesty's help against those emirs who governed Egypt.

Turanshah, who plunged into the Nile with a lance dangling from his ribs, was related to this sultan. Now, said the envoys, provided King Louis would help crush these loathsome emirs, the sultan would hand over Jerusalem. His majesty at length decided to respond through envoys of his own. And with them to interpret went Yves le Breton, a predicant friar who spoke Saracenic. And the message to the sultan of Damascus was this. King Louis would by no means ally himself with the sultan until he knew if the emirs would make amends for the outrages they committed.

So off to Egypt went Lord Jean de Valenciennes, charged by his majesty to find out how matters stood. Quicker than expected he came back with two hundred Frankish knights released from captivity as well as lesser folk. Among these knights were a good forty attached to the court of Champagne. I paid to have them fitted with tunics and green surcoats, thinking his majesty would offer them generous terms to serve under his banner. He listened to what they asked, but made no reply. A knight of his council rebuked me, pointing out that King Louis was thick enough in debt. The king, said I, had best not listen to you, considering how knights are in short supply. Having said as much, I burst into tears. His majesty ordered me to keep quiet and said he would give them what they asked. So he engaged them, posting them to my battalion.

Lord Jean also brought back from Egypt the bones of Comte Gautier de Brienne who was cousin to Madame de Saida. She buried them in the church of the Hospital in Acre, causing each knight to offer a wax candle and a silver denier while the king himself offered a candle and a gold bezant, all to the expense of Madame de Saida, which was a very fine thing to do.

However, the message Lord Jean brought from Egypt was not favorable. The emirs would accede to his majesty's demand for reparation only if he allied himself with them against the sultan of Damascus. His majesty responded that he would not consider an alliance until they sent him the heads of Christians they had suspended from the walls of Cairo. Further, they must give up all the Christian children they seized. And because he yet owed part of his ransom they should dispense with that. So the matter stood unresolved.

Friar Yves le Breton when he got back from Damascus told of a most remarkable sight. While he and the envoys were en route from their lodging to the palace here came an old woman crossing the street with a phial of water in one hand, a chafing dish of coals in the other. Friar Yves asked what she intended to do. With these coals I will burn up Paradise, said she. Next I will quench the fires of Hell, so neither will exist. Why do such a thing? asked Friar Yves. Because, said she, for love of God one ought to live honorably, not in hope of entering Paradise or from dread of Hell.

John the Armenian who had charge of the king's artillery also went to Damascus, I think to purchase horn and glue for crossbows. While bargaining in the marketplace he was hailed by some very ancient man who inquired if he might be Christian. John agreed he was. A long time past, said this ancient man, I saw King Baudouin of Jerusalem, by which he meant Baldwin the leper. With only three hundred knights, said this old man, King Baudouin defeated Saladin. But now, on account of your wickedness, we take you more easily than cattle in the field. To this John answered that the old man should bite his tongue, considering the wickedness of Saracens.

I have been foolish, the old man said.

How so? asked John.

I will tell you, the old man replied, but first I would ask a question. Have you a son or daughter?

I have a son, John answered.

Which would hurt more deeply? To be struck by a Saracen or by your son?

A blow from my son would hurt deeply, said John.

Now here is my reply, the old man said. Christians think themselves children of God and name themselves after Christ. Your God has given you teachers so you may discern truth from falsehood.

413

That is why He feels hurt more by your sins than by those we commit, since we are ignorant, thinking we may be cleansed of sin by washing our bodies before we die.

Almighty God did not create the world without variety. Therefore pagans as well as Christians may look up to the vault of heaven. Yet if this is true, how can a torrent of darkness issue from their hearts?

During the year 1253 came word that a Mongol prince, Sartuq, had converted to Christianity, which seemed to his majesty providential. He charged two Dominicans, William of Ruybroek and Bartholomew of Cremona, to seek out this Mongol and beseech him to aid fellow Christians in Syria. It had been, I think, four years since two predicant friars departed from Cyprus with a portable chapel for the great khan, yet never a word from Asia. We could but hope and speculate that somewhere these emissaries of truth should meet.

Also, during this time at Acre we heard from the Old Man of the Mountain. Here came deputies, a pleasing emir handsomely dressed, followed by two youthful Assassins. One youth carried three knives so cleverly wrought that the blade of one fitted snugly to the handle of the next, a gift for King Louis if the emir's reception proved less than cordial. Around one arm of the other was a roll of linen, a winding sheet in case his majesty disdained the overture.

After his majesty heard mass he received these deputies and wished to know why they had come, whereupon the emir presented letters of credence. My lord sends me to ask if you are acquainted, said he.

King Louis replied that he did not know the Old Man, but had heard about him.

Then I am surprised, the emir said. For if you have heard about him I should think you would send him large amounts of money to be assured of his friendship, just as the king of Hungary and the sultan of Cairo and others pay tribute year after year. But if you are unable to do this my lord will relieve you of the obligation, provided you relieve him of his obligation to the Temple and to the Hospital.

These two orders were much feared by the Assassins.

King Louis replied that he would see the emir that afternoon. When the emir came back he found King Louis seated between the Master of the Temple and the Master of the Hospital. The king asked him to repeat what he had said that morning. He refused. At this both Masters commanded him to speak, which he did. Then he was told in Saracenic to come and speak with them privately at the Hospital. There he was told that he had behaved rashly by delivering an insolent message and they would drown him in the putrid sea of Acre except that doing so would cast a shadow on the king. They told him he should go back to the Old Man but return in a fortnight bearing a letter of apology and such gifts and jewels as might appease the king's wrath.

These deputies returned in less than a fortnight. They brought the Old Man's shirt and a conciliatory message. As the shirt clings to the body, so does the Old Man cling to his love for the great King Louis.

Nor was this all. They tendered his ring, made of excellent gold, which had his name engraved, indicating close alliance, declaring his wish that henceforth they should be united as though espoused. They brought jewelry, crystal giraffes, crystal elephants, divers crystal fruits, gaming boards, and chess tables deftly inlaid with stone flowers. These all were embowered in ambergris, causing a fragrant odor to pervade the room. King Louis thought to reciprocate with equivalent riches and by way of these deputies sent lengths of scarlet cloth, gold cups, jewels, silver horse snaffles, and other magnificent things. And he charged Friar Yves le Breton to go with these deputies and find out what he could.

Friar Yves got back safely to Acre, albeit not many expected him to. He reported that Assassins follow the teaching of Mahomet's uncle, Ali, which none of us had known. We were informed that Ali raised his nephew to high estate, but instead of feeling grateful Mahomet despised and denigrated his uncle and proposed a different faith. Hence, Muslims who obey the teaching of Mahomet call the disciples of Ali misguided, whereas those who accept the latter call the former insurgent, much as we think Christian Greeks insurgent. Friar Yves explained that Assassins do not fear death because they think the soul of a man who dies serving his lord will be rewarded with a more attractive body.

We learned that the Old Man keeps in his bedchamber a book containing things spoken by our Lord Jesus to Saint Peter. Friar Yves when he saw this book admonished the Old Man to study it often because the words in it were both true and wise. The Old Man responded that he did often study this book. I have learned, said he, that the soul of Abel after death came into the body of Noah, and when Noah died his soul came into the body of Abraham, and when Abraham died his body came into the soul of Saint Peter, all of which occurred at the beginning of the world. Then, said Friar Yves to King Louis, I sought to explain how he was mistaken by expounding Christian theology, but I do not think he understood.

We learned that inside the castle walls are stately gardens where votaries spend their time inhaling the perfume of a thousand flowers. At length, when they grow mad with voluptuous dreams, each is given a knife sharpened to the edge of invisibility. One other thing did I observe, said Friar Yves. When the Old Man rides from his castle he is preceded by a herald carrying a Danish axe. This herald commands all to step aside for one who determines the death of kings.

Long ago in the city of Rayy this order was founded by a learned Muslim, Hasan Ibn al-Sabbah, who admired every sort of knowledge and exchanged verse with Omar Khayyam. Youths of impetuous disposition entered his service. They were taught the subtle art of courtesy and were privileged to meet travelers who spoke all the languages on earth. When they had become subject to the will of Hasan they were given brightly polished knives and charged to murder some lord of high degree. So they would go and spy upon the lord to acquaint themselves with his habits and kept their tongues oiled until they fulfilled the mandate. Thus, wrongly, did they anticipate heavenly bliss. They failed to perceive the sovereign light.

During the time of Richard Lionheart his nephew, Henry, chanced to be at Tortosa when a messenger arrived saying the Old Man wished Lord Henry to visit, saying he wished they might become friends. Lord Henry accepted this invitation. He was respectfully met by the Old Man at the fortress gate. If you command your men, said he, do they obey? Lord Henry replied that they did. Consider this, the Old Man said, holding up a white cloth at which every Assassin on the ramparts leapt to death in the valley below. Lord Henry marveled. As they went inside the Old Man pointed to a sharp iron stake and threw down the cloth, so the nearest Assassin lunged to impale himself. Count Henry begged him to prove his authority no further. And when it came time to depart the Old Man loaded Henry with gifts and vowed to murder anyone he named. Such are the Assassins, those who offered Lord Conrad de Montferrat a letter to read on the streets of Tyre. We know that our Sovereign rules by the helm of goodness, albeit we do not comprehend the turns and parallels of His universe.

King Louis decided near the beginning of Lent that we should proceed to Caesarea, a town forty leagues closer to Jerusalem, which the Saracens had destroyed.

While we were rebuilding and fortifying Caesarea as best we could here came a noble from Senaingan, Alenard, who said his vessel was built in the kingdom of

Norway, which lies close to the edge of the world. He had sailed around Spain and through the straits of Morocco, a perilous voyage. He said that in Norway it is possible to observe the sunset merge with dawn. Some believed this. Others scoffed. Alenard and his men betook themselves to hunt lions. They would spur toward a lion and shoot arrows, causing the beast to spring at them. Next they would drop a blanket or old tunic and the lion would tear it apart because he thought he devoured a man. All the while they kept shooting arrows. I do not know how many lions they killed. King Louis retained Alenard in his service along with eight or ten knights.

Philippe de Toucy arrived while we were at Caesarea. King Louis referred to him as cousin because he was descended from a sister of King Philip. He informed us that the emperor of Constantinople had struck up an alliance with Comans, who are devoted to war. The emperor and his nobles were bled, their blood poured into a large silver goblet. The Coman chief with his nobles did likewise. Water and wine were poured into this blood, after which all drank from the goblet. Next they formed ranks and made a dog run between them, slashing it with their swords, meanwhile shouting that whoever defaulted on this treaty would suffer the same fate.

Lord Philippe told us how an important Coman knight was buried. They attired the corpse handsomely and seated it on a chair in a deep grave. They let down the knight's favorite horse into the grave. Then his bravest sergeant bade the lords farewell. Each put silver or gold into his scarf, admonishing him not to forget what he had been given since they would want it back when they reached the other world. And the sergeant answered that he would faithfully account for it. Now he was handed a letter to the first of the Coman kings, which praised him as a trustworthy, obedient servant who should be rewarded. The sergeant next descended into the grave. Planks, stones, and earth were heaped on top, raising a huge mound in honor of the knight. Philippe said he witnessed this amazing spectacle while at the Coman camp. He remained in the service of King Louis for one year, after which he went back to Constantinople.

deus lo volt!

Now here came those predicant friars who departed from Cyprus with Christian effigies and a vermilion tent. Many among us had not thought to see them again. What adventures they recounted left us agape as if we heard some ancient epic, or looked upon some tapestry of days half remembered. These friars sailed away from Cyprus to Antioch, after which they traveled overland, riding ten leagues a day for one full year to reach the great khan of the Tartars. They rode past the ruins of cities destroyed by these nomads, which astonished them. They wondered at the devastation and inquired about it. They were told that once the Tartars lived on an immense sandy plain where nothing would grow, at the end of which stood huge and terrible rocks marking the edge of the world. Among these rocks lived the satanic nations of Gog and Magog, destined to march forth when Antichrist makes his evil presence felt. And since nothing would grow on this desolate plain the Tartars paid tribute for pasturage to Prester John, or as some called him Presbyter John, who lived very far to the east and was reputed to be Nestorian Christian. Some thought Prester John descended from the Magi because he ruled as they did and carried an emerald scepter. In such contempt did he hold Tartars that when they arrived with tribute he would not look at them. He turned his back. So finally the Tartars understood that if they wished to escape from bondage they must stop quarreling among themselves, which they did, enabling them to defeat the vast armies of Prester John and everyone else. It may be that Prester John fled to Egypt, mayhap Nubia, where he now lives and is at least two centuries old.

The friars told us that people in distant lands to the east are so frightened that they behave like oxen when Tartars ride into their villages and make no effort to defend themselves. A single horseman may capture an entire village. On one occasion a Tartar met seventeen Arabs, whereupon he demanded that they rope themselves together and follow him. They had begun to obey when all unexpected one lifted his head as though perceiving the light of the world and slew the Tartar. What should Christians make of this? Do we not see how pagans arrogate to themselves unwarranted jurisdiction over others? We thank Almighty God who is our bulwark against oppression.

We learned that Tartars do not eat bread but content themselves with meat and mare's milk spiced with herbs. Horseflesh is what they like best. They steep it in brine and leave it to dry until it may be cut like bread, but they will eat the flesh of any creature. When riding off to war they put slices of flesh under the lappets of their clothing and sit on it until the blood is pressed out, after which they devour it like animals. Some they keep in a leather pouch, dip into this when they feel hungry and choose the oldest meat first. I, myself, while imprisoned in Egypt saw one of my guards do this. He was a Khorasmin from Persia and the stench from his leather pouch drew vultures out of the sky.

Many other strange things did the predicants tell us. They spoke of Greek Christians among the Tartars, but could not say how this came about. If the Tartars decide to make war on Saracens they despatch these Christians to fight. Or, if they decide to attack Christians, they enlist Saracens. We were told that women without children accompany the Tartar fighting men and are paid the same. They take meals together, but the men do not seek relations with them. As we listened to such remarkable accounts we did not know what to think.

The predicants delivered a letter from the Tartar chief to King Louis, stating that nothing gratified him more than peace. If there is peace there is tranquility, said this letter, whence come all blessings. Animals graze unmolested and men till the fields without apprehension. But now you must listen to us. You cannot enjoy peace until you render obeisance. Prester John foolishly challenged us, as did the shah of Persia and others too numerous to mention. If you would remain at peace you will send money to us every year. If you refuse, we will ride against you and without mercy put you to the sword.

The predicants told King Louis that the great khan summoned princes who had not yet vowed allegiance and displayed the chapel his majesty had sent from Cyprus, together with little carved figures representing Nativity, Baptism, Holy Ghost, and so forth. He told them the king of France had sued for mercy and sent this tribute. Therefore, the khan told these princes, unless you likewise submit I will order the king of France to come and destroy you. At his words many shook with fright and pledged themselves vassals.

As to his majesty's thoughts upon hearing this, I do not know. He did not confide in me.

We stayed fourteen months at Caesarea. One day when I went to visit the king he brought up the fact that I had not agreed to remain past Easter and he asked how he might induce me to stay another year. I remembered quite well that he once called me difficult, so I said I would strike a bargain with him. If during that year I ask for something, I said, you will not become annoyed. For my part, if you fail to grant my request, I will not be annoyed with you. At this he began to laugh and told his counselors about the bargain we had made.

I had now been oversea with his majesty some four years and attempted to keep my life organized as best I could. I arranged my bed so that anyone entering the pavilion could see me, because I did not want anyone to suspect me of relations with women. I had two chaplains recite the Hours. At dawn one of them chanted mass. The other waited until all of my people were up. After hearing mass I would visit the king. If he wished to go out riding I accompanied him. Each year during the feast of Saint Remigius it was my habit to buy pigs and sheep and flour and wine and whatever else we might need to keep us through the winter because we could not depend upon vessels arriving. I would purchase one hundred barrels of wine and the best of it we drank first. Squires and servants got wine mixed with water, that of servants containing somewhat more water. As for knights at my table, each received a flagon of wine and a water bottle. How they mixed it was their own business.

During this time a certain knight unwisely visited a brothel where he was arrested. According to custom he might be led through camp

421

by the whore, bound with a rope and wearing only his shirt, or he might surrender horse and arms to the king. This knight would not submit to public disgrace, hence he was dismissed from the army. I then approached King Louis to ask if I might have the knight's horse for an impoverished gentleman. He said I was asking a lot because the animal was worth a good eighty livres. It appeared to me that he was annoyed so I complained that he had broken our agreement. He laughed and said he was not annoyed. All the same I did not get the horse.

Round about this time one of his sergeants who was called Le Goulu began trifling with one of my knights and gave him a push. Straightway I went to the king for satisfaction, but he did not think it important and advised me to forget the matter. I said I would not. Sergeants could not be allowed to jostle knights here or there as they pleased, said I, and if his majesty denied me justice I would no longer remain in his service. What moved the king to yield, I do not know, but the sergeant appeared at my quarters barefoot, wearing only a shirt. He knelt in front of the knight and said he had come to make amends. He offered the pommel of his sword, saying his hand should be cut off at the wrist. It seemed to me that justice had been done so I asked my knight to forgive the insult, which he did.

Seldom would King Louis be swayed by importunity. Brother Hugues de Jouy on behalf of the Temple went to Damascus and came back with an agreement whereby a tract of land should be divided, one half to the sultan, one half to the Temple. Brother Hugues brought a document proving it was so and was accompanied by an emir to represent the sultan. The king was much surprised. He informed the Grand Master that a treaty ought not to have been negotiated without his approval. Reparation was due, said the king. He ordered three flaps of his pavilion lifted so all might watch the punishment. He directed the Grand Master to walk barefoot through the camp attended by his knights, all barefoot. Thus humiliated they approached his majesty. He commanded the Templar and the Saracen deputy to seat themselves, after which he addressed the Templar in a harsh voice.

Master, said he, you will inform the sultan's envoy that you regret having made this truce. Further, you will release the sultan from all he has promised and you will give back the document.

The Grand Master complied, admitting he had done wrong to enter upon the agreement and regretted his temerity.

Now rise up, the king said, you with all your knights. And when they were on their feet he bade them kneel and repent. The Grand Master knelt, holding out the hem of his cloak, thereby offering to King Louis everything the Temple possessed. Next, his majesty expelled Brother Hugues from the kingdom. And not the queen herself, nor anyone, could prevent this.

Soon thereafter came his majesty's envoys from Egypt with a treaty drawn up committing us to help the emirs against the sultan of Damascus. In exchange, the emirs would deliver to us the Holy City. It had been agreed that we should march to Joppa while they would put ashore at Gaza twenty leagues distant.

To Joppa we went and set up camp in fields around the castle, which rises handsomely to overlook the sea. At once we undertook new fortifications and the king himself carried a hod filled with earth. The sultan of Damascus, when he learned how matters stood, despatched four thousand Turks to Gaza to prevent the Egyptians from joining us. As a result, the emirs did not keep their end of the bargain. Still, they did send us Christian heads that had been suspended from the walls of Cairo. His majesty buried these heads in consecrated ground. And they delivered captive children, albeit with reluctance. These children, too young to distinguish truth from falsehood, had been persuaded to embrace the iniquitous teaching of Islam. The emirs also gave his majesty an elephant, which he shipped to France.

423

How often are we led astray through error and foolish misjudgment. A Turkish noble thought to reap corn not three leagues from our camp. We went after him. The instant he saw us he flew away but a young squire pursued him, knocked down two of his knights, and thrust a lance into his body with such violence that the shaft broke.

The Master of Saint Lazarus, showing no better sense than this Turk, made up his mind to capture some animals in a valley near Ramlah. Off he went and did not inform the king. Turks fell upon him so briskly that of all his men just four returned alive. He himself came thundering into camp lifting such alarum as might be heard in Constantinople. I therefore armed myself and urged his majesty to let me go after the Saracens. He consented, but told me to order up knights from the Temple and Hospital. When we got to the valley we found the king's crossbowmen ahead of us. A Saracen and one of the king's men had rushed at each other with lances and both went down. Another of the king's men decided to steal their horses and was leading them off when the stopple of an old cistern splintered beneath their weight and down plummeted three horses and a thieving sergeant, all four to the bottom. I had a look. There was little enough to see. The cistern walls were falling in on them so they were about covered up. We then rode back to camp having registered no loss save that occasioned by the stupid Master of Saint Lazarus.

Now here came the youthful prince of Antioch into camp, accompanied by his mother. King Louis honored them and ceremoniously dubbed the boy a knight and gave leave to quarter his arms, which are gules, with the arms of France. In their company three minstrels from Armenia, brothers on pilgrimage to Jerusalem. These minstrels played horns so devised that the music seemed to issue not in front but from aside. They played such melodious and graceful tunes that people were reminded of swans on a lake. Also, they knew how to flip themselves over while standing on a mat. They could do this backward and forward, but the eldest would pause to cross himself before turning the somersault forward.

King Louis was informed that if he wished to visit Jerusalem the sultan of Damascus would guarantee safe passage. Not one counselor advised his majesty to go since he would be obliged to leave it in

Saracen hands. They spoke of King Richard sixty years earlier. They repeated the story, how one of Richard's knights shouted for him to come and behold Jerusalem. But he would not. He shielded his eyes, he wept bitterly and cried aloud. Dear God, suffer me not to see the Holy City for I cannot reclaim it! The counselors mentioned this because, they said, if his majesty should make the pilgrimage and return to France without loosening the Saracen grip, those who came later would feel satisfied to do no more. If he took this counsel to heart or some other reason prevailed, I do not know, but he remained at Joppa.

Anon the sultan's rage against those emirs who chased his cousin Turanshah into the Nile and butchered him like a pig caused him to march against Egypt. I have heard they fought savagely, gaining little here or there. The sultan boasted of victory yet with such losses that he returned to Gaza, he himself injured in the head and one hand. We observed his army withdraw, passing our camp less than two leagues distant, avoiding it as the traveler avoids the hedgehog. With the sultan, we estimated, went twenty thousand Turks and ten thousand Bedouin. We kept narrow watch.

This Turkish horde came next to Acre and threatened to ravage the gardens unless they got fifty thousand gold bezants. The lord of Arsuf, who was constable, answered that he would give them none. So they arrayed themselves to prepare a siege. Forth came the lord of Arsuf and took his position on Mount Saint John by the cemetery of Saint Nicholas to defend the gardens. Foot sergeants also ventured from the city to harass the Turks with bows and crossbows, but did not adequately consider the situation. The lord of Arsuf therefore directed a Genoese knight called Giannone to recall them. He was herding them toward safety when a Turk cried out in Saracenic, offering to joust with him, had he courage enough. Sir Giannone answered that quite willingly would he take the challenge. But as he was riding against this enemy he saw to his left a troop of eight or nine who had paused to watch the joust. He swerved toward them and skewered one. Another struck his steel cap a huge blow with a mace, whereupon Giannone drew his sword and there went the Saracen's turban flying off his head. Another Turk he slashed backhand so the enemy's spear flew off into the field. Then he brought back the imperiled sergeants. These fine strokes were observed by the lord of Arsuf, by important citizens, and by women who gathered on the walls to watch.

Next the infidels marched toward Saida, which they heard was poorly fortified. Lord Simon de Montbéliard, who had charge of his majesty's crossbowmen, retreated into the castle because he could not oppose such a multitude. We were told that he admitted to safety as many citizens as he could. The Turks got into Saida, butchered every inhabitant, and made off to Damascus with plunder. King Louis had wished to fortify some hillock that was a stronghold of Maccabees in ancient times, but hearing this sad news, hearing the barons argue against restoring a crumbled ruin, he decided we should go to Saida. Accordingly we broke camp on the feast day of Peter and Paul and some days afterward came to the sands of Acre. While we were bivouacked a troop of Armenians showed up. They had with them an interpreter so we learned they were en route to Jerusalem, having paid the Turks heavy tribute. They wanted a good look at our king. I therefore went and found him in a pavilion sitting on the sand without a carpet beneath his rump, resting his back against the pole. I explained about the Armenians waiting outside, how they besought me to let them glimpse our pious leader. For myself, I said, I have no desire to kiss your bones. He began to laugh and told me to bring them in, which I did. When they had their fill of gazing at King Louis they commended him to God. He, with inherent grace, returned the blessing.

Next night we camped by a ford with excellent water. People of that region use it to nourish sugar plants. Next we camped by Es Sur, which the Bible calls Tyre, and King Louis asked if we should capture the city of Banyas before continuing to Saida. The barons liked this idea but none wanted the king himself to join such a dangerous expedition. Only after much argument could he be dissuaded. Knights of the Temple and Hospital were chosen, along with the Comte d'Eu, Philippe de Montfort, Gilles le Brun, myself, and various others. We rode all night and got to Banyas just before dawn. Ancients called this place Caesarea Philippi. A spring rising within the city is known as the Jor. Another beautiful spring rising from the plain outside is called Dan. The river Jordan is formed where these two intermingle. Here was our Savior baptized.

When the Turks inside Banyas realized that our sergeants were breaking through the walls they lost heart. They fled toward the castle of Subeibah half a league up the mountain where the slope was strewn with rocks as big as hutches. I was directed to occupy a position on the slope but a troop of Germans belonging to the Comte d'Eu, seeing these Turks retreat, came flying past me to go after them. I called out that they were exceeding orders but they ignored me. Soon enough they saw they had made a mistake and turned back, whereupon the enemy regained courage, attacking with arrows and maces. My sergeants did not like the look of this because they were afoot. I said if they gave up our position they would be dismissed from the king's service. They pointed out that it was easy for me to talk, considering that I was on horseback. Very well, I said, if that troubles you, and dismounted and sent my horse to the Templars. A little while afterward one of my knights, Jean de Bussey, was struck in the throat by a Turkish quarrel. He dropped at my feet. His uncle, Hugues d'Escot, asked me to help carry Jean's body down the slope but I was angry with all who disobeyed orders. Bad luck to you and to anybody who helps you, I said, because you deserve it. I then added that he might lug his nephew's corpse to the dungheap by himself but as for me I would not move. I was told afterward that the barons of Languedoc had been informed of my perilous situation and urged to rescue me, but Guillaume de Beaumont said there was little sense worrying because I already was killed. I do not know who told him this. In any event, they decided to find out if I was on my back or on my feet so they could report to the king. Olivier de Termes, Jean de Valenciennes, and others came riding along the

427

slope and I think were surprised to find me upright. Olivier explained what I knew quite well, that it would be a good idea to get out of there, but I did not see how, since the Turks above us would come rolling down like an avalanche if we turned our backs. Olivier replied that he had a plan. All right, I said, tell us what to do. He said we should ride along as if we were going to Damascus so the Turks would think we meant to attack from the opposite side. Then after we got down on the plain we should cross the brook and do them some damage by setting fire to the corn in the fields. It did not sound like a good plan but I had no better idea. So, having got myself another mount, we did as he suggested and with the help of Almighty God made it to the cornfields. There at Olivier's direction we took hollow canes of the sort used in flutes, stuffed them with live coals and went around burning heaps of threshed corn. Some time later when we got back to camp, grateful to be alive, we learned that nobody had given us a thought.

Next day we continued to Saida where the king was. We were told that he personally supervised the burial of citizens murdered by Turks and helped carry putrid bodies to the trench, but did not hold his nose as others did. By the time we arrived he was meting out sites where we would camp. I had been given space not far from the youthful and spirited Comte d'Eu, which pleased me because I enjoyed his company. He reveled in pranks. I had my tent pitched in such a way that while at table we might take advantage of light through the aperture and he would often watch us. He constructed a tiny machine like a petrary from which he let fly pebbles, breaking several jugs and tumblers. Someone gave him a bear cub that he turned loose among my chickens. The poultry woman flogged the bear with her distaff but it killed a dozen before my men arrived and put a stop to the business.

We were busy fortifying Saida when some merchants appeared at our camp with news that a Tartar host had captured Baghdad. This was accomplished through treachery. After the city had been surrounded the Tartar chief sent to the caliph, saying he would like to arrange marriage between their children. The caliph agreed, however reluctantly, because he did not think Baghdad was strong enough to withstand a siege. The Tartars asked him to send forty members of his council who would swear to this marriage. He complied. Then he was asked to send forty notable citizens who would stand surety. This, too, he did. Now the Tartars would have forty more, chosen from among the wisest men at court. Again the caliph did as they requested. And the Tartar chief, having got all these important men in his grasp, lopped off their heads. Next he assaulted and took the city because he knew that without their leaders the people would not put up much resistance. We were told that he held the foolish caliph in an iron cage and for a long time gave him almost nothing to eat. Then he asked if the caliph was hungry. The caliph replied that he was nearly dead of starvation. The Tartar placed before him a gold dish full of jewels and asked if he recognized them. I do, said the caliph, because they were mine. Do you prize them? asked the Tartar. I do, said the caliph. Eat them, the Tartar said. They are not food, said the caliph. Now listen to me, said the Tartar. Had you bestowed this useless treasure upon your men they would have given their lives to defend you.

So much did these merchants allege. What became of the caliph, they did not seem to know. God affright misbelievers.

One morning the king asked me to go for a ride with him. While crossing a field we rode past a little church and since the doors were open we could hear a priest chanting mass. The king said this church was built to honor a miracle performed by our Lord. Then he said he would like to attend mass, if I did not mind. I told him that would be a good thing. We dismounted and went inside. The cleric who assisted the priest had a black and shaggy look and I could not help thinking he might be one of the Assassins, therefore when it came time to offer us the pax I took it from the cleric and brought it myself to his majesty. Afterward we continued riding and chanced upon the legate. His majesty complained of my behavior so I explained to the legate that I felt anxious for the king's safety because I mistrusted the cleric. The legate said I had acted properly. He did not, retorted the king. There in the field they took to arguing while I kept silent. This happened because the king was unable to imagine men less honorable than himself.

Anon, Queen Marguerite arrived by sea from Joppa where she had lately given birth to the Lady Blanche. I went to greet her and escorted her with the infant and her son Jean Tristram to the castle, after which I went looking for his majesty. I found him at prayer in the chapel. He inquired about them and I replied that all seemed in good health. This was the first time in five years he had spoken of them. Whether he talked about his family with others, I do not know. Nor do I understand how a man could be so distant from his wife and children. To me it does not seem right.

I asked his majesty if I might go on pilgrimage to the shrine of our Lady of Tortosa where numerous miracles had occurred. For instance, while we were in Egypt a man possessed by the Devil was brought to the shrine. As friends prayed to restore his health the Devil's voice could be heard from inside his body. She is not here! the Devil shrieked. Our Lady is in Egypt aiding the king of France! And the date of this was written down, the document later shown to the legate. He, himself, told me about it. Nor can the miracle be doubted since on that very day she helped our cause. She might have come yet more strongly to our aid, had we not angered her and the Lord Jesus. Be this as it may, King Louis gave me leave to go and he commissioned me to buy a hundred lengths of camlet in divers colors, saying he would give it to the Franciscans when we got back to France. At these words I knew we would not stay much longer oversea.

deus lo volt!

While we were in Tripoli and I had bought the camlet my knights began to jest, wondering what I would do with so much fabric. I returned them good measure. Perhaps, I said, I have stolen it and mean to earn a profit. We were nobly entertained by the prince of that city. He honored us and wished to give us valuable presents, but we accepted only a few relics in his majesty's name.

When we got back I instructed one of my knights to deliver four lengths of cloth to Queen Marguerite while I took the rest to King Louis. Later I was told that no sooner did my knight enter her majesty's chamber carrying a linen bundle than she mistook it for a packet of holy articles and knelt. My lady, he said, these are not relics but cloth sent by my lord of Joinville. At this she and her attendants began to laugh and she wished me the worst of luck for having made her kneel before my fabric.

While we were yet engaged at repairing the fortifications of Saida his majesty received a wonderful gift, a stone that could be split into flakes, over and over again. If one of these flakes or scales was lifted there could be seen a fish made entirely of stone, eyes, bones, tail, everything stone. We were amazed and swore these little fishes must have been alive. His majesty gave me a fragment containing a tench, brown in color, each aspect of a tench just as it ought to be.

Here at Saida in the year of our Lord 1253 we were notified of the Queen Mother's ascent to glory. The news was a long time coming, she departed six months previous. King Louis did not speak for two days. I was then told he wished to see me. When I came into his presence he stretched out both arms. Seneschal, I have lost my mother, he said. I replied that it must happen. Yet I wonder at this display of grief, I went on. As you know, Sire, a wise man long ago remarked that what pain a man feels in his heart should not be visible on his face, lest it delight his enemies and trouble his friends.

I believe the king scarcely knew his father. Louis VIII was by all accounts a vigorous young sovereign when he resolved to campaign against heretics in Languedoc and died unexpectedly at Montpensier. Most thought him poisoned. However it was, Queen Blanche thenceforth guided young Louis. He must listen to the hours of the Office each day. He must listen to sermons on feast days. I myself think, and heard it said, that she would rather her son incur temporal death than by any mortal sin displease the Lord.

As we later found out, in November of the previous year she retired to the Cistercian abbey of Maubuisson and devoted her last days to spiritual exercise while clothed in the habit of a nun. According to his majesty's brother Charles, when she felt death forthcoming she lost the ability to speak. Priests and clerics hesitated, uncertain what to do. But all at once she herself began to intone Subvenite Sancti Dei, muttering the prayer between her teeth, yielding her soul little by little as though reluctant to concede.

Toward young Queen Marguerite she behaved with uncommon harshness. Indeed, she would try to prevent the king from seeing his consort. The palace his majesty most enjoyed was at Pointoise, mayhap because his wife's chamber was beneath his own, the two connected by a winding staircase so they could meet without interference. They directed ushers to knock on the door with rods if the Queen Mother approached, whereupon the king would hurry up to his quarters. Once while Marguerite lay near death after childbirth the Queen Mother took his majesty by the hand and told him to come away because he was doing no good. At this Marguerite cried out and fainted. Only then did King Louis summon strength enough to withdraw from his imperious mother.

Soon after I had spoken with the king about his mother's death I was approached by Madame de Vertus asking me to go and comfort Queen Marguerite who was prostrate with grief. I found her weeping, which astonished me. My lady, I said, he who first observed that a man cannot know how a woman will respond spoke truly. The Queen Mother detested you. Now she is dead. Why do you grieve?

Not for her do I grieve, she answered, but that my husband should feel such loss.

His majesty held more than one office for the deceased queen and he sent to France a trunk full of letters addressed to all the churches, requesting prayers for her soul.

Now with Saida almost rebuilt he ordered processions through the camp, after each of which the legate exhorted us to pray that King Louis should do whatever most pleased God, whether he remained in the Holy Land or embarked to France. Later I was summoned to a courtyard where the legate ceremoniously informed me that King Louis was pleased with my service. Further, said he, I am to tell you that the king will return to France this coming Easter.

May it be so, I replied.

The legate asked me to his quarters. He led me to an empty room, shut the door, took my hands and began weeping. When he had recovered he told me how glad he was that we would soon escape this diabolic land. For myself, he went on, the thought of leaving such honorable company fills me with regret since I must go back to Rome and conduct myself as best I can among those treacherous people.

It seemed to me that our companions were less honorable than he thought. I had on one occasion told him of sins committed in the city of Acre as they were related to me by a priest and he responded that none knew better than himself what deplorable acts were done. It behooves God to avenge them, he had said, in such wise that the streets will be washed by the blood of citizens and others come to take their place. The legate prophesied much too well.

At the beginning of Lent we returned to Acre and King Louis supervised preparations for the voyage. His fleet consisted of thirteen galleys and sailing ships. All had been made ready in time for the king and his consort to embark on the vigil of Saint Mark.

Next morning the wind rose fair. His majesty told me that he was born on Saint Mark's Day, to which I answered that he might call himself reborn if one took into account what we had been through.

Saturday we came in view of Cyprus and the mountain that is known as Mountain of the Cross. Unluckily a mist blew down from

433

the island, so we did not know how close we were and fetched a sand-bank. Up went a huge cry with mariners shouting and wringing their hands in terror of being drowned. It happened I was in bed when we struck. I therefore got up and went on deck. Just as I reached the forecastle I heard Brother Raymond, who was a Templar in charge of the crew, order one of his people to throw the lead. Almost at once a sailor cried for mercy since we were aground. Brother Raymond howled that we were lost and clawed his beard and tore his garment. Now here came one of my knights, Jean de Monson, with a lined sur-coat to put around my shoulders because I wore only a tunic. I de-manded to know what use I had of a surcoat if we were going to drown, but he said he did not want me to catch a chill. The mariners shouted for a galley to rescue the king, but not one drew near. Later I understood the wisdom of this. We had eight hundred people aboard who would have hopped from our vessel like rats to save their lives and a galley would capsize.

By God's grace we drifted off the sandbank, although we did not realize this until the lead was thrown a second time. Brother Ray-mond went to inform his majesty and found him supine on deck be-fore the altar, arms outstretched to form a cross, barefoot and hair uncombed, ready to be drowned.

Next morning we understood how fortunate we were to scrape ourselves on the sandbank, for beyond it was a rock.

His majesty brought master mariners from other vessels who sent down divers to investigate the damage. Each reported a great length of keel missing. We think the timbers are out of joint, the mariners said, and they advised his majesty to board another ship because ours might fall apart. The king then consulted various lords including the archdeacon of Nicosia, chamberlain Pierre, Gilles le Brun who was Constable, Gervais d'Escraines, and myself, because he wished to know what we advised. We told him we thought it best to accept the advice of master seamen, for in worldly matters one should rely upon those with experience.

The king now turned to these master mariners. What would you do, he asked, if the vessel belonged to you and was freighted with your goods? Would you abandon her?

They replied in unison that indeed they would not, but would sooner risk drowning than spend four thousand livres on another ship.

Then, said the king, why should I quit her?

Sire, they answered, the stakes are not equivalent. Gold and silver may be weighed, whereas the lives of yourself, your queen, and your children may not.

I have listened to all opinions, said the king. Here is my judgment. Were I to board another vessel I would leave behind these hundreds of pilgrims, each of whom treasures his life as I do mine. Many would choose to land on Cyprus rather than subject themselves to a fitful sea. And these, perhaps, might never return to France. Therefore, he continued, he would not do such harm to his people but would entrust himself, his wife, and his children to the hands of the Lord.

In my opinion we had been tried enough, yet no more did we escape the sandbank than a fierce wind drove us toward the island. Anchors were tossed out to halt our progress but we drifted forward. We did not stop till the mariners had thrown out five anchors. Gilles le Brun and I lay miserably in the king's chamber when the door opened and there was Queen Marguerite looking for her husband. She wanted him to vow that he would undertake a pilgrimage of some sort if we might be saved, mariners having told her they could promise nothing. I did not know where the king was, but I said there was one thing she herself might do. She might promise the Lord that if we got safely home she would commission a silver ship to the value of five marks in the name of the king, herself, and their children. For, said I, only last night when we hit the sandbank I vowed to Saint Nicholas that if he would preserve us I would walk barefoot from Joinville to his shrine at Varangeville. The queen replied that she would promise a silver ship worth five marks if I stood surety for Saint Nicholas. I answered that I would. Then off she went, but in a

435

while came back to tell us that Saint Nicholas had listened, for the wind had fallen.

Now as the storm abated King Louis seated himself on the bulwarks and told me to sit at his feet. Seneschal, he began, our Lord has visibly manifested His strength in that with a single wind He might have drowned the king of France with his wife and children and all this company. The saints inform us that tribulation should be held as a warning, therefore we ought to look within ourselves to see how we have angered Him. And we should cast out whatever we find offensive, since otherwise He may smite us with death or some other calamity.

After a while he continued. You know, the saint addresses God in this manner. O Lord, why dost Thou intimidate us? Our end could not diminish Thee, nor could our deliverance enhance Thee. And therefore, Seneschal, admonitions arise out of God's vast love for us, that we may perceive our deficiencies and purge ourselves of what He finds abhorrent.

Then his majesty was a long time silent.

Olivier de Termes, a valiant knight who distinguished himself in the Holy Land, disembarked at Cyprus because he nurtured a fear of drowning. Such were the difficulties of travel that almost two years would elapse before he saw France again, although he was a wealthy lord with money enough for passage. Lesser folk might well be condemned to life on that island. So it may be seen how the king spoke truly.

After we had taken aboard fresh water and provisions we departed Cyprus and came to the island of Lampedusa. Here we caught a great many rabbits. Also, we visited a deserted hermitage among the rocks and saw a garden that was laid out by these monks. A pleasant stream trickled through it. We walked down the slope and entered a grotto in which we found a lime-washed oratory with a red cross made of baked clay. In another grotto we saw the skeletons of two men who lay as though asleep, the bones of their hands folded on their ribs. They were laid toward the east like those consigned to earth.

deus lo volt!

Upon returning to our ship we learned that a seaman had deserted. Our captain thought he might have decided to become a hermit. We left three sacks of biscuit where he might find them and continued our voyage.

Next we came to Pantalaria in the midst of the sea. Queen Marguerite wished to obtain fruit for her children, but his majesty was reluctant to put men ashore because the inhabitants of this island were Saracen. At last he consented and despatched three galleys, telling the captains they should not loiter but quickly rejoin the fleet. They pulled ahead in the direction of a small harbor. We did not see them when we passed by so we thought they must have been captured. Our seamen advised his majesty not to wait, pointing out that we were between Sicily and Tunis, kingdoms that did not love us. Give us leave to sail on and by dawn we shall pass through this strait, said they with anxious looks. His majesty refused to listen. He said he would not leave his people in Saracen hands and make no effort to rescue them. Turn your sails, he ordered, so that we may attack.

Now the queen became distraught and cried aloud that it was all her doing. Yet even as sails were rigged to catch a landward breeze we observed the galleys pulling toward us. When they got near the king asked why they dawdled and they answered that six young gentlemen of Paris had wandered about the gardens eating fruit and nobody could persuade them to leave. We could not abandon them, said the mariners, so it is not our fault. His majesty ordered these six young men put in a longboat, which is the place for cutthroats and thieves, whereat they threw up their hands and began to howl, imploring him to show mercy, saying they would be disgraced the rest of their lives. The queen and all of us joined this lament but nothing would dissuade King Louis from his purpose. Into the longboat they went and there they sat till we got to land, wretched and terrified by waves dashing in their faces. Yet his majesty was right, since by their greediness to eat fruit they had made us turn about and delayed us.

Before we made port one of the queen's attendants after seeing her mistress to bed quite foolishly set the queen's kerchief near a

437

candle. Then she went to the cabin where women slept. In due time the candle burned low, touched the kerchief, and flames spread to a cloth protecting her majesty's garments. I was told the queen hopped naked out of bed, tossed the kerchief overboard and extinguished the fire while our six cutthroats in the longboat began to shout. I myself, hearing some alarm, opened my eyes and there was her majesty's kerchief flaming lightly on the sea. If Saint Nicholas or another patron watched over us I could not guess, yet I think we were but moments from lighting up the sea in all directions.

One morning a wealthy gentleman of Provence, Lord Dragonet, lay sleeping on his ship, which sailed a league ahead of us. Early sun wakened him so he called a squire to cloak the porthole. The boy, finding he could not manage it from inside the cabin, climbed outside. His foot slipped and without any sound he vanished. My Lord Dragonet's ship being small and no dinghy to retrieve the squire, he was left behind. Several aboard the king's ship noticed an object fall in the sea but took it for a cask or tub since the boy did not wave his arms nor struggle to save himself. One of our galleys fished him up and delivered him to us for inspection. I asked the boy why he did nothing to preserve his life and he said he did not think it necessary because he commended himself to our Lady of Vauvert who came to his aid by holding him up till the galley arrived. When we got home I had this miracle pictured in my chapel and on the stained glass windows at Blécourt.

After ten weeks at sea we reached port two leagues from the castle of Hyères. Queen Marguerite and the counselors thought we should disembark, but his majesty declared he would not leave ship until we came to Aigues-Mortes. Nor could anyone persuade him otherwise. Our ship had two rudders attached so we could turn right or left as easily as a ploughhorse can be guided and the king beckoned to me while seated on one of the tillers.

Seneschal, give me your opinion, he said. What do you think of disembarking at this place?

I replied that it seemed a good idea, since if we did not we might deus lo volt!

emulate Madame de Bourbon who would not get off here but insisted on going to Aigues-Mortes, which through contrary wind
took six weeks.

His majesty summoned the council and repeated what I had said.
Everyone urged him to disembark, pointing out that by continuing
to Aigues-Mortes he would further imperil his wife and children. At
last he consented, which enormously relieved the queen.

While preparations were being made for our journey overland
here came the abbot of Cluny with two excellent mounts, presenting
them to the royal couple. Next day he reappeared. I did not hear
what was said, but I observed the king listen attentively. Later I asked
if I might speak my mind and he gave me leave. I should like to know,
I said, if you granted the abbot a favorable hearing because of these
two fine palfreys. The king thought a while. At last he replied that, in
fact, he did.

Sire, I continued, do you know my purpose?

The king told me to go on.

If, said I, officials of the realm who have sworn to dispense justice
are permitted to accept gifts you may be sure they will listen favor-
ably, even as yourself. Accordingly, Sire, I would urge you when we return to prohibit all benefaction.

The king summoned his counselors and repeated what I had said.
All made haste to agree that my advice was sound, yet one or two
looked at me without pleasure.

Another sort of cleric, Brother Hugues, a Franciscan much esteemed, was known to be in the vicinity of Hyères. The king sent for
him to come and preach. We saw him approaching a long way off,
which is to say we judged by the crowd following somebody that we
must be watching Brother Hugues.

My lords, there are too many monks at court, said this Franciscan
when he addressed us. Indeed, I count myself one too many. And
these monks have no hope of salvation unless Holy Scriptures lie,
which could not be. For we know that just as a fish cannot live away
from water, so a monk cannot live outside his cloister. If any would

maintain that the court of King Louis is a cloister I respond that it must be the largest ever seen, extending as it does from coast to coast. If they protest they live in utmost austerity for the good of their souls I answer that they feast on meat and drink sparkling wine. Had they stayed in their cells they would not enjoy such ease and comfort.

Thus did he begin with very harsh words. He told us he had read, along with the Bible, numerous works that help to clarify it, but he had not in any book learnt of dominions usurped or lost when claims of truth and justice were respected. Now take heed, said Brother Hugues to his majesty. Upon your return, take heed to govern equitably that you may deserve God's love and that so long as you live He shall not withdraw your patrimony.

Afterward I said we should try to keep Brother Hugues. King Louis said that already he had asked the friar to stay, but he would not. Then, taking me by the hand, his majesty suggested that both of us go and urge Brother Hugues to relent. This seemed a good idea. Our petition had no effect. I further beseeched him to stay with us, at least while the king was in Provence. The Franciscan took this badly.

God will love me better, he said, if I am elsewhere than the king's court.

One day only would he stay with us. Next day he left. I have heard that he lies entombed at Marseille where his bones work miracles.

When it was time to continue our journey we descended from the castle afoot because the hill was quite steep. The king lost patience with his old squire Ponce over some trifling matter and scolded him. I thought this unwarranted. Sire, I began, you should forgive Ponce much, considering that he has served not only yourself but your father and grandfather.

deus lo volt!

Seneschal, the king replied, my grandfather Philip advised me that we should value servants according to merit. By forgiving Ponce we subject ourselves to his ineptitude. That being so, it is we who serve the servant. Further, King Philip advised me that he is not fit to rule who cannot reprove as well as praise.

And I, hearing these words, discovered I was given much to think about.

We passed through the city of Aix where the husk of Mary Magdalene is said to lie entombed. There is a cave in a rock where she lived seventeen years as an anchoress and we went to look at it. Next we proceeded to Beaucaire, at which point I took leave of his majesty. I went to see my niece, the Dauphine de Vienne. I also went to see my uncle, the Comte de Chalon. And separately, because they were much at odds, I visited his son, the Comte de Bourgogne. After that I traveled to Joinville from which I had long been absent.

Presently here came a little silver ship from her majesty, not to the value of five marks but one hundred livres. On deck stood figures of the king, the queen herself, with three children, all most wondrously fashioned of silver. So were little mariners wrought from silver, the mast, the rudder, cordage, all silver, and sails neatly sewn with silver thread. I, for my part, walked barefoot to the shrine of Saint Nicholas at Varangeville to requite his custody and saw Queen Marguerite's ship placed in his chapel.

Some time afterward I rejoined the king at Soissons where he greeted me with such warmth that people whispered. Seeing him now among familiar vanities I thought how much was changed. He had lost his taste for beaver and squirrel fur, ermine, scarlet fabric, gilded stirrups, and the like. His garment now was gray wool, the covering of his bed lambskin or deerskin. At table he did not request special meats but ate what he was given, deprived himself of tender morsels, and did not salt his soup. Wine he tempered with water, more or less according to the wine, and drank from a glass goblet. Once on Cyprus he asked why I put no water to the wine. I said it was the physicians' doing for they told me I had a thick head and cold belly, hence it was not in me to get drunk. He answered that my

441

physicians deceived me. If you do not learn to water the wine until you are old, he said, you will suffer gouts and stomach complaints. Moreover, if when you are old you drink it neat you will get drunk, which is a passing foul thing.

Always he would look to see that his paupers had been fed and he sent money to distribute. If minstrels with viols came to entertain at supper he would not allow grace to be said until they finished singing. Only then did he rise and the priests stood before him to give thanks. If some Franciscan spoke of a book the king might enjoy hearing he would ask that it not be read, saying there could be nothing more satisfactory at table than good discourse.

Often at night he got up from bed to pray. Then the queen would rise and drape a cloak about his shoulders lest he catch cold. She told her confessor that the king seldom noticed. I think he discussed with her the possibility of abdication so that he might become a monk. Wisely she explained that by maintaining peace in the realm he would be more useful to God. I know that when writing privately to friends he called himself Louis of Poissy, referring to the little town where he was baptized. If some wondered that he disdained a royal signature he reminded them how kings are transitory.

Once I disputed Master Robert of Sorbon as to the qualities of a prud'homme, who is brave in body and the loyal servant of Christ. His majesty listened. At length he said he would dearly love that name. For, said he, it is so fine a thing that merely to pronounce the word prud'homme does fill up the mouth agreeably.

Bishop Guy d'Auxerre rebuked King Louis, saying that in his majesty's hands the honor of Christendom declined because no man stood in fear of excommunication. Therefore, said Bishop Guy, we require you to command your bailiffs and your sergeants to compel those who have been excommunicate for one year and one day to conciliate the Church.

Right willingly, his majesty answered, provided I am given knowledge of each case to see for myself if the judgment was appropriate.

Thereupon the prelates, having consulted, informed King Louis they would not divulge such information because it did not fall within his jurisdiction. Then, said his majesty, would he do likewise and withhold from them such knowledge as fell within his province, nor would he compel excommunicates to seek absolution. For if I did, he told them, it would be contrary to the law of God and every principle of justice.

Shrewdly did he administer the realm. He approved Étienne Boileau for the office of provost. And this deputy so upheld his task that scarce a cutthroat or thief ventured across the street. Most embraced the gibbet. Silver, gold, noble lineage, salvage of any sort, nothing availed to skip the noose. Also, his majesty issued a lengthy ordinance framing a more constant state in which he reserved to himself for public benefaction the authority to emend, adapt, construe, or disavow, according to his judgment. Thus the king's domain improved. Things fetched twice their previous value.

Yet here came a messenger from Germany with a letter to the court. And this messenger when he got back to Germany was asked if by chance he saw King Louis. He answered, mockingly, that he had seen a wretched papelard with a hood on his shoulder like a cleric. So did he interpret this exemplary king. Truly, there is error in our thought if what we meet does not meet our expectation.

We got word from the Dominican emissary, William of Ruybroek, who departed Acre in the year of our Lord 1253 with Friar Bartholomew of Cremona. They went looking for the Mongol prince, Sartuq, whom we thought had converted to Christianity. Friar William returned to Antioch on the twenty-ninth day of June in the year 1256, his head perched safely atop his neck, which is more than might be expected. From Antioch he proceeded to Acre and there composed his report to King Louis. We had difficulty believing what we heard as Friar William's account was read, so rare did the journey sound, so uncommon, as if these brothers traveled to the lip of the world. We wondered if we listened to some ancient myth. From Acre they rode to Constantinople, employing an interpreter named Homo Dei, and bought a slave boy called Nicolaus. Also in the party was a certain Gosset of whom Friar William wrote little. Across the Black Sea they went to a Venetian trading post. Thence by oxcart, wearing the garments Mongols wear, which is to say boots lined with felt and a sheepskin pelisse and a hood made of fur, encouraged by rumors of Christians ahead. At night they camped beside a small fire built with dung and cooked a bit of meat. They observed wild asses and numerous other animals on the plain. At the court of Batu, grandson of Genghis Khan, Nicolaus and Gosset were detained, for what purpose is not clear. With no companion save Homo Dei these monks were escorted to the camp of Mangu Khan. Here on the doorstep of a savage they folded their hands and sang joyfully, since it was Christmastide everywhere.

A solis ortus cardine et usque terrae limitem Christum canamus principem natum Maria virgine.

After they had been searched for knives they were led into the presence of the khan, a man of middling age and stature, his nose squashed like a bean. He lolled on a pallet draped with fur, beside him a young wife. His daughter Cirina by a different wife, some Christian woman lately ascended to God, lay on another pallet with several infants. Friar William thought Cirina horribly ugly. On the hearth crackled a fire made from wormwood, thorns, and cow dung. Gold cloth embellished the walls. They were offered mead, rice wine, or mare's milk. Friar William thought it courteous to sample the wine, which he found clear and aromatic. Homo Dei being offered a cup drained it without hesitation, after which he drained another and another so that very soon nobody could understand what he was saying. Mangu Khan himself get drunk. Indeed, if one credits Friar William, during the four months they visited this encampment the khan was all too often drunk.

In the month of April when they resolved to depart he spoke to them concerning his belief. Mongols believe there is but one God, he said. By Him we live and by Him we die. Before Him we are righteous of heart. But just as he gives the hand a variety of fingers, so has

He given mankind a variety of ways. To you has He given Scriptures. Why do you not abide by them? To us he has given soothsayers. We live in peace because we abide by what they tell us.

Friar William and Homo Dei then took leave, carrying a jeweled belt for protection against thunder and lightning. Friar Bartholomew remained at Karakorum because he was ill. As to his fate, God knows.

Friar William survived because he was a fat and sturdy man. Regarding the heathen prince Sartuq, he felt kindly toward Christians but that was all. As for Christianity in Asia, William reported that with Bartholomew he entered a Nestorian church in the village of Cailac and there sang, as loud as they could, Salve regina. Nestorians, he said, practice the faith in fifteen villages of Cathay and have a bishop. Outside these villages, however, the plains swarm with idolaters who wear yellow hoods. He said that hermits abound, living meagerly in the woods and mountains. Nestorians are ignorant of many things, yet contrive to say their offices and have books in Syriac, which they do not understand. Accordingly they sing as do the monks in Syria who are ignorant of grammar, so all is corrupt. They are usurers and drunkards. Some that live with Mongols have taken numerous wives.

He reported seeing a woman called Paquette from Metz in Lorraine who had been captured in Hungary, who prepared a banquet for them as best she could and spoke of all she endured. But now she was happy because she had married a young Russian carpenter and they had three children. She said there was at Karakorum a Parisian goldsmith named William Boucher who constructed a silver tree at the base of which stood four lions with mare's milk spouting from their throats. Gilded serpents writhed among the branches of this tree while rice beer, wine, and boal issued from their mouths. The goldsmith had a brother whose name is Roger who lives on the Grand Pont. This caused us to marvel.

Friar William also reported that while visiting Mangu Khan he

445

saw ambassadors from the sultan of India and they had brought eight leopards that were able to stand on the cruppers of horses. He reported further that the Caspian Sea does not anywhere touch the ocean but is surrounded by land, which contradicts the teaching of Isidore of Seville. All this we found astonishing. As to the Mongols, he did not think they could be converted. They appeared sympathetic to any religion but would submit to none. They were beyond understanding. As for sending aid to Syria, Mangu Khan would do so if Christian rulers acknowledged his sovereignty and came dutifully to pay homage. King Louis therefore felt disappointed because he could not treat on such terms.

During Lent his majesty summoned the barons to consult with him at Paris. I sent word asking to be excused since I was at that time suffering quartan fever, but he insisted. I got to Paris on the eve of Lady Day and could find no one to account for the summons. God willed that I should fall asleep. And while asleep I dreamt of King Louis on his knees before an altar. Prelates robed for service were about to vest him with a chasuble of Reims serge. When I awoke I sent for my priest Guillaume, told him my dream and asked what it meant. He replied that tomorrow King Louis would take the cross. When pressed to explain, he told me that the chasuble signified the cross upon which Christ died for us and was scarlet because of blood streaming from His wounds. Because the chasuble is coarse wool, Guillaume added, the crusade will bring scant profit. After hearing mass I went to the king's chapel and there he was by the scaffolding where relics are kept. A fragment of the True Cross was being handed down.

Next day his majesty took the vow, as did his three sons.

Clerics would remind us that vows of pilgrimage discomfit the devil. They speak of a knight en route to Paris who rode through a gloomy forest and heard frightful groans as devils bemoaned the loss of souls they thought belonged to them, shrieking the names of eminent lords. The knight felt terrified for himself and vowed at once to go on pilgrimage and made a cross of leafy branches to verify his oath. In Paris he told what he had heard, naming those lords named by the devils, and learned they had taken the vow at that same hour. Similarly, clerics remind us that in Flanders are numerous canals we are not able to cross except with much expenditure of time to reach a bridge. However, agile men take up a staff or perch or lance and with its help contrive at one leap to vault across the water. Thus do all who pick up the staff of the cross avoid the long pain of purgatory by crossing to heaven with a leap. Yet I think our saintly king had little need of instruction.

It seemed to me that those who encouraged him to undertake this journey committed mortal sin for he was at that time very weak. He could scarce mount a horse, nor ride with comfort in his coach. What his physicians predicted among themselves I do not know. It was his majesty's brother, Charles d'Anjou, a cold and merciless lord, who persuaded him that Tunis might be taken. The emir, Mustansir, did at times negotiate with Christians and King Louis perhaps thought the infidel ripe for conversion. Or should that plan slip, why then, Tunis ought to be an easy prize and here was a vast resource to use against Egypt. Charles, God help me, resembled his saintly brother as a toad may be likened to a prince. If Charles did not bulge with ambition, then never did any man. His wife Béatrice, avaricious as himself, hungered to wear a crown. So would he found an empire in the Mediterranean such as his ancestors vainly dreamt. So he argued that King Louis ought not squander funds in pursuit of the distant Holy City but go and capture Tunis, next to Cairo which was very rich. And with the king not apt to live much longer, who should benefit? Who might then call the sea his province?

I myself thought his majesty no longer showed good sense. Our beloved sovereign, whose intellect once was equaled only by his grace, now coursed with madness. For what is that we call madness, if not the compound of folly?

The last day I saw him, when I went to take leave, he allowed me to carry him in my arms as if he were a small child, from the house of the Comte d'Auxerre to the Franciscan abbey. He urged me to accompany him, but I said that while we were oversea my estates had become impoverished and my tenants suffered. I told him that if I wished to please God it behooved me to stay and redress what wrongs were done. For if, I said, knowing it would prove detrimental to my subjects, I once more ventured abroad I would not find favor with the Lord who sacrificed Himself for us.

His majesty sailed again from Aigues-Mortes, thinking to redeem the Barbary coast. I know little concerning that voyage. In view of Sardinia he dictated a will. He made land close by the castle of Carthage and nearly at once fell victim to flux. Some few days later he amended his will, replacing as executors two barons who had died from the illness gripping him. Now as he understood the desire of his spirit to leave this world he sent for Prince Philippe, instructing the youth to reign with dignity and consideration. When he finished admonishing his son he requested the sacraments, which he heard with a clear mind because it is known that he repeated each verse of the seven psalms chanted by priests anointing him.

On the final Sunday of his majesty's life Brother Godfrey de Beaulieu found him kneeling on the floor with hands clasped. The night preceding his death he was heard to sigh and twice murmured the holy name of Jerusalem. Shortly before the end he asked to be laid on a bed sprinkled with ashes. He looked upward and beseeched our Lord to show mercy toward Christians on that iniquitous coast. Later he spoke in Latin, commending his spirit to Almighty God. He said nothing else, but at the hour of vespers in the fifty-sixth year of life he departed. This occurred one day after the feast of Saint Bartholomew in our year of grace 1270. The shell of him they boiled in wine and water until the flesh slipped from his bones. These bones they conveyed to France, to Saint Denys where he wished to be laid. The cathedral of Monreale in Palermo received his heart.

Almost at once we heard of miracles worked before the tomb. His Holiness Gregory ordered an inquiry, naming Cardinal Simon de Brie as legate. Further, the pontiff asked Geoffrey de Beaulieu to prepare a summary of the king's virtues. Six years elapsed and the legate's report not finished, His Holiness ascended to God.

His Holiness Martin IV in the year 1280 instituted a public inquiry, this to be directed by the archbishop of Rouen. Sessions opened at Saint Denys. For ten months the commissioners listened. On the king's life, thirty-eight witnesses testified. Charles d'Anjou offered a special deposition from Naples on the virtue of his brother. I myself testified at Saint Denys for two full days.

Concerning miracles, more than three hundred witnesses testified. Among them Master Dudes, canon of Paris, who accompanied his majesty on the last crusade. Master Dudes subsequently fell ill with ague and fever, little hope obtained for his recovery. After settling his affairs, having made confession, he prayed to the king, saying, I beseech you to help me as I have served you. Then in a dream he beheld King Louis dressed all in white embroidered with gold, crowned, a scepter in his hand. The king touched Master Dudes on the head, removing an evil humor that had been the cause of illness. Next morning Master Dudes awoke in high spirits, confounding his physicians by requesting a goblet of wine and a chicken to eat.

The wife of a man who once had served the king testified concerning a flood in her cellar. She recalled that King Louis had given her husband some old peacock feather hats and despatched a lackey to make the sign of the cross over the flood with one of his majesty's hats. By evening curfew, according to what this woman said, the water had receded so much that it was possible to draw wine from casks that had been floating. And next day the flood disappeared, only mud to prove where it stood.

Not least, here was a shoemaker of Saint Denys who mocked

449

those who came to pray, who jeered them, claiming Henry of England was greater than King Louis. So a malady struck his leg and he was cured only by repenting his words and kneeling in prayer.

Twenty-eight years after King Louis ascended to glory he was lifted from his tomb, carried by a great number of archbishops and bishops to the dais where he would be honored. Brother Jean de Samois delivered the oration.

For myself, I thought of a vision I once had. King Louis stood in my chapel at Joinville, very pleased, as was I myself to find him there. My lord, I said, at Chevillon, which belongs to me, I would make a place for you. He laughed with delight, but said he had no wish to leave my chapel. When I awoke it seemed to me that I should build an altar, which I did. I endowed it to his memory and to the glory of God, that masses might be sung forever and forever. Here was the music of his presence.

In our year of grace 1305, by permission of the sovereign pontiff, one rib and the head of Saint Louis, excepting his jaw, were lifted from the crypt. King Philippe le Bel, attended by numerous prelates and barons, escorted these relics to Paris. On Tuesday preceding Japhe his rib was conveyed to the church of Notre-Dame, his head to the king's chapel. His gold cup, out of which no one afterward drank, and his missal were carefully preserved. With this, I think, the tapestry of his life was finished.

A carved stone effigy is but the semblance of this man I knew so well and loved past computation. Often I recall that moment in Acre when he put his hands atop my head and I, mistaking him for Philippe de Nemours, bade him leave me alone. I recall how gently he reproved me. Then does his majesty reappear as he once was and I am all but destroyed with love.

He rose to glory anticipating the redemption of Jerusalem. It was not to be. No more did we embark from Acre than what he effected in Syria began to lapse and sink, eroding like a sand castle. Once there had been unity, coherence, regulation. Now the kingdom suc-

450

cumbed to private interest, jealousy, rivalry, merchants quarreling. Genoese battled Venetians for control of trade.

Within two years the barons of Syria were divided, allied with one faction or another. Here stood the Ibelin family, Templars, Teutons, burghers of Pisa and Provence grouped round the Venetian flag. With the Genoese stood merchants from Catalonia, Hospitalers, and Philippe de Montfort who was lord of Tyre. Controversy blazed in the street as if a fire escaped the hearth. Venetians prevailed. Genoese retreated from Acre, gathering uneasily at the city of Tyre where Lord Philippe could protect them. In pursuit of wealth these people discarded their finest asset, which was their common cause, to cut themselves in half, as if the principles of their natures agreed on nothing but turbulence, as if a stream had overflowed the dike.

Bohemond VI, prince of Antioch, cast his lot with Venice. Bertran de Gibelet, his vassal, being of Genoese descent, could not but take sides with Genoa. So it came about that a peasant approached Bertran while he was in the vineyard looking at grapes, murdered him and carried off his head to show Prince Bohemond. These people had forgotten the light of the world.

Thus did Christianity oversea bleed itself while the Muslim waited.

Anon, Baibars ascended the throne of Egypt. Baibars, who split the hand of Turanshah with a sword, chased him toward the Nile. They say this blue-eyed Turk was bought at a Crimean slave market and brought to Syria roaring like a bull, huge, powerful, his right eye blemished by a milky spot. The emir of Hama thought him too loathsome to purchase, so he was relegated to the bodyguard of Sultan Qutuz. Through intimidation and murder he established himself. And growing conceited he demanded the governorship of Aleppo. They say Qutuz was offended by such arrogance. Islamic records tell how the sultan chose to spend a day at his favorite sport of hunting hares and in the company went Baibars. Some distance

451

from camp a retainer pretended to kiss the sultan's hand, which enabled Baibars to stab him in the back. Now with Qutuz bloody and dying the conspirators returned and Baibars entered the sultan's tent demanding homage. All bowed their heads submissively, whereupon he rode unchallenged to Cairo.

Arsuf. Caesarea. Joppa. Beaufort. Christian cities one after another submitted to Baibars.

Unexpectedly he rode against Safed but was driven off. Twice more he assaulted the fortress. Many of those who defended Safed were Christians native to Syria. Baibars therefore announced through heralds that Syrian Christians would be pardoned. These natives began to desert, which enraged the Franks. It is said there was fighting within the walls. And when a month went by the Franks despatched a sergeant called Leo to discuss terms of surrender because they did not think they could hold out. This man came back saying Baibars would allow them to depart unharmed. If the Franks trusted what they were told is much disputed. However it was, they gave up the fortress to Baibars and he cut off their heads.

He rode to the gates of Acre, his soldiers wearing Christian armor and helmets, waving lances, displaying banners seized from Templars and Hospitalers, all seeming to be Christian. Yet their black features disclosed the truth, nor did they sit their horses like Germans or Englishmen or Franks. The gates of Acre did not open.

Baibars retreated to Safed. Envoys who came looking for a truce saw the skulls of hapless prisoners decorating the castle.

On the fourteenth of May in the year of our Lord 1268 he surrounded Antioch, which had long been the most prosperous Frankish city. After four days his army breached the wall where it ran up the slope of Mount Silpius. By order of his emirs the gates were shut to prevent escape. Citizens caught in the streets were struck down, those found at home sold into slavery. So numerous were captives that not a soldier of his army but got a slave. At market one could buy a Frankish girl for five dirhems, a boy for twelve. Silver and gold bibelots were handed out like playthings, bowls of money given away.

deus lo volt!

Prince Bohemond chanced to be at Tripoli when Antioch fell. There exists a letter to the prince from Baibars, advising him of what was yet to come.

Do not forget how in the past we brushed your churches from the earth, how we killed your knights, enslaved your children, how Christian bodies rotted on the shore, how our soldiers who had no family all at once found themselves with countless wives, how Islamic ploughs broke the soil where once your houses stood. Had you but seen how we ravaged Antioch. Had you but seen how Saracen chargers crushed Frankish knights, how one gold coin purchased four noble ladies. Had you but seen leaves from your Gospel toss in the wind, crosses flung to earth, priests swallowed up in the flames of this world, sepulchers of your patriarchs defiled. Now the church of Saint Paul is rubble. Saracens tread upon your altar. Ah! Had you been there!

Soon enough Baibars came to Safita, white castle of the Templars. The Grand Master did not resist.

Next he appeared before Krak, mighty fortress of the Hospitalers. For two weeks incessant rain prevented him from using catapults. But on the fifteenth of March after a fierce bombardment his mameluks forced the outer enceinte. Two weeks later they broke into the fortress. Defenders held out ten days longer in the south tower, then seeing no hope for it they surrendered and were granted safe passage to Tripoli.

Now did providence intercede. Baibars died on the first day of July in that year of our Lord 1277, before he could subjugate Tripoli. By certain accounts he died of wounds. Others claim he drank too much kumiz, this being the fermented milk of mares. Yet again, some say he poisoned the prince of Kerak, who had insulted him, and thoughtlessly sipped from the fatal cup. What cannot be doubted is that he plunged head downward into hell, the gravest threat since Saladin to Christianity oversea.

Baibars' eldest son found himself unable to control rebellious subordinates. So now the emir Qalawun, who commanded Syrian

453

troops, marched on Cairo and declared himself sultan. Christians ignored such turmoil. Rather than exploit the weakness of Islam they fought among themselves.

Guy de Gibelet, vassal to Prince Bohemond VII, took up arms against his lord and promptly fled to the Templars for protection. Bohemond attacked certain Templar buildings and destroyed a forest they owned near Montroque. Templars demonstrated against him and burnt the castle of Botrun. Guy de Gibelet next thought to seize Tripoli but was betrayed, so he fled to the Hospital. Bohemond pledged to spare his life and the lives of his followers. Instead, what did Lord Bohemond do but blind them all, every one, save Guy with his brothers and a cousin, buried up to their necks in a ditch at Nephin and left to starve. Enemies of the Gibelet family celebrated. Merchants from Pisa staged a theatrical performance gleefully enacting the horrible death of Guy de Gibelet.

Thus, with foolish quarrels did citizens of Christ's kingdom ignore the Turk to set about their own destruction. All began to rot and decompose, fell apart like the body of Baldwin the leper a century before.

King Henry of Cyprus came to Acre in the year of our Lord 1286, expecting to govern the tumultuous remnant of Christianity oversea. He was fourteen years old and reminded everyone of a foolish girl. At times he would fall unconscious. His mouth watered. Attendants mocked him. Nevertheless his arrival brought joy and hope. Not for a hundred years had the kingdom witnessed such festive pageants and tourneys. They mimicked the Round Table, played at the Queen of Feminia where knights costumed as ladies jousted together. Knights garbed as nuns jousted pleasurably with monks.

They impersonated Tristan, Lancelot, Palamides, lost themselves in a frenzy of carnal delight as if they knew the Turk would appear.

Philip and Baldwin d'Ibelin, uncles to this girlish youth, counseled him wisely enough that a truce could be arranged with Sultan Qalawun, after which Henry returned to Cyprus. Meanwhile ships from Genoa and Pisa bombarded one another in the port. William de Beaujeu, Grand Master of the Temple, warned against civil war, pointed to Saracen armies north and south. Citizens jeered, beseeched him not to terrify them with rumor.

On the twenty-sixth of April in the year of our Lord 1289 the sultan appeared at Tripoli leading forty thousand horsemen. Genoese and Venetians hastily embarked with all they owned. Tripoli, pride of the Levant, fell in six days. The chronicle of Abul Feda describes people rushing toward the quai. Few escaped. Men were cut down, children and women enslaved. Qalawun ordered the buildings destroyed lest a new army of pilgrims try to recapture it. On a rocky islet offshore stood the church of Saint Thomas where hundreds sought refuge. Saracen horsemen urged their mounts into the water and swam to the islet, butchered priests, merchants, scholars, physicians, craftsmen. Abul Feda visited the church a little later but could scarcely breathe. He did not stay long.

Among those few to escape was the bishop of Tripoli who got to Rome and appealed for help. Also, the youthful king of Cyprus despatched an envoy. His Holiness Nicholas IV listened in sorrow. It is said he wrote to princes and sovereigns throughout the West and urged clerics to preach a new crusade, but there was little response save in the north of Italy.

Next summer the bishop came to Acre with a host of Tuscans and Lombards, not proud servants of Christ but unemployed rabble, peasants committed to nothing nobler than their bellies, dregs hoping to earn salvation while poking about for gold, pilgrims such as would not be understood by Christian kings of the past. They found the marketplace crowded, caravans arriving from Damascus thanks to King Henry's truce. Also, there had been a good harvest. What

455

happened next is argued to this day. It might be that some infidel took advantage of a Christian lady and her husband sought vengeance. Whatever the cause, these dregs of Italy rushed about looking for God's enemies, pushed drunkenly through markets howling of Muslim Vespers and laid the sword to hundreds. Bearded Greeks met the blade that fateful afternoon, mistaken for unbelievers.

Sultan Qalawun demanded the extradition of those responsible, which would mean their death. The barons debated. Should Christian pilgrims be surrendered to enemies of the Lord? However guilty, should they not be tried before Christian judges? The barons could not bring themselves to acquiesce, nor would the common people. Also, many in Acre considered the Saracens themselves to blame.

Now the sultan asked himself why he should respect King Henry's truce. He sent word to the governor of Damascus, Rukn al-Din Toqsu, to assemble troops at Caesarea. He ordered up the armies of Egypt, pretending he would move against Africa.

Grand Master William de Beaujeu again warned the Franks. Again they stopped up their ears. He sent an ambassador to Cairo with a proposal, hoping to mollify the sultan. Qalawun replied that he would spare Acre in exchange for as many Venetian pennies as there were inhabitants. Grand Master William therefore preached in the Church of Saint Cross, setting forth how he had prevailed upon Qalawun to fix the damaged truce with a single penny. Thus everything might be settled and quiet. He advised the people to accept, declaring that worse evil would follow if they did not. But the people cried out with one voice that he betrayed the city, that he deserved death for treason because he corresponded with those who hate our Lord. And the Grand Master hearing this tumult left the auditorium and scarce got out with his life.

Qalawun addressed a letter to the king of Armenia vowing that not until every Christian was dead would he leave Acre. He marched from Cairo on the fourth day of November but fell sick at Marjat, two leagues from his palace. Before expiring he commanded his son

Ashraf Khalil to devastate Acre, saying his body should not be buried while the city existed.

Ashraf Khalil prudently decided to wait for good weather in the spring. During this respite the barons sent Lord Philip Mainboeuf and a Templar, Bartholomew Pizan, to placate him but he would not receive them. Nor did these envoys return. If they languished in shackles for years or got their throats cut is not known.

Early in March this host of unbelievers moved north from Egypt, passing by Acre to Damascus where Ashraf Khalil lodged his concubines and assembled his armies. The chronicle of Abul Mahasin declares that soldiers came from throughout Islam, such was their zeal to participate in the annihilation of Christianity.

On the fifth day of April this multitude came to Acre. Soldiers pitched their tents side by side, yet they covered the plain as far as Samaria. Certain accounts place the sultan's army at six hundred thousand men arranged in three companies so that one hundred thousand might besiege the city while an equal number waited to relieve them. Two hundred thousand stood before the gates, the rest supplying what was needed. They brought with them numerous catapults to stroke and break apart the walls, more than ever had been gathered. One very large called Victorious. Another called Furious. They brought mangonels called Black Oxen.

Inside were no more than eight hundred mounted knights and sergeants with some fourteen thousand men afoot, considering those Italian dregs whose slaughter of peasants and merchants infuriated Sultan Qalawun.

For eight days Ashraf Khalil loitered in his vermilion tent, which they call dehliz, set on a pleasant hill with gardens and vines that belonged to the Templars. One entrance of his tent opened toward Acre, meaning he would go that way. For eight days Ashraf Khalil contemplated the city. When all had settled in his mind he directed his cavalry to advance, each animal carrying a log across its neck. So his cavalry rode to the edge of the moat and delivered logs to protect

457

miners burrowing at the walls. He directed mangonels to throw pots of explosive liquid. Now with fire and stones they assaulted Acre while the morning stiffened with arrows. A Christian knight preparing to hurl his lance found it notched by Muslim arrows before it left his hand.

Documents relate that one moonlit evening Grand Master William and Otto de Grandson, who commanded the English, led three hundred knights to burn a catapult. They got among the tents, but the man who should have thrown fire at the catapult was alarmed and threw it short and tent ropes entangled the horses. Eighteen Franks were lost, including one who fell into a cesspool. Those who got back boasted that they had killed many Saracens in the moonlight and displayed shields, trumpets, and kettledrums for proof. God's enemies also boasted. Prince Abul Feda, who commanded the Victorious, told how the Franks abandoned their dead when they retreated. Next morning, said he, my cousin al-Malik al-Muzaffar, who was lord of Hama, strung Frankish heads around the necks of captured horses to make wreaths for the sultan.

William de Beaujeu led another sortie through the gate of Saint Anthony some nights later, before moonrise. But the Turks had been expecting this. All at once torches blazed throughout the Muslim camp and by torchlight many Franks were slain.

King Henry arrived from Cyprus, forty vessels bringing one hundred mounted knights and two thousand foot soldiers, welcome reinforcement. With him was Archbishop John Turco of Nicosia, so the people lit bonfires to celebrate. Yet the boom of Muslim kettledrums resounded through the city. All understood that something must be done. King Henry therefore instructed two knights to speak with Ashraf Khalil and find out why he did not observe the truce. Discourteously he received the knights outside his tent. He demanded keys to the city. At this moment a stone loosed by a Frankish perrier struck not far away. Ashraf Khalil drew his sword a hand's breadth as if to kill these envoys, but was prevented by Emir

Shujai who implored him not to defile his blade with the blood of pigs.

Now the Saracens began to fill bags with sand, which they brought forward and threw down in order to level the ground. Meantime the sappers went about their work. Soon it became apparent that the old tower named for King Hugh could not be defended so the Franks withdrew, setting it afire. A few days later the English tower and that named for the Comtesse de Blois started to break apart. The wall near Saint Anthony's Gate began to crumble.

On the eighteenth of May just before dawn Ashraf Khalil ordered his men to take the city. Muslim regiments led by emirs wearing white turbans advanced through the almond orchards shouting insults and war cries, hidden from view by dense mist, encouraged by three hundred drummers mounted on camels. Cymbals and trumpets sounded. What happened that day was recorded in the Gestes des Chiprois, by the Templar of Tyre, by Ashraf Khalil himself in a letter to King Hethoum of Armenia, and by others.

These Muslims got in through the Accursed Tower, according to some. Others say they entered by way of a breach in the king of Jerusalem's castle. The first carried long shields, followed by those hurling Greek fire. Next came archers. Noble Christian ladies, girls, peasant women, nuns, all ran shrieking toward the harbor, some with babies in their arms. Saracens caught them. One would seize a woman, another would fling her baby into the street and horses would trample it. Or they would fight to have the woman but end by killing her. And because of Christian wickedness a furious storm arose, hindering the flight of any who would escape to Cyprus. Those on the quai beheld a roiling evil sea, green and black. Documents speak of highborn ladies rushing toward the boats with gold jewelry, crying for a mariner to take all their wealth and save them, transport them naked if need be, or have them for a wife. One whose name is not known accepted as many passengers as he could and bore them to Cyprus, requested nothing, and sailed on. Yet there was Roger Flor, a greedy Catalan,

459

who offered passage only to rich women in exchange for all they had, thereby pocketing a fortune.

King Henry with his brother Amalric escaped to Cyprus. Few thought he should have remained since he could do nothing and would add his name to the roster of Muslim captives. Nicholas de Hanapé, aged patriarch of Jerusalem, was helped aboard a skiff that would carry him to a galley offshore. He would not leave by himself, insisting they wait for others, whereupon so many struggled into the skiff that it sank, all drowned. Jean de Villiers, Grand Master of the Hospital, was brought to the quai leaking blood, meanwhile protesting that he should not depart.

William Beaujeu, Grand Master of the Temple, who vainly attempted to warn the citizens, was struck by an arrow near three o'clock that afternoon. He turned away from battle and some pilgrims from Spoleto thought he had lost heart.

My Lord, they cried, if you desert us the city will be lost!

He answered with a loud voice that he was slain and they saw the arrow buried in his side beneath the armpit. He twisted his neck, hurled the dart to the ground and almost tumbled from his mount. They lifted him down, put him on a long shield they found in the street and carried him to the Temple where he ascended to our Lord.

By sundown all belonged to Ashraf Khalil except that great Templar fortress jutting out to sea, sheltering a multitude of terrified citizens. Waves crashed against the walls, hammered bronze lions glared from the towers. For nearly a week it defied the Muslim horde. During that time women, children, and men who were unable to fight embarked on the few available boats, which departed hastily for Cyprus. Piteous cries from those left behind followed them out to sea.

Ashraf Khalil offered to let all in the fortress depart for Cyprus or any port they wished, if the ward and its goods were surrendered. Such terms being acceptable, the gate opened to admit one hundred mameluks and before long a white banner flew from the central keep. However, these Turks took to molesting Christian women and boys so the Templars killed them, threw the sultan's flag at the corpses and shut the gate.

Next day Ashraf Khalil invited Marshal Peter de Sevrey to come forth under guarantee of safe conduct to explain what happened. But when Peter de Sevrey approached the Muslim camp he was seized, trussed up, and beheaded. Now those in the fortress understood the situation and looked to their defenses.

Ashraf Khalil set miners to work digging at the foundation.

On the twenty-eighth of May the landward side of the Templar fortress cracked. Two thousand mameluks at once entered the breach, but Ashraf Khalil had not waited long enough. Stones began to fall. Now with a rush the central tower folded inward upon itself, crushing mameluk and Frank, pagan and servant of God. Not one escaped, as related by the Gestes des Chiprois.

Ashraf Khalil vowed that never again would Acre play host to Christian armies. Houses and markets were looted, burnt, watchtowers dismantled, broken walls left to disintegrate. It is said that people throughout the East grieved over this destruction in plaintive song as they are wont to sing over tombs of their dead, bewailing a grandeur none would see again.

Some leagues north the city of Tyre had twice withstood Saladin, but now it was lightly garrisoned. When those Franks noticed a shadow on the horizon they made haste to embark for Cyprus.

Further north at Saida the Templars prepared to defend themselves. For a month they saw nothing. Then came a host of unbelievers led by Emir Shujai so they retreated to an islet just offshore, whence the commandant embarked for Cyprus to levy troops but did not return. Those left to defend the islet fought valorously until Saracens undertook to build a causeway, whereupon they gave up hope and sailed further north to Tortosa.

One week later Shujai approached Beyrouth. He ordered the leaders out. When they anxiously complied he made them prisoner. At this the others fled, carrying off as many holy relics as they could.

Shujai tore apart the walls. He tore apart the ancient castle of the Ibelin family. He made the wondrous cathedral of Beyrouth a mosque.

Not long after this Ashraf Khalil took Haifa. He burnt the monasteries on Mount Carmel, killed the monks.

What was left? Castles of Athlit and Tortosa. Neither resisted. Offshore from Tortosa half a league stood the isle of Ruad. Some few Templars clung to it a while as falcons might perch on a remote cliff looking toward the vanished kingdom.

Ashraf Khalil marched along the coast destroying and scattering anything the Franks might use if they returned. So the peasants watching vineyards devastated and fields scorched thought they must find a way to live in the mountains. Those with Frankish blood prudently denied their heritage because centuries of religious loathing had put out the flame of tolerance.

As for God's servants who escaped the holocaust and got to Cyprus, what charity or love they met at first did not last long. Their presence on the island spoke loudly of Christian defeat. To this day old women on Cyprus wear black in memory of a lost kingdom oversea.

The sense of it, I, Jean de Joinville, do not presume to know.

Printed in the United States
by Baker & Taylor Publisher Services